In the
Shadow
of
Nuremberg

Based on a true story

Ellen Karadimas

In the Shadow of Nuremberg
Ellen Karadimas

ISBN: 978-1-7371700-0-6
Back cover photo by Regina Gerstner, Fürth, Germany, used with permission.

Dedicated to my parents
Irma and Photis Karadimas
And to my brother, Jim

AUTHOR'S NOTE

This book is based on a true story, as recounted to me via numerous interviews by families and friends who lived through the Nazi era. When necessary, the names and identifying characteristics of individuals have been changed to maintain anonymity. The chronology of some events has been compressed. Some conversations have been recreated and/or supplemented. However, the book is a truthful recollection of actual events in the lives of the characters herein.

CHAPTER ONE

H ey, Nazi Pig!"
The words served as a warning seconds before the unsuspecting girl was pummeled with ice-balls by a group of rowdy boys. Crowing atop an embankment of dirty snow, her assailants aimed their weapons with zeal.

Her trek home this dingy, winter afternoon had started like any other. Little did she expect a gang of boys were waiting to burst upon her. Shocked by the sudden, painful stings to her face, she dropped her books to the pavement and stared wide-eyed and disbelieving at their gleeful faces. It was a poor move on her part as it gave them a clear shot at her head. Another volley of ice-balls sped her way. This time the missiles cracked alongside her nose and spattered ice fragments into and around her eyes. Stunned by their impact, she attempted to cover her face from further attack. The boys were relentless. She froze, numb with fright, as her cheek and injured eye throbbed from the onslaught.

Why are they doing this to me?

She knew what a pig was. *But what is a Nazi? Why are they hurting me?*

Bewildered and shaken, she scanned the street for possible help, but most of her classmates had scrambled home and the path was empty.

The boys shouted out the words again:

"Hey, Nazi Pig!"

Another volley of ice-balls flew her way. She flinched as the chunks struck her small body, her second-hand coat offering little in the way of protection. The impact of the assault woke her from her daze. Scrambling for her schoolbooks, she ran as fast as she could from the vicious attack.

Although fear propelled her forward, she chanced a brief backward glance to see if they were following her. They were not. Headed in the opposite direction, she heard the boys snicker as they disappeared. Their sneering laughter made her wince; it pierced deeper than any shards of ice. She wished she were brave enough and strong enough to chase after them and strike back in kind; but she knew she was not. With aching head, and shoulders slumped, the bedraggled child trudged home through the slush-filled streets feeling defeated.

Except for a few swipes to her bottom by her parents when she misbehaved, she had never been struck by anything or anyone in such a heavy-handed manner. She fought hard to hold back her tears. The winter cold made the raw cuts on her face burn.

Trying to out-run the pain, she hurried past the hi-rise buildings lining each side of the avenue. They stood sentinel over her; yet no heroes had come forth, no rescuers had appeared at doorways to protect or comfort her. Her searching eyes noticed slight movements behind curtained windows; windows which veiled witnesses to her humiliation. She was glad they remained hidden away, as the shame she felt was keen. She did not want strangers seeing her cry, and she did not want their pity. She quickened her pace to avoid the prying eyes.

The girl and her family resided in the borough of Queens, New York. It was over a year since they arrived in America in the spring of 1952. The novice immigrant had tried to make friends in her new class, but it had not gone well; she often found herself excluded from activities at school. Yet she had never expected a cruel encounter. Touching her tender face, she winced from the pain, and her bruised eye began to water. She continued home, anxious thoughts driving her on. She could not understand what had gone so wrong.

Was it my fault? What did I do? What is a "Nazi Pig"?

At the start of her first school year, her teacher had presented each student to the class with a casual introduction. When her turn came, the teacher had informed the class, "This is Eleni, or Leni as she likes to be called. She and her family came all the way from Germany to live in the United States."

Her classmates had stared at her with intense curiosity. She had responded by squirming and turning crimson.

Why had they stared? Was it because I am German? Or because they did not like my name?

Reaching home, Leni trudged up the three flights of stairs, her head pounding, and pressed the buzzer to her family's apartment. Her mother opened it with a smile, but then gasped in alarm at seeing her daughter's mottled, swollen face, and her right eye squeezed shut.

"Was ist los, mein Kind?! What happened?" Her distressed mother reached for her and drew her in.

Leni flew into the outstretched arms, spilling forth a torrent of words which her parents and her four-year-old brother, Demetri, listened to with shock and bewilderment.

Encircling Leni's shoulders gently, her mother guided her despairing child into the living room and settled her on the couch. Her father, who had just arrived from work, rushed to get a damp cloth and soothing ointment with which to treat her injuries. Leni sat there disoriented. Her dazed and frightened mind was scrambling for answers. She knew being called a "Nazi Pig" was not a good thing.

"Why? Why was I called this?" Her eyes pleaded for an answer and relief.

"What's a Nazi, Mama?" she repeated between flinches as her mother swabbed the dirt from her eye with as much delicacy as she could. No answer was given just then, as the tenderness of her mother's touch penetrated the fragile barrier to Leni's long-held tears. Swathed in comforting arms, she sobbed and crumbled into the warm hollow of her mother's lap, the receptacle of all her childhood joys and woes. Seeing this, her little brother tried to pat her hand in comfort, but to no avail.

"Tell me why, Mama! Tell me why they called me a Nazi Pig!" she cried.

Her mother's arms tightened around her, and, with maternal ferociousness, she declared, "Du bist kein Nazi Schwein! Do you hear me? You are *not* a Nazi Pig, and you never will be! It is a dreadful story where such an awful name came from, and Papa and I will tell it to you when you are feeling better."

"Tell me now!" Leni begged in anguish. "Please tell me now! I do not understand! Why were they so mean?" Her eyes darted to her parents, "I hate America! I really hate it! I wish we had never come here!"

Stricken by her words, her mother and father glanced at each other. They beheld their distraught daughter and her now whimpering brother with dismay and sorrow.

Where do we begin? her parents pondered, as they turned woeful eyes toward each other.

There once was a girl...

There once was a boy...

There once was a monster who lurked in the shadows.

CHAPTER TWO

Fürth, Germany 1931

R osa Schmidt watched her youngest daughter with curiosity. The inquisitive child was leafing through periodicals as if she could read every word, with a serious scowl etched on her otherwise cherubic face as she spread the pages before her. Little Anya Margarete Schmidt looked quite ill-tempered.

It was a snow-bedecked day and Anya would soon be celebrating her fourth birthday. There was no cause for a puckered face. As she surveyed her daughter's delicate features, albeit in disturbed disarray, Rosa's mind felt a twinge of unease. Her little Anya, often commended for her tousled blonde curls, light green eyes, and a smile and a giggle that could soften the heartless, would, no doubt, grow into a beauty and attract attention as soon as she came of age. Attention, however, is not what Rosa wanted for the sprite.

She, herself, was an attractive woman with a good figure, light brown hair, soft green eyes, and fine features; but her appeal was subtle.

Anya's appearance was not her only concern; the child's stubborn nature and uncanny ability to speak her mind was the other. As Anya's little mouth contemplated and chewed on her next choice words, Rosa could swear steam escaped from her daughter's ears.

Having listened to "Dolf" on her grandfather's radio that

morning, and studied the newspaper photos strewn about, little Anya proceeded to voice her opinion with as much aplomb as a child could muster.

"He's funny looking and always yelling. I do not like him! And his hair is so stupid. He should be shot!"

Startled by her words, Rosa reproached her daughter with a swift warning:

"Child, where did you get such an idea? Please do not say such things or you will get us in trouble. You must never say those things to anyone, especially in front of your father! Promise me?"

Noting her mother's distress, Anya squirmed.

"I won't, Mama. I promise. Is it because he is a bad man? I heard Opa say to Onkel Willie that Dolf is a gangster and should be shot. What's a gangster?" Anya's forehead crinkled into a quizzical mien.

"Oh dear, I had better have a serious talk with your Opa. He should not be discussing such matters in front of you."

"Well, if I can't say it, can I think it in my head?" a pert Anya asked.

Her mother rolled her eyes and pulled her close.

"Only if you don't let such thoughts tumble out of your little mouth. Understood?"

Anya gazed up at her mother's serious face and responded with a submissive, "I'll try."

"Try harder," her mother implored, giving her a stern look. "Try *very* hard."

Rosa could not blame her child for feeling as she did. She felt the same way. "Dolf", as Anya had named Adolf Hitler when she was a toddler, was a canker on her own mind.

Seeing her mother's face turn sour, Anya tried to cheer her and pointed to a picture of Hitler balancing a young girl on his knee.

"Look, Mama. He looks like the Weihnachtsmann. Not so scary!"

Anya was right. Hitler exuded the air of a benevolent Father Christmas as he and the beaming girl were pictured in front of a bountiful Christmas tree. His benign gaze was centered on the happy child as she accepted a pretty porcelain doll from his hands. Anya watched her mother shake her head in consternation.

"Don't you like the picture, Mama?" Anya asked in surprise.

"Yes...yes. It's quite nice," her mother nodded in curt reply.

Having heard the men in her family refer to Hitler as a "dangerous political upstart", Rosa had a significant distrust of Hitler's motives as she pondered the picture. Charming children into his realm, was he? For what purpose?

"Mama, why doesn't Dolf grow whiskers like Opa? Wouldn't it be better than his silly mustache?" Anya noted as she studied Hitler's picture again. "Maybe he's afraid he'll look like a porcupine, huh?"

Picturing Hitler with quills, the unruly elf dissolved into a fit of giggles and, covering her mouth, tried to smother the resultant hiccups. One voluble hiccup, however, managed to escape her fingers, and the sound disengaged Rosa from her troublesome thoughts. Listening to Anya's chortles, she tried hard not to chuckle herself and struggled even harder to give her mischievous daughter a warning eye.

Anya's precocious banter, Rosa admitted, could not always be restrained, just as her own growing apprehension could not always be repressed. She emitted a loud sigh over this realization, which brought Anya's twitters to a halt. She looked at her mother's perturbed expression. *Mama is no fun today,* she decided and pounced up to leave.

"Where are you going?" Rosa demanded, glancing at her daughter with growing suspicion.

"I think I'll go visit Opa. Maybe he is listening to his radio again," Anya remarked, thinking it wise to disappear from her mother's view.

"Then wait, I will be ready in a moment, young lady, and go with you."

"Okay! I'll tell Opa you're coming!" she shouted while scampering off without so much as a by-your-leave.

Rosa looked askance at Anya's swift departure. She must speak with her father before Anya ingested more troublesome tidbits of information. She hurried to clear the room of the newspapers lying about and listened for Anya's assuring knock on her grandfather's study door.

Anya's grandparents, Johann, and Babette Bermann, lived in a three-story townhouse on a notable block of townhouses on the outskirts of Fürth, Germany.

The homes were inhabited by married couples who had fathered multiple children; an achievement the present government considered a boon to the country's population and rewarded with trite medals and substantial housing. Across the street was a small, tree-laden park and, in their backyard, a sizeable, fenced garden bordered by an immense, dandelion-dotted field that sloped downward toward town.

The nooks and crannies of her grandparents' home often enticed Anya away from her original destination, so Rosa was relieved to hear the heavy, study door squeak on its hinges.

"Come in!" Johann ordered.

Hoping someone was bringing him a cup of tea, he sat at his desk shuffling a few sheaves of paperwork to the side. Noticing it was one of his favorite urchins, he turned off the radio and motioned Anya toward his lap. Scrunching up her faded pinafore of brown muslin, she climbed into it with ease. Her well-worn, woolen stockings and scuffed shoes made her even more endearing to her Opa because she wore them without self-consciousness.

"Well, what can I do for my kleine Maus?" he asked.

"Oh, nothing, Opa. I just wondered what you were doing. It's almost time to eat supper, you know."

Pulling out his gold watch from his vest pocket, he concurred, "You are absolutely right!"

This delighted Anya as she informed him, "Oma is making Knödelsuppe today, so we should hurry!"

"Oh, is that what I smell? I like dumplings! Don't you like

dumplings in broth?"

"I suppose, but I would rather have a sausage with it," she admitted.

"Well, maybe someday. There must be some piglet out there that will sacrifice itself to become a plate of sausages for you. Right now, it seems to be hiding."

"Oh, Opa, you're being silly." Anya gave him a bright smile and giggled, but soon her mood turned. "I don't really want to see a piglet killed. That would be sad. I guess dumplings will do." She did not sound convincing, and he noticed the corners of her mouth take a downward turn.

"Well, maybe for your birthday we can come up with something better. I think I saw a big, fat chicken running about the backyard yesterday."

"That's not better!" She gave him an indulgent grin, then grew pensive again, "Opa, why do we have to kill things so we can live?"

He was taken aback by her question.

Johann, a veteran cavalry officer in the Prussian army, had spent the morning listening to the radio and worrying about his country's future and Adolf Hitler's place in it. Now he was faced with a question he did not know how to answer.

Where is my granddaughter's mind going with this?

Apparently nowhere, since in the next minute she was giving him a bright smile again, and smoothing out his white, handlebar mustache, and fluffing up his white mane of hair. Taking off his silver-rimmed spectacles, his blue eyes twinkled at her fussy gestures.

"You need to fix your mustache soon, Opa, or Oma won't kiss you anymore. It will look like a horse's tail. Look how beautiful you look in your picture!"

"Beautiful? Hmmm, don't you mean handsome?" he teased.

Anya was in awe of her Großvater, or Opa as most German grandfathers were nicknamed. A dignified and educated man, he towered several inches above the men he encountered in his daily life. When she learned he had been a brave soldier as a young man, she became enamored of the large portrait of him that hung over the bookcases filled with his favorite books. The painting showed him sitting astride a magnificent horse. Wearing an impressive uniform laden with silver buttons and gleaming medals with a pointed helmet of black and silver atop his head, Johann looked majestic in Anya's eyes. The hair was darker in the picture, but his nose remained regal and the eyes clear and sharp. Now in his senior years, he was still in possession of his handsome and dignified demeanor.

"Did you ride on the horse all the time, Opa?" she asked, looking at the grey stallion in the portrait and wishing she could ride as splendid an animal.

Johann shook his head and voiced a firm "Nein."

Her Opa had no wish to elaborate on his military experience, having witnessed atrocities during his service in the Prussian army that he could not and would not put into trite words. Granted an honorable discharge after his asthmatic attacks became chronic and debilitating, he was glad to be free of the war. The gunpowder polluting the air during battle had almost drained him of his last breath. Returning home, his medical condition and Germany's eventual defeat in World War I ended Johann's livelihood as a military officer both in the field and behind a bureaucratic desk. He still, however, maintained contact with his cronies who kept him apprised of general political and military situations in Germany.

Sensing her grandfather's reluctance to answer her question, Anya placed her small head upon his chest as if listening to his heart. She heard it beat in a slow and telling rhythm.

Anya looked up at him. "Are you sad, Opa?"

"Well, a little, I suppose," he confessed. "The news makes me sad."

"Then why do you listen to it?" she responded.

Her question made him study her in wonderment. The forthrightness of his little granddaughter often seemed to come with a nugget of acute intelligence.

"I guess I should not," he acknowledged.

"I'm sad too," she admitted.

"Oh? Why?" he asked with concern.

"Mama's mad at me because I said Dolf looked stupid and he should be shot."

"Oh dear," he replied, realizing that his dinner was going to be served with a generous helping of reproach from his wife and daughter.

Anya's mother walked in at that moment to underscore his discomfiting thought.

"Well, you two appear rather forlorn," Rosa scoffed, noting their serious faces. "Discussing world events again?"

Johann gave a brief snort in response to her jaundiced question.

"No, we are not," he avowed with as much calmness as he could muster, hoping to avert adding coal to Rosa's fire.

Sensing the tension between the two, Anya slid off her grandfather's lap as her mother reached for her hand.

"Sweetheart, why don't you go help Oma get the table ready," her mother firmly suggested.

"Is Opa in trouble?" Anya asked, perturbed at the thought.

"Well, a bit," Rosa gave Johann a pointed look.

"Well then I'm not leaving!" Anya retorted, running to his side, ready to defend her Opa from her mother's wrath.

"Anya, go to your Oma in the kitchen. She needs your help," Johann instructed with a gentle nod toward the door.

Anya hesitated. He gave her a smile, "Go. All will be fine. Listen to your Mama."

She smiled back and complied, but not before giving her mother an evil stare.

As the door closed behind her, Anya came to a standstill. Oma could wait another tiny minute or two.

On the other side of the door, her mother's voice drifted toward Anya's curious, perked ears.

"I do not want you and your ranting sons discussing Hitler or anything else of that sort in front of my daughter! You know she loves to babble away and will, most likely, say something in public she should not be saying. Or if her father hears, there will be war at home! You know how Oswald favors Hitler. I am sure her cousins have gotten an earful from all of you too. They have informed me that their teachers are trying to trick students into disclosing what discussions are going on at home. Can you not see the seriousness of this?"

Seeing the culpable look on Johann's face, Rosa lay a firm hand on his arm, but her tone softened, "Vater, you and my brothers cannot be careless about this. The children could get themselves and us in serious trouble. Anya is the youngest and will get hurt the most, because she has no idea of the consequences of her innocent chatter."

Johann emitted a long sigh at her censure and tried to respond in a sensible manner.

Outside the door, Anya did not dare breathe, anxious to hear what her grandfather had to say.

"Rosa, you cannot protect your two daughters forever, especially Anya. The world is in turmoil, and she has an inquisitive mind and sharp ears."

(Little did they know how sharp at that moment. Anya wondered what "turmoil" and "inquisitive" meant.)

"Bitte, Vater," Rosa clasped her hands in frustration, "I want to protect their innocence and their childhood for as long as I can. Anya and Hannah deserve that. All your grandchildren deserve that. They are growing up way too fast and suffering through enough hardship as is. Can you not spare them all this talk of Hitler, and politics, and the dark forces surrounding us as a family and nation? It will only cause fear and night terrors in them. And you know children often repeat what they hear. It will bring nothing but misfortune on us."

She bent down alongside him and putting her hand on his arm, stared up at his face.

"Please, Papa."

He looked at her and saw the desperate pleading in her eyes. Patting her hand in reassurance, he promised, "I will do my best,

Rosa. You are right. Forgive me."

She stood up and kissed his forehead in return, "Danke."

"However, might I suggest the mothers of my grandchildren become extra vigilant in herding them into another room, or shooing them out into the backyard, when my sons and I get into heated discussions?"

She stood up smiling and conceded "We will try our best to do that. I will remind them. Now come, let us get some supper."

As Rosa opened the door to head toward the kitchen, a faint scurry of little feet could be heard in the hallway.

"Tell me she did not listen at the door!" an exasperated Rosa cried out.

"Might I also suggest that you corral your little one and educate her on the dangers of snooping at doors?" her father proposed.

"That I will!" Rosa declared as she flew after Anya, while Johann chuckled and shook his head as a child's shriek was heard soon thereafter.

CHAPTER THREE

Johann's promise was fulfilled, and the days that followed brought a sense of familial peace. But behind closed doors, the discussions among himself and his sons remained vehement. They barely ceased by the time Anya's birthday arrived.

The day presented itself with a glimmer of sun, patterns of frost on the windows, and a generous dusting of snow on sidewalks, rooftops, and trees. Anya and her mother had stayed the night at the grandparents' house to get an early start helping with birthday preparations.

As the first light of dawn broke through the curtains, it brought a squint to Anya's eyes. Eager to begin her special day, she emerged from the duvet she shared with her mother, grabbed onto the bedpost, and sidled down the bed onto the cold, wooden floor as quietly as she could. Dressed only in her cotton nightshirt, she padded out the door and down the stairs in her bare feet, while the floorboards creaked. Her grandmother was surprised to find her stealing into the kitchen at such an early hour, instead of curled up in her warm bed on this wintry morning.

"Well, what do we have here?" Babette said, as she continued chopping stale slices of bread into bite-size croutons. Minute portions were centered in the raw, potato dumplings she planned to steam and serve later that day. Potatoes were plentiful, but meat for a roast was not. Dumplings with chicken would have to do.

"It's my birthday and it snowed!" a buoyant Anya proclaimed, throwing her arms into the air to punctuate her announcement.

"So, it is. But don't you think you had best wash up, get dressed, and wake your Mama first? You will catch your death of cold dressed like that. And no shoes again!"

"I guess I should get dressed," Anya agreed, but made no motion to move. She liked watching Oma prepare a family dinner. Approaching the warm stove that was emitting welcoming heat and wonderful aromas, she climbed on a nearby stool.

"Don't sit too close to the oven or you might get burned," Babette warned.

"What are we having for my birthday?" a curious Anya inquired.

"Chicken, pickled beets, and potato dumplings," the cook informed her.

Anya face could not hide a slight grimace, "Pickled beets?

"Followed by a giant, baked apple tart with dollops of Sahne (whipped cream) for your birthday cake," Babette added to reinstate a grin on her granddaughter's face.

"Really?" Anya asked, wide-eyed.

"Really, what?" inquired Rosa, as she walked into the room in her robe and slippers.

"We're having a giant apple tart for my birthday!" her rapturous daughter informed her.

"My, my, Oma must have hoarded the ingredients since Christmas. I thought fried bread would be all you would get today. You certainly are a lucky girl!" Rosa smiled at Babette in gratitude.

"Well, no one will get anything, if you two do not get dressed soon and help me out with my tasks!" Babette admonished. Right on cue, they ran up the stairs to do her bidding.

Later that morning, a tribe of cousins, aunts, and uncles arrived, wiped their boots on the front doormat with vigor, and shed their coats, hats, scarves, and gloves in the entryway. Squeezing around the kitchen table in the corner, and situating themselves on the bench, chairs and laps surrounding it, they chatted amiably with one another while Rosa and Babette began to set the table.

Soon plates were passed, silverware doled out, the main meal digested, and a cacophony of oohs and aahs emitted when the "saftiger Apfelkuchen", juicy and sprinkled with sugar and cinnamon, was offered up. Served like a revered delicacy worthy of any Viennese pastry shop, the birthday girl received the first piece and requested an extra dollop of whipped cream.

Born on the twelfth day of February 1927, in the quaint, medieval city of Fürth, Germany near Nuremberg, Anya was now officially four years of age. As they savored the sweet dessert, Tante Lotte, a teacher, informed Anya that she shared the same birthday as Abraham Lincoln, a famous American president.

"I was born on Mr. Lincoln's birthday!" she exclaimed to everyone, not quite sure who President Lincoln was, but she noticed most everyone looked impressed.

When bidden by Anya to explain the importance of this man to one and all, Tante Lotte described him as "a brave man, a wise man, a liberator of his people".

"What's a *librater*?" Anya asked.

"Someone who saves people from a bad situation," her aunt replied.

"What's a *sitation*?" Anya asked further.

Rosa looked at her daughter's puzzled face and rolled her eyes at Lotte. *This could go on all night!*

"How about you and your cousins finish up the last bit of cake and go play in the parlor," her mother suggested, "Tante Lotte will tell you more about President Lincoln later."

Her cousins opted for the leftover cake, and Anya, with tasty crumbs stuffed in her mouth, lost her desire to ask further questions and led them to the parlor.

When they disappeared, Rosa warned her sister, Lotte, "You do realize, by linking her to President Lincoln, Anya will wear that distinction like a tiara on her head. Next, she will ask how to get to America and become President!"

They both chuckled at the prospect, although Rosa did not relish the thought of Anya ever going that far away.

With the last bits of cake eaten, kisses bestowed upon the birthday girl, and the sparse presents oohed over, the men retired to Opa's study to listen to the evening broadcast on his radio. The children, in turn, followed Anya into the sitting room opposite the kitchen to chatter and play.

Rosa watched the young ones settle in across the way, then turned toward the women gathered in the room.

"How do you explain things to a child that are so difficult to explain?" she pondered out loud.

"Like any mother," Oma stated, "with your heart. Now come clear your head of cobwebs and help us wash all these dishes!"

Rosa, duty-bound, wiped her hands on her apron and helped clear the table. They all knew what she was thinking.

On this February 12th, there was no liberator in their own country. No one to free them from their own hardships. It was, as Anya stated earlier, a bad "sitation".

"What will the future bring, do you think?" Rosa asked her mother and sisters as they enjoyed a "child-free" cup of tea.

"I do not want to think about it. I have no idea what we are going to do if things get worse," a dejected Betty, Rosa's middle sister, pronounced. "Thank God we can count on each other to muddle through; otherwise, I doubt we would survive."

"I pray every night to the good Lord that things will get better," their pious, youngest sister, Gunda, revealed.

"I think you need to pray a little louder. He seems to have wax in his ears," Rosa retorted. The sisters laughed while their mother scowled.

"Years have passed since Oswald lost his factory job," Rosa told them, "If it were not for his monthly dole, we would have to move in with you and father...so you had better start praying forcefully, mother!"

Everyone chuckled but knew Rosa was somewhat serious. Many of their friends and their families were in the same economic state. Each day, calamity seemed to draw nearer; the news reports they read or heard were seldom optimistic and inspired little hope.

At present, the family existed in a country with spiraling and widespread inflation and unemployment. Poverty was rampant throughout due to the country's defeat in WWI and the treaty that required the German government to pay massive reparations for the destruction it had caused. In addition, the Great Depression of 1929, wherein the American banks withdrew their loans from Germany, was plunging their country even further into economic free fall. Many of their fellow countrymen felt disgraced and scared; and the Bermann family members admitted they did too.

Rosa, Oswald, Anya, and Hannah, (Anya's three-year-older half-sister, the product of a youthful indiscretion on their mother's part), lived on doled out rations while their parents scrounged for meager jobs and food.

"When will it get better?" Rosa wondered aloud. Her sisters and mother had no answer. The melancholic drone regarding the state of their nation wafted through the homes and streets of Fürth daily. It was becoming ever more audible.

Trying to get their minds off their woes, the sisters cleared the table, washed the last of the dishes, dried them, and put them away. They then sat down with Babette for another cup of tea. As they shared the spare brew amongst themselves, sharp snippets of conversation from their father's study drifted toward them. The women reared their heads in concern.

Rosa stood up, "I had best close the door to the sitting room to make sure the children do not hear."

She was relieved to find her girls and their cousins too busy playing and chatting to take notice of the discussion going on down the hall. They did not take notice of her as she closed the door.

Signaling to her mother and sisters, Rosa proceeded toward the study to get a whiff of the conversation behind her father's closed door. The voices sounded ominous.

Listening to the newscast on the radio, the primary topic of conversation appeared to be the health of Germany's President, Paul von Hindenberg.

"Hindenberg has grown too old and too sick to be an effective leader any longer. Hitler's sitting on Hindenberg's tailcoats," Johann stated with great solemnity, as his sons and sons-in-law listened and nodded in agreement.

"Ja, Vater, it is a disturbing situation, but verdammt! Was kann Wir tun?" ("What can we do?") Norbert, his eldest, asked, hoping a solution would miraculously present itself.

"Throw Hitler into the Pegnitz and let him drown!" piped up the youngest of Johann's boys.

They all laughed, but their laughter was half-hearted and tinged with unease.

Hindenberg's deteriorating condition, they were acutely aware, opened a perilous door; a door that would allow the charismatic and bombastic Adolf Hitler and the rising Nazi party to march onto Germany's political landscape. The men in the room dreaded such an outcome. It did not, however, faze Rosa's husband, Oswald. Having attended one of Hitler's first political rallies in Fürth, Oswald was inspired.

Convinced of Hitler's fitness to lead Germany, he asserted, "No need to look so morose; the Nazis will save us all!"

Outside the door, Rosa cringed at her husband's proclamation.

"From what?" his father-in-law retorted, "Themselves?"

Oswald remained silent, not daring to reply to his father-in-law's derisive remark. He sensed his ill-chosen words had diminished him, as they observed him with notable contempt.

By their silence, Rosa knew their conversation was at a standstill. She quietly returned to the kitchen and reported what she had heard, leaving out her husband's words. She did not see Anya peering through the sitting room door. The child's ears had heard much; but her young mind did not understand what she had heard nor how to process it. All she sensed was anger and fear.

CHAPTER FOUR

It was not until Anya celebrated two more birthdays that a news bulletin inflamed the populace of Germany as well as her grandfather.

"Hitler's voice is growing louder over the airwaves," he informed his worried family, "There is no doubt his heated and high-flown declarations are inciting political unrest in his listeners. It is what I have feared all these months."

Despite Hitler's grandiloquent assertions, only subliminal changes to their economic status had occurred. German citizens were still plodding along in their quest for survival. Little had changed in their immediate world in two years, but an undercurrent of enormous change was beginning to grip the city of Fürth, the Bermann family, and their entire country.

That winter of '33, as the children played in the snow near the stoop of their grandparents' home, a mad rush of footsteps stomped by, raced through the front door and into their grandfather's chamber.

"Why are your fathers running inside like crazy chickens?" Anya, now six, asked her group of cousins. They shrugged and continued their play, although with troubled faces.

"I'm going in there," she whispered to Hannah.

"You can't! We are not supposed to. Mama will get angry!" Hannah warned as she pulled her sister away from the front door.

"Stop it! Something is wrong!" snapped Anya. "I want to find out what."

But Hannah's grip on Anya's coat sleeve was too strong. They both fell backward into the snow, and their rowdy cousins joined in the fracas.

Anya's instinct was right. Something was wrong. Loud, frantic voices and crackles from the radio could be heard through Opa's window. Although they could not make out the words, the children noted the voice on the radio had spun the household into a furious frenzy.

"Willie, put me on your shoulders," Anya begged one of her cousins, "I want to hear what they are saying!"

To her annoyance, Willie made her take off her dirty boots first before complying, while Hannah covered her eyes thinking her sister was crazy.

In a serious voice, the broadcast announcer informed listeners that "President Paul von Hindenberg, nearing his death, has appointed Adolf Hitler to the second highest position in the nation, that of Chancellor of Germany."

The surprised gasps and groans from the adults in the room were audible to Anya's ears, but so many words were beyond her comprehension that the resultant conversation was lost on her.

Why did they have to use such big words? It was so unfair!

"Stop stomping on me!" Willie barked at her, "It hurts!"

Anya looked at him with disdain, "Don't drop me!" she hissed.

"Well hurry up! My shoulders are aching!" he retorted in annoyance.

Anya grunted at Willie, climbed down, clomped into her old boots, and headed for the house. It was her mother who, with a stern eye and arms folded across her chest, managed to stop her.

Inside, the conversation continued while Anya's ears strained to hear what was being discussed as she stood in the hallway, restrained by her mother from entering further.

"Vater, I have heard rumors that the President appointed Hitler with much reluctance," her Onkel Norbert professed.

"Ja, I have heard very much the same," Onkel Walter replied. Deflecting the blame from their dying leader seemed the sympathetic thing to do under the circumstances.

"I heard his advisors coerced Hindenberg into it. They believe Hitler's popularity will strengthen the Nazi party's position in Germany," her Onkel Hans proclaimed.

"Most likely, they fear the Communist party will overtake our 'democratic republic' if Hitler is not at the helm. It is the only explanation for this madness," Onkel Norbert stated.

It seemed all her Onkels had something to say as they interrupted each other.

"Humph," her Opa replied, standing up and smashing his fist forcefully upon the desk, "'democratic republic', mein Arsch! Hitler ist ein wahnsinniger Mensch! He is a lunatic!"

His explosive response, proclaiming Hitler a madman and bastard, stunned his sons. As the words boomed out the door and down the hall, Anya jumped.

Did Opa really say what we just heard?! Mein Arsch?! (My Ass?!) Where was Oma? Why didn't she scold him? This was serious! Opa said a cuss word!

Her mother ran toward the study, disturbed by the cuss-laden bellowing and intent on curtailing it. Anya followed. This time they were both stopped by Oma walking toward them from the back of the house.

"Let them vent. It is all very upsetting. They will calm down," she told Rosa.

It took a few minutes for her husband to do so, but his sons managed the feat. Once Johann curbed his vituperative rant and came back to himself, they hoped they could turn to the patriarch of the family for solace.

"Vater, what think you of all this?" Wolfgang inquired. "Wass will happen when Hindenberg ist tot?"

The thought of Hindenberg dying disturbed them beyond measure. If they wanted reassurance from their father, he could not give it to them.

"Adolf, no doubt, will grab the opportunity to obtain the supreme position of President of Germany in any underhanded way he can. My gut doesn't trust him," Johann confessed to his boys. "I do *not* trust him at all."

On the radio, the announcer reiterated that President Hindenburg was not expected to live much longer.

"Do you mind if I turn this off?" Johann asked. "I cannot bear to hear any more."

Neither could they. Neither could his young granddaughter who, when found eavesdropping at the door, was scooped away by her displeased mother.

Hear more they did as the weeks passed: Hermann Goering was named Prime Minister, Josef Goebbels became Hitler's Minister of Propaganda, and upsetting to all the family except Oswald, Hitler was granted dictatorial powers through the Enabling Act, a new law he proposed to the Reichstag which would give him, as Chancellor, the power to rule by decree rather than passing laws through the Reichstag and the President.

On March 23, 1933, Johann, with Anya at his knee, read his newspaper with alarm. With his fingers gripping the pages, the headline informed German citizens that the new law was enacted that day. It would transform Hitler's government into a legal dictatorship.

Horrified, Johann threw the papers to the floor with a vengeance. Anya's heart raced and lips quivered. She suspected great evil was happening in the world for her Opa to look so troubled.

Anya's grandfather was not blind. He was duly cognizant of the fact that, stealth by stealth, like a leviathan coiling itself around its intended prey, Hitler and his Nazis would crush democracy and leave Germany's freedoms choking for air. Most disturbing to Johann was the volume of people he encountered that were blind to Hitler's character and manipulations. Like lambs being herded by a cunning sheep dog, they followed where Adolf Hitler and his promises led. Their loyalty to, and praise of, Hitler was something Johann and his family could not fathom.

"Why can't they see him for what he is?" her tormented Onkel Norbert asked of his father, as Anya sauntered through the door examining a book of German folk tales. She had fallen in love with her grandfather's collection of books and often browsed through them, picking out whatever words she had learned to read.

Johann shook his head, "I suppose they are not yet skilled in separating a man's motives from his promises."

Onkel Norbert agreed.

Disturbed and perplexed by the political shift in their country, the men in the family held almost daily discussions in Johann's enclave. In fact, so many meetings that her mother dragged her from the room on a consistent basis. Anya's father was the only one who did not appear at these encounters. Oswald had been ostracized from the family early on because of his defense of Hitler.

Anya and Hannah spent almost all their after-school hours at their grandparents' house, helping their mother and Oma with spring cleaning.

That June, curled in her usual spot at the foot of her Opa's chair, scavenging through newspapers and magazines, two of her uncles, looking as if Lucifer himself was chasing them, charged through the door, and brought shocking news:

"Father, Röhm and his men have been killed!" they shouted at once.

Forgetting Anya was there, Johann blanched at this unfortunate turn of events and swiftly turned on the radio. An alert Anya sat immobile on the rug trying to comprehend bits and pieces of the news flash she was privy to.

Ernst Röhm and the SA party (Brown Shirts), three million strong, were the only opposition Hitler and the Nazis faced in their quest for total power. As everyone in the room listened with dread, the announcer stated that Röhm and high members of his cabinet had been assassinated.

"What does *assinated* mean, Opa?" an inquisitive Anya asked as she pulled at his pants leg to get his attention. He looked down at her in dismay.

"Gott in Himmel, the child is still here!" Johann swooped Anya off the floor and shouted for his wife to "Come get Anya, please!" Rosa was outside gardening, and he wanted to forestall any reproaches from her while the atmosphere was so heated.

Anya protested as she was grabbed by one grandparent, then the other, and swooped into the kitchen and plopped on a chair next to a placid Hannah. Her sister was munching on a slice of bread spread with homemade jam, appearing oblivious to the ruckus.

"You are so rude!" Anya angrily declared, glaring at both grandparents. Johann beat a hasty retreat, while her Oma tried to soothe her with a plate of shaved carrots sprinkled with sugar on top, one of Anya's favorite treats. The bribe kept her quiet when Rosa walked in a few minutes later, happy to see her daughters sitting there like innocent cherubs.

Back in the study, the men remained wordless as the voice on the radio announced further details. Norbert ruptured the silence, "I heard Röhm, and his top men were killed execution style. No doubt Hitler had his henchmen do it. Vater, I thought he liked Röhm? Verdammt! What's going to happen now?"

Johann sensed their dread but could not ease it. They needed to be aware of the truth, and he spoke without hedging.

"Total power. Hitler will obtain total power over Germany. He has the SA in his pocket and gotten rid of all his rivals."

His sons shook their heads as their tongues failed them.

The Sturmabteilung (Storm Detachment, or SA) was the Nazi party's paramilitary wing, which played a significant role in Hitler's rise to power through their covert operations.

Johann recognized the dangers.

"Worst of all, our countrymen are needy and seeking a savior; but, with Hitler at the rudder, that neediness will be our curse. It will put all of us in the dangerous position of being vulnerable to his manipulations. I know what a corrupt leader can do when the wind blows his sails in the perfect direction." He looked at his sons grimly. "Hitler worries me now more than ever. With his powerful oratory skills, his words can be very persuasive. We know well he has a voracious mouth on him. I fear he will devour Germany."

CHAPTER FIVE

Fürth, Germany 1934-1935

As the winter's chill yielded to the warmth of spring, it became obvious that Anya's, and Hannah's, childhood, as well as that of their cousins, was showing signs of strain. It had not been stripped away but was chaffing away. Anxiety and depression were beginning to corrode their youthful demeanor and the fault lines were evident to their parents.

Quiet frolics with Hannah and taking long, country walks with her parents and other members of her vast family became the mainstay of Anya's life and brought diversion. But each day she became more alert to the unsettling facts of their existence.

Her parents were not sleeping well. Lack of work or money made them angrier than usual with each other. One evening she heard their heated discussion through the thin wall separating her and Hannah's small bedroom from theirs. Unable to sleep amidst the noise, Anya tossed and turned in her cot and tried blocking out her parents' upsetting words by wrapping her pillow around her ears. When that did not work, she pounded at the cushion with her fists, hoping the effort would tire her out. It did not. Peering at Hannah, she was surprised to see her sister sleeping through the noise like a bear cub curled in its den.

"I think you need to stop attending all these political rallies and wasting your Pfennigs on beer!" she heard her mother hiss at her father.

"It's none of your God-damn business what I do! It's important I stay informed!" he growled.

"Informed by the Nazis? What a fine joke! They will tell you anything you want to hear, and you're fool enough to believe it!" she jeered in return.

"Shut up, Rosa. I have had about enough of your acid tongue," he shot back.

And so it went. Anya clutched her stomach as their words grew louder, fearing her father would harm her mother; instead, she heard a forceful creak from their bed and listened to her mother stomp with defiance from the room.

The door to her own bedroom opened with a soft squeak a moment later.

"Anya, are you still awake? What are you doing sitting up in bed?" her mother murmured in the dim light, hoping not to awaken Hannah who snored softly.

"I couldn't sleep, Mama," she replied, not knowing what else to say.

"Ahh, I see. Too much of a racket next door, huh?" Rosa admitted.

She walked toward Anya's bed and sat next to her. A welcoming shaft of moonlight peered through the curtain-less window and gave the floorboards and small cot a mellow glow. Anya saw her mother's face soften. Smiling, Rosa stroked her daughter's hair. It was butter-soft and framed her face with silky curls.

"I'm sorry. I know Papa and I should not be yelling so much. Things will get better soon. I promise."

"It's okay, Mama," Anya insisted, not being quite honest. Rosa could sense she was troubled.

"What is bothering you, sweetheart?"

Anya shifted a bit nervously, "Mama, is Papa a Nazi?"

Rosa sighed and put her arm around her daughter. There was no way to hide the truth anymore.

"It appears so. Although not like the brutish soldiers you see on the street.

He is more like a Nazi servant. He collects money for them, reports neighborhood gossip, and hangs posters around town for them. He does simple things."

"Mama...?"

"Yes, dear?"

"I'm ashamed of him." There, she had said it!

Her mother remained silent for a moment.

"I am too," she admitted in response.

Brandishing a smile, Rosa tried to reassure her youngest that things would right themselves and gave her a kiss on the forehead.

"Now that we have shared our deep, dark secret, please roll over and let your Mama get into bed. I am cold!"

Anya giggled and, feeling unburdened, curved herself against her mother's back. Rosa drew the coverlet over them. It was time to sleep and, hopefully, waken to a better day.

CHAPTER SIX

True to her word Rosa found work in a local Bierstube filling the Biersteins of the local gentry and the uniformed Nazi officers that were frequent customers at the pub. She quickly learned to keep her mouth shut, so as not to get into trouble, and put a pleasant, but businesslike, smile on her face, as she wended her way through the wooden tables and the exuberant bottom-pinchers in the smoked-filled rooms.

When a customer became too rowdy, she kept that pleasant smile on her face, and called out in a composed voice "Herr Meier, Hilfe bitte." It was a subtle signal to the barkeep to come to her aid. Herr Meier, a no-nonsense type, would then attempt to smooth the rambunctious guest's feathers by introducing him to one of the accommodating birds on hand (for the young girls did love the attention of a uniformed soldier!). When the coop was sparsely filled with chickadees, Herr Meier would implore, (with as much diplomacy as possible), the drunken lout's comrades take the sot (though not in those words) home and let him sleep it off.

One afternoon Anya and Hannah stopped by the pub with their father and were awed to see their mother carry four, giant Biersteins filled with foaming, amber ale, in her two hands.

"Mama, you did it without spilling!" Anya exclaimed while the patrons sitting near them chuckled at her amazement and pride.

Their father, not wanting to be upstaged by his wife in the eyes of his daughters, obtained work with the local butcher within a week of their mother's coup. Any position that could provide even a miniscule addition to their income, beyond their monthly dole, was a Godsend. However, the combined paychecks were yet to provide food beyond the essentials. On occasion the butcher who employed their father would surprise him with a pork chop or sausage to bring home. His boss apologized he could not be more generous.

"I am sure you can understand I must sell every bit of meat so that I can take care of my own family during these difficult times," he explained to a disheartened Oswald.

Anya and Hannah realized life was not plentiful when they listened to the symphonic gurgles in their empty bellies. Family meals, consisting of thin gruel or soup thickened with a bit of lard to give it substance, appeared on their table almost daily. Oatmeal, rice, potatoes, bread, and farina were also basic staples of their diet. Anya dreamed of the day she would not see rice on her dinner plate again. It seemed it was the only thing lining her stomach.

"Rice, rice and more rice! I am sick of it, Mama. When will we have real food?" She declared that someday she would "never eat rice again!"

Vegetables, a few fruits, and a smattering of anemic chickens were raised in the garden at Oma's and Opa's, but even those were sparse. Her grandparents often shared their meager bounty among their children and their abundant offspring. Meat, fish, or eggs were prayed for but remained scant on their menu. The fertility of Oma's few hens, or what the boys caught in the surrounding rivers with their fishing poles, would sometimes add to their larder.

One fine day, Anya's father, who had been busy at the butcher's, yelled up to their kitchen window, "Rosa! Rosa!"

Rosa opened it wide, "What are you shouting about? What's going on?"

"Come downstairs with the children and bring some newspaper!"

They did as he asked and followed him to a cobbled, side street off the center of town.

Rosa saw it first and threw back her arms to stop the girls from coming closer; however, she was unable to shield them from the sight. There, near the edge of the walk, lay a dead horse, most likely dead of starvation or being worked beyond its strength. Laying on its side to the rear was an old, broken cart filled with rotted vegetables and straw. As the distraught owner tried to clear the mess off the street, the town butcher, along with helpers wielding butcher knives, proceeded to cut the carcass into pieces and rinse them in buckets of water. The stomach and hindquarters of the horse were splayed open, and the skin stripped back, exposing a mass of horseflesh, veins, and sinews. The butcher had already bled out the animal and the sour stench of the blood running into the gutter was more than Anya and Hannah could bear, not to mention the black flies dotting the carcass like a disease despite the men batting at them. Seeing the red eyes of the dead horse staring at her, a nervous Hannah vomited. Then Anya, observing the flies feeding on the disgusting sight, vomited.

"Get over here!" their father ordered, as each wiped their mouth with their apron, "And bring some paper!"

His hands and clothes were streaked with blood. Hannah vomited again and wiped her mouth on her sleeve, and Anya bit her lip to keep from doing so.

Their mother smoothed out the pages of the newspaper with rapid swipes and gave several sheets to each child. With great reluctance, she nudged the girls forward to bring them to their impatient father.

"Spread out your hands with the papers!" he snapped.

As they obeyed, he placed slabs of bloody meat in their outstretched hands. They wrapped it up as best they could without dripping it all over themselves.

"Go! Get it home. Rosa," he instructed his wife, "Clean it and cook it as fast as you can. We should be able to eat it. The horse hasn't been dead long."

The girls and their mother dashed home laden with their bloody packages.

Meanwhile their father began bargaining with the butcher, offering him what little he could in trade.

When Rosa and the girls arrived back at their flat, Rosa followed her husband's instructions and asked the girls to set the table while she cooked. She did not want them getting any paler than they already were by watching her clean the mound of horseflesh. Once rinsed again, she placed the meat and some lard into the heavy, black skillet on the burner. The girls averted their eyes. Soon afterward their father came home. He had attempted to clean himself up in the basement washhouse, but his rough shirt and work pants were still damp and bore crimson stains. The girls tried not to smell him by holding their breaths at intervals.

"Now doesn't that look good!" he stated, "We are having meat for dinner! It should taste decent once your mother cooks it through."

"Go to our room and change before we eat. Try not to mess up anything. Then leave your clothes near the toilet. I will boil them later. They smell awful," Rosa ordered. The girls looked at their father and held their noses.

Once served, the horsemeat was, to their surprise, lean and tender with a sweet tang to it. At least it did not repel their empty stomachs. Rosa and her girls chewed the meat with zest and swallowed it without gagging. However, the sight of the animal as it was being filleted loomed large in Anya's mind and rice began appealing to her again.

CHAPTER SEVEN

The horsemeat did not last long. In the weeks that followed, the only respite in their paltry diet occurred when their father received his unemployment dole. Then he would announce jauntily, "We are going to Nuremberg on Sunday!" and they would scramble to ready their clothes for the journey to the neighboring city.

Like most low-income homes during that time, their apartment contained neither hot water nor an indoor heating system. A small oven, rudimentary furniture, two undersized bedrooms and a cubbyhole toilet were the only luxuries in their miniscule flat. Other impoverished apartment-dwellers were not as lucky: they would have to go down to the "Hof", the interior courtyard centered among the buildings, and use the communal toilet that was housed in a stall behind rough timber doors.

Anya, as she visited one of her school friends, found she had need of the facility. As she unlatched the crude door, stepped in, and lifted the grimy, wooden lid, she caught sight of the human droppings at the bottom of the stained pit. The sight and pungent odor caused her to heave, and she ran out and away from the stink of it all. She decided that she would much prefer to pee in her pants, then use that 'throne'. Her bemused friend watched as she fled to a nearby bush, where she was able to relieve herself without fainting or being seen. That night Anya fell to her knees, looked Heavenward, and with a grateful heart intoned, "Danke, lieber Gott im Himmel, das wir eine Toilette haben!"

Having an indoor toilet, even one as tiny as theirs, was a much-appreciated blessing. She later spoke of it to Hannah.

"You cannot believe what I lived through today!"

She could not wait for their trip to Nuremberg to get the image of the traumatizing toilet out of her mind and replace it with sights of the beautiful city.

On the morning of their excursion to Nuremberg, Rosa heated water on the stove before cramming her daughters into a washtub in the kitchen to be bathed. She, herself had used it in the early morning hours to have some privacy before the girls tumbled out of bed. Once dried and dressed in her slip, Rosa donned an apron over it to protect it from the girls' eventual splashes. Thankfully, it was a sunny, spring day and the girls did not have to shiver in a drafty kitchen watching each other's lips turn blue as they did on wintry days. Their father was downstairs in the cellar's communal washhouse where the laundry was done. He had heated water on the washhouse oven and was busy scrubbing his stout physique and shaving his rounded face before any neighbors formed a queue outside the latched door. The room was filled with steam.

Upstairs, the sisters lathered the coarse soap over their bodies then playfully splashed at each other with soaked washcloths.

"Stop that! You are getting the floor all wet!" their mother shouted, "Stand up! We do not want to keep your father waiting."

The girls hopped out of the tub and their mother wrapped their thin bodies in towels to dry them off. Hannah, overwhelmed with excitement, rushed to the toilet.

"Mama!" she yelled from the closeted room, "Please bring me more strips of newspaper! There's not enough here."

"Ach, that child!" Rosa picked out scraps from a nearby basket and handed them to Hannah through the crack in the door.

A few minutes later, they heard the *whoosh* of the toilet. Hannah emerged, picked up her sponge, immersed herself in the tub again, and washed the tender bum that was sore from using rough paper and smearing newsprint on it.

Rosa shook her head at the sight, "Here, clean yourself well and put some ointment there."

Anya curled up her nose and uttered a resounding, "Ugh", while Hannah stuck her tongue out at her sister before complying with her mother's wishes.

"Get into your dresses while I clean up," Rosa ordered. "You have five minutes! And put on your sweaters. There is still a chill in the air this morning."

In four minutes and thirty seconds, the girls, with hair plaited into slap-dash braids, were dressed and ready to embark for Nuremberg with their parents.

As they barreled down the stairs, the urchins flew by a startled neighbor holding onto the staircase railing for dear life.

"Guten Morgen, Frau Kraus! We're going to Nuremberg!" Anya informed her with glee as she and Hannah whirled by. The flustered woman received a quick barrage of apologies from Oswald and Rosa as they, too, hurried by to catch up with their children.

"Goodness me!" Frau Kraus declared, trying hard to maintain her footing.

Nuremberg, a seven-kilometer trolley ride away, never ceased to enthrall the sisters. As they sat down amongst the other passengers, and their tickets were stamped, Anya kneeled in her seat and turned to look out the window and enjoy the view. Hannah chose to sit ladylike next to their father, while their mother attempted to divert Anya's shoes from swiping dirt on her dress.

Anya remained oblivious to her mother nudging her feet away, so fascinated was she with the sights outside the trolley window. Inside, the occupants consisted of German soldiers, men, and boys in Lederhosen enroute to some country "Wanderung", and families in their Sunday best.

As the conductor routed the lengthy tram through the narrow, cobbled streets of Fürth, Anya peered with delight at the shop windows they passed along the way. Filled with fashions and merchandise for the well-to-do, their offerings left her agog. Catching sight of a pretty dress or a pretty doll especially thrilled her. She knew that her parents could not afford to buy many of the goods on display because they had often given her a firm "No" when she handed them an item and was instructed to put it back on its shelf. It was nice to look at and admire the things anyway, she decided. *Someday I might have the treasures I dream of.*

Watching people mill about on this summerish day provided even more entertainment. Everyone looked starched and new. Anya, herself, felt sparkly in her freshly washed and ironed, polka-dot dress and newly polished shoes. She only wished she had a pair of white socks to wear with them, instead of the grey tights. But no matter; someday, she decided, she would have a pair. She studied her mother, father, and Hannah. They looked fine indeed and happy, as the trolley continued along its path. Even Hannah, who was considered an ordinary girl with thick, brown hair, prominent nose, and slanted, brown eyes, looked vibrant in her blue and white gingham dress. They were sporting their Sunday best, the only dress-up clothes they had. Even her father wore his best suit jacket.

As they passed the town park and the train station, their trolley headed for the broad, tree-lined boulevard that would bring them directly into Nuremberg. On each side of the avenue, tall, Greystone apartments with fancy scrollwork and long windows appeared. The affluent townsfolk or officers occupied these buildings and Anya wondered what it would be like to live in one. She tried to catch a glimpse through the buildings' windows, but they were well-curtained and kept peering eyes at bay.

When the conductor clanged the bell and announced, "Nuremberg Centrum, next stop!" they, and several fellow travelers, prepared to disembark as soon as the trolley came to a halt.

Anya and Hannah jumped off at the first opportunity.

"Mama, Papa, hurry! We've only a day!" they implored, ready to run through the streets with the intent of exploring everything.

By noontime, after ambling through shops and byways, they were ready to eat. Their favorite pub, on a side street near the Nuremberg Marktplatz, awaited their appetites.

Jovial laughter, constant chatter, and delicious smells of sizzling food greeted them as they entered the quaint tavern. The ample space featured honey-colored wooden booths, several rustic tables and chairs at its center, and a stained-glass window depicting a prayerful saint kneeling in a glen amongst deer and flowers. Amber glasses and steins topped with foaming beer glinted in the hands of the sizeable crowd. The Schmidts were welcomed by a jolly waitress in a colorful dirndl of red, black, and green, adorned with a lace blouse and ample bosom spilling from it. Anya and Hannah slyly peered at their father to see his reaction to this bounteous display, but their mother nudged them forward as the waitress guided them to a table.

Seated in carved, wooden chairs, they ordered their usual modest plates of bratwurst, sauerkraut, and boiled potatoes along with a pint of "Dunkel" for the parents, and a small glass of lemonade for each of the girls. The girls drank in the boisterous surroundings with glee.

"Prost!" rang out often, initiated by the raising and clinking of Biersteins as they waited for their meal. Everyone appeared in good spirits, stoked by the beautiful weather outside and the dole inside their pockets. A few Nazi officers appeared at the door and joined in the fun, threatening no one by their presence. Rosa, afraid Oswald would go over to greet them, gave him a cautionary look.

Not today. Not with your children here, her eyes warned. He satisfied her wish.

Soon, the savory aroma of their spiced sausages browned in butter wafted in the air, and the girls ate their meal with delicious abandon.

"Anya, stop slurping like that! Chew your food thoroughly before you swallow it. And Hannah, you are dripping sauerkraut over the table. Use your napkins! I did not raise you to be monkeys!"

The girls giggled at the thought, and next dove into the golden Tartuffe Salat, stuffing multiple pieces of thinly sliced potatoes, drenched in oil, vinegar, onion and bacon bits into their mouths.

When the last speck on their plate was eaten, and the bill was paid, they departed. Outside, Anya and Hannah begged their father for a few Pfennigs to buy a small bag of cake crumbs from the Backerei next door.

"Bitte! Bitte, Papa!" He smiled and handed them the treasured coins and watched them romp toward the bakery.

Spending the rest of the day snacking on cake crumbs and absorbing the sights and sounds of Nuremberg was as thrilling as admission to an amusement park for the two exuberant girls.

Their next stop was the Nuremberger Hauptmarkt, the bustling square in the heart of the Altstadt, the older section of the city, with its daily displays of farm produce. Their mother examined the wares, as well as the fresh fruits and vegetables, before purchasing only what she required. The cost of the more exotic food items was beyond their means. Rosa tried to stretch the money as best she could and placed her meagre purchases into the small, netted bag that she carried.

Afterward, the family visited the nearby Frauenkirche, despite it being Catholic and they were Lutheran. Upon entering, they bowed before its majestic altar. Rosa and her daughters whispered a prayer and went to light a candle for the souls of the departed and the ill, performing this ritual with great solemnity as they stood beneath the soaring arches of the revered cathedral. Oswald stood back and watched. He was not devout and not the praying type and made no move to join in.

"Mama, may I also light a candle for Oma and Opa?" Anya requested of her mother as they stood at the vestibule. "They are getting old, and I want God to make them live forever."

"Is that what you are going to pray for? What about the sick and the souls who have gone to heaven?'

"Well, can't you light a candle and pray that someone doesn't get sick or go to heaven?"

An amused Rosa conceded and gave her youngest a few coins to light a candle for Oma and Opa. Hannah remained content with the initial candle her mother had lit.

Concluding this observance, they returned to the market square and hopped aboard a trolley heading to Nuremberg Castle and the Albrecht Durer house. Durer was Germany's distinguished Renaissance artist from 1509 to 1528, and the girls were proud to know such a famous person had lived not far from Fürth.

The house, of medieval architecture, was being converted into a secretarial school where Anya and Hannah would learn office skills when they came of age.

Winding their way around the Durer house, the family climbed the hill to the medieval Burg, or castle, with its sweeping views of the city and the Pegnitz River. Giving free reign to their imagination, Anya morphed into a princess while Hannah transformed into the evil dragon chasing her along the cobbled and curving route. Rosa watched their gaiety with a tranquil and grateful heart, as she and Oswald sauntered behind their daughters. It was a good day whenever they went to Nuremberg, and she felt serene as she watched her girls scamper about. Hannah was now ten and Anya seven and today they were happy, cheerful children. Rosa dared not ask for more.

Returning to their small flat in Fürth that evening, everyone remained in good spirits. The girls did not have to listen to their parents argue over food, money, jobs or all the other things parents squawked about and made mountains of. Being home, being together, and having full stomachs, was all they cared about, even if home was not a royal castle. Their home, they knew, was humble, but it was a roof over their heads, which was more than some people had according to their mother, and it was enough to be grateful for.

As the sisters lay down to sleep that night, deciding to share Hannah's bed, and voiced a sweet "Gute Nacht" to their parents, Anya and Hannah cuddled the cloth dolls their grandmother had made for them and felt content. They had a home shielding them from harm and the unpredictable moods of the weather. And, for one day, had been shielded from the unpredictable moods of their father.

"What was your favorite part of the day?" Anya whispered to Hannah.

"We weren't poor. I like it when we're not poor."

"Me too," acknowledged Anya, happily burying herself in her sister's bed.

"Guess what I have?" Hannah reached under the feather pillow and pulled out the last of the cake crumbs she had saved in the bag,

"Oh Hannah," Anya murmured with delight. Emitting soft giggles as they sprinkled the delectable crumbs into their mouths, they were, for a few moments, rich again.

CHAPTER EIGHT

Returning to their usual amusements in the days that followed, Hannah, along with the neighborhood children, played ball, marbles (using pebbles found in the street), or hide 'n' seek amid their more significant chores. Their favorite task centered around Herr Schumann's coal deliveries, and he was making a delivery that day.

"It's coal day! Let us see how many pieces of coal we can gather!" Anya cried out to Hannah and their friends, as Herr Schumann came spinning around their street corner in his company truck. Driving with deliberate zigs and zags down the road, ensuring that several briquets would spill out on the pavement, he navigated his way over the cobbled lanes with the bravura of a mad gazelle. The sisters, along with their neighborhood gang, ran into the street, grabbed the black lumps with glee and stuffed them into the flour sacks they carried or into any handy pocket.

"Look how many I have!" resounded from many a lad and lass.

When they returned home, the coal was stored in a bucket or large bin and was used to stoke the family oven on a cold day, or to cook meals as needed. There was also the matter of warm water for baths, washing clothes, and cleaning the grimy floors when a child was not careful with its collection, or used their apron pockets instead of flour sacks.

After Anya joyously, but carelessly, spilled her portion of coal into the bin, and Hannah did the same, their mother looked at their soot-covered clothes and streaked hands and faces and wondered if the harvest they reaped was worth the labor she expended to clean them up.

As the children played outdoors, the adults were always occupied with essential chores. Sometimes there seemed no end to it. Socks were darned and re-darned. Worn shoes were fitted with cardboard soles. Available fruits and vegetables had to be cooked and preserved. Meals, no matter how meager, had to be prepared. Clothing was maintained, borrowed, or passed from relative to relative, friend to friend, with rigorous care. Everything was precious; nothing was discarded.

The fashion-conscious ladies of the family, all with limited means, shared each other's clothes and, in warm weather, used an eyebrow pencil to draw lines down the backs of their bare legs to create the illusion of wearing stylish, seamed nylons. Like all young women, they wished to attract potential beaus.

"Mama, why are Marta and Regina drawing black lines down their legs?" Anya wondered as she moseyed through Oma's kitchen.

"They are practicing for summer," her distracted mother explained, picking at stitching on an old blouse.

"Practicing what, Mama?" asked her curious seven-year-old.

"To make themselves look nice, so they will attract nice boys," answered Rosa absentmindedly.

Anya ambled back to the kitchen, wanting to see her cousins' handiwork up close. They were gone. When she returned a short while later, her mother looked at her with dismay. The backs of Anya's legs were decidedly marked with thick, black lines.

"Gott in Himmel, what did you do?" Rosa exclaimed.

Anya's cousins had unknowingly left behind a stick of charcoal.

"I want to attract nice boys too!" her guileless daughter replied.

Rosa was wordless, while Oma, who had witnessed the interchange, laughed until her ribs ached.

"Wait until she starts school this fall. She will have your head spinning!" Oma declared, much to Rosa's annoyance.

As school drew nearer, Rosa transformed an old sheet into a dress for her growing daughter. The project was met with unaccustomed resistance on the part of Anya. While being fitted, she inquired, with a dubious expression on her face, "Who slept in my new dress? I hope it wasn't you know who," she groaned, referring to an elderly aunt who was known to be incontinent.

"Stop fussing. It has been boiled in soap and water and there are no stains on it. You look lovely in it," Rosa informed her.

Appeased, Anya danced around their tiny apartment in her handmade frock. Within a moment she stopped in half-twirl and wrinkled her nose, "It smells awfully funny."

Her father looked up from the table where he was reading the paper, "Wear it or you will get a good slap from me if you don't!"

At his words, Anya burst into tears and ran toward her bedroom, where her sister was quietly reading. A quarrel between her parents followed, upsetting her more. To Hannah's dismay, Anya collapsed on her bed bawling as if her heart would break.

"Oswald! Why are you so hard on the child lately?" her distraught mother yelled. "Things are difficult enough as they are!"

"She has to learn to be grateful for what she has and what she is given. You spoil her!" her father bellowed.

"Spoil her? With what? She is a child! A child I cannot even give decent food to! A child I cannot clothe warmly enough! A child who just for once wants something that is pretty and her own! She and Hannah have been robbed of so much and all you do is shout and make it unbearable for them. All they have known their entire childhood are difficulties!"

Her father had no reply as her mother ranted. Unbeknownst to Anya, his mind was in turmoil over his wife's bitter and truthful words. Anya muffled her cries into her pillow as she heard the door

45

slam and her mother break down in tears. Hannah lay down on the bed beside her and the girls huddled in their misery.

Within a matter of days, the argument was buried under chores that needed to be done and the arrival of grave news. Seated near an open window in the August heat, Anya overheard her parents discussing President Paul von Hindenberg in solemn tones.

"Is the President dead?" she asked with concern as her father read the paper, while her mother busied herself with needlework. Hannah had gone off with a friend, and Anya felt listless as the warm air drifted through the windows, doing little to cool down their flat.

"Nein, Liebchen. You do not need to worry your head about such things," her mother reassured her with a warm smile, "Sit by me. How would you like to learn to embroider like Mama?"

Anya sat next to her mother with interest, not daring to vex her father by refusing to do so.

At her grandparent's the following Sunday, she listened to further speculation about the President. As usual, her uncles were congregated around Opa's radio. They were doing this a great deal lately, Anya noted, feeling the weight of their routine wash over her as they listened for more news.

"Hindenburg is dying," one of her uncles announced with sorrow. "He can't rally the people any longer. Morale is lower than dreck right now. It is only a matter of time before Hitler is appointed and anointed Führer of Germany. Scheisse! Anyone but him!"

The somber look on Johann's face underscored what his sons were thinking.

"Ich kann nicht glauben Hindenberg made Hitler Chancellor. I cannot believe Rohm is dead. Hitler will now be Reichsführer of Germany for certain when Hindenberg dies," her Onkel Norbert stated. His ominous words made all in the room uneasy. With little desire to discuss the events further, the conversation ended in abysmal silence.

Anya did not understand much of the discussion. She had sensed the seriousness and deep sadness of the occasion and dared not emit a peep. To her surprise, her mother seldom blocked her from Opa's door anymore. Rosa realized her youngest would soon be entering school, and there was no way to protect her from the chatter of schoolchildren and teachers. Her young daughter would soon become a part of the world and, Rosa surmised, protecting Anya from it would only do her a disservice. Anya had to be made aware of what was going on, and how to safely navigate her way through it.

The summer passed without further dramatic incidence. The placid days were balm to their bruised souls. There were quiet walks in the countryside, amiable Sunday dinners with family, and muted discussions at home. But when the leaves began to fall in September of 1934, President Paul von Hindenberg was dead.

Young Anya cried for no reason except the fact that it was a sad event to have someone die. Her family was devastated. Only Oswald, her father, remained optimistic. Propagandized as Germany's only hope, Adolf Hitler, became President, and positioned his Third Reich to secure total supremacy over Germany.

Listening to Hitler rant over the airwaves, Anya and her family heard the new Führer promise deliverance from their destitution, and declare, with unmitigated bombast, he would make Germany great again. German citizens were persuaded to support Hitler and the Nazi party from thereon in.

Johann, disturbed by the turn of events, professed to his family, "Germany is in grave danger. No opposition; no choice in the election. Either you vote the way the Führer wants you to vote, or you can kiss your loved ones goodbye and order your casket now."

Anya did not know what to make of Opa's statement. She just held fast to her mother's and Hannah's hands as they listened to the Führer continue spouting promises on the radio.

CHAPTER NINE

No political promises were fulfilled straightaway, and the difficulties encompassing food or money did not ease. In the surrounding countryside, only the farmers managed to fare better. One October day, willing to forfeit whatever clothing or family heirlooms they could spare, Anya's mother, aunts and cousins trekked toward the surrounding farms in the hope they could exchange their limited belongings for food. Not all the farmers they encountered were willing to do so. If they did not want or have need of what was being offered, they declined to trade.

"Please, Herr Bauer, won't you consider these handwoven mittens in exchange for a chicken or some pork, or even a few eggs? Our children, as you see, are growing thinner by the day. We beg you. Winter is coming."

Anya and her cousins looked at Herr Bauer with expectant eyes. He placed a few items in their baskets and did not request a return.

"You are a kind man," Anya whispered. Then, to his delight, the pretty, little girl offered him a sturdy handshake and a hearty "Danke schöen!"

Emboldened by his charity, they continued their visits to other farmsteads in the area to find themselves greeted by either a generous spirit or waved off by a cantankerous, old sod or his equally cantankerous wife. If the latter, the children proceeded to yell "Alter Esel! Alte Kuh!" ("Old Mule! Old Cow!") as they scurried away to avoid the farmer's pitchfork.

When twilight came and the countryside quieted, their amber lanterns glowed as they turned toward Oma and Opa's house. They were grateful for the blessed food they had managed to obtain. A hen, a dozen brown eggs, two loaves of Bauernbrot, a square of butter and cheese, and two pails brimming with cow's milk filled their baskets and arms. A portion of this fare would provide a decent Sunday meal for the entire Bermann clan. Oma possessed a gift for stretching supplies. The goods prone to spoiling were stored in the cool cellar beneath the house for eventual use. This area served as a pantry of sorts, its shelves bearing jars of pickled vegetables and fruited jam.

As Oma emerged from her underground stockade, a squawking, orange-plumed hen was thrust into her broad hands. The distraught chicken was promptly penned up in the back garden for eventual plucking. Pecking away at the fresh seed strewn about, the unfortunate creature would see the blade of Oma's hatchet by the morning of the Sunday feast. Knowing this, her grandchildren were crestfallen as they contemplated the pending doom of the unsuspecting bird.

Tired from scavenging for food all day, they and their parents readied themselves for their departure home. Opa, ever the town crier, brought a cheerless news tidbit to their attention. The article he quoted made clear that foraging for food had become a pastime not only in Fürth but in the whole of Germany. Poverty was becoming an epidemic in their country with no foreseeable cure.

"Many more visits to the farmsteads will need to be scheduled, or we will starve," was Johann's dire warning.

CHAPTER TEN

The New Year brought a speck of hope. According to multiple news reports, it appeared the Führer would launch the rebirth of his nation and make good on his promises. Anya's family felt a tinge of optimism. The children sensed their parents were happier, and it put them at ease.

"Ah, listen to this bit of propaganda in today's paper!" Johann commanded when his family was gathered. "'Hitler has implemented Germany's transportation system, built new highways and low-income housing, developed new industries and more jobs, and created a piece de resistance, the Volkswagen Beetle... an inexpensive car as a mode of travel for the middle class,'" He put the paper down.

"Well, well, our generous savior reigns supreme! We are offered a Beetle, while he and his leeches ride around in a Mercedes-Benz," Johann spit the words out with utter contempt.

What was not made transparent in the article was the fact that Hitler had initiated the systemic eradication of Jews. That fact was kept from the world to ensure the prestigious Summer Olympics of '36 would be held in Berlin. Hitler wanted the prestige of being the host country to the greatest sporting event in the world.

Hearing mention of the Volkswagen, Anya, now nine years of age, asked, "Will we get a Beetle, Mama?" The trolley, horses, and flocks of sheep still ambled along the pathways of Fürth, but the inner city sported more cars on its streets. The automobiles enthralled

Anya.

"No, silly. Your father cannot drive," her mother responded. Then she sighed, "I would rather he put proper food on the table and acquired a decent job instead."

The economy was showing promising signs of a recovery. There was a glimmer of hope their situation might change soon. Anya's grandfather, ever vigilant, retained his doubts. In his estimation, the Nazi presence in Germany was reaching an ominous zenith. The boys of yesteryear, now grown men, were visible everywhere and leading the storm.

As early as 1925, Hitler's doctrines were driven into the impressionable minds of the German youth. It was during that year Adolph and his party launched the "Hitler Jugend". These Nazi youth groups consisted of male and female factions. Johann was sharp-witted enough to realize Hitler would benefit from the malleable psyches of the young. Eager students, they learned quickly and adhered to Nazi doctrines with rapacious devotion. Most cunning of all, they were encouraged to turn on their own parents if they proved disloyal to the Nazi party.

The Hitler Jugend, piloted by their passion and youthful rebellion against the establishment and the status quo, flourished and produced well-trained disciples that transmuted into zealous Nazi soldiers over the years. Nazi soldiers whose fanaticism was grounded in brutal and depraved behavior. When Johann's sons were of age to be drawn into the Hitler Jugend, he wisely procured jobs for his boys on outlying farms to keep them out of the clutches of the Third Reich.

"If they work for the good of the people, thrashing wheat and hauling manure, they will be safe enough," he reassured their concerned mother at the time.

In the Schmidt household, however, dispassion for the Third Reich on the part of Oswald's daughters and his wife reached a zenith one afternoon. Ear-splitting screams howled their way up the stairwell of their apartment building at the end of a school day.

Alarmed, Rosa listened as the wails drew closer and closer to her door. Opening it with caution, she discovered Anya shaking and crying in the hallway. Her daughter's eyes were red, wet, and filled with terror. Running up behind her was Hannah with an embarrassed look on her flushed face.

"Gott in Himmel, what is wrong?" Rosa asked in dismay, turning to Hannah for an explanation.

Rosa almost fell backward as Anya thrust her arms around her waist, clenching on to it like an oyster to a pearl. Rattled by her sister's extreme agitation, Hannah shrugged in nervous response.

"I won't go! I will not go, Mama! He cannot make me! He cannot make me!" Anya screamed.

Her cries generated such fierce hiccups, Anya began quivering and gasping for air.

"What in Heaven's name?!" Rosa snapped, giving Hannah a piercing look.

Taken aback by Anya's distress, Rosa sat her on her lap for comfort. Calming her daughter down took some effort.

She scowled at her eldest with suspicion. Rosa asked again, "What caused this?"

Hannah sighed as guilt washed over her face and confessed:

"It's my fault, well...sort of, Mama," Hannah began, "We saw a poster of a pretty girl with blonde braids, and she became upset."

"Well? What did it say?" her mother implored as Anya squirmed against her chest, "Tell me now!"

Hannah bit her lip, "It stated, 'Auch Du gehörst dem Führer!'." ("You too belong to the Führer!").

At Hannah's words, Anya grew agitated again and cried out, "I don't belong to him! He will take me away! He will take me away from you, Mama, and Hannah. I do not belong to him! I belong to you!"

Rosa held firm to a shuddering Anya, while Hannah, overcome by her sister's gale-force weeping, began to weep too.

"No, no, dear. He will not take you away. No, my sweet girl. Do not be afraid. You belong to me. You will always belong to Mama."

"I don't want to leave you, Mama! Not ever!"

"Look at me," her mother ordered. Anya emitted another sizeable hiccup, then obeyed with a whimper.

"I will always be here. And you will always belong to me. Understood?"

Anya nodded her head, still dripping wet tears, and hugged her mother tight. Rubbing her back until Anya was soothed and quieted, Rosa gave a discomfited Hannah a reassuring smile.

"Now both of you give Mama a kiss and let us see if we can find an apple for you to share."

Sitting at the kitchen table later while Anya slept, Hannah, with face flushed from guilt, placed her hand on her mother's.

"I'm sorry, Mama. I had no idea the poster would upset her so. I should have steered her away from it."

"It is alright, Hannah. Her nerves are just overwrought."

"Mine too, Mama," Hannah admitted.

Rosa nodded and patted her hand, "I know. So much has been going on since Hitler became Führer. It is overwhelming and disturbing, especially for young people like you."

"What is going to happen to us, Mama?"

Rosa noted the anxiety in her eldest child, "I do not know, Hannah. I do not know. But I promise you, we will get through it. We will."

Rosa wished it to be so, but her confidence was faltering.

CHAPTER ELEVEN

Rosa's concerns were not without gravity, and she often discussed them with her father. To the outside world, it appeared that Nazism thrust itself on Germany with swift and apocalyptic force. This she and Johann knew was a deception. The takeover was conducted in such a mundane and insidious manner that their fellow countrymen found themselves in the grip of Nazism before being fully aware they were being lied to, quashed, and turned into Hitler's lemmings.

In their walks around town, posters depicting an impoverished people read: "Unsere Letzte Hoffnung – HITLER" ("Our Last Hope - HITLER"). In the feigned 'democratic' elections that retained Hitler in office, there was only one political party to vote for. Germans had the choice of voting either "Ja" or "Nein" for Hitler.

"Will you vote Nein?" Anya asked her grandfather out of curiosity, as she sat in his office.

Johann grimaced. "Nein is not a choice; not if we value our life."

His terse and portentous reply stopped her from asking more. Grumbling and turning the dials on his radio, Johann scowled and appeared distracted. Anya proceeded to leave and heard distant and strange static as she closed the door behind her. *What is Opa listening to?* she mused, somewhat disturbed.

The Reich Minister of Propaganda, Joseph Goebels, had made radios incredibly affordable, thus ensuring their place in German households as a prime tool for spreading Nazi propaganda. The coveted radio came with a caveat: listeners were only allowed to tune into prescribed stations. Anything else, such as the BBC broadcasts out of Great Britain, were against Nazi law, and the non-compliant would encounter stringent penalties. The strange static Anya heard was her grandfather attempting to tune his radio to a secret broadcast...the BBC station out of London. He did not try this often; but, when he did, it was in seclusion. Even his sons were not aware.

The true purpose of this household device became the foil for private humor among neighbors and friends.

"Have you heard," they whispered, "an old woman took her little radio to church, and the priest wondered why. 'Oh,' she replied, 'it has to go to confession. It lies too much!'"

Its latest lie: The upcoming election for Chancellor of Germany would be a democratic one.

When time came for the presidential election, Anya's family, as other German citizens, were coerced to vote in person at the polls. They marched into the crowded building, flanked by armed soldiers, and found only one name on the ballot: *Adolph Hitler*.

On election day, if a person could not show up at the polls due to an infirmity, a member of the Nazi party arrived at their home to ensure their ballot was cast one way or another. One of Anya's aunts, weak and ill with the "Grippe" (flu) was dragged into the polling place attended by her son.

Meanwhile, Johann, hesitating in line as he stared at his ballot, felt the butt of a rifle slam into his back. The painful jolt left him winded.

"Sign it old man, and move along, or it won't be your back next time."

Johann marked his ballot with a reluctant check and dropped it into a designated box.

Norbert, who stood behind him, had shielded the exchange between his father and the soldier, from Rosa and their mother. There was no telling what Babette would do if she witnessed her husband being threatened or harmed. When his father exited the building, Norbert caught up with him and grabbed his arm.

"Are you all right, Vater?" Norbert's face looked as ashen as Johann's.

"I am fine. Look after the rest of the family. I will meet you all at home. I need to walk and get some air."

His son squeezed Johann's arm and returned to the hoard of people inside, but not without first ordering one of his younger brothers to accompany their father.

The volume of votes gathered throughout Germany were intended to show the world how esteemed Hitler was among his people. The ruse worked. When it was reported Hitler received 99% of the vote, world leaders were dismayed by his popularity. The Bermanns could only guess as to what happened to the one percent that voted "Nein".

Back at the house, Anya heard her uncles and Opa gripe behind closed doors,

"Let me take a rough guess *who* you voted for?" their soured father asked.

It had been a roguish election. Without an affirmative checkmark next to Hitler's name, voters knew they were signing their possible death warrant. Armed guards were always at the ready. The Bermanns, beholding their ballots, chose life.

Family get-togethers became gloomier as days then weeks passed by. Oswald, always vocal about his support of the Nazi party, was seldom home anymore, choosing to do his "duty" instead. Rosa, not clear on what his "duty" entailed, pledged Anya and Hannah to secrecy as a cautionary measure. They were never to repeat to their father what they heard at the family gatherings.

Without Oswald's presence, the Bermann men shared their true political feelings without restraint, but always behind closed doors. Opinions overheard by the wrong person could lead to severe consequences, and not just at the hands of the Nazis. One evening they discussed Hitler so vehemently that their descriptions of Adolf torched the ears of the women and children sitting in the kitchen. Anya's grandmother and mother took up their brooms and banged mightily on the study door.

"We will thrash you if you do not lower your voices!" the ladies threatened.

The culprits made a solemn vow to reduce their braying if the women took their thumping broomsticks elsewhere.

When the female stampede returned to the kitchen to finish washing the dinner dishes, a curious Anya sneaked down the hallway to listen to the latest political discussion.

"That maniac actually believes his own bullshit. Das grösster Arschloch der Welt" is convinced that he is Germany's redeemer," muttered one incensed uncle. Anya, at her secret post, reddened at the words she was not supposed to hear. Her male cousins had once used them in her presence when she stumbled upon them playing a heated game of stickball in the park. When she repeated the curious words, they laughed and told her what they meant, leaving her appalled. *Just like now,* she thought, *I never expected cuss words to be so plentiful around Opa and my grown-up uncles! Calling Hitler the "biggest asshole in the world"...wow!*

"That is the problem," Johann stressed, as she stuck her burning ear to the door. She was almost ten and was beginning to understand and absorb more with each conversation she overheard. Anya gathered she was getting a unique education.

"A man who has such strong confidence in his own beliefs will be able to convince others. Hitler, unfortunately, has become the voice of Germany's tribulations and the lifeforce behind their hopes. Do you know what I fear?" he paused, contemplating the words he was about to utter, "I fear his vision will damage Germany, not redeem it."

There was silence in the room after her grandfather spoke those words. Anya sensed they were thinking about what he said.

"What a paradox Hitler is," Johann continued. "He seemingly sustains his people and yet does not trust them to be loyal and vote him into office democratically. He is a complete cynic in his political tactics. It is an unusual mental aberration in the mind of a dictator. I guess we will never understand such men."

"Power and control are their addictions," her usually quiet Onkel Hans commented, "I think Hitler is being heavy-handed because he wants to avert a coup. He is, no doubt, terrified of it happening."

"I dread that it might be more than that," Johann stated. "I think Hitler is going to use Germany as a weapon to fulfill his own ends. He is Austrian! He has no allegiance to this country. What the hell is he up to?"

Anya, listening intently, wondered what a cynic and a coup was, but did not dare ask her mother, who was beckoning her to come away.

"What are you doing, dear?" Rosa asked her snooping daughter.

Until now, Rosa had been too busy washing dishes to notice that Anya had strolled away from the kitchen and toward the study.

"I went in to collect their empty bottles, but they were busy talking, and I didn't want to interrupt."

"What are they talking about? Good old Adolf, no doubt, huh? And it has you curious?"

Anya nodded, flustered that her mother was often aware of her true motive.

"Well, I think it is time you, Hannah, and I went home before your father comes after us. I am sure you have heard enough to turn your brain into strudel."

They readied themselves to leave.

"Mama, why doesn't Papa come here with us anymore? What are the Nuremberg Laws?"

Her mother sighed and did not answer, and Anya sensed she should not ask again nor repeat what she had heard. They gathered up their coats, gathered up Hannah, waved their goodnights, and strode into the darkened street not knowing what would greet them at home.

CHAPTER TWELVE

Her mother's eventual explanation of the Nuremberg Laws left Anya horrified. They were anti-Semitic and racist, but in her young mind they were simply hurtful to people she had grown up with and liked. Established in 1935, she had little knowledge of them until now. Hitler had suppressed their implementation until the 1938 Summer Olympics were over. Germany was the host country, and Adolf ensured the honor would not be stripped away from the Reich.

The laws excluded German Jews from Reich citizenship and prohibited them from marrying or having sexual relationships with persons of "German or related blood." And a person was considered a Jew not primarily by their religious affiliation, nor by the fact that they identified as one, but by their lineage. Anyone who had three or four Jewish grandparents was considered a "Jew". The Nuremberg Laws were the first step in subjugating people of the Jewish faith or heritage in Germany.

"Why are they being treated so meanly? Why does the Führer hate them so much?" a perplexed Anya asked of her mother.

"I do not know the answers to that, child. I wish I could tell you, but I cannot," was her mother's troubled reply.

The depth of Hitler's anti-Semitic hatred became all too visible one day as they walked from town to Oma and Opa's house.

As they neared the slope that curved upward toward the

Bermann's neighborhood, two open lorries approached a house along the road and pulled up in front of it. A cluster of Nazi soldiers poured out, hammered at the front door with their rifles, and shouted instructions to the inhabitants. A middle-aged couple, their daughter, and a dark-haired man Rosa had never seen in the area before were dragged out of the home and thrust toward the back of one truck. The dark-haired man tried to run but was seized and placed against the wall at the front of the house. He stood there trembling with his hands on his head not daring to say a word.

In an action that lasted mere seconds, a rifle was raised, and a series of rat-*tat-tats* pierced the air. Horrified, Rosa and her girls watched a human face transformed into a ripe tomato and its pulp sprayed across a barren wall. As the lifeless body of the man slinked to the ground, the soldiers grabbed it and unceremoniously threw it into the truck like a sack of grain. The other occupants screamed and prostrated themselves in submission to their fate.

When the driver revved up the engine, Rosa grabbed the girls and darted for safety.

Neighbors who had heard the commotion remained hidden behind their curtained windows. They knew this atrocity on the part of the Nazis was to serve as a warning to them all.

As Rosa dragged her daughters away with tremulous hands, air stabbed at her lungs from the effort. Once the three made it around the corner, Rosa pounded on her parents' door with the fierceness of a mother bear. Alarmed by the noise, Johann and Babette came running and, opening it guardedly, found their daughter and granddaughters looking wild and anxious. A breathless Rosa rushed them into the parlor and tried to explain to her startled parents what they had just been witness to. Shocked by the news that something so violent had occurred in town, Babette and Johann sat them down and noticed the pallor of all three. Hannah and Rosa were crying, but Anya stood frozen, her eyes reflecting the terror of what she had seen. When the child began shaking uncontrollably, Babette jumped to her feet and barked orders.

"Johann get blankets! Rosa, warm some tea for her!"

Anya was soon encased in woolen coverlets, as Babette and Rosa rubbed her hands and feet and rocked her back and forth to flow life back into her numbed body. After Anya drank a bit of warm tea, and her breath returned to a normal rhythm, they lay her down on the sofa and watched with relief as she drifted off to sleep. Hannah, wrapped in her grandfather's protective arms, also calmed down. It was not long before she too fell into a deep slumber.

The three adults sat there for a good hour, listening only to the soft breaths of the children and the *tick-tock-tick-tock* of the mantle clock in the sitting room. Outside, the world appeared as usual: the moon shone bright, leaves rustled in the breeze, and the distant rattle of neighboring voices could be heard.

Rosa wiped her eyes and emitted a slight sob.

"I think it was the Stein family. I did not know them very well. Did you?"

Her parents nodded a grim "yes" and said little else.

"I am so sorry. I did not recognize the dark-haired man," Rosa told them.

Her father cleared his throat, "I believe they were hiding a Jewish friend in their cellar."

Rosa gazed at her father in disbelief, "In their cellar? Did you know?"

He did not answer.

Rosa shuddered and closed her eyes tight, "I pray I never see anything like that again. It was...it was," she could not finish.

Johann had seen violence all too often as a soldier and put a knowing and comforting hand on his daughter's shoulder.

"Father, how can people kill other people so easily? Just kill or imprison someone for wanting to save or protect another human being...how?"

Her father looked grieved, "I have no words, no answers."

"You know what the worst part of it was? The soldiers laughed! They dumped the body in the truck, and they laughed," she looked up, her face full of dread.

"What are they doing to these people?"

Seeing her alarm, her mother reached out to her, "Rosa, why don't you take Hannah and go rest upstairs. Wrap yourselves warmly. I will watch over Anya and check on the two of you later."

A saddened Johann picked up the sleeping Hannah, while a spent and forlorn Rosa followed behind. They headed up the stairs, while Babette wiped tears from her eyes watching a troubled Anya moan in her sleep.

CHAPTER THIRTEEN

Having witnessed the ruthless ascent of Nazi aggression, Anya and Hannah were tormented by their father's political association and his alienation from the rest of the family. They assumed he had, as he had explained (and they wanted to believe), joined the Nazi party in the hope of securing a proper job. *But was that the truth?* their minds kept asking.

"Who are you Papa?" Anya inquired one day.

"What do you mean, who am I? What a stupid question!" Her father was plainly irritated with her, and she did not repeat the question again.

Sneered at as a Nazi sympathizer by their mother's family and unwelcome in their homes, their dislike and mockery of him, as well as Rosa's disrespect, increased the fierce arguments at home. Anya and Hannah often covered their ears to shut out the blistering words their parents hurled at each other.

"I am trying to save my family! Why can't you see that?" their father often hollered before running from their mother's lashing tongue and slamming their apartment door with a vengeance.

"Get out of my sight and stay out, you Nazi whore!" Rosa would shout after him.

It would be many hours and many beers before he returned. If he returned.

They were aware their father was a man of limited education, and the years of unemployment left him with profuse angst. Becoming familiar with the National Socialist party, he attended their monthly meetings first out of curiosity then out of duty to an organization he felt would rebuild Germany. Anya, young as she was, could understand his frustration in trying to make a better life for his family. But his true motives and allegiance came under scrutiny, and it maddened him to no end.

Did he seriously believe all the Nazi rules and policies? Anya had been given no definitive answer when she was brave enough to ask. Oswald was never clear on that point. But Anya's family was clear on their position regarding him.

Although it changed nothing where his relatives were concerned, to Oswald's relief his commitment to the party was rewarded with a position as a machinist in a local factory that built airplane parts. Hitler's growing militarization of Germany was a boon to their town. Fürth was developing into a hub of transportation in and around Bavaria. The growing industry resulted in the expansion of the local job market. Her father, now in his forties, felt empowered after years of laying fallow.

In addition to his factory duties Oswald was assigned, their vexed mother informed his daughters, he was also going to be a collector of dues for the Nazi party on the street where they lived. This position was part of the "block system" initiated by the Nazis to maintain close control of individuals from the standpoint of their political reliability. Part of their father's job was to report any gossip he heard regarding people or plans that might be a threat to the Third Reich. To their dismay, and their mother's chagrin, the head of their family was issued a standard brown uniform signifying his status on the lowest rung of the Nazi hierarchy.

"Doesn't he look like the cock of the walk strutting about the streets in his brown feathers," Rosa taunted as she and his daughters strode behind him on one of their treks through town. Outraged when he heard them twitter at his back, he turned on them and sputtered, "Have you no respect? I am your father!" He punctuated his words with a swift flick of his hand to the back of Anya's and Hannah's heads while glaring at his wife.

At home he continued to pressure Rosa and the girls to register with the Nazi party.

"You will be protected and secure jobs in the future. Stop being foolish and sign on!"

They refused, and his constant coercion evolved into a splintered relationship with his wife and daughters. At the Bermann home, although Oswald never betrayed their political leanings, he remained persona non grata.

The crack in their family life widened into a major fissure on the day Anya balked at his insistence she join the female offshoot of the Hitler Jugend known as the JungMädelbund (Young Girls League for ages 10-14).

As her father pontificated on the glories of joining such an honorable group, Anya turned her back to him and walked away from the dinner table. His response was apoplectic. Picking up a serrated dinner knife, he flung it toward her. The blade punctured the calf of Anya's right leg and remained imbedded there.

Horrified, Rosa flew from her chair, screaming in fury, "You maniac! Are you crazy!?" as she rushed to the aid of her injured and shrieking daughter.

Hannah, petrified, not daring to move, stared in disbelief at the rivulet of blood coursing down her sister's leg. Their father, as soon as he heard Anya's anguished cries, grew quiet and looked confused by what he had done.

"You are always beating her! Why? Why? And now this!" yelled Rosa.

Stunned by his own action, he answered as if in a trance, "She needs to learn to obey."

"Verdammtes Arschloch! The Nazis have made you crazy!" Rosa fumed.

Kneeling in front of Anya, she tried to calm her daughter. Flustered, not knowing quite what to do, Rosa untied her apron and hoped to pull the knife out to staunch the bleeding. The injury was not as deep as she feared, but deep enough. Anya screamed and turned deathly white as the knife was slowly drawn from her leg. It was not the wisest thing to do, as it could have caused more damage to the muscle, but Rosa saw no alternative.

"Get me a washcloth and towel...and a belt!" she called to Hannah. Rosa's apron was seeped through with blood.

Within moments an uncomfortable silence fell on the room except for Anya's groans and Rosa's labored breathing. Discomfited, Oswald rose and left to go, unsure of what to do next.

"Get out and stay out," Rosa rasped through gritted teeth, as he walked to the door, head hanging low, and closed it behind him.

Concentrating on stemming the flow of blood, Rosa, with Hannah's help, bound the gash as tightly as she could before heading to a nearby clinic. As they held Anya up on each side, she limped down the wooden staircase moaning in pain and feeling faint.

At the clinic, Anya's wound was cleaned, stitched, and bound before the doctor allowed her to hobble home with her mother and sister.

"I have administered a shot both against infection and for the pain. She should sleep soundly tonight." He then asked grimly if Rosa wanted to file a report with the police, but she declined.

"It was an accident. My husband thought he saw a rat scurrying across the kitchen, and our daughter stepped in the way just as he threw a knife toward it."

The Nazi police, she secretly determined, would only side with Oswald and sneer at his errant child. Anya would be the only one in trouble.

Once home, she and Hannah put Anya to bed, hoping the medication would mute the pain and allow her to sleep. Their father did not return.

Day after day, Anya began to heal, but their spirits did not.

Not long after, while sitting at the kitchen table at her parents' house as the girls rested and read in the sitting room, their mother broke down in tears. Babette held her hand as a concerned Johann looked on and asked, "What's wrong, Rosa?"

Before she could answer, he noticed Anya and Hannah looking sadly toward the kitchen. He rose and gently closed the door between them. They knew something was wrong, and they hoped their grandfather could make the awfulness go away.

Returning to the table, Johann looked at the bowed head of his grown daughter.

"I cannot do it anymore, Papa," Rosa declared between tears, "I cannot live with what Oswald has become. He struts around in that uniform, goes drinking, comes home and screams at us and beats Anya if she takes a breath sideways. And then he throws a knife! Her scar might be permanent! No doubt his stubborn nature will create difficulties with his officers and be a continual problem for us. I cannot bear it any longer. I want out of this marriage."

"Did you ever think that maybe he hates what he has become?" her father pointed out gently, while her mother stroked her hand.

"What do you mean?" Rosa asked, confused by the question.

"According to him, he took on a job with the Nazi party to put food on the table. Now the job is costing him more than he expected, and he does not have the courage to get out."

"Or he wanted to be there in the first place," retorted Rosa. "He was an unemployed peasant, nothing more! The job gives him respect and power. He loves to flaunt it over people!"

"Rosa," her mother interjected as peaceably as she could, "you must think this through. Oswald has not reported us to the authorities as possible dissidents. He gave you and Hannah a home when you needed it most. He was not Hannah's father. A man you loved threw you away. Oswald took you both in, married you, adopted Hannah, and was good to you. You now have two children to care for."

"Then tell me why he beats his own child and is lenient with Hannah?"

"Hannah is submissive; Anya has a mind of her own. You know

that."

"It does not excuse him. I need to protect my children! Hannah fears him now and Anya defies his wishes to the point where I fear for her."

Her mother sighed, "If you must leave him, you and the girls have a home here. We will make room. But give it serious thought. You will need to take care of them on your own. Make wise moves, Rosa. Your life and that of your daughters depends on it."

Walking home that evening, Anya and Hannah held on to their mother's hands. A desolate Hannah looked up and murmured, "Do we no longer have a father?"

CHAPTER FOURTEEN

With their father seldom home, and their mother aware she could not survive with her girls on her meager earnings, nor wanting to be a burden to her parents, they remained in their flat. Within two weeks, Oswald returned home, churlish and belligerent. Nothing had changed. Rosa sensed she had made the wrong decision.

Despite suffering her father's wrath, Anya remained persistent in her refusal to attend gatherings of the JungMädelbund. Oswald, equally stubborn, registered his daughters against their wishes. Fueled by the anger of what he had done, Anya reinforced her stance. This time her mother and sister were behind her.

"How could he do this, Mama? It is so vile and unfair! I hate him for it! I will not go...I just won't go!" Anya declared.

Her father, however, would not back down. Anya remained obstinate and refused to attend any meetings of the JungMädelbund, and future participation in the BDM (Bundes Deutscher Mädel for girls 14-18 years of age). As a result of her standpoint, she suffered not only paternal abuse but also the admonishments of the Nazi party itself. In retaliation for her non-compliance, the Nazis threatened to cut off Anya's allotted food stamps as punishment for her "no-shows".

Hearing of it, her vexed grandmother decided to take matters into her own hands.

"What nonsense is this, taking food from the mouth of a child!?" The thought had her tearing around her kitchen like a maimed tigress. Anya watched her grandmother pace with a mixture of fascination and dread.

Babette was a formidable woman who had borne thirteen children (receiving an Iron Cross for the deed, not because she wanted to increase Germany's population, but because she was fertile and could not resist her husband's charms). She had also in her younger years taken in children from destitute families and lost three of her own to childhood diseases and accidents. It riled her that anyone would withhold food from her malnourished grandchild. Small in height, but of robust stock, she wore her hair in thick braids crisscrossed atop her head like a crown and sheathed herself in practical smocks of a nondescript color. They were her fashion statement: "I am here to work, not to shirk!"

Anya admired her grandmother for it; yet feared her wrath when she was provoked.

A literal queen Babette was not; but she was matriarch of their huge family and ruled her kingdom with a mighty hand. That hand, angled to the right because of severe arthritis, did not keep her from whacking the head off a chicken when the need arose. Anya had seen it herself and marveled at how a cook, a baker, and a baby-maker could find the gumption to handle such a grisly task. An astute chicken never presented itself in her Oma's backyard when dinnertime approached.

As caretaker of her burgeoning family, which presently included six sons, four daughters and seventeen grandchildren, Babette grabbed her twelve-year-old Anya and steered her to Nazi headquarters in Fürth quicker than a hen outrunning a fox.

"We are going to settle this problem, if it is the last thing I do!" she crowed, as a flustered Anya strove to keep up with her as they burst through the door of the Nazi bastion.

Trapped under Babette's clucking wing, Anya grew light-headed when her grandmother announced to every official within hearing distance, "This child will eat with or without you! We won't let her starve!"

Well-known to the Nazi bureaucrats in the room, they did not dare defy the roar of a woman who had borne and added a baker's dozen to the Reich and won a medal to prove it.

"Frau Bermann, your granddaughter is not complying with our rules. She refuses to attend mandatory meetings for girls of her age," the head officer recounted.

"She is a shy girl. Very self-conscious. She would rather hide in a corner than face a crowd of cackling girls who will make fun of her lack of social and athletic skills. You must understand!"

Anya gazed at her grandmother. She never realized until now that Oma could lie so well. *Shy? Lacking social and athletic skills?* Why just yesterday she had whooped down the hill into Fürth on her cousin Willie's rickety bike without any qualms about her safety!

"Frau Bermann, you must listen to reason...." the official demanded.

"Reason? What reason is there in making such a sweet, young girl so miserable?" she implored.

Upon her grandmother's cue, Anya attempted to look as sweet and miserable as she possibly could.

The magistrate scrutinized the girl fidgeting in front of him. Anya remained mute, eyes and mouth downcast, and clung to her Oma's arm.

"Frau Bermann, she must comply with...." he sputtered.

"Comply with what?" Babette demanded. "What is one less girl in that herd of prancing foals? My granddaughter is a lamb. She does not belong there!"

The commandant looked at his assistant, who appeared taken aback by the ferocity of the notable Frau Bermann. He again studied the downheartedness of the delicate girl before him and sighed.

After a few minutes of reiterating "the rules", Frau Bermann and her granddaughter were dismissed from the chamber. Both had been strongly admonished, but Anya retained her food stamps.

Licking the cream from their Cheshire cat grins, they walked toward the main door in triumph. A well-intentioned member of the Nazi party accompanied them. As a former neighbor, he had known the Bermann family for some time and took it upon himself to discreetly advise Frau Bermann. He hoped he could inject some sense into the woman. She had always been known to be headstrong when it came to protecting her family members.

"Frau Bermann, you know this will not end. Might I suggest you have your granddaughter participate in the youth meetings a few times to keep her safe? She might not have to participate in every gathering. She can sit or stand on the sidelines and pretend she is bashful."

Anya sensed his knowing stare and tried to remain calm.

"Think about it," he continued. "It will keep both of you out of consequent trouble."

"Do not worry, we will protect her," her grandmother replied. Grabbing Anya's hand, she stormed off pulling her along in the tow. Deep inside they both knew the man was right.

"Oma, I think maybe I should make an appearance, as he suggested. I don't want to get all of us in trouble," Anya decided on their walk home.

"We shall see," her Oma replied, "We will discuss the problem with your grandfather and your mother and come to a logical solution."

The logical solution they agreed upon was for Anya to participate in a few initial meetings. As it turned out, after the first two, she began to enjoy them somewhat. She listened little to the speakers; but, according to the pamphlet she was given, there were picnics and hikes in the countryside, swim meets, and volleyball games to look forward to. And the girls at the meetings seemed nice enough, not like the Nazi brats she had heard about and anticipated. Some girls, she was happy to discover, had also been cajoled by nervous parents into attending the gatherings after their initial reluctance. Within a short time, they recognized a kindred spirit in each other and formed their own hush-hush clique. Of the group, Lisbeth Holzinger would prove to be a crucial friend to Anya.

CHAPTER FIFTEEN

Her grandmother's assertiveness at headquarters, unfortunately, did not go unheeded. Her husband told her she was naïve to think that it would. Living in a neighborhood suspected of being inhabited by anti-Nazi and Communist sympathizers, the home of Anya's grandparents and those of their neighbors were put under surveillance and searched without warning on numerable occasions. The surprise intrusions rattled their nerves and proved disruptive to their lives.

Anya witnessed such an invasion when the Nazi police came knocking at the door and stormed through her grandparents' house looking for the slightest bit of paper that would link Babette and Johann Bermann to the German Communist Party.

"I do not mind you scavenging through my house," she heard her Oma shout, "but must you make such a mess!?"

Anya cringed at her grandmother's quarrelsome words and watched the Nazi police throw things helter-skelter with increased frenzy.

They found nothing; but the family recognized the implication of these searches. A week later, two of Anya's uncles were taken to Nazi headquarters, interrogated, and jailed for several days. A great sense of unease engulfed the family.

Babette remained defiant and impatient during these intrusions (much to the exasperation of her husband, who had given up long ago trying to tame his wife to keep her from harm). When a Nazi guard blitzed in one day and pointed to an item protruding from a kitchen cabinet demanding to know what it was, she eyed him with disdain and declared, "It's a machine gun. What does it look like?"

Aggravated by her reply, the sassed officer examined the object and realized it was a simple coffee grinder. He was not amused and scribbled in his notepad. Nazi police, Anya noticed, were always scribbling in small notepads.

As reprisal for her grandmother's blatant insolence, several of her uncles were recruited into the German army with abrupt speed. It was mandatory for male youths 18 or older to join up, but the Bermann boys were swept up with little notice. Johann refused to speak to his wife for days and locked himself in his study. Anya's anxiety increased, and she felt helpless, not being able to help her cousins. She would miss Willie most of all. He was her partner when it came to having mischievous fun…like riding tandem on his wobbly bike or makeshift sled and scooting down hills with only their feet for brakes. Many a bloody scrape needed tending after such feats of bravado.

The day before Willie departed with his brothers, he showed her an old suitcase filled with pictures he had drawn.

"I didn't know you could do that!" Anya exclaimed in surprise.

Willie, who was usually gruff around girls, blushed, "I'm not sure they're any good. Please *do not* tell anyone. I don't want my brothers thinking I'm a sissy and laugh at me," he confessed.

"Willie, they are more than good; they are beautiful," she noted with astonishment as he pulled out penciled portraits of familiar people, and finely rendered scenes of their town.

"I knew you'd understand and like them. I've watched you draw some pictures too when you thought I wasn't paying attention," he admitted.

"Nothing like these, for sure!" she declared, "You'll make a great artist someday. I know it!"

He gave her one of his big, lop-sided grins.

"I'm going to leave my suitcase of pictures with Oma and Opa for safekeeping. My father might throw them away as wasteful if he found them."

The thought saddened him, as it did her.

"I'll make sure they always stay safe until you come home, don't worry."

"Thanks, Anya, You're a good cousin. Now, should we go for one last ride? Not down a hill though. I'm not allowed to break a leg!"

They laughed and ran out the door.

Early the next morning, after tearful and ample good-bye hugs, the sons of Johann and Babette Bermann were rushed to the recruitment office in Fürth and transported to parts unknown.

Johann shut his wife and daughters out of his study the next few days. Feeling guilt-ridden, Babette dared not disturb him, and prayed all would be forgiven.

After the boys were taken away, a heightened sense of intimidation beset their household when they became the target of yet another harrowing investigation. Because Johann and Babette had a decidedly Jewish-sounding surname, a background check was done on their lineage. Although it did not uncover any incriminating evidence against them, they became acutely aware that Hitler abhorred Jews. It was no secret that bigotry against them was prevalent in much of the world even before Hitler's time. Using them as the scapegoat for the economic chaos of his country, with his reasoning being that Jews owned too many businesses and were profiting from them while the German populous suffered, Hitler encouraged anti-Semitism through a massive campaign to that effect.

Walking through Fürth, Anya found herself subjected to abhorrent posters emblazoned with "Juden sind hier unerwunscht!" ("Jews are not welcome here!") "Deutsche! Wert Euch! Kauft nicht bei Juden!" (Germans! Defend Yourselves! Don't buy from Jews!")

What had these people ever done to us to earn such hatred? The question baffled Anya's mind.

Rosa, who worked as a maid for a Jewish family in years past and was treated kindly, struggled for answers too.

On a winter evening in November of 1938 any illusion of improving the Jewish condition in Germany was figuratively and literally shattered.

CHAPTER SIXTEEN

As the girls and Rosa slept, their father crept up the stairs late that fateful night. Shoes in hand, Oswald turned his housekey with caution so as not to waken them, and headed for the kitchen window where a sudden, red flicker caught his eye. Curious, he pulled the curtains apart and gasped in disbelief.

A strange, orange glow illuminated the evening sky.

My God! What was happening?

The previous summer the Nazis had destroyed the Nuremberg synagogue. He gazed at the rising inferno with dread. The fire was in the direction of the synagogue in Fürth and nearing the town center. His heart pounded at the sight of the blistering catastrophe.

Are the Nazis trying to burn down the city? raced through his mind.

Oswald prayed the flames would not reach their section of town, even though the smell of smoke wafted through the window. The fire seemed consigned to the central part of the city, but the wind could turn and bring it their way. Pulling up a stool to the window, he remained riveted on the scene. He did not want to frighten Rosa and the girls unless the danger neared. Weary and mystified, he sat there the remainder of the night watching the blaze burn, then smolder, and finally subside. Thick trails of black smoke rose from buildings and streets, but he saw no flames.

Rosa woke first and found Oswald slumped in a chair, his head resting on the kitchen table. Bleary-eyed and still wearing his clothes from the evening before, he stirred to the sound of her voice.

"What's going on? Are you drunk?" she asked as she took in his appearance. With his clothes bedraggled, and his eyes red and watery, she assumed Oswald had spent the night guzzling beers at the local pub.

Needled by the remark, he brusquely informed her of what he had witnessed. Rosa fled to the window at his words, and saw the heavy, black smoke rising in the distance.

"Gott in Himmel!" The sight shook her. She turned to Oswald, in dread of what the day would bring. "Do not tell the children. We must keep things as normal as possible; otherwise, it will frighten them," she instructed.

"What are we to tell them? Are you sending them to school?" Concerned, he felt that might not be a good idea.

"I will tell them there was an accident at one of the factories. Yes, I think they should go to school, and we leave for work. Look outside; our neighbors are already departing. The fire is out. It should be alright."

She did not realize how wrong she was.

The startled girls were roused swiftly, informed of the situation, and instructed to get dressed and go directly to their respective schoolrooms. Drowsy and confused, they complied and, after a sparse breakfast, headed out the door. Rosa gave each a kiss before they departed.

"Come back as soon as school is done. Do not loiter in the streets," their father ordered.

They nodded at his words and scooted down the stairs.

On the long walk to school, Hannah, inhaling some of the dense smoke that lingered in the air, began coughing and covered her mouth to forestall an asthma attack. She had forgotten her medicine in the rush.

Their mother had informed them about the fire, but said it was safe now. They did not feel safe as they approached their school. It was closed. There were Nazi soldiers with guns guarding the building.

"Go home, children! Didn't your parents hear the orders!" one of them shouted, as more young students approached.

Hannah and Anya backed away, unsure of what was happening.

They knew they should head home to their apartment, but their developing curiosity led them to the center of Fürth instead. What they encountered there revolted and wounded them.

Scores of people wandered about in bewilderment and shock, as they wended their way through the central market square. Many were trying to clear away the mess in their path. The sisters were startled to discover the store windows of the Jewish-owned shops were demolished or in the process of being destroyed by scores of the local militia. Most of the shops' merchandise had been removed or thrown helter-skelter into the streets and were looted by passersby. Armed guards yelled at the gathering throng to "keep moving and go home!" while herding crowds of people away to prevent pillage in the area. The cobbled streets were a sea of glass shards, debris, and store goods. Hannah and Anya, dazed by the increasing chaos around them, picked their way over the splintered windowpanes and strewn wreckage with extreme caution, while the acrid aftermath of the fire burned their nostrils. The girls turned in panic to escape the site.

"Hold my hand, Hannah," Anya begged. Hannah grabbed it and continued to cover her mouth and nostrils with the other, coughing and shaking as she tried to steer them home.

"Let's go, Anya, I need my medication!"

Walking through the teeming streets, they watched as masses of people wearing the black bands with a yellow star were shepherded aboard a convoy of trucks. The girls knew the yellow star was known as the Star of David and signified the person was Jewish. The passengers looked perplexed, and their terrified children wept or screamed in their mother's arms. Anya recognized one girl in the crowd. It was her best friend, Paulina.

"Hannah, where are they taking her? What is going on?"

"I don't know. I think we best hurry home," she replied, gripping

Anya's hand tighter.

"No! I want to talk to Paulina!" Anya yelled, "Let go of me!" She broke free of Hannah's hold and ran in the direction of the truck, rushing through the frenzied crowd without thought of safety.

"Paulina! Paulina! Where are you going?" she shouted toward one of the trucks.

Paulina, seeing her German friend break through the throng, could not respond with more than a weak wave of her hand. Her eyes and face were etched with fright and despair.

"Paulina! Paulina! Do not leave! Where are they taking you?"

Frantic, Anya ran after the vehicle, but Hannah, gasping for breath, caught up with her and pulled her back.

"Let go of me!" Anya screamed, trying to break free of her sister's grasp. The truck carrying Paulina wended down the street, away from them, and soon disappeared amidst a caravan of lorries heading out of town.

"Hannah, we have to ask someone where they are going! Please!" Anya begged.

"No! Do *not* ask questions," Hannah, trying to catch her breath and stem the pain in her chest, pulled her away. "The soldiers all have guns. Something bad might happen. It's best we leave." People were weaving helter-skelter all around them.

"But I can't leave my friend! Paulina, come back! Paulina!" Realizing the truck was gone from view, Anya fell to her knees and cried.

"Paulina. You cannot leave. Please come back. You can't leave us."

Hannah bent down and tried to gently lift Anya up, as passersby gave them a brief stare and rushed on.

"She's my best friend! Where will they take her?"

Hannah looked down at the misery on her sister's tear-stained face and wanted to take her in her arms and soothe her, but there was no time.

"Come, we need to go home. I'm not feeling well."

Anya's pained face scanned Hannah's, and she stood up in obedience.

"What will happen to Paulina?" Wiping at her tears and trying to keep panic away, she drew in great gulps of air.

"I don't know, Anya, I don't know. Come, we need to get away from here."

"Why is it nobody knows anything anymore? If I hear 'I don't know' one more time, I pray God plucks my ears off!" With that statement she seized Hannah's outstretched hand and followed.

Clutching onto each other, the sisters picked their way through the rubble, the broken glass, the plunderers, the soldiers with guns, and the people wandering around like sheared lambs bleating over their lost wool. Smoke and the smell of petrol filled their nostrils as more truckloads of captives rumbled by. At each turn of a corner, bedlam filled the street. Hannah, stopping every few minutes to catch her breath, finally spotted an escape.

"Schau, Anya, eine Gasse!"

It was a narrow alleyway that funneled out of the city center and might lead them home. They scurried through it and, finding the broad avenue that led toward the residential streets, ran in the direction of home until Hannah's lungs could bear no more.

Near collapse as they entered the flat, Hannah ran toward the cabinet that held her medication, while Anya bolted the door. Crumbling on the couch, they waited for their mother and father to return with nervous anticipation.

Their parents arrived sooner than the girls expected. A state of emergency had been declared throughout Fürth, and Rosa and Oswald, desperate to get home, prayed they would find their daughters there and safe. They hugged with relief when Anya opened the door.

"Gott Sei Dank," their mother exclaimed, looking heavenward, and thanking God her girls were unharmed.

The remainder of the day both children were listless and asked few questions. Their parents, aware of their unspoken distress, tried reassuring them that everything would be restored to normal, but the girls were unconvinced.

"You will have a few days off from school. Isn't that good news?" their mother asked with as much cheer as she could muster, but her voice sounded strained.

"No. My friend Paulina is gone, Mama," Anya stated, "Where did they take her? Can you answer that?" she asked and waited for a response that did not come, "You 'don't know', right?"

Rosa did not answer, and Anya went to her room bereft of feeling.

Both girls retired to bed early that night without a word. Hannah drifted into an uneasy sleep, while Anya lay in bed gazing out the small, moonlit window thinking of what she had witnessed. Soon the heavy weight of sorrow lay its head on her breast, and she began to cry. Nearing twelve, she could feel her childhood slipping away. It drifted down a street filled with madness, followed trucks that took good people away, then turned a corner and said goodbye.

What had happened? What was happening? What is going to happen? She continued peering out into the night; her mind disquieted by the unanswered questions swirling in her head. Tomorrow she would visit Opa, she decided. She would read his newspapers and listen to his radio. She would ask for the truth. She would no longer be a child. That was her plan.

CHAPTER SEVENTEEN

In discussing the destructive event, which became known as "Krystallnacht" ("The Night of Broken Glass"), rumors stated it was a reprisal for a wrongful assassination. The rumors were proclaimed factual through the Nazi propaganda machine. The misguided attempt, as Johann predicted, would become Hitler's scapegoat for his escalating vendetta against all Jews. Anya was part of the group that listened to the speculation at her grandfather's door. She was no longer barred from his study. Anya had steeled herself against her mother's protests and this, at first, distressed Rosa.

"I want to learn, Mama, and I want to understand. Not knowing is more frightening to me," Anya explained, "I want to understand why my friend, and the others, were treated in such a heartless way."

Rosa feared her youngest would become hard-bitten by her difficult experiences, instead it seemed to foster Anya's empathy and compassion. To Rosa, that alone was a miracle, and she was grateful for God's grace.

In Hannah's case, although she was three years older than Anya, there was little resistance to keeping her distance from Opa's study. All the narratives and news therein stirred enough anxiety in her to trigger an asthma attack, and she was glad to stay away.

Johann discovered through his military cronies that the German newspapers, after Krystallnacht, were virulent and misleading. They proclaimed that a Jew by the name of Herschel Grynbszpan had allegedly ignited the current situation. Grynbszpan had attempted to assassinate the German Ambassador, Count Johannes von Wleczek, at the German Embassy in Paris. Instead, he shot six bullets into the wrong man. The victim, a young diplomat named Ernst von Rath, later died of his wounds.

"How could anyone attempting to assassinate a known government official shoot six bullets into the wrong man?" Johann could not fathom it. "Does Hitler expect us to believe that this vendetta was instigated by one, disgruntled young man? Does he think all Germans have sausages for brains?" he asked his gathered family.

His anger and frustration were severe, as everyone in the room, including Anya, watched him throw aside the papers in fury.

Know your enemy! Know your target! had been drilled into Johann in the military. He knew Hitler had identified his enemy and chosen his target.

The German populace were ignorant of the fact that a pogrom against the Jews had been covertly organized by the Nazis months before Grynbszpan's folly. Anya's disbelieving grandfather suspected that the young man's foolhardiness was the Nazis' convenient excuse for the eruption of Krystallnacht.

Within a short time, his cronies informed him over 20,000 Jews were imprisoned, more than 70 killed, and strident decrees were being issued eliminating Jews from the economy. In the Jewish community in Fürth and other German cities, Krystalnacht was an epiphany. Their lives had been reduced to prisms in a shattered glass.

CHAPTER EIGHTEEN

When the vestiges of Krystallnacht were cleared away and the situation taken in hand, Anya, and Hannah returned to school. In doing so, they discovered all their Jewish classmates had disappeared.

This added to the burgeoning angst of the students. The remaining classmates asked innumerable questions of their teacher, Frau Speyer, in the days that followed. They had previously learned that throughout Fürth's history, the ancestors and families of their missing classmates were instrumental in the development of the town since the Middle Ages. Up to the present day, Furth's Jewish citizens had maintained a decent relationship with their community. They had established their own synagogues, their own schools for teaching the young ones Hebrew, and their own cemetery.

Frau Speyer informed the class, "It seems only now, facing uncertainty and perhaps danger, they have decided to keep to themselves as much as possible or leave."

"What kind of danger, Frau Speyer?" Anya asked.

The teacher realized she had let slip too much, and Anya noticed she was staring at the classroom door nervously and wringing her hands.

"I didn't...I do not mean *danger.* That is too strong a word. Of course, there is uncertainty as to where they have gone. Perhaps they are simply being moved to areas where they can build their own neighborhoods. Their culture is quite different from ours, and this would make more sense. Separateness could be a good thing for them," she stressed.

The bell rang.

The bell always rings when the class has more questions, a perturbed Anya concluded. The questions seemed cleverly relegated to the end of each day's lesson plan.

Gathered with her family for Sunday dinner in the Bermann kitchen, she repeated what her teacher had told her and pointedly asked, "Do you think our friends and neighbors have left or are leaving because they *want* to?"

Johann looked at his granddaughter and saw that she would not broach dishonesty in anyone's answer. She trusted him for the truth.

"No. I do not believe they have left of their own free will."

"Then why are they being taken away?" Her piercing eyes were aimed at her grandfather.

"I do not know, Anya. They have done no harm and there has never been religious strife in our city. They worked hard, lived in fine houses, and owned many well-established shops in town. I am certain the trouble lies with haters, like Hitler and his Nazi party. He has made it known he detests Jews. I venture to guess some of our friends moved to where they would feel safer or were taken to towns where they could live amongst their own culture."

"Where is that?" she asked.

"I do not know," Johann replied while Anya grimaced.

"Don't you think someone should find out? Nobody seems to know anything around here, not even my teacher!" she bristled.

Don't you think someone should find out?

It was such a simple appeal from a frustrated schoolgirl, and yet people were reluctant to search for an answer.

Commerce certainly was not the problem for the exodus, her

grandfather acknowledged. Their fellow townspeople had done constant business with their Jewish brethren. Even after the Nazi-imposed boycott, they continued to do so, but now in secret.

When anti-Jewish edicts were first passed, one of which eliminated Jewish tradesmen from Fürth, Anya, Hannah, and their mother had sneaked off in the night to the homes of the former shopkeepers. There, hidden merchandise was sold in a secret room. With great prudence, many locals found their way to these hidden enclaves.

Anya's family spent mournful days after Krystallnacht shaking their heads trying to come to terms with what was happening around them. Many assumed Hitler was just crying wolf on the radio and relations with their Jewish neighbors would improve as the economy improved. As her Opa noted, some had wisely left for safer havens before the troubles started, traveling as far away from Germany as they could. Others had not anticipated what was to come and chose to stay put. Now they too were gone.

"Where did they go? America?" Anya asked. America was where most people went, she heard her relatives say, but they were not sure. When Frau Speyer was asked the same question by a student, she ignored him and gave no answer. She could not answer his question. She was not sure herself...or her mind refused to acknowledge her suspicions.

In the aftershock of Krystallnacht, four words reverberated in German households: "I do not know."

But certain people did know. The Nazis had secretly begun building concentration camps and boycotting Jews from business and German society since 1933. These camps also held political dissidents.

According to the Third Reich, millions of Jews had been 'graciously' shipped to such propagandized 'resorts' as Dachau, Auschwitz, Belsen-Belsen, Buchanwald or Treblinka (to name only a few). 'Resorts' which were staged, filmed, and shown to world leaders as offering a plethora of swimming pools, sports, dances, games, and barbecues for Germany's Jewish comrades to enjoy. Whether world leaders believed what they were shown remained questionable. What would become clear to the Germans and the world at large is that a blind eye can only be cured by hindsight, if it can be cured at all.

CHAPTER NINETEEN

O ne year later, in 1939, when Anya turned twelve, Hitler and his Nazis invaded Poland and World War II was launched, much to the horror of people around the globe. The Führer's need for "Lebensraum", more "living space" for his nation, consisted of stretching the Third Reich's borders as far as he could. His quest became ruthless and fathomless.

Ironically, saccharine photos of the Führer interacting with German children were often seen in newspapers and magazines.

"What a hypocrite!" Anya heard her grandfather spew. "With one hand he lovingly pats them on the head while maintaining a chokehold on their future with the other!"

Anya herself was soured by these pictorials, knowing full well Hitler stole her childhood from her.

Her mother was wretchedly aware of that fact, as she observed her daughters each day. Anya was, as Rosa predicted, growing into a beauty and Hannah into a pleasant-faced young woman. Both had become more introverted and, although cordial to their peers, their once carefree joyfulness appeared dimmed.

Adding to everyone's anguish, was listening to the astounding newscasts, or reading the unnerving articles that bore witness to the Nazis' growing invasion of Europe, North Africa, the Ukraine, Russia, Greece, and subsequent attacks on the United Kingdom.

"There will never be an end to that maniac's ambition, power, or greed!" an incensed Johann decreed. What incensed him most was the fact that Hitler was heading toward hell and taking the country with him.

By 1941 Germany was engulfed in full out war with its neighbors. For Anya and Hannah, it hit home when the British RAF bombed Nuremberg.

The sisters cried, remembering their outings in that beautiful city, and prayed the damage was not as brutal as they had heard. Banned from traveling to Nuremberg by their parents, they tried to ferret out news from their friends. The reports were daunting and left the sisters fretting over their future.

"What will happen to us, Mama? What will happen?"

Their fate became clearer soon thereafter: A reluctant Anya found herself recruited into the "Labor Services" with compliments of the Nazis. This time she could not escape Nazi orders. It was mandatory for 14-year-old girls, who had graduated from preliminary school and had no physical handicap, to serve for one year as a housemaid for a high-ranking Nazi family. This was in addition to completing their lessons at a trade school for two more years. In between attending first-aid or secretarial classes, Anya was instructed to serve in the home she was assigned to and do what was demanded. Her father ensured she followed through on her duty. Her sister, however, was freed of the same fate. Oswald acquired a medical dispensation for Hannah due to her asthmatic condition. Shortly after her fourteenth birthday, a hard-pressed Anya reported to her appointed workplace.

Walking two kilometers in the snow from school, she approached the assigned house with trepidation. As she strode down its circular driveway, Anya found it to be quite an opulent home. The large, golden eagle knob at the front door intimidated her, and she knocked it warily to gain entry. A well-dressed and well-coiffed woman threw open the massive door and greeted her in a perfunctory manner. The woman was of trim body, and she looked well-cared for. Dressed in a pale silk blouse with her blonde hair twisted into an elegant chignon, Anya noted the woman's face was not softened by the delicate silk. She had the look of a stern matron who found nothing in life humorous.

"Heil Hitler," the woman stated curtly.

"Heil Hitler," Anya murmured in response.

"I assume you are the new girl here to serve us... Anya Schmidt?

"Yes. Yes, I am," Anya confirmed with a shy dip of her head.

"I am Frau Webber, madam of this house. Come in. Please make sure to wipe the snow and mud off your shoes before you enter."

Anya did so, then followed the mistress down a long hallway flanked by a marble staircase. At the end, she was led into the main living quarters. A massive library was at the left, and the living room was at their right. The living room left Anya breathless. It was laden with priceless artifacts, well-appointed furniture, and a massive fireplace aflame at its center.

"Sit," the woman ordered.

Anya sat promptly, feeling awkward in her unaccustomed setting. Clothed in a worn woolen coat, over a plain woolen dress, with her woolen leggings tucked into her worn, sensible shoes, she felt like a misbegotten orphan being sized up for a potential adoption.

"Herr Webber and the children will be here shortly to meet you. It is imperative that you get along well with my young son and daughter while you serve here."

"Ja, Frau Webber. I am good with children."

"Well, we shall see," Frau Webber retorted, giving Anya a pointed look. "Meanwhile I will take you on tour of the house and make you aware of your chores and our expectations."

"Ja, Frau Webber," Anya mumbled, and off they went.

Her chores, Anya discovered as she and her affluent employer examined the kitchen, the bathrooms, the parlor, the study, and the upstairs bedrooms, were plentiful. She was expected to cook, clean, do laundry, and baby-sit for her assigned family for a major part of each day. While hopping between the Webbers' elaborate home and lessons at school, she was informed she would receive two meals a day and 10 Deutsche Marks a month in payment for her labor (a pittance in Anya's already beleaguered mind).

When Frau Webber finished her litany of rules and chores, they returned to the living room where a swoop of the front door and a clattering of footsteps could be heard.

A formidable and well-heeled Herr Webber was the first to enter the room, followed by his exuberant off-spring. Anya jumped up at their entrance. The master of the house was a rather portly man, with thinning hair, a flaccid face, and well over six feet tall in stature.

"Heil Hitler!" he intoned, as he and his mimicking children extended their right arms.

Anya followed suit, "Heil Hitler."

With these words, she found herself an indentured servant to a Nazi family.

Anya wanted to spit whenever she raised her arm and uttered "Heil Hitler" in daily obedience to the patriarch of the Webber family. At school, she was required to greet the teacher in the same manner. She wondered if a broken right arm would be a curse or a blessing. Unfortunately, she could not conjure up a painless way of acquiring a painless fracture.

Her routine, Anya found, was a challenging one. During the cold winter days, she arrived half frozen from the long walk from one destination to another. (She assumed during the summer she would, no doubt, swelter in the heat.) And then there were the wet days, soaking her through in their misery. On frigid days, her first chore was to start a fire in the central oven in the kitchen, then stoke a roaring one in the living room fireplace. The house was to be heated before the master, his mistress, and their rambunctious children roused themselves from the comfort of their featherbeds each morning.

Most days, instead of being dismissed at 7:00 p.m. as the Webbers were expected to do, they did not dismiss Anya from her chores until much later in the evening. And often it was without the courtesy of providing a supper for her. Arriving home at 10:00 p.m. one night starving, cold, and weary, her parents noticed the drain on her physical being with alarm. Minutes later Anya collapsed from exhaustion on the couch.

"Papa, please help me," she begged as her worried mother and sister fed her warm soup and placed her in bed. Observing her strained face, her father's stance softened as she lay there and tried to tell them of her plight. The paleness of her face and the sight of her wisp-thin body under the blanket, startled him. When Rosa threatened to go to the Webbers herself, he acknowledged he needed to do something about the situation.

The next day, fully dressed in his brown uniform, Oswald confronted the Webbers and demanded they send Anya home at a decent hour and feed her sufficiently or he would report them to headquarters for not following proper guidelines. Despite his lower rank, his threat worked. Her father knew no high-ranking officer wanted to cause trouble and have his reputation besmirched in front of his superiors or peers. The Webbers agreed Anya could stay home for a few days until she felt better. She slept for a week.

Seven days later, Anya was back at her duties. The adult Webbers eyed her with their usual disdain but eased their treatment of her. The children tumbled about as children usually do, but they heeded Anya's orders and were politer.

CHAPTER TWENTY

Beyond the domestic upheavals in Anya's world, the war in Europe advanced. To boost solidarity with their cause, the Nazis organized massive gatherings at the venue bordering Nuremberg's Dutzendteich (Dutzend Pond). The stadium, designed by Hitler's architect, Albert Speer, boasted a 40-foot-long podium. With microphones and speakers implemented throughout, it allowed the Führer to make good use of his oratory skills and charisma, as well as display Nazi military prowess via massive parades.

Rosa was adamant her grown daughters refrain from attending these rallies when scandalous tales of a lascivious nature reached her ears. Allegedly, in the heat and fervor of Nazi rhetoric at these assemblies, and surrounded by handsome Nazi soldiers, young women were busy mating with said soldiers in camps set up along the Dutzendteich. The Reich wanted Aryan babies, and Rosa supposed this was their way of propagating the race. Rumors declared that several hundred girls were pregnant as a result. The notorious camps were scheduled to be abolished in the foreseeable future, but at present Rosa was taking no chances that her daughters be seduced into any disreputable behavior.

"But Mama, the rallies could be such fun!" the naïve girls declared, unaware what kind of 'fun' might be in store for them.

"No, you are not going, and that is final!" she told her disappointed offspring.

Their father, however, was adamant that they be allowed to watch Hitler parade through Fürth enroute to the latest Nuremberg rally. After much volatile debate, Rosa conceded just to keep the peace.

On a beautiful, unclouded Sunday, Anya and Hannah caught their first glimpse of the man behind the radio rants. As Hitler rode through the streets of Fürth in a chauffeur-driven Mercedes headed toward Zeppelin Field, Nuremberg's outdoor arena, they were stunned to be in proximity to him. An unnerving sense of awe, fear, and disgust jumbled through Anya as she watched the "Dolf" of her childhood stand upright in his limousine and give the horde his palm-up salute. Her own arm, as if a separate entity, raised upward in response to "Heil Hitler!" as the crowd roared. It was surreal. The man she had read and heard so much about was streaming by in the flesh, and all she could think was how much he looked like a peahen preening in front of his audience. Her father stood at her side beaming with pride until his persistent grin appeared grotesque to her. Her mother had refused to come, pleading a headache. Hannah stood to her left, dazed by the unexpected throng and commotion. For a moment, all three stood in a freeze-frame of astonished disbelief.

Lost in their individual observation and reflection, Anya, her father, sister, and fellow gatherers were startled when an onlooker reared up and threw tomatoes at Hitler's car. The force of it left dripping blotches of red against the vehicle's side door that looked much like blood. The gesture, Anya noticed, delighted several bystanders around the culprit, but left the vast majority aghast and did not amuse the soldiers guarding the Führer.

With a grim look on his face, she watched Hitler sit down in haste and the Mercedes pick up speed. As the crowd buzzed about, punishment for the offense was swift. Nazi police descended upon the perpetrator, clubbed him until his head was as red as the tomato he had thrown, and dragged him off. Oswald and the onlookers were acutely aware it would be the last time such a grave incident would occur. The Nazi police, always watchful and standing guard to ensure their Führer received the respect he deserved, would not forebear another transgression such as this. If spectators did not wave and cheer in response to the Führer's greeting when making public appearances, the scorching wrath of Hades awaited them. The tossing of vegetables soon gave way to a fervent, "Heil Hitler!" from all citizens who swarmed to see Hitler, enthusiasts or not. Prompted by Oswald, Hannah and Anya raised their arms in the mandatory salute, as the soldiers swept over the crowd with a keen eye. It sickened the girls to do it, because inwardly they felt ashamed.

Malignant vigilance by the Nazi militia prevailed day in and day out to ensure all laws were obeyed. A short while after the tomato incident, Anya learned how truly inhumane the Nazis' handling of certain transgressions could be.

A young schoolmate of hers, who suffered from hunger as food became scarce and rationing tighter, sneaked off on occasion with his friends to steal a chicken from a local farm. Afterward they brought it to an elderly neighbor to clean and cook it for them. The risk they took filled their stomachs, but they were caught. The old woman was dragged away never to be seen again, and their schoolmate and his friends were shot to death.

"Why did they shoot them? Why? They were only boys!" a traumatized Anya shouted at her mother.

Rosa tried to explain the current rule of law to her daughters as they clung to each other for solace. She tried hard to speak words that would make sense of the boys' execution and ease their fright, but their mother's words were not audible to their ears. Fear had numbed their senses, and they had shut down.

The requisite "Heil Hitler!" permeated each facet of their everyday life. Many cheered with enthusiasm, others less so. Hitler's grip prohibited most all from exercising their free will, as he steeped them, and their fellow Germans, ever deeper into the hellhole of his ambition.

When Benito Mussolini became a Hitler ally, Anya was able to see him in the flesh too. The Italian dictator, traveling through Fürth on a slow-moving train, waved to the people from an open window, allowing them to catch a glimpse of the infamous El Duce. Anya had gone by herself this time, as her father was needed at work, and Hannah had no interest.

When the clacking of the train slackened, bystanders cheered and greeted the Italian ally with German hospitality. Anya noted that Mussolini soaked up the attention like spaghetti sauce on a bed of noodles. She was curious but felt no excitement at seeing the man. When he did trail by, standing at the window, conferring impervious waves and nods to the cheering crowd, she was left cold.

Barrel-chested, jowls hanging from a gluttonous, round face, he wore a strange, ornate, black pillbox hat on his bare head and a steel-grey uniform sporting several medals, as well as a sash across his broad torso. To Anya he looked like a bulldog on a leash. She headed home, devoid of enthusiasm, and never mentioned seeing El Duce to anyone. Her scorn deepened as she contemplated a partnership between Hitler and Mussolini. "Dick und Doff" (Fat and Stupid) came to mind. They were the perfect Laurel and Hardy sidekicks to cause trouble across Europe.

CHAPTER TWENTY-ONE

Fürth, Germany 1939-onward

The early years of the war were a constant struggle but calm in comparison to what Anya, her family, and her countrymen endured during the latter part of the conflict; a conflict which had exploded into World War II against the Allies.

The Americans were not involved in the early battles in Europe. Except for the solitary hit on Nuremberg, warfare entailed scattered and limited bombing in locations usually distant from Fürth. The British RAF, in its initial skirmishes with Germany, used bombs that were not of the magnitude the Americans would use later. It was not until early 1944 that the massive bomb raids on German cities and towns began. In the interim, the air assaults were destructive enough.

Entering her mid-teens, Anya felt more vulnerable and endangered than ever. Day by day, she did not know if she would lose her family or her own life. She could not foresee the future, and that terrified her.

There were often mad runs to air raid shelters in the middle of the night when sirens blared warning of another attack. Grabbing whatever food and water they could, in case she, Hannah, and their mother were trapped in a shelter for a long period of time, they dashed down the stairs and toward the nearest refuge. Her father often shut himself up with his cronies, since he was at work or at a pub when sirens blew. At home, they slept in their day clothes with their shoes always at the ready and acquired methods to help them survive. Along the way they grew up before their time. Childhood was a luxury Anya and Hannah could no longer afford.

Often sequestered in an air raid shelter with their mother, the smell of the refuge seldom left them. The stench of people holed up in close quarters, and children and the elderly reeking of urine and excrement, were ills they had to forbear. In the winter, coughs and sniffles, and the guttural explosion of phlegm irritated their senses. In the summer, it was the pungent odor of sweat.

Then there were the rants of those with claustrophobia, men and women who would rather risk running into the open streets than being enclosed in a shelter.

But the worst was the silence, as they listened for the whistling bombs to fall.

It was in these precarious places that Anya began to worry what her future would be like or if she had any future at all. As she and Hannah curled against their mother on the couch that evening, an idea to find a possible answer brewed in her mind.

"Let's go visit the gypsy camp and have our fortunes told!" an eager Anya proposed when she met up with her friend, Lisbeth, the next day with Hannah in tow. "Don't you want to know what our future might hold?"

Lisbeth was enthralled by the suggestion, while Hannah was alarmed.

"You mean go to the gypsy camp all alone?" she asked, horrified at the thought of walking into such a foreign and uncertain place.

There were Roma living on the outskirts of Fürth. Some of these gypsies were Romany transplants from Hungary known to possess a flair for creating fascinating bits of jewelry, colorful handwoven rugs, and embroidered blouses. They also had a dubious talent for discerning the future via the reading of one's palm.

Anya and Lisbeth, eager to go, steadied Hannah's fears by insisting it would be an enjoyable entertainment.

"Don't you want to know what the stars have in store for you? Come with us!" her sister demanded.

Anya and Lisbeth badgered the poor girl until, with some misgiving, Hannah agreed to accompany them one Sunday afternoon.

Bravely marching toward the outlying forest surrounding their town, the two adventurous, and one semi-adventurous, "gallants" found their way to the Romany enclave. Fascinating to behold, it consisted of colorful, horse-drawn wagons that served as their homes. Situated near a stream, the girls encountered several grazing horses before finding the courage to approach the most ostentatious carriage in the row. A Roma woman by the name of Setta Magdalene, renown for the service they were seeking, lived there.

As they neared her wagon, Lisbeth sprinted ahead to knock on the door while the girls waited behind. She recoiled when an awe-inspiring woman with mahogany skin, dark raven eyes, and a wild mane of rust-colored hair burst the entry wide open.

"Yes? What do you want?" the bejeweled woman barked, eyeing the startled girls with a slight tinge of humor.

Lisbeth, straightening her spine, tried to appear mature and non-plussed. The gypsy woman, with her flamboyant skirts and bangles, was daunting, but Lisbeth took command of her nerves and remained cool.

"My friends and I would like to have our fortunes told. If you are Setta Magdalene, would you be so kind as to help us?'

The gypsy eyed the girls and turned back to her wagon, "Come in, but only if you have the money to pay."

As they entered, Setta Magdalene surveyed the three young girls who were foolhardy enough to risk walking into a gypsy camp on their own.

They must really want to have their fortune told, she surmised, *and who am I to disappoint them? It certainly will not disappoint my pocket.*

The wide-eyed girls, entranced by the vibrant interior, were led to a candle-laden table. There they dropped the coins the woman requested into a silver tray and were told to sit down.

"So, which one of you will be first?" the woman asked, turning a baleful eye toward them as they surveyed their surroundings.

A nervous Hannah was the closest to the table, thus the girls pushed her forward.

"Give me your hand," the gypsy commanded of the shaking girl, "What is your name?"

"Hannah...Hannah Schmidt," she replied, embarrassed by the nervous crackle in her voice.

Setta Magdalene rubbed the tops of Hannah's fingers to calm the girl down. Then she turned Hannah's hand over to read and analyze her palm.

"Hmmm, you have an easy hand to read," the seeress said, "I see a simple life for you. Yes, in fact, quite a simple life. You will marry a local fellow and have several children."

This pleased Hannah to no end, as she dreamed of having a large family and had no desire to do anything more exciting.

"But" the gypsy said, studying Hannah's hand with undue gravity, "you must be careful and listen to people. If you do not, there will be consequences. Otherwise, your wishes will be assured."

Hannah beamed. The gypsy looked at her with keen eyes.

"Remember, you must be careful and listen to people."

Hannah thanked her and switched seats with Lisbeth, who offered her palm with aplomb.

The gypsy examined it, turning it this way and that for a few moments. As she did so, a deep furrow appeared on her forehead.

"You will find romance, but you must take heed. You have an impetuous nature, yes?"

Lisbeth admitted it was so.

"You must not let your impulsiveness reign, or your life will prove difficult. Keep your head about you and protect your heart, and you will be fine."

"Will I get married and have children too?" Lisbeth asked,

hopeful she would.

The gypsy scrutinized her palm again, "In time."

Lisbeth leaned back in her chair and appeared dissatisfied.

"How long must I wait?" she wanted to know.

The woman gave her a piercing look, "As long as necessary, until you find a man you can trust." With these words, she dismissed Lisbeth with a forced smile and waved to Anya to join her at the table.

Sitting down in the chair vacated by Lisbeth, Anya thrust out her palm in expectation of learning her prospects. Her eyes challenged the fortune teller to deter her growing skepticism.

Unperturbed, the woman scrutinized Anya's palm for a long while.

"Hmmm...your palm tells a very interesting story."

"A good one, I hope," Anya said with piqued curiosity.

"An intriguing one," the gypsy murmured, looking solemn as she continued, "You will take a long journey some day at the hands of someone quite mysterious. Beware of your heart too, for it can lead to trouble like your friend's here," indicating Lisbeth. "You must let your head rule, or your emotions will get the better of you. I can see you are very mature in your demeanor, but still innocent in the ways of human nature."

"Will I 'get married and have children' too?" Anya countered.

"Yes. *If* you are *patient*," the woman shot back. "Now, that will be all, unless you wish to pay more for my services."

There were no more coins in their pockets, so they rose (albeit with reluctance), thanked the strange woman for her time, and left.

After clearing the grove amid the stares of its inhabitants, Anya gave Hannah and Lisbeth her honest summation of the fortune teller and her predictions: "I think she's a fake. A long journey? I have barely enough money to make it to Nuremberg! And who is this mysterious stranger I am expected to meet? She sounded so ominous in telling our fortunes, didn't she?"

Little did Anya know that "a mysterious stranger" was heading toward Fürth that very day. Kreon Kalanis, age 26, a foreign laborer from Greece trying to overcome a distressing history of his own, would soon cross her path and lead them on a perilous journey.

CHAPTER TWENTY-TWO

Massachusetts, USA, 1915-1921

On the 4th of May 1915, Kreon Kalanis came screaming into the world, all eight pounds and two ounces of him. Perhaps he knew what was coming. At the first sign of his pending birth, Kreon's father, Demetrios Kalanis, summoned the local midwife to aid in the delivery.

Once born, cleaned, bundled, and handed to his mother, the boy's birth was duly recorded at his place of origin, Lowell, Massachusetts, USA. Kreon (Kree-ohn) was a first-born American in the Kalanis family and his father's pride.

Demetrios and Eleni (nee Parapanisious) Kalanis had emigrated from the northern village of Trikala, Greece and sailed into Boston Harbor in 1912. They had joined Eleni's sister, Fotini, and her new husband, Andreas Stanos, in the land of hopes and dreams. Andreas had provided their passage.

Their new home was a tenement on Worthington Street in Lowell, near the industrial core of the city. Demetrios obtained employment as a laborer in one of the textile mills while Eleni, unable to read or write English, made as comfortable a home for him and their children as she could under the limitations of their finances.

It was obvious to their kin that they shared a great love and were devoted to one another. This was punctuated by the fact that their offspring arrived in rapid succession. Their eldest girl, Vasiliki, had been born in Greece prior to their journey to America. Their first-born son, Kreon, a second daughter, Sonia, and a baby boy, named Apostolones, filled their home and were duly baptized. The parents gave alms to their Greek Orthodox Church in gratitude and preserved a remnant of each child's caul in a small leather pouch, as was their tradition. It was a time of joy.

It did not last.

By the age of six, Kreon, his sisters, and their baby brother were motherless.

Eleni, at the age of 32, once lively and vibrant, did not withstand the assault of the influenza that gripped her body so soon after giving birth to their fourth child. Her weakened frame succumbed to the illness, and she passed from their lives.

The evening of her death, their Uncle Andreas brought the three eldest children to their mother's room, to say their final good-byes.

As they entered, their mother lay on the bed as if she were sleeping. Their Aunt Fotini, sitting on the edge, held the hem of their mother's skirt against her cheek and sobbed. Their father, kneeling by the bed and holding their mother's hand, prayed for God's mercy in his grief. Candles illuminated the room, and the smell of incense was heavy in the air.

"Go," their uncle quietly instructed, as he guided the weeping children forward, bound in sorrow, to kiss their mother good-bye.

Vasiliki and Sonia approached their mother's body first, kissed her cheek, then clung to their father, who remained deep in prayer.

Kreon was next. Gazing at his mother, he moved a few steps forward. The room felt suddenly chill, and he shivered. Watching his family mourn added to his growing despondency. As he neared the figure on the bed, Kreon stiffened. The sight of his beloved mother, her eyes closed, her body lifeless and unmoving, stunned him. In obedience to his uncle, he bent to kiss her pale cheek. It was cold and felt like hardened clay. He cringed, and his head jerked backwards. Nudged on by his uncle, Kreon kissed her again, with more care.

As he did so, he heard his uncle say to his father, "I have contacted the undertaker." At these words, a torrent of emotion raged through Kreon.

"No!" he screamed, "No!" and ran from the apartment, down the stairs, and into the street before anyone could stop him. His shocked uncle raced to retrieve the distressed boy.

The next morning Kreon stood stone still as his mother's body was removed from their home. After the church service, attended by family and friends, he remained unmoved at the gravesite, and held onto to his father's shaking hand. With the benediction of a Greek Orthodox priest, they placed Eleni Kalanis, blessed wife and mother, into the earth.

A few weeks later, in the throes of inconsolable grief, their father made a wrenching decision: his two-month-old son, Apostolones, would be given up for adoption to family friends who wished for a child. He, with his remaining three children, would return to Greece to begin a new life in Athens. The Stanos family begged him to stay, but his heartache over losing his beloved wife was unbearable.

"How can I stay," he cried, "when everywhere I look, I see her? It is agonizing and will drive me mad. How can I stay in the land that has taken her from me? I cannot breathe without her."

"But she is buried here," Fotini exclaimed in her sadness, "Her body is here. You can visit and talk to her at her grave, as I do."

"Yes, her body is here," he replied, "But not her spirit! It never left Greece. Nor has mine."

He soon booked passage with a portion of the money he had saved.

He and Eleni had doted on each other. She had been beautiful, but temperamental, a source of infinite exhilaration and warmth in his life. Her temper would flare red hot at times, but only against the neighbors that irritated her in the tenement where they lived, never against her adored husband. He had to leave. The torment of his memories and the reality of his loss was scalding and bitter. Guilt, too, was driving him away.

If only I had not gotten her pregnant again, perhaps she would have remained strong and lived.

He could no longer function in their home in America.

The day of their departure from Boston Harbor, Kreon and his sisters stood at the pier overwhelmed by the turn of events.

"Patera-mou, where are we going?" they asked, their faces showing bewilderment. Their Aunt Fotini, clothed in a long, somber suit of dark linen with matching gloves and wide-brimmed hat, knelt to gently explain.

"You are going to a lovely land with your father. There will be huge mountains and olive trees to climb, and a blue sea to swim in. It is where your parents and Vasiliki came from. You will like it."

The younger children were not convinced, especially when Vasiliki did not remember a place like that.

"Well, Vasiliki was only two when your parents came to America," their Uncle Andreas informed them, dressed in mourning clothes like their aunt and their Papa. "You will like it."

A loud blast sounded from the steamer, and their father shuffled them forward with their aunt and uncle behind the small brigade.

"Come, we must get on board," he instructed his children firmly.

Aunt Fotini watched them near the gangplank and dabbed a lace handkerchief at her reddened eyes and nose.

"Why are you crying, Aunt Fotini? Do not be sad. We will come back again. I will make father return," Vasiliki promised.

This evoked even more tears from their aunt, and they watched as she returned to the comfort of their uncle's arms.

Their father shook hands with Uncle Andreas, "Thank you for everything. I will write as soon as I can. Take care of my baby boy." The words brought a catch to his voice and Demetrios tried to choke down the emotions that would overpower him if he allowed it.

Seeing his struggle, Andreas gave him a somber nod and pat on the back. Aunt Fotini broke away and flung her arms around their father.

"Demetri, why must you go?" she cried, "Your family belongs

here! Your baby belongs with you!"

Their father, with tremendous effort, gently removed her arms and kissed her on the cheek.

"Fotini, please understand," he begged with crushing sorrow in his eyes.

Defeated, she backed away and locked arms with her husband.

"God protect you," she whispered sadly. With that blessing, Demetrios Kalanis steered his three glum children up the gangplank of the freighter. They waved one last time from the railing before disappearing into the bowels of the ship. When the final horn blew, the steamer set sail for the open sea and they into an uncertain future.

CHAPTER TWENTY-THREE

Athens, Greece 1922

The children remained listless and morose during the long journey across the Atlantic, mirroring their father's own despondency. Only when dolphins sprang from the steel grey waters did they show a bit of interest in the life around them. The trip was uneventful as the seas were calmer than normal and the weather dreary; thus, the days were endless and numbing in their monotony. It was not until they transitioned from the Atlantic to the blue waters of the Mediterranean Sea that their spirits lifted a little.

When they at last neared the port of Athens and prepared to disembark, the children were more than eager to explore their new home. Athens with its beaches, its sprawling array of white stucco homes, historic sites and statues, and the majestic Parthenon at the pinnacle of the city, was guaranteed to reignite the lifeforce within them. Or so Demetrios hoped.

In preparation for their arrival, their father had written a friend in Greece to acquire a small flat in the outskirts of the city for them. Demetrios had sent money for the first month's rent in advance, and the pocket-sized living space awaited them upon their arrival. Unfortunately, the new domicile could only accommodate one occupant comfortably on a day-to-day basis. For their first few days, the children had to share a bed, while Demetrios fashioned a makeshift mattress for himself on the floor.

Within a week, out of necessity, their father settled his children into gender-specific orphanages nearby, not having the resources to take care of them. By a stroke of good fortune, he secured a position as a doorman at the orphanage where Kreon was placed, and not far from his two daughters' residence. It gave him the opportunity to visit his children daily if he so chose.

Bewildered and frightened, Kreon, Sonia, and Vasiliki submitted to their father's will and tried to adjust to their new environment. The sisters had each other, but Kreon was alone and disheartened.

For him, there was no softness to turn to; no comforting arms to be wrapped in. His mother had adored her son. Almost seven, he was now on his own. A tremendous sense of loss washed over him the first night he lay on his cot in a room full of strange boys. His unmuffled sobs woke his neighboring bedmate.

"Are you crying?" whispered the youngster to his right.

Kreon quickly wiped his tears away in the dark and lied, "No."

"I cried when I first came here," the lad told him, "Everything scared me. I think most of the boys here cried when they arrived."

Hearing his words, Kreon shed more tears.

"It's okay. Don't be sad. I'll be your friend," he whispered, "I'm Nico."

Kreon turned toward the boy in the dark, "I'm Kreon," he whimpered in response.

"It gets better. Wait and see," Nico assured him, "It's just scary when you are new."

Some of the light sleepers near them stirred, hearing the muted chatter, and mumbled a "Hi" before turning over, wrapping their blankets tighter, and returning to sleep.

"We'd better lower our voices, so the house master doesn't hear," Nico instructed, then whispered, "Why are you here? What happened to your family?"

It took a moment for Kreon to divulge his story.

"My mother died in America. But my Papa is still alive. He

couldn't take me and my two sisters to live with him when we came here."

With those words, Kreon's sobbing resumed.

"I really miss my mother," he confessed.

"You're lucky, though. You still have family. I don't have anybody," Nico told him, with only a shred of self-pity.

Kreon was dismayed, "Nobody?" he asked.

"No. Nobody. Not even an aunt or uncle to take me in," Nico answered.

Kreon found this incredulous, "How did that happen?"

"Train accident. My parents and I were heading toward the sea for a holiday. I survived and a few others. Was in the hospital for two months and no one claimed me."

"No one came to visit you or look for you?" Kreon, still incredulous, asked.

"No. No one. Some people from the orphanage came to check me over, and the doctors and nurses were nice, I guess. I was only three years old, and I don't remember much of it."

"That's so sad. I'm really sorry." Kreon did not know what else to say and fell silent.

"It's okay. This place is all I know. The boys who stay are my family," Nico told him.

"You don't remember your parents at all?" a stunned Kreon asked.

"No, nothing. But I was given some pictures of them that my father had in his wallet. They look nice. I'll show you tomorrow." Nico decided to change the subject, "Why can't you live with your father?"

Kreon shrugged. "His place is small. And he said he didn't know how to raise us without our mother."

"How hard can raising children be?" Nico pondered.

"I don't know. I never had any," Kreon replied. Nico chuckled at his answer.

He peered at Kreon in the dim light, "It looks like you're feeling better. We better go to sleep before we get in trouble. I will teach you everything you need to know about this place tomorrow. Promise."

"Thank you. Good night," Kreon murmured. Both boys rolled over and shut their eyes. Kreon slept better than he thought he would. It felt good to keep the nightmares away.

CHAPTER TWENTY-FOUR

Nico was true to his word and taught Kreon to focus on his daily routine. Life in the orphanage consisted of structure and discipline. Kreon's hair was shorn off the next day and a uniform issued. During the daily routine, he was checked for lice, ears and nails checked for dirt, his body for disease, and to ensure his teeth were brushed well. Having his teeth and gums checked made him feel like a horse.

Much like good soldiers, they rose at 5:00 a.m. and did their calisthenics before breakfast. Their schedule was regimented and demanding. It was not without its good moments, Kreon discovered, because it included many sports competitions and trips to the beach to learn to swim.

The bus trips to the shore were his favorite. He loved swimming in the wide, open Aegean, smelling the salt air, and listening to seagulls caw as they swooped above the surf or strutted on the sand. The white-capped, pounding waves exhilarated him as he and his mates splashed under the blazing Grecian sun.

"Greece and this orphanage are not so bad after all," he admitted to Nico.

At the orphanage Kreon was allowed visitors, mostly his father, as he had not yet made friends outside his current residence. Kreon had no serious complaints. He made friends easily among the boys, especially when they learned he came from the great land of America, which made him popular. Bullying was kept at bay through swift and harsh punishment which consisted of solitary confinement and severe flicks of the headmaster's switch on their bare behind. Few if any wanted to chance his wrath and be humiliated in front of the entire assembly.

Despite a tolerable life and decent schooling at the orphanage, Kreon still ached to be with his family in their own home, as did his sisters. They longed for freedom and fewer rules and pleaded with their father to let them live with him and make their family whole again. But their father could not fulfill their wish.

"Papa, we miss Mama so much. Can't we stay with you?" they often beseeched him.

"No, it is not possible," he informed them resolutely, "I cannot afford a larger place, and with me working each day, what am I to do with you?" he asked, frustrated as much as they were by the bounds of their situation.

"We could go back to America and be with family," Vasiliki, his eldest, proposed one day.

"No. I have no more money to make that happen, nor the heart. And I will not beg your aunt and uncle for it," their father decided.

It was wrenching to see their discouraged faces as he stressed his words. There was no mother to take care of them, and he could not bear the thought of remarrying and replacing his beloved wife. Kreon and his sisters would not get to leave the orphanage until they turned eighteen. And that was final.

Not all proved bleak. Kreon was able to see Sonia and Vasiliki on holidays and intermittent visits. It became the extent of their closeness until such time all three siblings were released and could blend their lives.

As the days drifted into months and then years, Kreon fostered his dream of returning to America, the land of opportunity for strong, young men. He was reading and hearing so many extraordinary things about the United States and often tried discussing with his father his desire to return. His father did not want to listen, and it caused many disputes between them. "Barba Dimitri", as he was eventually called by the locals (a nickname given with affection to a gentle, old soul) was loyal to his homeland and kept telling his son, "The streets are not paved in gold in America!" although Demetrios, himself, had defied his parents and run off to Argentina in his youth to search for that very thing.

One day, while taking a walk together around a local park, Demetrios confessed to his son, "It is not just loyalty to Greece that makes me want to keep you here. I lost your mother to America. I gave my youngest son to America. I don't want to lose my eldest son too."

Kreon had not seen his father crumble since the evening of his mother's death. He beheld the ageing, frail man before him, this man who was shattered so long ago, and enfolded him in his arms. His father's legs were dependent on a cane and the strong arms of others now.

"I will stay with you. I will remain in Greece." Hearing those words, Barba Demetri rested his head against his boy's shoulder.

"I hope so, my son. I hope so."

CHAPTER TWENTY-FIVE

Kreon's eventual release from the confines of the orphanage in 1933 was adrenaline-charged. He was a hot-blooded male of eighteen. There were microbursts of energy as he discarded years of constraint. Wiry, handsome, and with enormous, dark eyes and thick, dark hair, he enjoyed the company of the entrancing Greek girls who flitted about like hummingbirds seeking a bud. Having finished trade school, he apprenticed as a machinist in a manufacturing plant to pay for these pleasantries and attempted to save what he could. The girls liked Kreon a great deal. He possessed a good sense of humor and was fun. But they soon discovered there was an edge to him that prevented them from getting too close. None became serious relationships, and, for now, he liked it that way.

"Kreon, where are you?" a female companion pointedly asked one evening as they rested on the beach watching the sun set.

"I am right here. Where else would I be?" he answered, perplexed.

"No, you are not. Your body is here, but your mind has migrated elsewhere."

The statement pricked his conscience because he knew he was not being fully attentive to her, nor to any girl he met. Most girls were toys to him, always ready to play, always ready to be cajoled into carnal games. Many girls he knew were brazen like the sun, ready to jump into the Aegean Sea from heady cliffs and taste the sparkling clear waters below. Marriage was a weak desire in the heated days of his youth.

Much to his displeasure, those youthful days were at risk when the Greek army summoned him to headquarters with the intention of enlisting him. Some madman named Adolph Hitler, up north in Germany, was stirring up dust in Europe. The commanders of the Greek Army wanted to be ready in case unwelcome grime blew into their country.

Appearing at the recruitment office, Kreon handed over his identification papers to the officer in charge.

"What is this?" the officer asked, holding up the thin sheaf of papers.

"My American citizenship papers, Sir, and my birth certificate," Kreon replied, "I was born in Lowell, Massachusetts in the United States. The papers will acknowledge it, Sir. I hope they suffice for your purpose."

They did not.

After verifying the documents, the assistant deemed Kreon ineligible to be recruited into the Greek army because of his American citizenship.

Leaving the enlistment office with mixed feelings, Kreon reported the news first to his father, who now had a room in a home for seniors and was relieved his son would stay in Athens. Later he met up with Nico at a favorite café for some Ouzo to catch up on their lives.

"They would not take me," Kreon confessed to his friend. "I considered joining voluntarily, but it meant sacrificing the one thing I value most, my birthright. I still dream of returning to America someday."

"Well, they took me," Nico informed him, bemoaning his fate.

" *What?*" Kreon blurted out, looking stupefied, "I was not aware you were being recruited!"

"A few days ago; I had no choice. I leave on Tuesday...which is much sooner than I expected."

"Are you planning on serving only your term or what?" It

disturbed Kreon that he might not see his friend for a long time, if ever.

"Am seriously thinking of becoming a career soldier," Nico admitted, "It's honorable enough and will pay me more than I am making as a barkeep."

"Stop bull-shitting me! You just want to wear a uniform and attract every available girl in Athens, don't you?"

Nico grinned, "Well, that's part of it too!"

"And here I thought you would go to America with me some day," Kreon sighed.

"Never say never, my friend," Nico chided him, "keep holding on to that dream of yours. You never know what this crazy world will bring."

Today, a little of that dream was fading away.

CHAPTER TWENTY-SIX

By 1941, the year Kreon turned twenty-six, the Nazis invaded Greece and seized its factories. Reality sucked his lofty dreams down like quicksand. Kreon lost his livelihood and found himself scrounging for food. And a uniformed Nico had disappeared into the hills of Greece to fight the German enemy.

The war soon impinged on the daily life of all Greek citizens. The constant search for jobs, food, and housing kept Kreon and his family members scattered throughout the towns surrounding Athens. Vasiliki had married, but not to a man of any substantial means. Sonia, their younger sister, won a speck of money in a church lottery and nurtured dreams of her own. She absconded from Greece without so much as a backward glance with the jackpot winnings and her suitcase in hand. A brief note stated she was looking for job opportunities elsewhere.

"Where do you think she has gone?" her distraught father asked. Neither Kreon nor Vasiliki knew and could not bear the hurt look in their father's eyes.

"Better to ask why she left without saying goodbye. Or why she did not help her family with the money?" an incensed Kreon remarked to his eldest sister.

Sonia's abandonment left them puzzled and bitter, but their search for her had to wait. The wind from the north was raging.

Thrown into the maelstrom of war, Kreon, Vasiliki, and their father were torn apart and found it increasingly difficult to keep track of each other's whereabouts. Worse yet, the food shortages became unyielding. Sanctions imposed by the German and Italian occupation of Greece led to the secret storing of food and goods by those operating the Black Market. It kept Greek citizens impoverished and groveling for rations.

As families became scattered, Kreon launched a desperate search for his father, who was now 74 years of age and relocated to a distant home for the elderly and infirm. Barba Dimitri was unable to contact his son to inform him of his current whereabouts, and Kreon's frantic search for his father proved futile until one fateful morning.

An area doctor managed to track Kreon down and contacted him through a local phone service.

"Is this Kreon Kalanis?"

"Yes."

The doctor introduced himself, then stated his mission.

"I am very sorry, Mr. Kalanis, but I have very sad news to report to you."

Kreon listened to the words in silence. When the man finished speaking, Kreon uttered a faint, "Thank you, for letting me know," and hung up.

With heartfelt regret, the doctor had informed him that his father had died three days ago in a neighboring village. Demetrios Kalanis was found starved to death in a field trying to eat grass. Dehumanized, reduced to bones, Barba Dimitri's body had been tossed into a mass grave with other victims of the Nazi-induced famine.

Realizing he would never see his father again, never be able to speak to him again, never be able to hold him, Kreon fell prostrate to the ground. His chest was overcome by pain as silent screams constricted his lungs and would not let go. The inhumane way his father died tormented him without mercy and would manifest itself in a chronic nightmare of an old man crying, "I am hungry! I am hungry!" The passage of time would not obliterate that vision, and

Kreon's anguished cries in the middle of the night could only be assuaged by morning light or a gentle nudge by an understanding hand.

In the ensuing days, his father's demise, and his burial in such a horrifying manner, festered into a wound beyond grief. The acute loss purged and humbled Kreon. Feeling gutted and adrift, he did a dance with the devil and battled for a hold on his sanity and his life. His elder sister, Vasiliki, tried to be his stronghold, but she, too, did not bear the loss well.

"Why could God not grant our father a gentle death? Why did he have to die in such a dreadful and undeserved manner?" she raged in anguish.

The relentless famine, the churning war, the torment of losing his father (and, possibly, the absent Nico), pushed Kreon to seek whatever ballast he could to keep himself from drowning.

I want to live. I want to live for my father!

Survival in Greece was honed to a stringent matter of life or death for all its citizens. Work and food for their empty stomachs became an obsessive need. Not only were the old dying of illness and starvation but the young also.

One afternoon, wandering without purpose through Athens, a flyer was thrust into Kreon's hand by a Nazi soldier. It offered jobs to "foreign laborers", specifically factory workers and machinists, in Germany. As Kreon read the printed words, the soldier pointed in the direction of Nazi headquarters and made a scribbling motion.

"I guess that's where we are expected to sign up," a potential recruit standing nearby holding the same flyer pointed out.

Kreon took a deep breath, "I suppose you are right."

With myriad laborers fighting on the battle fronts, Germany was in desperate need of replenishing its work force. Germany offered food. Germany offered jobs. Germany dangled the carrot of survival in front of foreigners willing to work in German factories.

Days later, called to Nazi headquarters in Athens after filling out the required forms, Kreon walked in feeling like a piece of meat beset by flies. Within a few hours, they sized him up, prodded his arms, and checked over his body.

"He's thin, but he's wiry, well- muscled, strong. He is trained as a machinist. He will make a good worker. Check his paperwork and sign him up," the overseeing officer ordered.

Kreon understood none of their babble, but he assumed he had passed their assessment favorably when he was shuffled to the finish line. There, a hurdle was placed in his way. He found the chief commandant reviewing his paperwork with a troubled eye and waving an interpreter over:

"Ask Mr. Kalanis why he was not recruited into the Greek army."

Questioned in his native tongue, a dispassionate Kreon replied, "I am an American citizen, Sir."

When the interpreter informed his superior, the commandant looked displeased but instructed his assistant to "Check out his citizenship papers and then get him processed."

Given a dismissive once-over before being ordered by a guard to gather his belongings, Kreon was unsure if he was being recruited or consigned to a firing squad.

Wending his way through the hallways, he received a reassuring pat on the back from the Nazi's interpreter who calmly told him,

"Don't look troubled, my good man. You will have a job. A roof over your head. You will be fed. Not so bad, is it? Good. Good. Right? Come along."

Rushed down another corridor, more paperwork awaited him, and more eyeballs focused on him as if he were a zoo animal. Following a brief interrogation and given instructions by the interpreter, Kreon received his shots, was checked for lice, and had his transport pass validated. He would be departing for Germany within a few days. Kreon was astounded that his American citizenship had not deterred the Nazis from recruiting him.

Apparently, the Germans were determined to fill the vacancies in their factories as efficiently as possible. No time was to be wasted in filling the needed quotas for manpower. Unbeknownst to Kreon,

40,000 laborers would soon find themselves in box cars headed for various locations in Germany.

Less than a week later, after a tortuous good-bye with Vasiliki wherein they hugged, cried, and tore their hearts asunder, Kreon boarded one such train.

"Promise me! Promise me you will return!" Vasiliki begged of her brother as he departed her home. "Write to me, Kreon! Write to me!"

"I will. I will try to send you some money too if I am able. Take care of your family."

"We love you, brother. Never forget that."

He nodded, kissed her cheek, and waved back one last time before turning the corner on his way to the train depot.

CHAPTER TWENTY-SEVEN

Preparing for his departure at the train station, Kreon surveyed the area around him. It was wrenching. Men, women, and children were everywhere, wailing their final good-byes to each other. Trains were stoked with coal, emitting smoke, and blowing their shrill whistles. The air smelled of bustling people and the fumes of transport vehicles.

Kreon took one last look at the scenery beyond. The sight of Athens and its surrounding mountains, brilliant in the sunlight, distressed him.

I am saying good-bye to everything I love.

A sharp order to "Move forward!" cut his thoughts short, as he and several foreign laborers found themselves shuttled to a nearby cattle car. Pushed toward its entry to board, Kreon gripped the outer bar of the rough door with his strong hands and hoisted himself into the boxcar as fast as he could. Straw was strewn all over its wooden floor, and he nearly slipped trying to gain his footing. Inside, men peppered the ground or leaned against the walls to catch glimpses of their loved ones or homeland through the slats. To acclimate himself to his new surroundings, Kreon concentrated on finding a decent spot within the crowded confines. A large, wooden barrel took up room in a corner, he noted. Its smell stung his nostrils, and he decided to avoid that area for a while. In the other corner, several uneasy men stared his way, and he gave them a sociable nod.

Outside, armed Nazis crawled everywhere as they oversaw the boarding of the trains. The laborers pushed and shoved to enter the locomotive before it chugged its cumbersome haul down the track.

It was spring in Athens and warm. Kreon, brandishing a used coat under his arm, tightened his hold on the small valise of clothes his sister had managed to scrounge together for him. His American citizenship papers were tucked under the insoles of his shoes. The Nazis had instructed him to bring a good pair of shoes. The ones he wore were the best he could forage out of his brother-in-law's closet, when given permission to do so. A picture of himself as a boy with his father and sisters remained stashed away in an inner pocket of his jacket. He took no risks in losing any of his precious cargo.

In the minutes left to them in their homeland, Kreon and his fellow passengers attempted to make themselves as comfortable as possible in the cramped quarters, or peer through the slats one last time. When the train whistle blew, the people outside milled around the cars, waving, weeping, and wailing once again. Children shrieked in their mother's arms amidst all the chaos. Kreon viewed this sea of sadness and breathed deeply hoping to achieve some inner sense of calm.

Having found a spot on the worn floorboards among amiable men, he placed his suitcase in an upright position and sat upon it to rest. A stream of light filtered through the planks offering ventilation. He had no interest in looking through them for last views of Athens. At present he was weary in spirit and not inclined to assess where they were headed, nor view what they were leaving behind.

The massive, movable doors were slammed shut, and the convoy of box cars, better for transporting cattle than men, began to chuff out of the station and clack down the tracks in a monotonous rhythm.

The men, anxious about the journey they were embarking on, eased the tension by breaking into noisy chatter. Some burst into jovial renditions of Greek songs to forestall the sadness.

Hazy tendrils of smoke, the stuffiness of their enclosure, and the undulating rhythm of the train as it lumbered down the tracks caused many passengers to yawn and nod off. Kreon, in no mood to converse with anyone, pretended he was dozing off too. He appreciated the fact that conversation was welcome but not necessary. He was aware, if he expected to endure this voyage, friendships would eventually need to be forged. Over two hundred and fifty men were packed on the train that left Athens for an unknown future in Germany.

As the truth of their destination settled in, none dared to dream of a perfect life awaiting them. Grim reality had to be faced and dealt with. Awakened from their uneasy slumber, becoming lucid once more, the disconcerted passengers made a sincere effort to bond. There was little choice to do otherwise when they considered their circumstances. Their voices soon overpowered the din of the iron wheels clacking down the railroad tracks.

"What's your name? Where do you come from? How is your family?" flew around the enclosure in the days ahead, as did speculation about the country they were being transported to.

"What is Germany like?"

"Anyone know?"

"Anyone been there?"

Their curious and concerned chatter rambled on.

Whether talking or trying to rest, most passengers, like Kreon, sat on their suitcases or stretched out on the floor and used their balled-up jackets for pillows. There was little opportunity for complete relaxation as the train jerked and screeched to a halt several times during its 10-day trek from Athens to Germany. The travelers found themselves jostled like saplings in the wind and fought to keep their shoots planted in the ground.

After the last violent jolt, one ingenious fellow suggested they create a buffer by sitting shoulder to shoulder to prevent crashing into each other, or worse, crashing against the rough-planked and nail-imbedded walls. They braced themselves and did as he said. It worked.

"Well, we have one fellow among us who has a brain!"

They cheered him and laughed.

Often the abrupt halts were due to problems on the tracks: munitions needed to be loaded, soldiers and trucks needed to pass, water needed to be fetched. Most disruptive and alarming were the bombings along the route causing fretful and unpredictable delays. When the train screeched to a halt again, there was a collective sigh.

"What is it now?" they asked of the men peering through the slats.

"The sheep need to be cleared away," they were informed, "They are very upset."

"What, the soldiers?"

"No, the sheep."

Loud bleats were heard, and the men broke into guffaws.

"Looks like the Nazi boots are knee-deep in sheep shit."

Sequestered on the train for hours, Kreon and his compatriots welcomed the scheduled rest stops for their daily meal. It enabled them to stretch their cramped legs, escape the stench of their quarters, breathe fresh air, seat themselves on proper benches and eat the bowl of soup and bread that was handed to them. They were allotted one meal and one snack per day. Back in their box car, they persisted in rooting out the humor in their situation. It kept them sane.

"So, my good fellow, which piece of bread did you find the tastiest, the one in your hand, or the one the Nazi dropped on the floor."

"Lucky Kreon found a fly in his soup! Why were we not served some meat?"

The foulest part of the trip, short of when the hapless odor of bodily gas was emitted, occurred when someone needed to relieve himself on the moving train. There was no toilet except for the barrel filled with straw and doused with a pungent-smelling antiseptic (which was emptied out at scheduled stops). When the barrel reached its limit before such a stop could be realized, another solution was found.

Pulling open one of the heavy, sliding doors a foot or so, two men would hold tightly onto the man whose bowels or bladder were calling for relief. When the humiliated traveler projected his hind quarters or aimed his appendage out the door, his ability to do so with grace was dependent upon which direction his body part faced and which way the wind blew. The wind never seemed to cooperate. The interior of the box car, as well as its passengers, would often be sprayed with human waste. A frantic covering of mouths and noses (amid disgusted grunts or bursts of amusement) would follow as the producer of the volley of excrement tried to restore his mottled dignity. They all stank, and they knew they stank. The stink was not discriminatory. All they could do was wait for the next stop to clean themselves off as best they could. Some of the men tried to seat themselves nearest the widest slits in the boxcar's walls to obliterate the smell until the train pulled into a station. They then headed for the latrine, attempting to wash the foulness off their clothes and skin.

CHAPTER TWENTY-EIGHT

Fürth, Germany 1942

The migration of these displaced souls ended a week and a half later, in late April of 1942. As acrid steam spewed from its engine, the train gave a warning whistle and arrived at its destination: the Hauptbahnhof of Fürth, Germany (its main train station). Kreon's birthday was a few days away, and he would enter his twenty-seventh year in a new country.

A city of approximately 84,000 inhabitants at the beginning of the war, Fürth's feudal history was prominently on display as they disembarked. The city boasted more historic buildings in proportion to its inhabitants than any city in Bavaria...over 2,000. In the past century, it had become an important transportation hub for rail travel and the transport of goods, human or otherwise. Located next door to Nuremberg and north of Munich and the Bavarian Alps, it possessed a romantic charm despite its progressive activity. Kreon had never seen anything like it and viewed his surroundings with sharp interest, as he and the men were hustled outside the station by German foot soldiers.

Stepping into the sunlight, the eyes of the Greek laborers widened in awe. Before them stood a massive fountain depicting a Centaur, a creature half-man, half-horse, holding sway over the rotund piazza in front of the train station. Flanked by a faun performing on its flute, the Centaur reared in majestic splendor over its watery domain. What better welcome could there be for these men of Athens than to be greeted by an icon of Greek mythology? Kreon's heart brimmed with optimism. It was also the Sunday of the Greek Easter.

"It makes you feel hopeful, doesn't it?" said a fellow traveler to his left.

"Yes. Yes, it does," Kreon replied, smiling at the sight.

Gazing at the medieval buildings festooned with window boxes dripping cascades of flowers, Kreon liked Fürth right away. The graceful city was in the flush of Spring and on vivid display. The sky was as azure as the Aegean, and puffs of clouds moved along with the breeze. A unique trolley car clanged, glided, and curved its way through cobblestone streets. There was a lush green park not far from view, and wet dew still lingered on the lawns around it. Bright yellow and orange daffodils, forsythia and multi-colored tulips bloomed everywhere. The air was rife with the floral scents of the season, as birds chirped and flitted around swaying branches, and people strolled about or sat on benches feeding pigeons. Amid all this, children squealed with delight as they played.

Kreon was enchanted by the quaintness of his new surroundings. The town was picturesque, unique and, most of all, pleasurable in its beauty. The only blemish that marred its charm were the red, black, and white flags bearing the Nazi swastika jutting from the windows of nearly every edifice in sight. Colorful as they were waving in the breeze, he envisioned tearing them down with a vengeance in the name of his father. He had seen these flags rippling throughout Athens and remembered all too well what they had taken from him and from Greece.

As anger threatened to overshadow his initial elation, Kreon turned his eyes back to the Centaur. His contemplation was brief as uniformed guards gathered the newly arrived "Fremd Arbeiters" (Foreign Laborers) and hurried them into waiting lorries. Kreon and his Greek cronies seated themselves on rough planks inside the nearest truck and viewed the people through its tied-back, canvas flaps.

As he watched the townsfolk pass by in their turned-out best, Kreon noticed something unusual about several of the wanderers. Nudging a fellow seatmate, he nodded toward the group.

"Do you know why they are wearing those strange bands on their arms?"

Kreon guessed perhaps they were blind, as the blind often wore similar armbands in Greece to make people aware of their affliction.

The man stole a quick glance, dropped his eyes, and whispered a cautious warning: "I heard those bands signify they are Jewish. Do not ask any more questions, especially around any Nazi soldiers. Keep your mouth shut and make yourself invisible if you can."

The black bands bore the yellow, palm-size Juden Stern (Star of David) and were required to be worn, Kreon discovered later, by every Jewish person above the age of six.

While driven through the town, Kreon continued his observation of the men that bore the insignia, noticing how they walked with their heads down and avoided eye contact with the soldiers milling about. He had heard vague stories of the Jewish plight in Germany, of the segregation of their families and intermittent disappearances.

Were they true? The thought perturbed him.

Kreon scrutinized the soldiers patrolling the area: their helmets, their rifles at the ready, their hard, leather boots. Perhaps it was best to heed his friend's advice.

As the trucks departed the main hub of the city, the foreign laborers onboard were subjected to a roll call, had their passes examined again, were ordered to hand over their required documents and were transported to their work camp.

Kreon kept his citizenship papers hidden in his shoe.

Arriving at the base they found the barracks decent but inadequately heated, as they unpacked and headed for the showers with fresh clothes. Their filthy clothes were to be cleaned and returned later that day. Fifty men had been assigned to each building and were grouped by nationality. They lived in a dorm-like setting: a narrow, numbered cot and locker were provided for each man, and a large washroom provided sinks, toilets, and the showers. Each man was issued a towel, washcloth, soap, toothpaste, and toothbrush. Their bodies were to be kept clean. Kreon felt like he was back in the orphanage.

The recruited laborers were advised work would begin at a local factory at 7:00 a.m. and end at 6:00 p.m. each day (half days on Saturday). They were informed they would earn a decent wage, be allowed to entertain themselves at the canteen and local establishments, be required to adhere to a strict 9:00 p.m. curfew, and follow established rules "or else". Holiday and vacation time would also be granted, but they could travel no more than 30 kilometers from Fürth without an authorized visa.

Properly indoctrinated, the men ate their evening meal in the canteen and retired to the spare, albeit comfortable, cot assigned to them. Too fatigued to chat, they soon fell asleep. Kreon remained awake.

Thoughts of his father and the Nazis roiled in his head. He wondered if the people wearing the obtrusive black bands with the gold star would meet the same fate as his father.

Will I? was his last thought before nodding off.

In the morning, after a breakfast of cooked oats and a slab of buttered brown bread was dished out on tin plates to each man, the Fremd-Arbeiters boarded the trucks that would transport them to their assigned factory. Anxious as to what was in store for them, they had not slept well, and most appeared bleary-eyed. Kreon was no exception.

Arriving at the designated facility, he and his fellow workers discovered the plant manufactured airplane parts. Duly cleared for admission, they were guided to their individual workstation and given their task. Kreon examined his space and noted it was clean and well-organized. While scrutinizing the tools provided for him, the factory foreman appeared and welcomed the new recruits with equable acknowledgment. Then the managers of the varied workstations began their tutorials and the men, some smelling of nervous flop sweat, obediently commenced with their tasks. A burring of machines was soon heard throughout.

Their first day progressed without incident, as the laborers were trained in their duties. Kreon and his comrades kept their heads low and their voices mute, only asking questions when necessary. After a full day of work, they were returned to their barracks. That night they ate, relaxed, and openly discussed their new situation.

"Not too bad, eh?" declared one worker in their midst. Most nodded and agreed. Kreon studied their faces and chose to keep his opinion to himself. Uneasy thoughts were niggling at his head.

CHAPTER TWENTY-NINE

It was "not too bad" for a beginning. The foreign laborers adapted to their routines, made tentative friends with their co-workers, and picked up fragments of the local language. On their first Sunday outing, Kreon and his Greek cohorts visited Nuremberg. They headed for the Dutzendteich (Dutzendt Pond) and stadium where they heard Hitler liked to give his imperious speeches. Germany's Führer was not visiting that day, so they did not expect to see him. They hoped they never would. Most disturbing during their explorations of the city was the realization that the people wearing black and yellow bands were becoming fewer and fewer.

Kreon and his friends, being strangers to this land, felt uneasy, although they had no obvious cause to be. The German people, while not used to having these foreigners in their midst, treated Kreon and his countrymen with respect and decorum. The townsfolk proved helpful and sympathetic, rarely derogatory (at least not to their faces). The laborers were aware that if they followed the rules established by the Nazis and acted in a civil manner, they could avoid trouble and remain unharmed.

"The rules bring an order to things," they were told.

The kindness they experienced did not always stem from intrinsic German hospitality though. Rather, the German populace received mandated instructions from Nazi headquarters to "be courteous to the foreign laborers to sway their allegiance toward Nazism and the

Nazi party itself".

One essential tenet in their day-to-day dealings with Germans, or even amongst themselves, was that you did not discuss politics. The directive, unspoken but clear, was, "You can look, you can listen, but keep your mouth shut."

This rule they could comply with; but one troubling tenet disturbed them:

On a Saturday afternoon while exploring the center of Fürth, Kreon and his buddies heard the air raid sirens. The piercing wail had them running for the nearest shelter but, to their dismay, they were not allowed entry.

"What is this?! We are not allowed to get out of harm's way?" an agitated Kreon shouted at the entryway.

"Nein! Verboten!" the local gentry responded while pushing him and his cronies away.

"We need shelter!" Kreon yelled louder this time.

"Verboten! Verboten!" the frantic crowd repeated as people squirmed past him to gain admittance. One German pointed down the street, where only shops could be seen.

"This is insane!" Kreon said, observing his group's plight with dismay, "What are we to do? Stand in the doorways of the shops and wait for a bomb to hit us?"

Luckily, they ran toward a shop that had a deep alcove. Managing to squeeze themselves into it, Kreon and his colleagues jumped as British planes soared overhead and bombs detonated in the distance.

When the alarm was over and they returned to their barracks, the men complained about their treatment, only to be informed there was a rule that forbade foreigners from seeking refuge in the Luftschutzkellers. These underground shelters were only permitted to be used by German citizens; foreigners were excluded due to "lack of space".

With increasing frustration, the non-nationals found themselves scrambling for safety whenever warning sirens blared. Nothing seemed safe to them anymore, not when they stood in the hallways of the factory, or doorways of homes or shops as the deadly bombs fell. Kreon and his compatriots came to know their true place in German society. They knew they worked hard and suffered because of this country. To be left to their own devices and treated as vermin in these shelters when they needed protection, resulted in bitterness they could not expel.

CHAPTER THIRTY

Fürth, Germany

May 4, 1942
My dearest Vasiliki,
I do not know if my letter will reach you, as I have received no response to the brief note I sent informing you of my safe arrival. If it is delivered, I pray it finds you and Alexi secure and in good health. Please try to get word to me so that I know you and your husband are alive.

I have been in Germany almost a month now and thought I would write and be with you in spirit on this, my 27ᵗʰ birthday. I wish I could be with you and Alexi, sharing a bottle of wine at the temple of Sounion, watching that glorious sun dip into the Aegean Sea. How far away that all seems!

Life here is bearable. It is much like the orphanage: a strict routine, many rules, and punishments, of course, if we disobey them. The German people treat us decently, but I wonder if it is their true nature. I have heard that German citizens were given orders by the Nazis to treat us graciously so that we might be swayed to their cause...whatever that cause may be. You know how I feel when I look at their swastika-emblazoned flag and watch the Nazi soldiers patrol the streets. I think of our father. What more can I say?

Homesickness washes over me as I think of Greece. I especially miss swimming in a bracing sea while the heat of the Grecian sun burnishes my skin. Oh, to feel that again! And how I miss the cawing of seagulls as they soar into that sapphire sky!

Germany is scenic too, but in a much different way. There are hills and forests and lush fields of green, with rivers and streams running through it. The nearby villages and cities are very quaint, quite different in architecture from ours; very medieval. The most wondrous thing I saw on the journey up here was the Alps. Such majestic mountains! They are covered in snow at the top, then slope downward into fields of green that are dotted with cows of milk chocolate color with bells around their necks. And the Alpine villages are comprised of rugged cottages that spew colorful flowers from the flowerboxes at each window. When I viewed this wondrous sight, I was astounded that such a beautiful land could sprout such ugly "weeds" in its midst. I guess they need a better gardener to rout them out.

Anyway, my dearest sister, I have established a routine for myself. I work in the factory all week and ½ a day on Saturday. During my free time, I explore what I can within the 30-mile radius we are allotted. Thus far, I am staying out of trouble and keeping my mouth shut. It is the best way to live if you call this living. Again, please write and try to let me know how you are doing. I worry about you, as I know you worry about me. You and Alexi are missed terribly. Until we meet again, dear Vasiliki, God keep you in the palm of His hand.

Your loving brother, Kreon

Kreon did not want his sister to worry, so he did not write of his exclusion from the air raid shelters. There was also another matter he omitted from his letter to Vasiliki, knowing she would fret about his penchant for the opposite sex.

A formidable and strictly enforced law in his new country was:

"Foreigners are not allowed to date, marry, or have intercourse with German girls."

It was "VERBOTEN"! Hitler wanted to propagate a "reine, Deutsches Volk" ("pure-bred Germans") not a race polluted by the blood of foreigners.

The day Kreon Kalanis set eyes on Anya Margarete Schmidt, that rule faced a dangerous test.

CHAPTER THIRTY-ONE

Each day, Kreon made sure to arrive at his work bench ready to do his assigned task. He was a machinist. He knew what was required of him. He knew he was obligated to do his job "or else".

After work, he and his companions often enjoyed dinner and a beer at a local pub. On Sundays they spent free time surveying their allotted 30-kilometer region. Afterward they returned to their barracks, slept, and the work week began again. Kreon lived life by rote. He liked it that way. It calmed his thoughts and dulled his senses.

But one day he looked up from his workstation and all things changed. He thought he saw an angel. He had once read that a silver string connects lovers together when they are born and then, in due course, draws them together in life. He had scoffed at the overtly romantic sentiment. He was not scoffing now.

Mesmerized, he watched as the angel floated down the long aisle between workstations and miraculously headed in his direction. The lithe figure looked ethereal as she glided by earthy men who gazed with appreciation at her beauty. Kreon noted her sweet face, framed by waves of honey-gold hair, possessed the most beatific eyes he had ever seen. She bowed her head shyly, blushing at the men's responsive stares. Dressed in a simple white blouse and tan skirt, striding gingerly on pumps that made the workers aware of her legs, she became their instant fantasy.

Watching her, Kreon turned to the friendly, attractive woman working near him. It was Rosa Schmidt. He liked her; they got along. Giving a little point, and trying to act nonchalant, although his heart was quivering wildly, he asked, "Do you know who that pretty girl is getting all the attention?"

Rosa smiled.

"Oh yes, her. That is my not quite sixteen-year-old daughter," she revealed, emphasizing the word *sixteen*.

Kreon gulped and glanced at Rosa in disbelief. Then he recognized the resemblance.

Having begun a new job as an office intern that day, Anya was perturbed to find she had to walk by rows of ogling men to meet her mother for lunch. Young and inexperienced, she was not accustomed to the male attention she was arousing, and it discomfited her.

"Grüß Gott, Liebling," Rosa murmured as she welcomed her daughter with open arms and a peck on the cheek. Turning toward a dumbstruck Kreon, the bemused mother introduced her daughter to him.

"Anya, this is Herr Kalanis, or Kreon if you will. Kreon, this is my young daughter, Anya, or Fraulein Schmidt to you." He noticed she stressed the word *young*.

While shaking Anya's delicate hand, he peered into the girl's pale green eyes. The Nazi rules barring foreigners from German girls drowned in them. Kreon's good sense was the second casualty.

As mother and daughter walked toward the factory canteen, male eyes followed their every movement until they disappeared through the door. Then in swift succession his Greek buddies encircled Kreon.

"It's time for our lunch break. Think you can eat some food?" a friend inquired with amusement.

"Looks like he's dining on love," another chided, noting the enthralled look on Kreon's face.

Kreon took no notice of them. He remained focused on the canteen door.

"I am going to marry that girl someday," he pronounced in a voice strengthened by concrete certainty.

The men burst into stunned guffaws, then reverted to abrupt silence. The German workers were staring.

"Marry! A skinny, bug-eyed Greek like you?" one whispered.

"With the blessings of the Third Reich?" murmured another.

Jorgo, his closest friend, put an arm around his shoulder.

"Come, Kreon, you need to eat and clear your head before you find it on the factory-room floor."

Steering Kreon away from his work bench and toward the canteen, they agreed it was time to instill their Greek wisdom into the bedazzled fellow before he stumbled into serious trouble.

Learning that Fraulein Schmidt, although many a man's dream, was presently no man's reality, Kreon failed miserably in resisting the virtues of Rosa's beautiful daughter. Despite his comrades' warnings, he began his campaign. It took weeks of prudent but determined maneuvering and bits of his limited German to draw near to her.

Whenever Anya appeared for lunch with her mother, he grabbed his chance to break through her shyness by remaining polite and avoiding tripping over his own tongue.

While at their neighboring workstations, he attempted to hide his feelings from Rosa so as not to alarm her. In his free time, he improved his language skills by paying a bi-lingual friend 10 Pfennig for every German word he would teach him. Kreon focused on learning German phrases appropriate for courting. He had a gift for mimicry and within months recited the words without a hint of an accent.

Heartily on the lookout for her each day as she met her mother for lunch, Kreon ran into Anya while walking along a factory hallway one wintry day. It was the first time he caught her alone. Feeling emboldened at the sight of her alone, he discretely sidled up to her and asked if she would like to go for a walk or movie with him some Sunday afternoon. He stumbled over his German words, but hoped she understood.

Anya, a tad panic-stricken, hoping no one would come down the corridor and see them together, did not know what to say or make of him.

Is he crazy? Doesn't he know the rules? He looks at me in such an odd way...like a child looking at a favorite treat.

Although a handsome man, Kreon had grown lean from lack of proper food, and his eyes were enormous, quite like the Byzantine pictures she had seen in her schoolbooks.

What was wrong with him? What does he want of me?

She was familiar with the edicts regarding socializing with foreigners, but she, admittedly, was beginning to experience baffling feelings toward this strange man she saw almost every day when meeting her mother.

Pity or something else? Her mind was reeling.

Anya was not sure. Her conflicting thoughts and feelings left her bewildered. She had no experience in these matters and did not know who to ask without tripping headlong into the lion's den. Annoyed at his boldness, she pretended not to understand what he was asking.

"I am not in the habit of being cornered in a hallway by a stranger I hardly know!" Shaking her head, a flustered Anya trotted away.

Reproved, and sensing her reluctance, Kreon remained calm yet resolute in his courtship. His gentle persistence ultimately melted her reserve. She finally agreed to meet him for dinner at a local pub and recruited her fellow co-worker and best friend, Lisbeth, to act as a cover and lend support. Anya did not dare turn to her mother for guidance nor permission!

Being her best friend and a lover of romance, Lisbeth, a smidgeon older and wiser, prepared Anya for her very first date the following Friday evening.

As she stood in Lisbeth's cubicle of a room after work that Friday, Anya launched into a conversation with the mirror on the wall.

"Am I crazy? Am I doing the right thing? What if my parents find out? What if the Nazis do? What will happen to me? Oh, this is so wrong!" Anya exclaimed and plopped herself on Lisbeth's bed. Lisbeth calmly dug into her closet and pulled out a simple dress of navy-blue wool for her young friend to wear.

"Here, try this on," she proposed, throwing the garment Anya's way, "You can wear it with your trench coat. It'll look smart."

Anya pulled the dress over her head and struggled to button up the front with twitchy fingers. She looked at the faded, tan coat lying on the bed. It was second-hand and frayed at the collar.

"I'll look awful! What is the use! I'll get drenched in this weather!" she wailed. Lisbeth surveyed her with exasperation. The evening had brought intermittent rain, but Lisbeth was not going to let her boggle-minded friend get discouraged.

"Trust me, he won't be looking at anything but your pretty face. In fact, here, let me pinch those cheeks and get a little lipstick on you!"

"I've never worn lipstick," Anya disclosed, intrigued at the prospect. Lisbeth stood in front of her and began tweaking her friend's face.

"Ouch! Don't pinch my cheeks so hard!" Anya exclaimed.

"Do you want to look like a slab of fish or a healthy, young woman? You need some color!" Lisbeth shouted.

Listening to her reasoning, Anya allowed one more tweak.

"What can I do about my open-toed shoes in this rain?" She looked balefully at the toes of her stockings, then at Lisbeth.

"You can wear my pumps. I have an old pair I can wear. Here..." Lisbeth pulled off her black pumps and handed them over to Anya.

"Danke, Lisbeth. You are such a good friend." Lisbeth was pleased to know she was appreciated.

Anya sat back on the bed as she put on the shoes. They were a pinch too big, and she was not sure she would be able to walk in them without tripping or losing a shoe.

"Here," Lisbeth suggested, "stuff some of these tissues into their fronts."

Anya did so, and they fit better.

"Lisbeth, am I crazy to do this? What's possessed me?"

Lisbeth, sensing Anya's angst, sat next to her and took her hand.

"Kreon is charming, and he likes you. And you like him. In fact, I think you like him very much," Lisbeth declared, staring at her friend's red-faced expression.

Anya blushed deeper at Lisbeth's gaze and conceded with a nod, "He's been very nice, but it's such a risk."

"Nowadays, getting out of bed, or even staying in it, is a risk. Do *not* be afraid of your feelings or of life, Anya. You're stronger than that," Lisbeth contended, "You deserve someone who truly loves you."

"Do you think he might?" Anya felt anxious over the idea, yet there was also a strange longing.

"We'll soon find out. Finish up! We don't want to be late!" her friend commanded.

Pulling on their coats and grabbing umbrellas, Lisbeth mused, "Kreon's sexy, especially when he has a stubble. Have you ever wondered what he's like in bed?"

Anya froze. Her eyes broadened like a deer caught in the beams of the Red-Light District. It took Lisbeth's assurances that she was only joking to thaw Anya out and make her blink. Locking arms, she guided her faint-hearted friend out the front door.

Through a fortuitous stroke of providence, Lisbeth's parents had a dinner date at the home of friends that evening and did not see the girls make their escape.

The weather was not as accommodating though, as they marched into town.

Lisbeth held Anya's shivering hand as they ambled toward the designated meeting place. The sky remained molten grey, and the cobbled walkways were puddled with rain as passersby, hidden under umbrellas, sloshed past them, and the odd vehicle splashed down the road. Only another block or two needed to be traversed before they arrived at their destination. Kreon had arranged to meet them at a reputable bistro near St. Michel's Church. It was situated on the corner of a plaza bordered by lanterns that provided a welcoming glow. Less than a block away, they spotted an anxious Kreon gazing at his watch, wandering back and forth under his dripping umbrella.

Anya sneaked a peek at him from under the darkness of her own umbrella and stopped. The darkened figure pacing back and forth brought forth an image of a roving panther. Anya tried to move forward, but her feet betrayed her; they turned colder than the cobblestones she was standing on. Grabbing Lisbeth's arm, she pulled her surprised friend in the opposite direction, blurting, "Let's go back!"

Flabbergasted, Lisbeth made a desperate attempt to calm Anya's overwrought nerves but could not. Giving up, she scurried after Anya, who was already 20 paces ahead and retreating to the comfort of the "familiar". A disappointed Lisbeth surmised Anya was not yet ready to jump into the "unknown".

Half an hour later, despite his valiant courtship, a sodden Kreon realized Anya had stood him up. His feelings were scorched to cinders as he returned to his barracks in the unsympathetic downpour.

Remaining at Lisbeth's overnight as they planned, the ladies got little rest. Anya talked incessantly, trying to sort out her feelings, and Lisbeth listened with one eye open and the other semi-closed.

By the time they arrived at the factory the next morning, a sleep-deprived Anya had sorted things out in her beleaguered mind and regretted her rash action of the night before. She stoked up her courage and approached Kreon during a suitable moment in the hallway to apologize. As she began her nervous and weak defense, he simply ignored her and walked away.

As such things happen when it comes to the mysteries of love, Anya's vulnerable heart burst wide open and was game for Cupid's arrow. She realized, through his constant and steady attention, Kreon was a secure figure in her ever-unstable world. She loved him for it and did not want to lose his friendship nor his presence in her life.

Desperate to atone for her unkind behavior, Anya begged Lisbeth to speak to Kreon on her behalf. A weary but sympathetic Lisbeth agreed to help. When the opportunity presented itself the following day, Lisbeth appealed to Kreon's chivalrous nature on Anya's behalf. With serious and truthful intent, Lisbeth beseeched him to relent.

"Kreon, you are her first, earnest suitor. You must understand, Anya is very mature, but still young in the ways of men. And you are older, Greek, and forbidden by law to court her. What can you expect? Yet she has feelings for you and is willing to be a friend."

Lisbeth rattled on, trying to reignite a spark of empathy toward her chum within Kreon.

Kreon listened. Kreon thought about Anya. Kreon succumbed.

CHAPTER THIRTY-TWO

Kreon and Anya's subsequent dates were pleasant but disquieting. They knew they would face great trouble if the Nazi henchmen became aware of their private encounters. Most often, there was the occasional meeting at a discreet pub with Lisbeth and Costa, a friend of Kreon's, accompanying them. If trouble brewed, the girls took off arm-in-arm, like two friends meeting for a meal, while the men stayed behind. Their dates also remained chaste, which took immense restraint on Kreon's part, but he sensed that the natural progression of their relationship must go slow and easy, if he did not want to scare Anya nor get them into a more flagrant and dangerous position.

There were several precautionary measures taken, especially on Sunday strolls in the countryside or local villages. The two ladies usually walked in front and the two gentlemen not too far behind as subterfuge. When Nazi soldiers crossed their path, the girls swiftly walked in one direction while their beaus turned down another, acting as if they were strangers. Few people knew of their courtship, and those who they entrusted with their secret, mainly Kreon's friends, aided them when they could. Her mother and grandparents were unaware, although Anya guessed her mother harbored suspicions.

Their fondness grew, but the effort to see each other kept them on edge. Despite the strain, there were moments of laughter, especially when Kreon mangled a German phrase or two in conversation or hand gestures were misread and became comical. To Anya's amazement, Kreon picked up the regional German dialect with speed and with no noticeable foreign accent. The local jargon proved not as complicated nor tongue-twisting as the sophisticated "Hoch Deutsch" (High German) spoken in more urban settings.

"I swear some of the German words are longer than any foreign alphabet! City folk speak to you as if they had a ramrod up their ass," one disgruntled comrade complained after being patronized by a group of businessmen at a Nuremberg pub. "They're all a bunch of high and mighty bastards!"

Kreon agreed the language seemed pompous, but he continued with his German lessons, which consisted of the more "user-friendly" Bavarian dialect. His diligence and gift for mimicry soon had him speaking the language easily. Despite all the dangers, subterfuge, and work that entailed courting Anya, he knew it was worth it. He was feeling something beyond sadness once again.

"Look at the joy on his face!" his compatriots teased, "Wonder what 'Schnapps' he is drinking?"

When a glorious, sunlit day presented itself, the foursome ventured into Nuremberg. The sprawling city with its hilltop castle, numerous pubs and bustling life proved a safer haven than Fürth for clandestine meetings. There was little chance of running into people they knew. Disembarking from the trolley, the girls walked several paces ahead until they felt secure enough to walk arm-in-arm with their companions.

Lisbeth and Costa headed to a nearby café where they agreed to meet up later.

"Come," Anya implored, linking her arm with Kreon's in a genial manner, "I want to show you something."

Standing in the Hauptmarkt of Nuremberg flanked by the Gothic Frauenkirche and the city's medieval town hall, she led him to the exquisite gold fount at the center of the plaza. He had seen it before on one of his visits but was not aware of its background. Anya informed him it was not a fountain but a church spire which stood almost twenty meters high.

"It was originally intended to cap the Frauenkirche centuries ago, but the Medieval inhabitants found it so striking they wanted it to stay at ground level."

As she spoke, she noted the look on Kreon's face, "Very impressive, isn't it? It's called the "Schöner Brunnen" (Beautiful Fountain) and something special was created for it."

He looked at the numerous, ornate figures surrounding the spire.

"No, not the saints. Look, here it is."

She pointed to a gold ring encircling one of the metalwork spears. The ring had no noticeable seam, and it was a mystery as to how it had been forged.

"It is said if you spin it, it will bring you good luck. Go! Spin it!"

He did as he was told. The ring spun two, then three times with the thrust of his fingers. As it did so, he heard her tinkling laughter behind him.

"What is so funny?" he asked.

"Legend says that you will have a child for every spin that you achieve!"

He saw the grin on her face and could not help but smile himself. She looked radiant as she placed her arm through his, and it made him happy.

"Come," he commanded, "let us go get something cool to drink and sit down with our friends. All this walking is making me hungry!"

After satisfying their stomachs, the four comrades took the trolley to Nuremberg's famous Dutzendteich. The area, comprised of two large ponds that were part of the recreational "Volkspark" (people's park), was bucolic in nature except where it bordered Zeppelin Field. This vast arena was where the Nazi rallies were held. Kreon steered them away from the site and toward more pleasant grounds.

Viewing the city in the far distance as they walked, the scene invoked a feeling of unease.

"How awful it would be if bombs fell again on Nuremberg. How much of it, or Fürth, will be left in ruins?" Anya mused out loud.

The British and American air raids were becoming more frequent and more frightening.

Somber in thought, they sat on a park bench surveying the vista, while Lisbeth and Costa sauntered ahead. Sitting side by side, Kreon was pleased when Anya locked arms with him.

"It's beautiful, isn't it?" Anya sighed, breathing in the fresh air.

"Yes. In this moment everything is beautiful. It's a summer day, the sun shines warm upon us, there is no air raid, and war seems far away," a contented Kreon replied.

"Wish it could stay this way," she said wistfully.

"Someday it will. Nothing bad remains forever," he said, hoping to lighten the mood.

"I hope we all survive, Kreon."

"We will, Anya. Although, hope is fickle, isn't it? Comes and goes as it pleases."

"Has it ever left you?" she asked, turning to him.

He gazed off into the distance, "Sometimes."

"When your father died?"

"Yes. And my mother before him. Losing someone you love is a wound you never recover from. And the way they die...well, that can change you in many ways."

"I hope our world will get better," Anya prayed.

Kreon smiled at her use of the word "our".

Clasping her hand, he proclaimed, "In this moment, it is better. Very much better."

She returned his smile. "Kreon, what do you wish for your future?"

"Hmmm...right now, I want the next moment to be as good as this one," he confessed.

"No, really. What do you wish for your future? I'm serious!"

He took in her intent stare, "I have dreamed of returning to America."

"America! So far away? Not back to Greece and your sister there?"

"I doubt I can return to Greece anytime soon. Things are not going well in Athens. There is a civil war brewing there. Besides, Vasiliki is married and is expecting a child. She will be too busy to deal with her errant brother."

Anya chuckled at his assessment of himself.

"I'm sure she misses you very much. I can't imagine ever leaving my family." She grew silent at the thought, then asked, "What attracts you to America?"

"Freedom. Freedom to do as I please. Freedom to grow as I please. There are no limits there. Plus, I have Greek family members I want to see," he inhaled a breath, "and my mother's grave to visit."

"You must have some happy memories there, don't you, of your childhood?" She pressed his hand in comfort, which touched him deeply.

"Only dim ones, and they are growing dimmer each day," he admitted. He turned toward her, "Well, now you know a little more about me. What about you? What do you wish for your future?"

Anya felt awkward saying, "a family of my own, a good husband, children, perhaps a small home. I wasn't made for much else."

"Oh, but I think you were meant for so much more! A mansion! Servants! A glamourous life!" he blustered, all the while grinning at her.

She laughed, "Your dreams are quite extravagant, Herr Kalanis!"

"Yes, they are! Yes, they are," he replied, as they stood up in good spirits and rejoined their companions.

That evening Kreon made a bold move and escorted Anya to the door of her grandparents' home where she was staying the night. Before turning the key in the lock, she surprised him with a peck on his cheek, and then shooed him off. As Kreon stood in the street, he gave her a little wave and, with a broad smile on his face, began trotting to the bus station in town to return to his barracks.

After watching him disappear around the corner, Anya turned

the lock and entered the house as quietly as she could. She was startled, as the hall light was switched on, to find her mother standing there with her arms crossed. Her grandparents, too, were still up and staring at her from the kitchen.

"Don't you have something to tell us?" her mother asked, her brooding eyes fixed on her daughter.

CHAPTER THIRTY-THREE

Anya could do little but confess that she was seeing Kreon. The admission was met with dismay and a litany of their concerns, countered by a litany of Anya's reassurances. Her mother finally diffused the situation by conceding that she liked Kreon. Working side-by-side at the factory, she found him to be a hard worker and a kind and decent fellow. She also guessed that he was smitten with her daughter by the way his eyes lit up whenever Anya came to meet her for lunch. Rosa acknowledged that Kreon always treated them in a respectful manner. Her remarks somewhat appeased Babette's concerns about Kreon, but "What about Hitler and his goons?!" her grandfather, Johann, wanted to know.

"We'll be as vigilant as we can be," Anya insisted, trying to hide the fact that she was not confident their vigilance would always protect them. Where Nazis were concerned, she and Kreon needed eyes behind their heads.

Anya's grandparents acquiesced to her wishes, but their frowns did not leave their faces as they headed upstairs to sleep an uneasy sleep.

She and her mother stayed behind, brewed more tea, and sat at the kitchen table mulling the situation. After a few awkward moments, Rosa broke the silence and delicately, (because delicacy was called for when dealing with her sensitive daughter), inquired of Anya, "What made you fall in love with Kreon?"

After a moment of inward contemplation, Anya replied, "It was the day Kreon and I went with Lisbeth and Kreon's friend, Costa, to the countryside for a stroll. We were walking in a field and Lizbeth bent down and plucked a flower to hand to Costa, but Kreon bent down and tenderly handed one to me. I realized in that moment how kind and good he was. He will not hurt me, Mama. I'm not afraid of him anymore, and I trust him."

Rosa nodded. She understood her daughter's position but was concerned about her idealistic nature.

"Please be careful. As romantic as it is, it is extremely dangerous. And do not rebel for the sake of rebelling. You must have purpose! You will only harm yourself if you do not follow reason."

"I know, Mama. I know," she placed her hand on her mother's shoulder to soothe her.

"You must also understand that a man will say "I love you" to get what he wants and not necessarily mean it," Rosa informed her.

Anya, repelled by the unseemliness of what her mother was alluding to, pulled her hand away.

"Kreon is not like that, Mama!"

"Well, he may not be the wolf I imagine most men to be, but please be careful. That is how I wound up being a young mother to Hannah. And never let your father find out. You are a mature and wise sixteen, but still sixteen. Kreon is twelve years older. Your father will thrash the both of you if he becomes aware!"

Rosa's warnings were unnecessary. Anya and Kreon were all too conscious of the lurking dangers as they continued their relationship. The streets at night, in both Fürth and Nuremberg, were pitch black, with cars reflecting only small slits of light to keep enemy planes from spotting their targets. This darkness proved menacing. They were never sure who would come out of the shadows and catch them together.

Although there was little ordinary crime committed by German citizens because of Hitler's police state, Anya and Kreon could not escape the reality that extraordinary crime was sinking its heinous teeth into the heart of German life.

The shadows they feared most were those of the SA, the Nazi members who wore the brown uniforms with the swastika insignia on their arm; or the SS, men dressed in black uniforms with the flash of lightning emblazoned on their sleeves. Or, on rare occasions, the Gestapo, the Secret Police, who operated primarily in the larger cities and incited absolute terror when they appeared. Then there were the most treacherous of all...the Nazi sympathizers who did not wear uniforms. They came in the form of deceitful friends, co-workers, or even relatives who might give them away.

It was not long before danger showed its menacing teeth. Walking to the barracks alone one night, having dropped Anya off near her parents' flat, Kreon heard the heart-stopping crunch of boots behind him. He tried to speed up his gait, but within moments he was accosted and beaten by ruffians who warned him, "Keep away from German girls!" as the sharp points of their shoes kicked at his ribs. He did not recognize their faces, nor did they seem to be wearing any uniform of significance with which he could identify them. When they were done, they left him so savagely beaten that he required emergency medical treatment; and the violent blows to his head would long affect his hearing.

By the grace of God, Kreon managed to stagger back to his barracks and inform the guard, and later the hospital medics, that he was the victim of a racist attack.

"They called me a stinking foreigner!" he fumed, not mentioning his assailants' actual warning.

When Anya saw his face several days later, her gasp spoke a thousand words. She held him tight, willing the bruises away, but Kreon's painful wince made her jump back.

"Why did they do this to you?"

He did not tell her the truth, reiterating instead that the attack was racist in nature. She stood there looking at the severity of his injuries.

"Did they see you with me? Is that why they did this to you?" she asked outright.

He looked up at her distraught face, "No," he answered with all the firmness he could muster.

The truth was attacks on foreigners were increasing and often occurred under the blanket of darkness. One night, shortly after Kreon was settled back in his quarters, another compatriot crawled back to the barracks and called out to his roommates for help. He had been pistol-whipped for dating a German girl. And another foreign laborer had downright disappeared when accusations against him were made.

Martin Bormann, Hitler's personal secretary, had sent out specific instructions to the Nazi commandants that, if foreign laborers broke any rules, the punishment be just and equal to the crime, not more, not less. Those mandates were often overlooked by the public and by the Nazis that caught the offenders, and especially by Anya's father.

CHAPTER THIRTY-FOUR

It was to be expected. Secrets cannot be hidden from a vigilant parent. Having heard of their trysts, Anya and Kreon were startled to find her father waiting for them one evening in an alley near the family flat. Anya's instinct was to run, but Kreon knew he had to face the Goliath.

It did not go well. Although they swore their involvement remained chaste, Oswald went after Kreon like a rabid dog.

"Get over here you miserable, sonofabitch!" Oswald yelled as he grabbed Kreon by the collar and kicked him without mercy. Kreon's arms rose to defend his bruised ribs, but he refused to retaliate.

"Stop it Papa, can't you see he's already hurt! Stop hitting him! He did nothing!" Anya begged her father while stragglers passed by the melee with little curiosity. Not privy to the particulars of the fight, they assumed the men were involved in a drunken brawl and walked away from the unpleasantness.

Kreon struggled to keep Oswald at bay, but his bruised body was no match for her father's wrath. Despite Anya's cries, Oswald would not diminish his blows until his anger was completely unleashed and spent. At that point, concerned bystanders did attempt to separate the mad dog from the object of his fury.

Kreon, bloodied and battered, rose to stand up and face Oswald squarely,

"I love your daughter," he said calmly and turned to leave the scene.

Refusing Anya's arms, Kreon limped down the street accompanied by two mates, and heard Anya's father spit after him while the small crowd dispersed.

Kreon could not blame Oswald Schmidt for the beating. Oswald was a father afraid for his daughter. Anya could be put away, or worse, for dating a foreigner. Plus, he was much older than Anya, and her father did not know what Kreon's intentions were. During the war, many foreigners were impregnating German girls then abandoning them after leaving their seed behind. Kreon considered it might be best if he broke things off with Anya. *But can I?* was the vital question rumbling through his mind.

When Anya returned home that evening, Oswald's skirmish with Kreon led to a furious battle between father and daughter.

"You never gave us a chance to explain!" she yelled, "All you did was act like a senseless animal. Is there no humanity in you anymore?"

"I will not have my daughter run around with a foreigner and act like a whore!"

Anya blanched.

"That is your summation of me, your own child? And of Kreon? Your mind is as low as the pigs you once butchered!"

"Don't you dare talk to me like that," he spewed.

"Don't worry, father, you won't hear my voice again. I'm leaving this place!"

Her mother and Hannah did not interfere as they listened to the scathing words. Mistrals of emotion thundered throughout the rooms of their flat that night.

"I've asked to live with Oma and Opa. I cannot stand this endless strife and your abuse anymore. Nothing but war inside this house and war outside this house. When do I get the chance to breathe, father? When do I get the chance to be happy for one moment? Tell me, father? When?"

The utter despair on her face stopped him from responding to her words. His arms sagged and he turned to leave the apartment, slamming the door behind him. Only then did her mother and sister take her into their arms.

It was not long after that Hannah, herself, prepared to leave and move in with an aunt who lived in the neighboring town of Zirndorf. She needed fresh air to combat her asthma, and the stress at home exacerbated her condition. Rosa was saddened by the exodus of her two daughters, but she understood their grievances and did not wish them to be harmed any further. They needed a safe house, and both of her children's locations were easily accessible for visits by her.

When Oswald, still infuriated, heard Anya had seriously moved in with her grandparents, he rushed to the Bermann home, grabbed her by the arm as she exited the door, and tried to drag her back to her parental home. Anya shook him off with a vengeance and refused to return. He countered by threatening to check on her each evening to ensure she was obeying the Nazi rules "or else!"

When her father did come to investigate, her grandmother, who trusted Anya and permitted her to see Kreon, told him that she was asleep upstairs. Johann was not yet privy to his granddaughter's escapades and remained oblivious in his study with his radio and newspapers until it was time for bed.

On subsequent evenings when Oswald came to check on her, he was mollified by Babette's assertion that Anya was sleeping soundly and safely in her bed. This was not always the case. Anya often slipped out to meet Kreon whenever she was able.

On the evenings she expected to come home late, she and Babette had worked out a system which allowed Anya to sneak in the house without waking her grandfather. The window near the front door would be left open wide enough for Anya to pass her arm through it and unlock the door from the inside. On occasion she would freeze when the latch squeaked on its hinges, but she always gained entry, and had a grin on her face when she did.

Oma and I make a great team!

Pressing on the doorhandle with utmost care, she would quietly let herself in, take off her shoes, and pad up the stairs to her room. Her grandmother would always hear her, for her maternal radar was fine-tuned, and she could not help but worry until Anya was back in her bed.

A lovestruck young woman is a resourceful woman. Nothing could deter Anya from seeing her Greek suitor again. Whether Anya was seeing Kreon out of defiance or out of love, Rosa realized her daughter's relationship with Kreon was strengthening. Yet she was unsure if Anya and Kreon were strong enough to endure whatever lay ahead. She feared they would get careless in their euphoria. Her thoughts left her on edge, and there were nights she could not sleep.

CHAPTER THIRTY-FIVE

There was no doubt in Rosa's distraught mind that Kreon and Anya's ever-growing bond would put them in harm's way. One evening at a local pub, it did.

A female co-worker spotted Kreon helping Anya on with her coat. A simple gesture, but a profound one. The next morning the woman reported it to their mutual boss.

"Herr Speyer, I feel it is my duty to make you aware of something...."

Her words to her boss were over-heard by a passing co-worker.

Sympathetic to Anya's plight, the co-worker quickly informed Anya she had been spied upon. Thanking the kind woman for alerting her, Anya braced herself for a call to the front office. The call came later that morning.

As Anya approached her manager's door, her heart pounded to the staccato rhythm of Nazi jackboots. She imagined a brigade of Hitler's soldiers coming for her. Pulling herself together, she reached for the handle to her manager's office. She hoped she could mask her fear. She had to if she wanted to talk her way out of this situation and survive. Anything less would result in a work camp for her, and worse for Kreon. Taking a deep breath, she turned the knob.

"Heil Hitler," she intoned tersely as she entered the office and gave the requisite Nazi salute.

Her boss looked up from his paperwork, "Heil Hitler," and

grimly added, "Sit down, please, Fraulein Schmidt."

His interrogation was firm and direct regarding her alleged "indiscretion" with a foreigner possibly from his factory. Sitting poised in her chair, but quaking internally, Anya managed to convince him that she did not know the man who had helped her with her coat the previous evening.

"I am only sixteen, Sir, not yet allowed to date. And certainly, would not do so with a foreigner if I were allowed!"

Her indignant replies to his questions appeased him and he chose to believe her. Then he called for his secretary to bring the informant to his office, while Anya sat there speculating what would come next.

The woman appeared, trembling and unsure of herself. Their manager explained that it was all a misunderstanding on her part and ordered the woman to apologize to Anya for the accusation she had made. Astonished, the co-worker took a deep breath and did so without defending her actions. She knew it was wiser to do as one was told and not question authority. Anya, too, was astonished by the outcome, but hid her feelings and accepted her accuser's apology with a ladylike nod. The informant received a curt dismissal and was warned not to make such rash accusations again. After a moment, Anya too was dismissed, but with more graciousness.

Once in the hallway, Anya rushed to the bathroom and encased herself in a stall. As her strung-out nerves unraveled, she began shaking with such severity, she thought it would never stop.

Oh my God, how close have I come to disaster? Will he inform the Nazis? Will my father find out?

The contents of her nervous stomach heaved, and she retched until her muscles could take no more.

Washing her face afterward, she tried to quiet her anxieties by thinking rationally.

My boss was kind. He asked the woman to apologize. He did not believe the accusation. He would not report an unfounded story.

Her nerves were not buying it, and she collapsed against the sink with little relief. She thanked God that no one was on break and could walk in on her.

As her thoughts lurched about, one thing became clear: she knew her boss liked and valued her.

Had he known the truth? Kreon and I need to be more careful.

Taking several deep breaths, Anya composed herself, returned to her workplace, and made herself as inconspicuous as possible for the remainder of that morning. It was the end of the work week and she, blessedly, would have Saturday afternoon and all of Sunday to gather her wits about her.

Returning home that afternoon, she did not tell her grandparents what had transpired for fear of worrying them. She also feared that they might stop her from seeing Kreon again. That thought was unbearable to her. She was preparing to meet him the next day for a picnic. Until then, she begged off dinner, pleading a headache, and retired to her room. She was still unnerved, and when she finally fell asleep, specters in a nightmare were waiting.

CHAPTER THIRTY-SIX

Anya rose the following morning from an agitated sleep and began to dress. It was a sunny day with a nip in the air. Her stomach was feeling a nip too, the remnants of the day before. She darted out of bed, eager to get out of the house. After washing up at her basin and pinning up her hair, she chose a simple, white blouse and pale blue, cotton skirt to wear. Her beige sandals with the frayed straps were the best she could do. Pinching her cheeks to get color back in her face, she draped a brown cardigan over her shoulders and headed down to the kitchen where her grandmother was peeling potatoes. A straw picnic basket was waiting for her on the table.

"I have packed a few things for you. Not much, but it will do. You look very pretty, dear," Babette observed, "Do you want any breakfast?"

"No thank you, Oma," Anya gave her an appreciative smile, "If I know Kreon, we'll be emptying this soon." Grabbing the basket, she vowed, "I'll be home before dark," and kissed her Oma good-bye.

Anya hoped to escape before she was asked any further questions.

Rushing to the small park across from the house, she found Kreon sitting beneath a tree. A rolled blanket was cradled under his arm.

Wearing tan khakis, a white, open-collared shirt, with his dark hair newly trimmed, Anya noted he looked quite handsome this morning. But, as she walked toward him, Kreon noted her wan face and sensed her fragility.

"What is wrong? Are you not feeling well?" he asked, as he stood up and took the basket from her.

"Why don't we walk as I explain? I desperately need to breathe fresh air."

Ambling along the path dotted with small cottages and colorful gardens on each side, they headed toward the cool confines of the distant woodland. Little by little, she told him of the events of the previous day. He remained silent as Anya recounted her dire morning. Aware her shoulders were shaking; he wrapped his arm around her as she continued to speak. Kreon soon felt her body relax.

Once she finished her tale, Anya said little else as they carried on with their stroll. Sauntering quietly, they allowed the beauty of their surroundings to act as balm on their troubled spirits. It was early Sunday, and few people were about. Some were at church, while others slept in after a tiring week of work. The few people they did encounter nodded and moved on. Birdsong is all that Anya hoped to hear that day instead of the chatter and clatter of townsfolk milling about.

When they reached a shaded glen, Kreon put the basket and blanket down; but, before he could spread the coverlet on the ground, Anya flew into his arms. He hugged her tight and stroked her head.

"I am so sorry you had to go through that," he uttered with deep regret, understanding too well what she had endured.

"I was so scared...so scared," she admitted.

His hold tightened, and it made her feel secure.

"We will have to be more careful. Right now, in this moment, we are safe," Kreon assured her.

His easy comfort proved soothing. She marveled at how protected she felt whenever he was with her. She did not want to leave his embrace as they settled down on the blanket.

They sat motionless for a while, her back leaning against Kreon's chest with his arms circled about her. Inhaling deeply, the serenity of their surroundings enveloped them.

In the silence, a pensive Kreon contemplated the horrors, no doubt, going on in other lives in that exact moment.

Will Anya and I always be as blessed as we are right now? Or will we too become victims?

The thought was sobering, and he stroked Anya's hair to forestall his darkening mood.

"Why don't we have some food," he suggested.

"I'm not sure I can eat much," Anya confessed.

"Good, then there will be more for me!"

They both laughed at his remark. She knew how hungry Kreon always was.

"What's in the basket?" he asked while his curious fingers poked at it.

"We shall see!" Anya chortled as she proceeded to pull the items out, "Hmm...freshly baked bread, wedges of cheese, two juicy apples, and a thermos of refreshing tea...my favorites!"

"My, my, no wine? No nectar from the Gods?" Kreon teased as he reached for a slab of farmer's bread and a thick slice of cheese.

"We could make believe we're drinking champagne," Anya proposed, "and make a toast to us." She raised the thermos of tea, then poured some into a spare cup and offered it to him.

"Danke Schöen. To us!" he exclaimed, raising his mug in a toast.

"Ja. To us!" she repeated, evading his eyes. Her mood too was changing.

"Something wrong?" He eyed her with concern.

"Nein, Kreon. Nothing."

He watched her, "Anya, tell me. Let us not keep secrets from one another."

She twirled a loose curl of hair before speaking, "You have never...." She stopped.

"I have never what?" Kreon flipped through the catalog in his head to find an answer.

She blushed, "I can't say it."

He put a finger under her chin and turned her face to his, "Say it."

"How come you've never tried to kiss me?"

Her question startled him. He leaned back on his elbows and began to chuckle. She eyed him with annoyance.

"What's so funny about my question? Why have you never kissed me?" she demanded to know.

Kreon was aghast, "But I have!"

"Yes, a peck on my cheek, or my forehead, or my hand, but never a real kiss!" Anya declared.

"What do you mean by a 'real' kiss?"

His question irked her, "You know what I mean." She blushed.

He grinned, "Well, it was not from lack of wanting to. I simply did not want to scare you away. You have to admit you have been very skittish about any such intimacy."

"Well, I'm not so skittish anymore. Do you think of me as a silly girl? I'm not, you know," Anya emphasized by straightening her shoulders.

"No, I do not see you as a silly girl. Where did you ever get such an idea? You are quite the young woman. Frankly, I think you have never had the chance to be a girl."

"What do you mean?" A wrinkle furrowed her brow, as the question perplexed her.

"You have had so many responsibilities from what you told me: a difficult family life, servitude to a Nazi family, and a war to contend with. How could you ever be silly and carefree? The remarkable thing about you is that you have not become bitter."

"Sometimes I am. But not when I'm with you." She took his hand. "I try hard not to make bitterness a part of my nature."

"I doubt it ever could," Kreon stated tenderly. "You are the kindest person I have ever met. Instead of reacting to your circumstances, you act, which is a very mature thing to do. You are better than I am in that regard."

"I don't think so," Anya replied, "I think you act very well in certain circumstances. And right now, I would like a kiss." She was aghast at her sudden boldness then admitted shyly, "I've never been truly kissed before."

"What?" He regarded her with feigned bewilderment. She reddened.

Bemused by her confession, he said, "Truly?"

"Truly," she admitted, ignoring his jocular tone.

He was inwardly pleased at the prospect of his kiss being her first.

"Hmmm, I guess I might have to kiss you after all, before a wolf beats me to it." Kreon drew her toward him, and she puckered her lips in response. He tried not to let his amusement show.

"Relax," he instructed her gently, "and close your eyes."

He leaned in and kissed her with less chasteness than he had first intended. She liked it more than she had first anticipated. Her arms tightened around him.

"More," she said, while her eyes remained closed in a dreamlike state.

He kissed her again, a bit longer this time. To his surprise she pressed herself against him daringly and kissed him with increasing passion. Flabbergasted by her fervor and his own increasing response, Kreon withdrew Anya's arms from around his neck and pulled away.

"We can't do this," he murmured, trying to catch his breath.

Her eyes flew open, "What's wrong?"

"Nothing's wrong," he avowed, "It's just..." he fumbled for words, "It's just...I think we should go for a walk."

"A walk? Now?" she sputtered.

"Yes!" He appeared riled. "We can't do this!"

Pulling her arms from around his neck, he drew her up from the blanket.

"Do what? Kiss?" she asked, confused by his sudden turnabout.

"Kissing is fine. It's just...it's just that it leads to other things...like trouble."

"Trouble?" She scanned his face, "You mean my father? Are you afraid of him? I'm not."

Frustrated, he jumped up and proclaimed, "I don't want to risk getting you pregnant!"

She gawked at him, "Pregnant," she repeated, then clarity dawned, "Oh."

Kreon felt guilt-ridden at the sight of her humiliated and crestfallen face.

"Anya," he took her right hand and kissed its upturned palm in a weak attempt to placate her, "German girls have, and German girls might, but for you and me, a foreigner and an Aryan girl, pregnancy means imprisonment or death. And our lives are something I will not risk. Do you understand me?"

A downcast Anya nodded and said not a word as reality reared its unromantic head. To hide her discomfort, she stooped to fold up the vacated blanket.

"I think our future will consist of some very long walks for a while," Kreon insisted, as he took the blanket from Anya and led her to the road that beckoned toward home.

She gazed at him. "With a once-in-a-while kiss?" she asked coyly, as her humor returned.

"With a once-in-a-while kiss," he conceded.

Anya smiled. Kreon did not.

CHAPTER THIRTY-SEVEN

Returning to her grandparents' home later that afternoon, Anya found a glum mother and Hannah sipping tea at the kitchen table with Oma. Opa was in the sitting room engrossed in his papers as usual.

"Sit down, child," Oma beckoned her toward a kitchen chair, "Would you like some tea?"

"Yes, thank you. That would be nice. I am a bit chilled."

Her grandmother instructed Rosa to reheat the kettle and fetch a cup and saucer.

"So," her mother asked, "how did your outing go? You returned early."

Anya tried to act casual, although she knew her mother was smart enough to see through her diffidence. Rosa was keenly surveying her and had something on her mind. A serious discussion was forthcoming.

"Kreon, I know, is a good man," her mother began, "I've worked with him long enough to know that much. But I want you to be especially careful," Rosa warned.

"He wouldn't harm me," Anya reminded her mother, frustrated by where the conversation was headed again.

"You know what I mean," Rosa interjected.

Anya blushed and stiffened her shoulders.

"We haven't done anything wrong if that's what you mean,

Mama. He's very mindful of the dangers and makes sure I'm mindful of them too."

"Yes, I'm sure he is. Well, you know foreigners are forbidden to fraternize with German girls, and you know what will happen to Kreon. But do you know what can happen to you if you get pregnant?"

"Yes," she turned to her mother dryly, "Father will kill me."

All four burst out in unexpected laughter over her statement.

"True," Oma agreed. "He will surely spare the SS the trouble."

Hannah, cringing at what the consequences could be, spoke up, "Death would be easier than what happened to Lisbeth."

"What are you talking about?" Anya bristled with annoyance when faced with riddles. She had seen Lisbeth a few days ago.

"You haven't heard?" Perplexed, Hannah turned to her mother for guidance.

"Heard what?" Anya shouted, wanting to shake her sister's brain back into place.

Unnerved, Hannah rapidly informed her, "She became pregnant by that foreign fellow she was seeing."

"Costa?" Anya was shocked by the news. Lisbeth had told her nothing!

"Yes," Hannah affirmed, "and he's gone."

"Costa? Where has he gone?" Anya implored.

"No one knows." Hannah informed her, shrugging her shoulders.

"And what of Lisbeth and the baby?" Anya glared at her sister with an increasing desire to strangle the words out of her.

Hannah cast her eyes toward Rosa, begging her mother to proceed.

"I am sorry to tell you this," Rosa began, gazing at her youngest with compassion as she spoke, "Her parents beat her when they found out. They pushed her beyond endurance..." Rosa paused to take a deep breath, then blurted, "Lisbeth tried to abort the baby and is now under hospital care."

Anya was stunned by the news and sprang from her seat, "That's horrible! Is Lisbeth alright? I need to see her!"

Her mother grabbed Anya's arm and pulled her back.

"Sit down and listen! Lisbeth is alive and so is her baby, but I do not want you going near her!"

"Why not?" Anya asked, feeling her world spin in the wrong direction.

"Because..." Rosa hesitated, "because the hospital reported Lisbeth to the authorities, and they are monitoring the situation."

Anya collapsed in her chair.

"Oh God, Mama, what will they do to her?"

Rosa looked at her daughter's anguished face and explained as steadily as she could, "You know that abortion is punishable by imprisonment or death."

Anya nodded and began to cry.

"Lisbeth is a pretty young woman, blonde, blue-eyed, and pregnant," Hannah added plaintively.

"And?" Anya looked at her mother, exasperated by Hannah's vague and nonsensical statement.

Rosa continued, "If the Nazis relent, she could be taken to a Lebensborn facility where she will be well cared for until she gives birth."

"Lebensborn? Does it still exist?" Anya turned to Rosa in shock, "I've heard rumors of it but didn't believe them." She shook her head in abhorrence, "Lisbeth, forced to mate with SS officers to make Aryan babies? No. I can't believe this!"

Anya had heard terrifying tales of the secret project that Heinrich Himmler was said to have initiated to increase the German/Nordic population and develop an Aryan "Master Race". Lebensborn, the "Wellspring of Life", recruited young women who were "racially pure", blonde-hair and blue eyes being the preference, to meet at a clandestine facility and allow themselves to be impregnated by SS officers who also met the same Aryan criteria. The babies were then given to the SS organization which took charge of the child's adoption and education.

"Well, believe it," her mother continued. "Sadly, it still exists. I ran into her mother at the market. The woman is beside herself with fear and guilt. She is pleading with the Nazis to be kind to her daughter."

"Kind? The Nazis?" Anya retorted, "When have they ever been kind? And what of her baby, Mama? It is Costa's. What if it has dark hair and dark eyes and doesn't look Aryan at all?"

Rosa answered her with direct honesty, "The baby will probably be placed in an orphanage. At least we pray it will be."

Anya had heard of more sinister outcomes for foreign babies. "I don't believe this," she groaned, head in hands. "I don't want to believe this. Are you telling me that Lisbeth will lose her child and be expected to produce more by coupling with Nazi officers? That she will be imprisoned or killed if she doesn't obey?"

The thought of Lebensborn horrified her.

Rosa stroked her daughter's hand and said nothing.

Anya professed with certainty, "My friend would rather die than have her baby ripped from her. I doubt Lisbeth wanted to abort it. I think she wanted to kill the baby and herself to spare them both."

Her mother, her sister and Oma remained silent while Anya attempted to sort out her painful thoughts and feelings.

Rosa knew the news had been brutal; but she knew both her daughters needed to hear it. Anya was seeing a foreigner twelve years her senior, and Hannah had recently taken up with a local man twenty years her senior. Her girls were embroiled in a world they could only hope to understand and attempt to navigate with success. She beheld her burdened daughters with deep sadness.

Stirred out of her tumultuous thoughts by her mother's warm hand, Anya pondered the situation, "Why is Hitler so crazed about creating a nation of blonde and blue-eyed Aryans when he, himself, has dark hair and dark eyes? Why is he so prejudiced?"

The question was left unanswered. There were no answers to give when contemplating the labyrinth that was Hitler's mind.

"I hate my fellow Germans," Anya proclaimed.

"You mean you hate the Nazis, not your fellow Germans, don't you?" her mother countered.

"I doubt, in time, there will be any difference anymore. The Nazis have the power to brainwash or intimidate us as much as they want to. They will do everything they can to bring German citizens in line," Anya concluded.

Rosa looked at her troubled daughter and placed a steadying hand on her arm.

"You don't mean that."

"Oh, but I do, Mama. Oh, but I do. It's already happening."

She thought of Kreon and their situation, and recognized with painful clarity what kind of world they were living in.

"People still have the choice to make moral decisions," her grandmother pointed out.

"But will they, Oma? Will they? I doubt it very much where the battle for survival is concerned." Anya said nothing more, and they stared at her uneasily. Her question pricked their mind.

CHAPTER THIRTY-EIGHT

While the women in the Bermann household tried to come to terms with Lisbeth's dilemma and Anya's pronouncement, across town Kreon was attempting to make himself comfortable on his cot. He had come back earlier than usual and found his room in the barracks empty. His comrades were out on their Sunday jaunts, and, on this balmy spring day, he assumed they would not return until supper or before curfew.

Picking up a crumpled magazine hoping it would distract him, Kreon found Hitler's face plastered on its cover. He flung it away in fury. Putting his hands behind his head, he lay there fuming, and stared up at the ceiling to clear his mind. It was Jorgo, his closest friend, who returned first and discovered Kreon in that position.

"Finding the solutions to your problems up there, my friend?" Jorgo joked.

Kreon let out a sardonic laugh. "If only it were that simple. Why are you back so soon?"

"A man can only strut around Nuremberg so much with a glorious woman on his arm before he collapses," he joked. "Frankly, I am dog-tired. I have not been sleeping well and decided to catch a nap before our comrades show up," Jorgo explained. "Have you been here long?"

Kreon nodded, "Beat you by an hour."

"Did Anya forsake you?"

"No." Kreon let out a deep breath. "You could say I had to forsake her. At least for today."

"On such a beautiful day! What is the problem?"

"Hormones."

"Ah, yes," Jorgo shook his all-knowing head and settled himself on the neighboring cot. "When hormones start to flow, you swim in the river of no return."

"How very poetic," Kreon smirked, "You do Greek culture proud."

Jorgo contemplated the wretched face of his friend.

"You have two choices, Kreon" he proclaimed, "One: You can have sex with yourself, although there's not much opportunity for that in our crowded quarters. Or, two: You can find a woman on the side who is not as big a risk as the girl you want to protect."

Kreon looked at him with sharp eyes, "What do you mean?"

"There's a lady I know. She comes from Czechoslovakia. She has a boy whom she needs to keep fed as well as herself."

"So? Where is the father?"

"Shot in front of their eyes by a rebel group for being German. The Czechs deported her and the boy back here after her family pleaded for their lives."

"Shit."

"That pretty much sums up her situation."

"Is she a whore?"

"No. A friend," Jorgo insisted. "She's a nice woman. Very selective about the men she opens her door to. And she is clean and has access to birth control."

"Jesus. Does the boy know?"

"Not sure. He acknowledges nothing. Hardly talks. Most of the time he remains invisible; he is either out on the street or in school. She tries to be discreet but, he is twelve, and I don't think he's stupid."

"What a way to live."

"Well, don't judge her. She is not the only woman to compromise her virtue to survive a war. She can help you with your problem if you help her with hers. I give her what little I can."

"You are seriously suggesting I have sex with the same woman you are having sex with?"

"Why not? We're already sharing hell!"

Kreon snorted in response. Jorgo looked at him without amusement.

"Want her address?" he asked.

Kreon hesitated.

"Be clear-headed, my friend," Jorgo warned, "It will save Anya from your raging hormones. Problem solved."

There was no argument there.

"Give it to me. I will think about it."

Jorgo wrote the address down and handed Kreon the slip of paper. "I have already told her about you and Anya."

"Did you?" Kreon noted the address with minute interest and pocketed it. "The world has gone mad."

His comrade agreed, "How many times has that been said in the past, my friend? How many times will it be said in the future?"

CHAPTER THIRTY-NINE

The following Monday, Anya's world morphed into chaos again: She received a written summons to report to a "farming camp" within a week's time. Overcome with dread, speculating if she was indeed being sent to a farm to aid with chores or being sent elsewhere for a more ominous purpose, she sped to her boss' office to inform him of the news. Whether out of charity or not, he delivered her from peril once more. Asking his secretary to place the call, he resolutely informed Nazi headquarters that he could not spare her.

"I need Fraulein Schmidt to continue working in the defense plant as she is of enormous assistance in maintaining the smooth operation of this office."

He requested she remain in his charge instead of being relegated to "farm duty". His request was approved.

Anya, astonished by his help once again, realized that perhaps there were still good people in this world. Through his benevolence her manager had extricated her from two dire situations. Bowing her head, she thanked him with a humble heart. As he watched color return to her ashen face, he shooed her out of his office with a smile. She breathed easier as she exited, little aware of what was yet to come.

CHAPTER FORTY

Kreon, having often missed the strict 9:00 p.m. curfew in recent days, impelled the German gatekeeper in his barracks to give him a strong warning: "If you are late one more time, I will report you."

Not a clock-watcher when it came to any rendezvous with Anya, Kreon turned up late again despite his resolve to be more mindful.

The next morning at breakfast, two bearish-looking men in black uniforms marched up to Kreon's table, glared at him with menacing eyes, and jerked him to his feet. Aware they were SS, Kreon had no time to disguise his alarm. The startled faces on his fellow diners conveyed their own terror. A secret cacophony of beating hearts amongst the on-lookers could be sensed in the room.

"Are you Kreon Kalanis?" the head commandant asked.

With his heartbeat pounding in his ear, and rivulets of sweat running down the sides of his face, Kreon gave a slight jerk of his head. His voice was lost to him. Grabbing him by his arms, the uniformed guards 'suggested' he come with them. Within minutes they rushed him to police headquarters in Nuremberg for interrogation, and he soon found himself sequestered in a nondescript room with a wooden chair and table at its center where, he knew, they would besiege him with questions.

Kreon hoped his bowels would not give him away, as sweat soaked through his shirt and betrayed his inner turmoil.

"Kreon Kalanis, where were you last night?"

The question was punctuated with a fierce and unforeseen kick to his spine and a command to "Tell the truth!" before he had a chance to reply.

Aware the beating would increase in severity if they discerned the truth, Kreon lied through gritted teeth as he flinched with each painful blow. Blood gushed from his nose, and he felt a sharp pain in his ribs. The blows to his head left his mind staggering. Trying to protect himself and Anya, he struggled to remain conscious and swore again and again that he was keeping company with a Czechoslovakian woman, not a German one. It was a falsehood he repeated numerous times that morning.

I want to live for my father! was his guiding light.

The truth was he had not kept company with the Czechoslovakian woman as Jorgo had suggested. Instead, he had developed a slight bond with her when he sent along a bit of money to feed her boy. Jorgo told him it was the first time he had seen her cry. Kreon prayed she would cover for him if questioned.

Once given the chance, he mumbled through bloodied lips, "There is a piece of paper with her address on it in my pants pocket."

The ploy worked. The beating ceased, but its psychological impact began to fester.

"Lock him in a cell while we check this out," the commandant instructed.

Kreon was dragged to a prison cell and thrown into it without ceremony. He writhed with pain on the rough floor but was thankful for a reprieve from further assault.

In the interim, the Czech woman found herself accosted by two uniformed men at her door. Quickly sizing up the situation when questioned, she managed to uphold Kreon's account of their relationship with miraculous calm. She had learned the lying game well when confronted by militia and knew how to play it. Yes, she was his lover. Yes, for several months now. She uttered the words with such conviction that the subterfuge worked. Kreon's neck was ultimately saved by her "confession", but Nazi justice still had to be served.

Despite his injuries, which resulted in his ribs being rebound, Kreon was imprisoned and sentenced to three weeks of hard labor for breaking curfew. Anya, who had arranged to meet him the evening of that unfortunate day, was instead informed of his incarceration while lunching at her mother's apartment. Rosa felt it wiser to stay away from the crowd in the canteen when she broke the news. When her mother informed her, Anya rushed to retch in the toilet as Rosa prepared a wet cloth to wipe her face with.

That evening Anya prayed for God's help in keeping Kreon alive, while her mother gazed up at the heavens and prayed for her daughter.

CHAPTER FORTY-ONE

Kreon stayed focused on seeing Anya again to forebear his situation. Spring rains and the cold temperatures added to his misery. Each morning, accompanied by guards, he and the other prisoners cleaned the streets of the rubble left over from recent bombings. They were given only a small amount of food, little warm clothing to wear and, most crucial, no gloves. Their hands became raw and blistered from the wet and jagged rocks they had to handle. No amount of warm breath blown on their fingers could diminish the impact of the stormy winds. At night they slept on concrete floors with only a thin blanket for insulation. His cellmates were a mixture of nationalities including French and German dissidents. They seldom spoke to each other. Speech had its price; it robbed them of their energy.

One bitter morning, finding himself detained in the prison yard, Kreon witnessed an influx of people being pulled off lorries and shuffled through the prison gates. It was a sight that left a distinct imprint on his psyche. To his dismay, the Nazi guards were marshalling several hundred men, women, and children toward the prison buildings. The black bands with the yellow Star of David bobbed everywhere, creating a striking mosaic against the bleakness of their setting. Chained hand-to-hand and shivering from the merciless cold, they were ordered to move forward by armed guards. As they did so, many a lip turned blue, while snot trailed from the noses of wailing infants. The women cried quietly, while the men marched stoically to the demands of their jailors.

Leaning against the barbed wire fence, Kreon pulled his thin jacket about him and tried to stand upright and move in their direction. In his distraught mind, he wanted to do something, but knew he could do nothing. He was stopped by the sharp butt of a rifle slammed into his shoulder and fell backward to the ground.

"Get back to the fence, du verdammter Idiot! Where did you think you were going? You think you can save them, fool?"

The butt of the rifle was slammed into his chest once again, this time causing Kreon intense pain. Sprawled on the frozen ground, gasping for breath, he watched as the prisoners were hustled into the buildings, while the shrieks of their children echoed in his ears.

Fight! he wanted to scream, *Fight!* But he recognized it as a futile word best left unspoken. If they protested, they would be shot. If he protested, he would be shot. No one was being passive; everyone was simply in fear of the rifles cocked by men who had no mercy. Kreon sat motionless as the human chain was led away.

With eyes focused on their hopeless plight, Kreon wondered what happened to the young man he once was...the youth who jumped from daring cliffs into the Aegean Sea, fearless and bold. Today, he realized he had been pushed over a cliff into a sea where the tide had gone out. His illusions of being a hero were hurled upon the rocks.

Bearing witness to this pitiful scene, Kreon concluded the Nazis were converting humanity into their own ecosystem: the insane devouring the sane.

Hitler and the Nazis are the scourge, not the Jews, Kreon surmised in his rage. *How many of Hitler's followers have secretly come to that conclusion? How many will let him continue with these atrocities?*

Witnessing the imprisonment of these terrified people was not the last of Kreon's ordeal. A few nights later, as he sat on the cold floor of his cell, a German boy of about 16 years was incarcerated in the jail. Thrown into a cell down the hall from where Kreon and other foreign nationals were locked away, they were forced to listen to the boy's anguished screams all night long. The youngster knew he was to be executed in the morning.

Had he, too, stolen a chicken from some farmer because of his gnawing hunger? a sardonic Kreon mused. *What other excuse did the Nazis need to satisfy their cold-blooded lust for murder?*

Unable to escape the boy's torment, the horrorstruck prisoners squeezed their ears shut against the agonizing wails. Throughout the long night their wits were shredded by the child's fervent pleas.

"Bitte! Bitte! Ich habe nichts getan!" He did nothing, he kept screaming, nothing! But the words fell on inhumane ears.

What kind of human beings are these that could be so merciless, so pitiless, toward a young boy, toward women, toward children, toward men in chains who could not defend themselves? thundered through Kreon's mind.

The realization that the robotic Nazi machine had neither brains nor a soul was reinforced in him. White hot fury surged through Kreon by dawn and turned venomous when he heard the well-aimed crack of a rifle shot.

CHAPTER FORTY-TWO

Released three weeks later, Kreon was transported back to the barracks in Fürth. It was late afternoon and his roommates had not yet returned from work. Finding himself at odds, he headed for the Bermann homestead hoping Anya would be there. She was. Quickly pulling him into the house before the neighbors could see, he drew her into his arms as she sobbed with relief. Taking note of Kreon's condition, she flinched at seeing the bruises on his face and body. Enveloped in her caring and warmth, Kreon realized the dream he held in his arms was worth the nightmare he had endured.

With haste, Anya heated some broth, stirred in vegetables from the garden, and fed his emaciated body as her benevolent grandparents helped where they could. The wounds to his psyche were invisible, but they were easy to sense. While tending to his injuries, Anya and Babette bombarded him with questions, causing Kreon to stiffen. He was not ready to talk at length about his experience and preferred his feelings remain contained.

"He needs sleep," a watchful Johann informed the two women. They looked at the weakened person under their care and stopped their chatter.

Under Johann's instruction, Anya set up a bed for Kreon on the couch. Settling him down, Johann removed Kreon's shoes and covered him with a warm blanket. It took mere minutes for Kreon to fall into a fitful sleep.

Waking later in the evening, his body more relaxed and pliant, Kreon sat up and joined them for tea. Johann headed for the kitchen and returned with a long-stored bottle of schnapps and passed a measure of it to Kreon. As the liquid coursed through his body, it eased his aches and calmed his mind.

Overjoyed at having Kreon back safely, even in his reticent state, they were oblivious to the hourly chimes of the church bells. Anya turned to him in alarm when she realized the bells had long since signaled the evening curfew! Kreon did not care.

"The Nazis can go to hell," he blurted, shrugging off Anya's pull on his arm.

Anya and Johann were stronger and persisted. Against his will, they carted the reluctant swain off to his barracks and delivered him to the front entrance.

As Kreon sauntered through the gate, the overseer, astonished by the man's repeat transgression, took one look at Kreon's bruised face and was sympathetic enough not to report him.

His reappearance in his sleeping quarters was also met with astonishment. As soon as Kreon sat down on his cot, his curious compatriots came over to greet him and assess his condition. His wounded face made them gasp. Within moments a cold compress for his temple made a quick appearance, as they fluttered about him like rattled ostriches. Kreon could not pretend all was "fine" around his companions. The truth cannot be hidden from experienced men. They deduced he was seething inside although his outer countenance was stony.

Glowering with bitterness, Kreon declared, "We are not foreign laborers. We are their prisoners! Damn their rules and their God-damned curfew! God damn Hitler to hell! God damn the Nazis! God damn this entire country! We foreigners are under siege!"

A firm arm on Kreon's shoulder restored his stability.

"When did you get out of prison? What made you late again?" one friend asked kindly.

Kreon did not answer. He did not have to. They already knew.

"Kreon, we Greeks understand that this young woman is the link to your soul. We understand. Truly."

The man's words were placating, and he recognized the compassion in his comrade's voice.

"But you must think of us too. We are begging you not to make things more difficult for us. Like you, we are trying to survive. We ask little. Just try to come back on time. That is all we want."

Kreon nodded. They deserved his respect and obedience, "Yes...yes...I will."

After they thanked him and drifted away, he lay down on his cot hopeful of obtaining the oblivion he craved. Closing his eyes, Kreon prayed sleep would serve as a sedative. The men, meanwhile, returned to their evening chatter, keeping their voices low. They left him in peace but kept a concerned eye on him.

"God knows what he's been through with those bastards," one said.

"If it is anything like what Max and I witnessed today, those Nazis have gone out of their goddamn minds," stated another, "I can only imagine what they would do to a human being they consider an enemy or who breaks one of their laws."

"What are you talking about?" Jorgo asked, curiously looking at Sergei, the man who had spoken.

"Max and I were returning from the city with the Rothman boys when their neighbor, Frau Brunner, came screeching toward us followed by her two crying children," he shook his head in disbelief remembering the incident. "'Our Hannelore is dead! Our Hannelore is dead!' she kept yelling. I did not know who she meant, but she and her children seemed inconsolable. Max took hold of her and told her, 'It's okay, Frau Brunner. Calm yourself! We are here now. Calm yourself and tell us what happened.'"

Sergei eyeballed the men around him and continued, "Once she quieted herself, the story she told was unbelievable. Hannelore, you see, was their family cat."

He paused.

"And?" piped up one of his enthralled listeners.

"The cat had jumped the garden gate and scooted down the lane. Frau Brunner, when she noticed it scurry by, ran after it into the street, as did her children. However, before she could catch their pet, one of the Nazi soldiers patrolling the area shot it. Shot it right in front of them! But it was not dead yet, so he shot it again! According to the neighbors, Frau Brunner and the young ones went berserk. She called him every cursed name she could think of and screamed at him while the children wailed like sirens. The neighbors came running and were sickened by the sight.

"'Why did you kill our cat? Why did you kill our cat?' Frau Brunner kept shouting. Do you know what the stupid ass told her?"

He looked around at the men to watch their reaction.

"The lunatic told her, 'I killed it because I thought it was a Jewish cat.'"

"'You thought it was a *Jewish* cat?' Frau Brunner yelled at him, 'You killed it because you thought it was a *Jewish* cat?'"

"'Yes,' the idiot answered, 'I thought it was a Jewish cat. Jews lived in your neighborhood, didn't they? And they were not allowed to have pets! When I saw this one straying about, I thought it had been left behind. I thought it was a Jewish cat!'"

"When she heard that, the curses Frau Brunner spewed at him even I wouldn't repeat. My dear, departed mother would slap me from her grave. Can you blame the woman for reacting as she did... she and the children seeing their pet cat killed that way? Well, when she refused to stop cursing at him, the jerk threatened to report her to Nazi headquarters for her insolence, him being a reputable Nazi soldier, etc....talk about bullshit. We found out later he had not reported her. I guess the ass realized how foolish he would look in front of his superiors."

There was another silent pause. The storyteller shook his head. "He shot the cat because he thought it was a Jewish cat. If they do that to a cat, what would they do to a Jewish person?"

The sudden creak of a cot caught their attention. They turned to look at Kreon. His back was still toward them, but there was a slight twitch to his torso. And then there was wracking laughter amid wracking sobs. The sounds coming from him were all too familiar. A man's psyche could only endure so much.

"He shot the cat because he thought it was a Jewish cat," one murmured dazedly. And no more was spoken.

It was Spiro in their group who, watching Kreon, finally broke the silence.

Speaking in a subdued, matter-of-fact voice, he stated, "I envy people who can cry. I cannot cry any longer. I am not human. I am a machine. I get up every morning. I piss in the pot. I wash myself. Clean my teeth. Rake a comb through my hair. Put on clothes. Go to work. I meet the requirements of the day. I keep my mouth shut. I survive."

"Perhaps it's the wisest way to live," Jorgo said. The men murmured in agreement.

"No," said Spiro. "Living this way does not spring from wisdom. It springs from fear. Fear of losing your job, fear of losing your family, fear of losing your life. This fear drinks us dry, day in and day out, day in and day out. In the end, it will degrade and break us. I am not a man of wisdom. I am a man of fear."

He walked over to Kreon's cot and sat on the edge of it. It squeaked soundly from the drop of the man's weight. Kreon stirred, as his mind emerged from its shadows.

"My friend," Spiro said, "do not let these monsters devour your soul. You are human. You want to live. That is human nature. We do the best we can. God understands."

Kreon beheld the clear-sighted eyes of the comrade who faced him, and he grabbed his hand.

"Thank you...thank you," he mumbled like a man pulled from the wrath of the sea.

CHAPTER FORTY-THREE

In compliance with his comrades' wishes, Kreon adhered to the curfew as he promised. To soothe his frayed nerves, he took quiet walks with Anya and struggled to speak of his pain. She listened. It was all she could do. In trying to help him, she quieted her own mind.

Around them, the war escalated into a frenzy. The air raids intensified in the winter months of 1944 and life in Fürth became increasingly perilous. The Americans bombed German cities with bigger and more sophisticated weaponry than the British ever had. In addition, they were now bombing cities and towns that housed munitions factories. Hitler, wanting to preserve the young, mandated that school children be evacuated from dangerous areas and brought to safer locations in the countryside. Farmers were ordered to take the children and their mothers in and provide them with room and board.

On a sparkling, early spring morning, a precursor to what could be expected in the year ahead, made its presence known in Fürth.

It was a beautiful day. So beautiful, in fact, that during their lunch break several workers roamed in the field adjacent to the factory; Kreon and his friends included. Anya and her mother chose to have lunch at Rosa's nearby apartment. As they prepared their meal in the kitchen, a loud whistling noise and a tremendous crack outside the window startled them. They ran to it and watched in horror as the tower of the factory building exploded not far from their street. Stunned and panic-stricken, Anya and her mother scrambled for some food and water and ran for the door to find shelter. Another whistling noise sounded. This time it hit the building they were in. Crawling under a table, they watched as debris flew.

Kreon, not far away, was trapped with friends in the open field. The warning sirens had begun howling a short time before, but the workers assumed the Allied aircraft would strike elsewhere. They did not expect to be bombed in what was, primarily, a residential area.

Instead of sitting for long hours in the "Luftschutzkeller" (Air Raid Shelter), which was in proximity, the German workers who were allowed to utilize it chose instead to take a walk or sit in the neighboring field to enjoy the warm sun. Kreon and his fellow foreigners, who were still forbidden to seek protection in the shelters, were returning to the factory, chatting about mundane things when, to their disbelief, an unexpected "marker" was spotted falling from the sky. These "markers" were phosphorous, usually glowed at night, and allowed bomber pilots to find their target.

Within seconds, several hundred planes, like migrating silver birds, flew over Fürth and dumped their leaden droppings as they passed by. One savage bomb after another gave a shrieking whistle as it descended, then detonated, upon factory and field. Fire, ash, debris, and the acrid smell of smoke and burning flesh spread everywhere. It entered lungs, stung throats, and permeated nostrils. Shrill screams resounded throughout as people panicked in the streets and rushed to the nearest shelter.

The exposed laborers in the field collapsed to the ground and watched in terror as the factory received one enormous blow after another. The massive bombing in the surrounding area continued for over half an hour.

When the ordeal withered and the fires dissipated into smoke, the sirens gave the "all-clear" signal. Kreon and the surviving crew quivered and stumbled toward the heavily damaged factory. More than half the building had been pulverized to rubble; walls had given way and machines were skeletons of metal. Strewn about the ruins were the bloodied and grotesque bodies of the dead, the dying, and the wounded.

Within seconds of their return, the remaining workers were ordered by a foreman and an emergency fire crew to retrieve what tools they could and then leave for their homes. The shell-shocked laborers did as they were told and sifted through the chaos. Saving what was salvageable, they held their breath and averted their eyes from the mutilated flesh that lay exposed among the debris. Kreon and several men stood in reverence over the casualties that were still recognizable, as emergency crews lifted them onto stretchers and gurneys. Some made the sign of the cross, as casualties were carted away. When the survivors departed, the suffocating dust and the sickening stench of dead bodies trailed after them.

At Rosa's damaged flat, Anya and her mother, shaken and covered in grey ash, stood up and dusted themselves off. As they surveyed the damage, they were alarmed to discover huge holes in the walls separating them from the neighboring apartment. Glass, wire, and rubble were strewn everywhere, and they proceeded to pick their way through it with caution.

"Mama, what are you going to do?" Anya asked after assessing the damage.

"The family will help. The family..." her mother crumpled into a chair, as Anya ran to the window. The sound of more explosions not far off were heard.

"Come, we need to get out of here. Come!" Anya yelled, grabbing her mother's arm, "I need to find Kreon."

As Anya pulled Rosa toward the hallway a movement near the gaping hole caught her eye, and a shrill voice in the adjacent room reached their ears.

"I will not leave without you and our daughter!" a woman shouted.

Herr and Frau Schilling lived in the apartment abutting theirs with their two young children, and they were in severe distress. The boy was crying, the mother beside herself, and the father barking orders. Anya made her way through the wreckage to find Herr Schilling kneeling beside the bed in which his four-year-old daughter, Renate, lay. His wife and son were locked out of the room, and Frau Schilling was banging on the door trying to get her husband to open it.

An exasperated Herr Schilling gazed up at Anya and Rosa peering out from the ruins of the wall.

"Be careful, plaster, wires and timber are still falling from the ceiling," he warned. His eyes were pleading for their help.

"Herbert, open this door! I'm begging you!" his wife screamed.

"What is going on, Herr Schilling? You and Renate must get out of here!" Anya shouted.

"Renate is unwell!" he yelled back, "She is sick with diphtheria! I was unable to get her admitted to the hospital because it is full."

Anya walked cautiously toward the bedroom and tried to enter it.

"Do not come closer," Herr Schilling warned, "She is burning up with fever and contagious. They will not allow Renate in any shelter. I must stay with her. Please get my wife and our son out of here and to safety. I beg you!"

The child on the bed was barely breathing. Flushed and soaked with sweat, Renate was flicking her head from side to side in her delirium.

"Herbert, let me in!" Frau Schilling shouted as their boy, Karl, sobbed behind her. Anya nodded at Herr Schilling.

"My mother will get them to safety. You needn't worry," Anya reassured the frantic father. Just then a gas explosion could be heard outside.

"Drag her if you must...but go! We will be alright. I will stay here and watch over my daughter. Get yourselves to safety!"

Propelled by his intensity, Anya scrambled over the rubble, kicked up a swirl of dust, and headed toward the front door. She turned back once to see Herr Schilling kneeling in prayer beside his daughter's sickbed.

Out in the hallway she found her mother dragging Frau Schilling and Karl down the stairwell amid the woman's protests.

"It will be alright. You must be brave," Rosa was telling them as she pushed the woman and the boy along, "We need to get to a shelter. Herbert and Renate will be fine. It sounds like the planes are now further away."

Forgive me the lie, Rosa thought to herself, *but if it calms the two of you down, I will lie until the devil himself is disgusted with me.*

Feeling somewhat reassured, Frau Schilling and her son allowed themselves to be led into the street to search for refuge. People were scurrying like crazed mice to the nearest Luftschutzkeller, and Rosa headed them there.

When all four were safely settled in the shelter, Frau Schilling began wringing her hands and mumbling prayers under her breath, while Karl clung to her and flinched at the fearsome noises outside. Anya, troubled by the intense sounds, headed for the exit. Her mother grabbed her arm.

"Mama, I need to find Kreon!"

"You cannot leave now! Do not even think of going out there! Kreon will take care of himself. He is resourceful. He will be safe." Pulling Anya back in, she led her to a makeshift bench. "Sit!" Rosa ordered, "When it is all over, we will look for him. I promise."

The anxious crowd and Anya recoiled when another blast shook the street above them. Anya decided to pay heed to her mother and settled down next to her. The lone little girl sitting across from them shuddered at the thunderous noise and dissolved into inconsolable tears.

"What's wrong, child?" Anya asked, "Are you by yourself?"

With shaking head, the girl nodded, and Anya noticed she was shivering.

"Come here," she said, reaching for the poor lass' hand. The girl grabbed it as if Anya were saving her from wild dogs. Anya wrapped the gasping child in her arms.

"Where is your mother, Mädchen? Did you get lost?"

The girl shook her head, "Nein." And a fresh waterfall of tears flowed down her cheeks.

"Mutti is home. I am supposed to go there when the sirens sound, so she knows I am safe. But when I was walking to our house, someone pushed me in here. Now she will not know where I am! I have to get to Mutti, so she will know I am alright!" The girl jumped up, ready to run.

"Whoa!" Anya caught her by the waist, much to Rosa's relief and those of the people around them. "Come here and sit with me. I want to run too, but we must stay here until it is all over. Won't you keep me company?"

"No! I have to go home to Mutti!" the girl wailed.

"Oh, let her go!" one of the exasperated matrons nearby bellowed, "Let her go before she frazzles our nerves completely!"

"You expect me to throw her out?" Anya held on to the girl and glared at the woman. Others were staring at the crone too.

"Why not? We have been listening to her bleating since she got here. She obviously wants to go home. Let her cry there!"

Hearing the heartless words, the girl collapsed against Anya, and Anya placed consoling arms around the distraught child.

"It will be over soon," she reassured her, "then we'll take you to your Mutti. Don't listen to the mean old lady." Holding her tight, Anya asked the young girl her name.

"Monica," she sniffled, "My name is Monica."

"Well, Monica, my name is Anya. I will protect you, and later we will go find your mother. Okay?"

Pacified, the girl quieted down, while Anya gave the old crone a malevolent stare.

"Kindness goes a long way, does it not?" she stated loudly. Her audience cheered her words, while the sour woman huffed and turned her surly face away.

A collective sigh of relief was emitted when the aerial attack was over and the "all clear" signal sounded. People streamed forth from their bunkers, thankful they had made it through. When Anya and her mother exited their shelter with Monica, the child had the good fortune to bump into a neighbor who offered to escort her home.

Wishing Monica well and hugging her good-bye, Anya and Rosa rushed toward the factory. Cleaning up and salvaging the apartment would have to wait. Their priority was to report back to their workplace. Upon arrival, they were embraced by co-workers thrilled to count them among the survivors. Devastated by the gruesome damage they encountered, Rosa inquired about the co-workers in her unit, while a frantic Anya kept her eyes and ears open searching for Kreon. News was he had survived and was helping with the clean-up in another section of the factory. Rosa and Anya were soon assigned a similar task.

CHAPTER FORTY-FOUR

Within a stone's throw of the factory, Frau Schilling and her son exited the shelter, rushed to their apartment building, and were relieved to find it damaged but still standing. With grateful hearts they found Herbert and Renate inside unharmed. The child's face was not as flushed, and the parents began doing what they could to get her better.

As people streamed out of the Luftschutzkellers and private hideaways across Fürth, the air was thick from fires still burning in various parts of the city. Relief over the air raid's end turned to despair as they viewed the destruction done to their town.

The factory withstood the heaviest damage. Anya and Rosa, distraught over the immense wreckage surrounding the building, watched their co-workers shuffle about in a stupor. Both shuddered when they saw why. Bodies, or parts of bodies, lay everywhere, or were being taken out on stretchers.

Scanning the crowd inside and outside the plant in desperation, Anya's anxiety was alleviated when she caught sight of Kreon and he of her. Their elation was palpable as they struggled to keep from running into each other's arms. They longed for one shred of solace in the madness and horror of the day but knew they could not acknowledge or comfort each other without jeopardizing their secret relationship. As their eyes caught, Anya gave him a slight smile. In resignation they departed with heads held low, each embarking on a separate destination. Their only consolation was knowing they had, on this day, survived the madness of this world together.

The next morning the surviving factory workers, including Anya, her parents, and Kreon, returned to the factory in turmoil. The bodies of over 150 victims were laid out in the hallways. These had been their co-workers and had been their friends. The victims had wives and husbands and children and grandchildren, and myriad relatives and friends who had searched for them or waited for them to come home. The dead had been good people.

Had! Had! Had! seared through Anya's tortured mind. Their deaths were incomprehensible. The factory had become a morgue for the unimaginable.

Anya and Rosa wept and tried not to break down or retch at the sight. They had known many of these people all their lives. Seeing their pain, Kreon wanted desperately to take Anya and Rosa in his arms to console them any way he could.

Look, but do not touch! The law, and fear of reprisal against all three of them, kept Kreon at bay. It was torture to watch mother and daughter in such heart-rending circumstances and only be able to offer the sparsest support: a pat on the back, perhaps, or an understanding or comforting word, but little else. Rosa and Anya staggered through the factory in a daze. He trekked behind them and hoped the power of his compassion and love could be felt by them in some mystical way. Perhaps just being there was enough.

As if sensing his will, Anya turned toward him, and they faced each other head on. He was startled to notice a remarkable change in her demeanor. The hell of the day had burned away the last vestiges of her girlhood, and from this hell emerged a woman. Her face was scored with passion and purpose, and he responded in kind. In that moment, Kreon and Anya became one against the world.

Proceeding through the devastating mass of bodies and debris, the dreadfulness of what they had witnessed shattered or hardened the living. The bloody and dismembered bodies, headless or limbless, dead eyes staring or gouged out, split open or burned, lay there like victims of a carnivorous beast. The residual mounds of human flesh, some covered, some not, remained exposed for the purpose of identification by their survivors. Friends and family members despaired as they struggled to find their loved ones. Moaning throughout, they covered their noses with handkerchiefs or rags to keep the smell of death at bay. Several fell to the ground in anguish, keening in grief as they discovered the remains of one held dear. Others sobbed dully, unaware of the tears that streaked down their face. Most were in the icy grip of trauma, never having beheld anything like this before.

All day they continued moving, prodding, praying to find traces of a relative or friend that could be removed by the undertakers and prepared for a decent burial. On the main floor, a platoon of soldiers bagged unclaimed limbs and body parts then carted them off like so much human offal.

To distract themselves from the chaos, the remaining laborers made a concentrated effort to clean up their former workplace and restore it to approximate use.

When the horrendous day was over and Anya sat at the kitchen table with her grandparents and mother that evening, no one could eat the food before them.

"Where is God in all this?" Anya asked, her usual optimism overshadowed by the bleakness of the day.

Her grandmother studied her, "He is here." It was a quiet but resolute statement.

Anya scowled. "You still believe that? After all this?" she retorted.

"Yes," answered her grandmother, beginning to bristle.

"After all He's allowed to happen?" her granddaughter fired back, shaking her head in disbelief.

"Enough! God did not allow this to happen! The devil did! The devil does evil to us, and it is God who gives us the strength to endure!" Her grandmother uttered the words with such vehemence it left no room for argument.

Anya did not attempt to contradict her. If this belief is what kept her grandmother strong, then it must be so. She did not have the strength to form a rebuttal. Her religious beliefs had been lashed by this storm. She and her family had not been to church since the day the Nazi flag was placed near the pulpit. Anya found herself questioning all the doctrines she had been taught there.

The next day the Nazis sent one of their top leaders, Hermann Goering, on a brief visit to Fürth to encourage the survivors not to give up hope. He assured them their town would recover and the factory would be restored.

"Everything will be well again," Goering informed them.

Well again? Anya wondered. *How do you become well again when friends and family members cannot be restored? When you see them maimed and tattered beyond recognition? Where a ring on a finger, or a watch, or a minute piece of clothing is their only identification? How the hell do you become well again?*

Even she, unaccustomed to swearing, thought Hermann Goering could stuff his "well again" up his "verrückter Arsch". The man, in her mind, was a "crazy ass".

Kreon and his comrades, reacting to what they had witnessed, mocked Goering behind his back without qualms.

"Ja, ja, sure," they piped to one another. The Nazis were always delivering messages of hope over the radio. Even when facing defeat, Hitler's voice would proclaim, "We are winning!"

Goering delivered his brief address to the workers, then dashed off to his chauffeur-driven Mercedes and sped away.

Kreon, observing Goering's exit, later told his roommates, "He scurried like a rat toward a morsel of garbage. Hitler is probably waiting for his report."

Their work was not done. Day by day, the workers cleansed and resurrected the factory with as much grit as they could. But, without gloves to wear to withstand the cold that had set in again, their progress was difficult. Huge cast-iron stoves were brought in and placed on the factory floor to provide heat against the unrelenting weather. The cauldrons did little good. Incessant wind gusts would swirl through the damaged building and cool the cauldrons down. The survivors' one consolation in coming to terms with the destruction was that the "Pulver Fabrik" (ammunitions factory) in town had not been hit. The resultant explosion and fire would have entailed complete disaster for Fürth. They were lucky, they were told. *Lucky like stepping in a pile of dung,* Kreon thought, as he surveyed the ruins around him. What would the bombs hit next?

CHAPTER FORTY-FIVE

From that day forward, full-scale war came to Fürth. Residents who lost their homes were in dire search of living quarters in bunkers, or with family and friends who had a room to spare, as the American raids prevailed throughout the year. Anya's aunts and their small children migrated to the surrounding countryside to live and work on farms in hope of keeping their offspring safe. Pastureland was seldom destroyed, and the next generation needed to be "conserved for the grandeur of the Third Reich", as Hitler often pronounced.

In Germany's final and most intense year of combat, both young and old were drafted into the German army to bolster the ranks on the battlefronts. Anya's father, at age 44, found himself delivered to the Russian front without benefit of a uniform nor much else. He and his compatriots did not go in the name of duty, but rather from coercion. Nine months later Oscar Schmidt would return to Fürth wearing rags on his scarred feet and tattered clothes on his back.

"This is what Hitler and the Nazi party brought him to," Anya told Kreon, with a tinge of scorn. "My father has finally seen the light. Now he knows that Hitler and the Nazis are not the 'saviors' of Germany. It took the Russian front to teach him that."

Her father's stubborn refusal to acknowledge this fact from the beginning, and disavow his allegiance to Hitler, ruptured and ultimately destroyed his marriage. Rosa Schmidt planned to divorce him as soon as the war was over.

On the home front, low wages and food rationing continued; but, as the bombings and resultant destruction increased, these forms of sustenance soon came to an end. With homes damaged or payments in arrears, garden huts and over-crowded bunkers were utilized for living quarters, sometimes with considerable strife amongst its occupants. Food stations with scant offerings were positioned around Fürth to feed the hungry.

On weekends, Anya and her grandmother attempted to smuggle extra food to Kreon who, like his fellow co-workers, looked gaunt and exhausted.

More distressing than the loss of food rations was the growing loss of lives. The incessant raids increased the fatalities among the people Anya and her family knew and loved and led to the demolition of many familiar homes.

After one violent bombing, the charred torso of one of Anya's and Hannah's childhood friends was found in the debris. The sisters were plagued by bad visions thereafter.

Another airstrike claimed nine members of a neighborhood family as they ascended from an air raid shelter, thinking the raid had ceased. A casket filled with charred human remains was carried out of another neighbor's ravaged house.

One heartbreaking day bled into another until it came to a standstill at the Bermann's door. Anya, sitting with her grandparents at the kitchen table, was present for the unexpected presentation of a telegram by one of her aunts. Seeing their daughter Gunda's face, Oma Bermann grasped her husband's arm as he unfolded the merciless piece of paper.

The telegram stated tersely that their beloved grandson, Willie, who had been drafted into the storm troopers at age 16, was dead. During a mission over Holland, he had parachuted onto a land mine and was killed on impact. The news arrived one day before his 18th birthday. Joyful, talented, fun-loving Willie was gone.

Their grief was terrible. Anya, hearing the news, barely ate for weeks. She and Willie were near the same age. *He cannot be dead!* her mind told her. Willie was her buddy, had taught her how to ride his bike, steal pastries from Oma's pantry, and stand on his shoulders to mischievously peek through windows. Anya could not process that he was gone.

The worst part of Willie's death...there was no physical body to bring home. No physical body to hold and cherish one last time; no decent burial to honor a young soldier. When Oma and Opa Bermann's house was damaged soon thereafter, the only thing they had left of Willie, his beautiful artwork, was burned to cinders.

The vivid memory of Willie leaving home, proudly dressed in his soldier's uniform, never left Anya. Hurting and despondent, she told friends, "Before he went around the bend of our street, he turned, waved, and gave us one of his big grins. It was the last time I saw him. I never thought it would be the last time."

Kreon tried to console her, but Anya's emotions were too raw to accept any comforting salve.

"He always dreamed of becoming a well-known artist," she told Kreon. Haunted and bewildered, she asked, "Why does God put a dream in one's heart, if it's not supposed to come true?"

"I suppose, while people are alive, they have to honor who they are and what they want to be, no matter the outcome. It keeps people going," Kreon spoke from his own experience. Anya recognized that and tried to find comfort in it.

Willie's mother, too, was bereft beyond words, but focused on protecting and supporting his siblings who suffered and missed their brother. It was Oma Bermann who was shattered most by Willie's death. The fatal landmine had detonated the heart of her family. She had helped raise her grandson and loved his happy-go-lucky spirit. For her, there were days of wretched weeping, of self-recrimination, and of abysmal silence.

As time passed, one could observe the profound change in Babette. Fighting internally to keep from being consumed by grief's unrelenting power, Babette became more and more impassive and tight of lip. She continued to take care of her family and was considerate of them, but her last residue of joy and tenderness went by the wayside. For Babette, joy and tenderness came at a premium; it constituted a melt-down of her reserve. It meant allowing herself to be vulnerable again. The emotional outlay was beyond what her worn spirit could endure. And, for the first time in her life, Anya's grandmother was having an internal battle with God.

CHAPTER FORTY-SIX

The war's intensity reached monstrous proportions in 1944 when Anya turned seventeen. She and her family were astonished by their ability to survive day by day, week by week, month by month. She felt fortunate to be surrounded by a large, close-knit circle of relations and friends who helped each other cope. She cherished them, and she cherished Kreon. Their assignations were sporadic but no less intense and sincere. They buoyed each other as they faced their tribulations.

As the combat between Germany and the Allies grew, Kreon's survival techniques were once again tested when the Nazis relocated him far from Fürth.

With roughly twenty-five other Greek workers, Kreon was transferred to a work camp near Innsbruck, Austria. There they labored in a quarry amid the Alps, pulverizing rocks into gravel for use in German cities. It was arduous, back-breaking labor and Kreon surmised the Nazis were trying to work him and the others to death.

A month later, weakened by extreme hardship and unaccustomed to the glacial ice and snow, the laborers fled without benefit of authorization. Kreon was among them. Their escape attempt was an immense risk, because none of them had German identification papers nor a visa in their possession. All Kreon carried on his person was his American birth certificate still hidden in his shoe. The other papers were officially stored at the barracks in Fürth. Dumb luck and a determined will helped them return to Fürth without getting caught by the Nazis. Their tumultuous journey was comprised of hitch-hiked rides from sympathetic Germans and the density of the surrounding forests for cover.

On February 12, Anya's seventeenth birthday, she went to visit an aunt's house for lunch and found Kreon sitting at the dining table. If that was not enough of a surprise, he astonished Anya by presenting her with an engagement ring. It was fashioned out of a German dime and smuggled home in his pocket. The question, "Will you marry me?" was answered with an exuberant "Ja!" and a jubilant kiss as Kreon placed it on Anya's finger.

As common metal is wont to do, the cherished ring became tarnished. Kreon, reinstated at his former factory due to the labor shortage, took the ring with him to the machine shop with the intent of polishing it up. When his foreman caught him doing this, he began thrashing Kreon for this "offense", striking severe blows to Kreon's head. The workers witnessing the assault were appalled by the man's viciousness toward Kreon and began to protest. The bullish assailant silenced them into submission by threatening to have them sent to the Russian front if they did not keep their mouths shut.

Kreon's simple polishing of a ring resulted in a transfer to another distant labor camp; this time he was transported to Bad Tolz outside of Munich.

Anya did not learn of his plight until two weeks later when she received word via mutual friends. The news had her lighting candles and praying fervently to a God she hoped was devoid of a hearing problem.

To help Anya stay sane, Rosa suggested she write out her pent-up feelings in a notebook. Amenable to the idea, Anya created a small volume of poetry and loving thoughts as a gift for Kreon upon his yearned-for return. When she put ink to paper, she felt connected to him in spirit, and it bolstered her belief that he would return. *How could he not?*

CHAPTER FORTY-SEVEN

Mein Lieber Kreon
Wir waren uns fremd,
Wir lernten uns kennen,
Wir hätten uns lieb
Wir müssten uns trennen
Ich bleib Dir den noch lieb und treu
Und wenn Du wieder bei mir bist,
Dann bist Du stets wie einst,
Der aller liebster mein.

My darling Kreon
we were strangers when
we came to know each other
we fell in love
we had to separate.
I will remain loving and true.
When you are at my side again
you will be my "one and only"
and, with all my love, mine.

The labor at Bad Tolz was grueling and dreary, and Anya's absence from Kreon's life was maddening. His days were filled with missing her; his nights with longing to be "home". He was desperate to get a message to her.

Was Anya all right? Was she even alive? When would the damn war be over?

The burdens of his mind tortured him each miserable day.

I must return! I must!

When his situation became unendurable, Kreon and two comrades decided to escape their hellhole and return to Fürth. Again, without a visa and little money, they found a wormhole that might accommodate their escape. It was in the form of a German soldier who did not care what they did. In the soldier's mind, the war was already over. The signs were there, the news of a German victory, bleak.

Let them go home. Let them all go home. Verdammter Krieg! Damn the war!

As fickle fate would sometimes have it, Kreon and his compatriots jumped on a train where, to their misfortune, two sentries demanded they show their "Ausweis" (visa). No Ausweis, no Fürth. They were carted off to jail when the train stopped in Eichstadt.

Imprisoned, they resumed their struggle with the bitter weather and meager food supply. For three weeks, bereft of gloves and wearing only thin jackets, they sawed wood for the Nazi officers and their wealthy colleagues in the area. Shivering, their hands rubbed raw, Kreon and his cohorts swore they would return home no matter what it took.

CHAPTER FORTY-EIGHT

Mein Lieber Kreon....
Dich, suchen am Tage meine Gedanken,
Dich, suchen meine Traume bei dunkler Nacht

My dearest Kreon....
My thoughts seek you during the daylight hours,
My dreams seek you in the dark of night.

Anya wrote in her journal each day, scribbling down the feelings that were roiling in her. Vigorous walks in the countryside with Hannah or an understanding friend also helped clear her head and eased the stress her thoughts and emotions were creating. Evening strolls with her mother, after work was done and dinner served, were the most soothing of all.

"Mama, what if something happens to Kreon? What will I do?"

"He's a strong and resourceful man. And you are a strong and resourceful young woman. No matter what happens to either of you, you both will go on. You love life too much."

Anya could not fathom her life without Kreon, but she took comfort in her mother's faith that she had the ability to survive.

There was only one vexing problem that Anya was not sure she could overcome without stirring up trouble. As her mother had predicted, Anya had grown into a beautiful and thoughtful young lady, attracting a great deal of male attention.

"Mama, how do I handle the men who are starting to take an interest in me and ask me out? Most of the time I just want to yell at them to leave me alone!"

"Tell them it is kind of them to ask, but your parents feel you are still too young for male company. Do not become exasperated and throw them away. Always put people on a shelf gently. You never know what life will bring and your need of them."

"What will life bring me, Mama?"

Rosa did not answer, instead she squeezed her daughter's hand. They continued their stroll in silence.

CHAPTER FORTY-NINE

Spring was nearing and Kreon's deliverance from his circumstances seemed slight. His hope of an escape was dimming until one fortuitous stroke of luck came his way. A landowner appeared at the prison with a Nazi official and inquired if anyone among the crew knew how to farm. He needed manpower and was authorized to choose a potential farmhand from among the prisoners.

Kreon immediately recognized his opportunity. Knowing nothing about farming, he raised his hand without trepidation. He knew he was strong and wiry and a fast learner.

Maybe that is enough? he thought. *Cannot be much harder than what I have already done and am doing.*

Kreon's hand was the only one raised. The farmer sized him up. He did not ask about experience, as the prisoner was the only volunteer.

"He'll do," he told the official at his side.

"Come with me," the farmer directed, as the Nazi overseer signed the papers that committed Kreon into the custody of his new employer.

As he exited, Kreon nodded a curt good-bye to his former cellmates. They nodded back, aware of his lack of farming experience, and said nothing.

Within a short time, Kreon found himself living in a small room on the farm and working from daybreak to sundown. He took to farming like a woodpecker to a tree and was well fed for his efforts.

Besides strenuous physical labor, the only other requirement was that he join in prayers each morning. It was by no means a taxing demand; it trounced prison labor in his mind. Although Greek Orthodox and not Catholic, Kreon reckoned he knew how to pray. Falling to his knees, he lowered his head and mumbled reverently along with the others.

God must have heard him for it was not long before another unexpected opportunity presented itself. He found himself alone in the Bauernhaus one Sunday morning. The family was attending a country fair after church, and they had sequestered him in his upstairs room. Without hesitation, Kreon seized the day.

Grabbing his shaving kit, checking to make sure his birth certificate was safe in his shoe, he pulled on his well-worn trench coat and winged out the second story window.

He landed atop some well-placed bushes with a notable thud. Rolling off the thicket with a voluble groan, he stood up and examined his body to ensure nothing was broken. He found a few bloody scratches, some sore spots, but nothing crucial. Brushing the grass and twigs off his clothes, Kreon sprinted toward the woods nearby.

The next few hours, filled with breathless walking and running through forest and glen, he managed to cover several miles. But then he came to an abrupt halt. A road sign he ventured upon made it quite clear he was heading in the wrong direction. His feet were leading him south, instead of north to Fürth. Reversing his course, he stomped once again through the sheltering forest. The sky was darkening and the crunch of pine needles, dried leaves, and fallen twigs beneath his feet made him edgy.

What if a wild animal in the forest heard? What if, upon discovering my absence, the farmer sent his dogs after me?

Despite his fear of being attacked and chewed, Kreon found the forest provided several hidden pathways and nooks in which he could hide. Nevertheless, every crackle, every unexpected movement amongst the trees, became a threat to his safety and made him jump. He knew his escape had set him on a hazardous journey. He did not dare think about what would happen if he were caught by the Nazis.

As the afternoon sun began to wane, a figure wearing a tattered German uniform appeared in the distance. Kreon hid behind a tree but was soon spotted. The remote figure began to approach, and Kreon's body stiffened.

"Hallo? Hallo," the man called out, giving an uneasy wave. "Freund? Ich binn Freund."

Realizing the man felt as nervous as he did, Kreon approached the stranger with caution but soon held out his hand. The traveler looked harmless enough despite the uniform.

"Ja, Ich binn Freund. (I am a friend)," Kreon declared.

The man, relieved beyond measure, extended his hand in reply. Both men were exhausted from their trek, but thankful their dread of encountering an enemy, human or otherwise, was dispelled for now.

"Sit, please, for a little while," the stranger beseeched him and beckoned to a patch of grass under a nearby tree.

Kreon did as was requested. He needed a rest too.

"Mein Namen ist Mikel."

"Ich heisse, Kreon."

They continued speaking for a few moments. Mikel told him he had escaped from a bedraggled band of German soldiers who all seemed in a hurry to get home.

"The war will soon be over," Mikel informed him.

"You think?" Kreon was not so sure.

"Yes. The German army is in tatters. And the soldiers I have met, like myself, do not give a hoot anymore. Except maybe Hitler," he spit the name out with disdain.

"Where are you headed?" Kreon inquired.

"Back to my family in Stuttgart. And you?"

"Fürth, near Nuremberg."

"Ah, yes! I know it well. Nice area."

Kreon did not say much more. Mikel scrutinized him. Kreon appeared hungry and drained.

"Would you like a heel of bread?" Mikel offered, "I stole a small loaf from someone's kitchen windowsill this morning,"

Kreon nodded eagerly at the sight and smell of it, "Yes. If you have any to spare."

"Here," Mikel handed him half, "I'm too fat anyway."

They laughed; Mikel was as slight as a reed in the wind. Kreon thanked him for his generosity.

When they finished eating (with Kreon retaining some of the bread in his pocket) they rose, shook hands again and, wishing each other well, headed on their respective journeys. Watching Mikel disappear in the distance, Kreon felt bereft as he found himself alone again.

How odd to befriend a German soldier; at least he was not a rabid Nazi.

Trailing through the pine-scented woodlands, Kreon kept an eye out for other wanderers as well as the creatures whose habitat he was invading. He had no wish to grapple with a fox, a wolf, a wildcat, or an antlered deer. Either one could leave teeth marks or a dent in him.

Nearing a graveled road, a young lad carrying a bundle of twigs and branches on his bike whizzed by startling Kreon. The exuberant youth gave a jolly wave and shouted "Grüss Gott!" before he could respond in kind. Watching the boy vanish, he took a deep breath to steady his nerves. Regaining his composure, Kreon crossed the road and wended his way through the trees again.

For two days he wandered, picking berries where he found them, drinking water from streams, and pulling his coat tight around his shivering body. The screech of a hawk, or howl of a wolf, were unsettling when he lay sheltered under a tree at night. Gathering sticks and branches, he was able to make a fire with the matches he had hidden in his pocket; and he used the branches for cover for the few hours he slept. The one blessing was the weather; getting away from the mountains, it was milder, and there was no rain or snow to drench him nor muddy his path. The brisk air kept Kreon's limbs in motion.

By nightfall of the third day, his stomach pinched from hunger, his need for food, drink, and a decent place to sleep became critical. He staggered on through the shadows, until he could find a hamlet that might provide refuge.

Approaching a small village in the late evening, Kreon was disheartened to find that most of the inhabitants had settled in for the night. There were few lights illuminating the homes. One residence did have a welcoming lantern at its door, and he knocked on it, hoping for a response. A gruff landsman and his anxious wife unbolted it with caution. Eyeing Kreon with suspicion, trying to discern if he was in trouble or came to cause trouble, they blocked his entrance to their foyer. The head of the household, he noticed, carried a shotgun under his arm. In his best German, Kreon explained that he was supposed to meet his sister in Nuremberg but had lost his way.

"Bitte, mein Herr, would you be so good as to help me? I will cause no trouble. I only require shelter for the night."

Not saying a word as they sized him up, Kreon was surprised when they allowed him to enter. Guiding his way, they led him to a wooden table near their kitchen's warm oven. He could not keep his empty stomach from stirring when he smelled the delicious aromas in the room. The matron of the house, recognizing his hunger, did not hesitate to conjure up a plate of rabbit stew, boiled potatoes, and a cup of hot tea to place before their ravenous visitor.

"Danke! Danke!" was all he could utter in response to her generous hospitality.

After having his fill, he was beckoned toward a room at the rear of the house that contained a bed, a dresser and little else. The bed was all he longed for. Repeating his heartfelt appreciation, he sank onto the blessed mattress after they left. As he did so, Kreon was unaware that their son had notified the local police of his presence.

Kreon was also unaware that Nazi mandates had once again been sent out to German citizens reiterating the fact that they should treat all foreign laborers and visitors with the utmost consideration in the hope of persuading them to join the Nazi cause in its final thrust. The family that had opened their door to him felt it Christian to be cordial but wise to be prudent. The local police would settle the matter.

In short shrift a town constable arrived, and an exhausted and rattled Kreon was recalled to the main room of the house. The constable wasted no time in interrogating him in an amiable but firm fashion. Tired himself, he wanted to get the interrogation over with and return to his wife and his own hearth.

The questions came in rapid succession: "Who are you? Where do you come from? Where are you going?"

He replied with fabrications, but they sufficed.

Satisfied that Kreon was not a criminal, the constable departed and left him to his hosts. They in turn led their guest back to his room, bid him a goodnight and locked him in as a precaution. Hearing the turn in the keyhole, Kreon understood their need for safety. He quickly rid himself of jacket and pants, and once again collapsed on the bed, this time falling into a bottomless sleep.

In the morning they unlocked his bedroom door and, as soon as Kreon was washed and dressed, fed him a hearty breakfast. When it came time to depart, they shook hands cordially, wished each other well, and sent him off (in the proper direction) with a modest package of sausages, bread, and a bottle of beer. He thanked them again for their big-heartedness and for the bounty. He was especially pleased that, this time, his trek would commence with his stomach full, his body intact, and without the necessity of jumping out a window. All Kreon now desired was a safe path home.

Miles away, in his longed-for destination, Anya was scrawling words into her journal, her mind feverish with troubling thoughts.

"Anya," her grandmother yelled up the stairs, "Are you coming down for breakfast?"

She placed her head in her hands, pressing hard against her temples, trying to deter the questions in it.

Where is he? Is he hurt? Is he alive? Or is he dead?

CHAPTER FIFTY

Tramping through the woods and down dirt roads that morning, Kreon came to a sudden halt and slapped his head. He had forgotten to write down his hosts' name and address as he had hoped to do. This deed had been waylaid by his rush to continue his journey. It bothered him. He had hoped to repay their kindness whenever the war was over. They had taken a chance on a fellow human being. Kicking himself for the oversight, he prayed God would reward the family on his behalf.

By late afternoon, his worn and blistered feet began to ache. He decided it was time to hitch-hike along a main road as soon as he came upon one. It was a rash move, he knew, but he was desperate to return to Fürth and Anya. When sundown approached, with reserves low, his spent legs could only shuffle along. Watching him drag himself along the road, serendipity took pity and blessed Kreon with a ride on a truck headed to Fürth.

Home to Fürth, at last! Kreon's spirit soared and his nerves relaxed. Yet danger had not sheathed its claws. As he ran toward the cab of the truck, he noticed a Nazi soldier dozing next to the driver. The soldier had a rifle nestled in his lap.

Shrouded by nightfall, the driver motioned Kreon toward the back of the truck. Duly warned, Kreon changed direction and hopped onto the rear of the vehicle. Keeping his body low to avoid being snared, he crawled to a corner like a snake on its belly and managed to stay out of view.

As sweat beaded on his forehead at the thought of being discovered, the uniformed Nazi turned out to be the least of Kreon's worries. Surveying the interior of the truck, he was alarmed to find he was traveling in a vehicle transporting V-2 rockets. A large sign warned, "NICHT RAUCHEN!" ("DO NOT SMOKE!") He was thankful he had never picked up the habit. Now all he had to pray for was a ride devoid of potholes.

The trip proved nerve-wracking as the lorry struck ruts along the way. Kreon, thankful the soldier remained asleep and stayed oblivious to his presence, was afraid to nod off himself. Fearing the rolls and pitches of the truck might knock him into one of the rockets, he remained wide-eyed all night long.

Arriving in Fürth late the next day, he was worn-out but whole. Disembarking the truck cautiously, he gave a quick salute to the driver and hurried away.

Having no other place to go at that hour, Kreon returned to his former barracks. He was perplexed to find the place almost deserted. Sneaking back into his old unit, he found an empty cot and settled in. Across the hall two fellows were snoring and whistling in a sonorous musical competition. He was too weary to wake them and ask questions. He would search for Anya in the morning. First, he needed sleep, a shave, and a good wash. He smelled of sweat, and the goose-shit and cow piles he had stepped upon along the way.

Sunday morning dawned bright and reassuring. A few surprised friends had dribbled in during the night and greeted him warmly. Re-energized, Kreon dashed for one of the showers, scavenged a razor, clean clothes, and a few Deutsche Marks, then grabbed a quick coffee and warm roll at the local kiosk before heading into town to find Anya.

The destruction he encountered in Fürth left him riddled with fear.

Where is Anya in this mess?

Dashing from one location to another, he discovered her parents' flat had been damaged during the air raids, and her grandparents were staying with relatives in the countryside. Neighbors had no idea where Anya or Rosa were.

Frantic with worry, he tried to recollect the locales of her other relatives. Rifling through the muddle in his mind, he recalled the street address of her Tante Bette. Speeding there like a race car driver aimed at the finish line, Kreon ran up the stairs and knocked on Bette's door.

During his long absence, Anya, beset with wild imaginings of Kreon's fate, pondered whether he had been shipped back to Greece or, worse yet, killed. She only found comfort in the assurances of her mother and grandmother, "Don't worry, Anya, your Kreon will come back. We feel it. You will see."

She deduced it was sympathetic claptrap, but it worked. Day by day, Anya embraced their words and made a shield of them to dispel the pessimistic thoughts that threatened to engulf her.

Believe in miracles became her mantra.

As time passed and Kreon did not reappear, she fortified her faith in positive outcomes until that faith became ingrained. Optimism was the war's gift to Anya. She recognized it as a potent force in battling life's misfortunes, and she honed that gift to perfection.

When Doubting Thomases stated grimly that Kreon, being a man and a foreigner at that, would most likely not return, she scoffed at their words and responded, "If he *can* come home; he *will* come home."

Throughout those challenging days, Anya spent quiet hours with her widowed aunt, Tante Bette, chatting, having tea, and keeping busy with needlework and her writing. And then, one extraordinary Sunday, hearing a knock on the door, Anya rose to open it, and there Kreon stood.

Crying with joy, she flew into his arms. Tante Bette, standing behind them, savored their reunion with delight. Gazing at the haggard, young man with the large, soulful eyes, and the young woman standing on tiptoe hugging and kissing him, she could feel their bliss. Bette reveled in the warmth of the moment but was soon snapped out of her reverie by the creak of a nearby door. At its sound, she grabbed the bewildered lovers and pushed them inside.

"Kreon cannot be seen by the neighbors," she explained, "An edict has been issued by the Nazis commanding all foreigners to 'disappear' as they suspect a massive military invasion by the Allies is imminent."

Kreon and Anya were perplexed as to why foreigners had to "disappear" during this juncture in the war.

"It is because certain German citizens do not think it fair to accommodate foreigners in the limited and overcrowded shelters of their cities," an embarrassed Bette informed them. "Most foreigners have been forced to hide in the countryside or in the homes of their German friends or girlfriends," she continued, looking ashamed, "We will have to find other quarters for Kreon in the morning or we will all be in trouble." They understood and told her not to worry.

Sitting on the couch later in the evening after a good meal, Kreon held Anya close as she rested her head on his shoulder. They were listening to the radio while Bette sat in an armchair trying to concentrate on her needlepoint. The word on the street was not good for the "Heimatland", and certainly not good for Hitler. Yet, the radio newscast swore Germany was winning against the invading Allies. Having heard enough propaganda for the day, they turned it off and headed for bed. Tomorrow was a new day.

"Maybe this invasion will bring an end to the war," Kreon mused. His words were met with a weak response.

Turning in, Bette and Anya settled into the ample-sized King bed with its goose-down comforter and pillows. They invited Kreon to sleep there too, as there was room for all three to slumber in comfort, (albeit in their clothes and with shoes at the ready). They were surprised when he chose to take a pillow and blanket and sleep on the floor next to the bed instead. Anya could not believe it; but Kreon knew what he was doing. After being gone for so long, fighting to stay alive, dreaming of returning to her and longing to hold her, how could he sleep next to the one person he loved the most and keep from crushing her into his arms and more?

He looked at her as she fell asleep, while Tante Bette snored beside her.

How could this young woman be so innocent and not realize how I wish to make her my own? How could she not know how difficult it would be for me to share that bed?

He smiled at the beautiful face that was so oblivious to his roiling emotions. Her hand was dangling down to where he lay. Kreon touched a soft fingertip. Drowsy, she turned her head toward him. Her eyes remained closed.

"Can't get to sleep on that hard floor?" she murmured.

"I am fine," he assured her.

"Hmmm...." She opened her eyes a bit and gazed at him. "What are you thinking?" she asked.

"I am wondering what you see in an old man like me?"

"An old man?" She emitted a faint chuckle, "Oh yes, I forgot you will be thirty soon."

"And you are all of eighteen," he affirmed.

"Yes. Eighteen. A problem?"

"No. But what do you see in me?"

She took his hand, "I see a very honorable and patient man." She smiled, then her eyelids fell limp again.

"Go to sleep," he ordered, giving her fingers a light kiss.

"Are you really going to sleep on the floor?" she yawned.

"Yes."

"Güte Nacht, Kreon. Ich liebe Dich." Anya's words were barely audible. She closed her eyes and burrowed her head deep into the pillow.

"Und Ich Dich. Güte Nacht, Liebling," he whispered, but she had already drifted off.

He pulled his blanket tight around him and closed his eyes. Adam lay on the floor, Eve in the bed, and the unbitten apple between them.

CHAPTER FIFTY-ONE

Leaving Tante Bette's residence early the next morning, they were astounded to learn the Americans were attacking the outskirts of Fürth.

"My God, they have already arrived! We must find shelter!" Kreon began to rush them out of the building.

He and Bette implored Anya to stay with her mother, who was now living in a bunker with her co-workers. Built by the factory owners to sequester machinery, tools, and an underground operation, the bunker and factory were heavily guarded against outside intruders.

Bette professed, "It is the least perilous refuge for you, Anya. Rosa will disown me as her sister if I do not encourage you to go there. I will stay at my son's shelter. And I promise you, I will find a secure refuge for Kreon too. There is a concealed room near Fürth's city hall that your uncles made me aware of in case we cannot get into a shelter. It belongs to one of your grandfather's friends."

As night fell, Kreon found himself relegated to what was no more than an oversized closet with a bed, a lamp, and a chamber pot in it. Since there was nothing to do but yawn, Kreon lay down, wearing his day clothes, and mulled over his situation. Should artillery fire or a bomb draw too close, his shoes were at the ready in case he needed to run. Alone, in the dark, he listened for the dreaded whistling sounds before submitting to sleep.

CHAPTER FIFTY-TWO

In the early hours of the following morning, the American Allies bombarded their way into Fürth by shooting rockets into its center. One missile blasted away the tower of City Hall, and an alarmed Kreon scrambled for his shoes and ran out of the building to save his life.

But where should I run to?

His eyes frantically searched for shelter as the melee in the streets gathered momentum.

Caught in the vortex of exploding rocket fire and fragments of mortar and glass flying about, Kreon held his shoes tight and darted barefoot toward Rosa's bunker hoping to find Anya. His feet bled from dashing over the splintered shards of glass and rubble.

Not far off, hearing the explosions and feeling their impact, Anya rushed out of the bomb shelter and ran toward City Hall to seek Kreon. Rosa had shouted after her to stay put, but Anya bolted for the exit. As she ran, wild with desperation to find him, Anya was unaware that Kreon was running up one side of the street while she ran down the other. Their mind and heart were beset with the same anxious question: *Where is she? Where is he?*

People staring out their windows, or from sheltering doorways, watched with alarm as this crazy young woman darted through the streets. They screamed at her to take cover, but Anya kept moving. No one could stop her. The only words she heard were her own, *I must find him! I must find him!*

Not far from Anya was the "Wiessengrund", a wide, open park from which the Americans caught sight of her without obstruction. By some miracle, they did not shoot in her direction. A damsel in distress was not their target, the buildings of Fürth were.

Moments later, with a stampeding heart, Anya arrived at Kreon's hideout. It was empty but intact. Her relief lasted only a second before it gave way to dread. Her reeling mind tried to guess where Kreon might have headed. Rushing back into the street amid a chorus of shrill warnings from people observing her, Anya charged toward the public bunkers, praying to find him in one. Her panic increased as she swept through one shelter after another to no avail. Not too far away, Kreon was on a similar course.

Their persistent search for one another finally paid off. With sheer relief they found each other in the town plaza. He grabbed her, as spectators pulled them into a doorway.

Kreon and Anya did not say a word; she simply collapsed against him.

"We need to get back to my mother," she whispered, as curious ears perked up around them.

Breaking free, running again, they wended their way through the chaos and headed for her mother's bunker. Arriving breathless, they entered it as subtly as they could. The overseer, recognizing Anya, allowed them to pass. Stepping around people's legs and feet, keeping their heads low, Kreon and Anya searched for a spot to wait out the American assault. Rosa, praying for and awaiting their safe return, had cleared space for them and made sure they, especially Kreon, would be accommodated when they appeared.

As the uproar outside turned voracious, Kreon and Anya sat down and huddled together for comfort. Despite the explosions nearby, Anya felt a strange calm befall her with Kreon's arms wrapped around her. She recognized it for what it was; she was no longer afraid. With Kreon by her side, Anya was convinced she had nothing to fear, and gladly rested her head against his chest. The

American gunners, however, were positioned to erode her confidence.

CHAPTER FIFTY-THREE

In the world beyond their underground bunker and Fürth, devastating destruction had commenced throughout Germany under the orders of Hitler himself. The Führer did not want to leave any spoils to the victor.

The day after the American assault on Fürth, April 19, 1945, the American troops declared the war was over.

Kreon and Anya were standing out in the open when the American soldiers marched into town. Family, friends, and neighbors hugged each other with abandon.

"The nightmare is over!" they shouted from windows and throughout the streets. "The war is finally over!"

People kissed each other, kissed the ground, and even kissed the American G.I.s that poured into town. The townsfolk were relieved it was the Americans advancing into Fürth and not the Russians (who, via reports, were known to be brutal toward the defeated.) The townsfolk around Kreon and Anya roared with pleasure at seeing the American flag.

Anya and her family rejoiced over the laying down of arms and cheered the American victors as they trekked through the streets. No more bombs, no more fighting, no more running for shelter or hiding. The war was over! Everyone in Fürth, no matter what nationality, appeared blessed by the news. One could sense their collective gratitude toward the Allies that had put an end to WWII on the European front, a feat that seemed almost insurmountable a year ago.

Kreon and Anya were beyond ecstatic over the outcome; they no longer had to conceal their relationship.

"Gott Sei Dank," ("Thank God"), Kreon breathed into her ear while embracing her openly with enormous pleasure, "We can finally be together without fear."

Anya grinned broadly at him. Emboldened by his love, she wound her arms around his neck and kissed Kreon with such passion, he thought they would be permanently glued in this position. Anya was neither worried about who could see them like this, nor of people's reaction. *We are free!* With that delightful thought, she hugged Kreon until he laughed and begged her for mercy.

As the day of liberation progressed, German soldiers, who sought refuge in the bunkers, were tramped out with their hands on their heads. Soon thereafter, the American militia requested that the people of Fürth hang out a white flag from a prominent city building as a mark of surrender. This was to be done, the American officers stated, to offset any continued attacks by their military.

Anya, Kreon, and the townspeople darted around to find a suitable white flag to signal their surrender. In no time, not just one, but an array of white sheets, white pillowcases, white tablecloths, white towels, and even white undergarments were gathered to be displayed from windows and spires in Fürth. Bemused by their response, the commander of the American troops informed the citizens and officials of Fürth that only a single white sheet was required, not an entire laundry list.

As the day passed, most citizens of Fürth saw the American soldiers not as their enemy, nor as their victor, but as their savior. Hitler and his Third Reich had died an ignoble death.

With the flag of surrender risen, the American army proceeded to march out of town and head south to Nuremberg. Novice German soldiers, most in their mid-teens wearing oversized uniforms, with hats too big and sleeves too long, were rounded up and ordered to march beside the G.I.s. Not knowing what the upshot of their future might be, the boys joined the contingent with enormous apprehension. However, many had refused the advice of family and friends to discard their uniforms and change into civilian clothes to save themselves. Kreon, watching the boys march by, realized these young men preferred honor in defeat. Trooping side by side with the G.I.s, the German lads felt less apprehensive as they listened to the cheering crowd and received friendly thumps on the back from their champions.

The entire military contingent was on their way to Nuremberg for a victory celebration. Unbeknownst to them, they would be greeted by a devastating sight: 95% of Nuremberg had, unfortunately, been demolished by Allied bombs.

CHAPTER FIFTY-FOUR

With a new regime trying to establish itself, upheaval followed in the streets of Fürth. The looting of stores became a given. The American troops themselves emptied Fürth's City Hall of goods covertly stored by German officials and dumped the items on its front steps.

Kreon, because he was American born, and all other foreigners were permitted to take whatever clothes, blankets, boots, or sundry items they needed from the massive pile. Germans were excluded from the scavenge, and the Americans burned what was not claimed.

In acquiring what he could for Anya and her family, Kreon was heartened by the compassion the G.I.s demonstrated toward the local children.

Perhaps the soldiers missed their own children back home, he mused.

Or perhaps they understood all too well what these harmless children had been through.

That evening at Tante Bette's home, Kreon unearthed his birth certificate from his shoe and showed it with pride to Anya. Buoyed by the events of the day, he began dreaming of the future.

Anya's day had not been as buoyant. Everywhere she walked she had seen nothing but destruction. Nuremberg was in ruins, and she had no desire to go there and see the once beautiful city maimed beyond recognition. She consoled herself with the fact that the lights were back on, Germany was experiencing some semblance of peace, and she did not have to sleep in her day clothes anymore.

Having done that for so long, Anya and her family found it unbelievable that they could don proper sleepwear again and rest through the night. Kreon, clothed in new pajamas he had acquired from the City Hall stockpile, had also upgraded to a comfortable mattress on the floor at Tante Bette's, while Anya continued to share the bed with her aunt.

Rosa had moved back to her parents' townhouse. They had managed to patch the roof of their home and make it livable again.

All were grateful to be in proper nightwear again, and for the quietude they needed for a decent night's sleep. Sleep, however, would sometimes betray them. They were often roused by nightmares, shaking and sweating, dreaming the war was still raging.

There was also the disturbing awareness that, although the bombings and shootings were over, the pervasive evil of Nazism had not died the day of the Armistice. The Germans and the American military knew there were still Jew haters and devotees of Hitler lurking about. They had simply slithered underground to draw attention away from themselves. The Allies, however, were determined to ferret them out, bring them to trial, and ensure that all convicted war criminals were incarcerated or executed.

"I wonder what Hitler's last thought was before he shot himself?" Kreon asked Johann one day after hearing of Hitler's suicide.

"Probably contemplating how to conquer hell and teach the devil to goose step," was Johann's sarcastic reply.

They both chuckled at the vision.

They were not laughing a few days later when Anya barged into the Bermann home with temper blazing.

"How could that ugly, old cow say such a thing!"

"Who are you talking about?" Babette demanded, while Johann

and Kreon regarded Anya with intrigue. It was not like Anya, who was usually charitable in her assessment of people, to call a fellow woman a cow.

"Your neighbor, Frau Strauss!" Anya retorted.

"What did she do?" a mystified Babette wanted to know.

"That ignorant woman said," Anya mimicked Frau Strauss' nasal voice, "'With all the chaos and foreigners running about, we need another Hitler. Not a big Hitler, just a little Hitler'. Is that woman completely insane?! Who would want any kind of Hitler?! I could punch her!"

The picture of petite Anya taking on the monumental Frau Strauss, elicited guffaws from everyone.

She turned on them, "What's so funny? You think I can't whip that woman?"

"No," Kreon said between chuckles, "We are laughing because we know you can, and we fear for the poor 'cow'!"

Once cooled down, Anya did not pursue her pugnacious inclination. She was placated when new faces as well as long-hidden ones returned to Fürth, despite the Frau Strausses of the world. Most surprising was the influx of displaced people who were determined to reestablish themselves in the town they had been exiled from. A great deal of their homes had been destroyed, and they had to start over with meager resources. Showing enormous fortitude, the returnees proceeded to rebuild, resettle, and regenerate their roots.

But then the world fell to its knees.

"I can't believe this," a horrorstruck Anya murmured, gazing at the newspapers strewn about in her grandfather's study.

The articles and graphic pictures sickened her.

It was obvious that those who survived Hitler's regime were lucky to have anyone left to come home to. The day's papers were rampant with depictions of what the Allies found when they swept through

Germany in the aftermath of the war.

Anya dropped one periodical to the floor as she viewed the monstrous pictures on its front page. The photographs were accompanied by articles filled with appalling revelations. The news coverage made it abundantly clear that the Jewish population, and those not conducive to the "Master Race", had not been deported to another country, nor been sent to German 'country clubs' such as those depicted in Leni Riefenstahl's propaganda films (to appease foreign dignitaries and the German populous). They had been incarcerated, tortured, experimented on, and worked beyond endurance. As a final heinous act on the part of the Nazis, they had been stripped of their clothes and human dignity before dying. Through Hitler's "Final Solution", the articles stated, millions of human beings had been steered into fabricated 'delousing chambers' expecting them to be showers. Instead, they were gassed to death, and their bodies dumped into mass graves filled with the skeletons of the victims before them.

Subsequent reports stated that General Dwight Eisenhower, commander of the American forces, ordered films be recorded to document the carnage and be shown to the public. Eisenhower wanted to ensure no one could ever deny the reality of what would be termed "The Holocaust".

"How could human beings inflict such demonic horror on other human beings? How is this even possible?" Anya asked of no one in particular. No one in the house said a thing, too shocked to respond.

Similar questions reverberated in households around the world as the abomination came to light. The news had not entirely surprised Johann. His summation of Hitler had been on point. He had intuitively known the madman was capable of anything, and news of the gas chambers only unscored Hitler's murderous lunacy. However, the scale of it was beyond anything Johann could have anticipated.

Entering his study that morning, Anya came upon a man alarmingly altered from the proud and stoic man she knew. Her grandfather was crumpled in his chair, sobbing over the soul-crushing news.

Seeing his pain, she enfolded him in her comforting arms and lay her cheek next to his.

"I know, Opa, I know."

"This atrocity...." he stumbled over words as anguish wracked his body, "...killed worse than animals," His tears fomented into rage, "Why did the ones who bore witness in the camps not stop it!? Why?"

"I don't know, Opa. I can only guess their own lives were at stake," Anya stated, still holding him.

"Hitler has destroyed our country." He waved at the papers, "This is not who we are, Anya. Is it?" He looked at her with suffering eyes.

"No, Opa. This is not who we are. The world will see that one day. This was the work of the devil."

Johann acknowledged her words, but his heart remained shattered.

CHAPTER FIFTY-FIVE

For the survivors of the war, the restoration of their life, livelihood, and living quarters began its arduous journey. Cities had to be rebuilt, families had to go on without loved ones, prejudices had to be overcome, and faith in humanity and a better world had to be reinstated.

Kreon and Anya were determined to get married as soon as possible to begin their journey together. Within days after the cease-fire, they initiated plans for their wedding and new life. Acquiring a miniscule, garret apartment not far from the center of town on Mathildenstrasse, they commenced to spruce it up with whatever household goods, paint, and pieces of furniture they could conjure up.

Their future domicile was situated in a corner building that housed a shop where featherbeds and mattresses were sold. The building itself was an old, stone edifice in a block of grey, stone edifices. Kreon and Anya's tiny loft was accessed by climbing a dark, wooden staircase that spiraled up to the top floor.

Its miniscule kitchen contained a small sink, second-hand cot, stove, a table with two chairs, and a drafty window that overlooked the slanted, tiled roof. The kitchen was situated on one side of a long hallway, a small bathroom at its middle, and their bedroom at the other end.

Anya made certain their cozy nook was painted and spotless

before they moved in their meager belongings. Her family dubbed it Anya's "Puppenhaus" (dollhouse) as it was diminutive in scale and made charming by her touch: a pillow here, a doily there, a vase of spring flowers, and second-hand curtains enhanced and enlivened the pale, yellow rooms.

"What do you think, Kreon?" a buoyant Anya asked her fiancé once finished.

"You are a housekeeper extraordinaire!" he declared and punctuated his summation with a pat on her bottom.

"Go back to cleaning the toilet, Herr Kalanis, or we'll never get done!"

Within days the loft was deemed ready for its future occupants. As they stocked the kitchen cabinets with last-minute items, the long-patient lovers made quick work of the chore, then headed for the room that had been uppermost in their mind.

Free of restrictions, Kreon and Anya spread their new duvet over the sturdy bed and decided to put both to proper use. Grabbing a giggling Anya, Kreon lifted her up and threw her atop the fresh sheets, supple pillows, and goose-down duvet. Joining her, and plying her with fervent kisses, Anya rid herself of her shyness and Kreon of his restraint.

Not knowing what to expect, nor knowing precisely what to do, Anya, raised on the romantic books she read, found their first time to be awkward and messy. At the point of her deflowering, she gasped more from discomfort than from pleasure, and gave Kreon a quizzical look. It seemed to say, "Is this it? Am I bleeding?"

Kreon, realizing his passion had overpowered the proceedings, enveloped her in his arms, saw to her comfort, and kissed her multiple times with as much romantic verve as he could muster. It warmed Anya to him.

"It will get better. I promise," he whispered in her ear, while his hands, lips, and tongue began to explore her with the languor of a summer day.

Anya was happy to discover that Kreon was a man of his word.

CHAPTER FIFTY-SIX

On a beautiful May morning in 1945, blessed by sunshine and a light breeze, the engaged couple led a procession of friends and family to the Rathaus (City Hall) in Fürth to exchange their matrimonial vows.

Churches in Fürth had not yet been reopened; therefore, a religious ceremony was not a consideration. The 100-year-old Rathaus, modeled after the Palazzo Vecchio in Florence, Italy, boasted a 55-meter tower (damaged but in a state of repair) and its interior was closed to the public. The stairway to its main entrance served as the temporary site for civil weddings, and the somewhat impatient officiate was waiting there for Anya and Kreon's party to arrive.

As they marched toward it, the only notable lack that fine day was the absence of the father of the bride. Oswald Schmidt was not expected to show up for his daughter's wedding. Alienated from the family and discomfited at the idea of facing Anya and the foreigner he had beaten and objected to, Oswald chose not to attend. Anya's Onkel Otto, husband to one of her aunts, had the honor of escorting the bride up the City Hall steps. Also missing were the uncles and cousins who were held in Russian and French prison camps and not expected to return until a few weeks later.

In their place were two honorable people to make up for the deficit: Lisbeth, the first to arrive, warily acknowledged the greetings of the people who had missed her presence. Anya and Kreon embraced her warmly, and Rosa drew Lisbeth under her wing for the day. The grief the young woman suffered after losing her dark-haired, dark-eyed child to the merciless Nazi system, and suffering further indignities at the hands of the German soldiers who leered at and used her body, could never be erased. Those who cared about Lisbeth could only hope that by surrounding her with acceptance and love, her pain would be eased. She had been welcomed to stay in the home of friends, after refusing to return to her parents' house. Anya and Rosa promised they would do everything they could to make Lisbeth feel safe again.

The second surprise guest was the lovely Czechoslovakian woman on the arm of Kreon's best man, Jorgo. Anya was quick to walk up to the quiet woman and take her hand in hers.

"You saved my man's life," Anya told her forthright, "and I am so glad you could come. Thank you, Catrina."

Catrina gave Anya a grateful smile, pleased that Kreon's soon-to-be wife acknowledged her and knew her by name.

While the women chatted a bit, Kreon smirked at his pal, "Should I expect to hear an engagement announcement anytime soon?"

Jorgo grinned, "Perhaps."

Kreon shook his friend's hand then Catrina's before the wedding ceremony commenced. Nothing would please him more than Jorgo showing a heart toward this woman and her son. Sporting a grin, he turned toward his bride.

Anya looked radiant in her wedding attire, as her beaming groom stood by her side. Her outfit consisted of a black satin skirt, dark nylons, and pumps (bought by Kreon on the black market), and a sheer white blouse custom-stitched by her mother and worn over a simple chemise. Anya was not aware the blouse had been created from the veil of a young bride who had been killed on her own wedding day. (Rosa had been adamant that this knowledge be kept from the sensitive bride, but a chatty cousin blurted out the secret while they were getting dressed that morning. A livid Rosa thought the cousin had done it out of jealousy, but Anya, instead of being upset, surprised everyone when she stated that she treasured the garment even more after the revelation.)

The ritual proceeded without any disruption, although passersby stopped to gape at the wedding party on the stairs. Kreon, entranced by his beautiful bride, missed his cue when asked by the officiating cleric if he would "take this woman to be your lawfully wedded wife." Jorgo, acting as best man, gave the bridegroom a notable prod, and Kreon blurted out a hasty and exuberant, "Ja!"

The wedding rings they exchanged were humble but no less valued. Kreon's ring was made of aluminum, which he had crafted himself. Anya's band was of an inexpensive, gold metal. She had saved the faux gold ring for several years. When a school chum purchased the ring at the local Woolworth, the cheap metal turned her finger green. Disgusted with the ring, she removed it and threw it into the street when they took a walk one day. Being a practical child, Anya retrieved it and asked if she could keep it. With her friend's approval, she placed it on her left hand and wore it from then on. The ring had not turned Anya's finger green, instead it betrothed her to Kreon. On their wedding day, as is German custom, he placed it on her right ring finger while he recited his vows. With that gesture, capped by a jubilant kiss amid much applause, the bride and groom were deemed "Herr and Frau Kreon Kalanis".

Adding to their joy, they harbored a secret: Anya was hiding a pregnancy of only a few weeks.

Slapping Kreon on the back, his new family exclaimed, "You are one of us now!" At their words, Kreon's grin broadened and, drawing his new wife close, felt a contentment he had never known before.

The festivities stretched into a two-day celebration. More than sixty guests, German, Czechoslovakian, and Greek, attended the wedding reception held at a local pub. Everyone contributed what food and drink they could, and the beer flowed freely. A cousin played the button-accordion to pump up the gaiety. On the second day, the celebration was moved to their modest apartment. The small rooms, hallway, and staircase were crowded with merry revelers, and their neighbors joined in. The partying ended by 7:00 p.m. each evening to comply with the curfew that was enforced by the American occupation.

Via a previous German law that was still in place, until a new government could abolish it, the moment Anya Schmidt married Kreon Kalanis she was considered "Stadtenlos". This meant Anya was stripped of her German citizenship, as well as the right to acquire ration cards for food and goods, for marrying a foreigner. During the heady days after their wedding, Kreon and Anya did not allow these setbacks to burden them. A pastoral honeymoon, consisting of bike riding and hitch-hiking to the German Alps with one of Anya's favorite cousins, Hildegard, and her husband, Helmut, was first on the agenda.

With the two ladies riding tandem on the bike, the two gentlemen, each with a small suitcase in hand, kept pace on foot. When they tired, they would hitchhike to their next destination via the lorries that populated the byways.

Each evening they would search out a barn where a charitable farmer might allow them to spend the night. Their sparse wallets precluded a stay at an inn or hotel, so a hayloft suited them fine. Honeymoon bliss created a world where discontent was not welcome. Even Anya's occasional morning sickness could not dim their humor.

"Are you fertilizing the grasslands with your breakfast to make the cows happy?" Kreon would ask, as he held her head and wiped her brow in sympathy. After resting a few minutes, they would be on their way again.

During their happy travels, the budding spring weather and scenery was a wedding gift in and of itself: yellow and red poppies dotted the verdant countryside; flowers of every hue dripped from chalet balconies; recently threshed wheat sweetened the air in the fields; and even cow manure took on the familiar and pungent scent of the earthy life that was in bloom again.

Curled up in her husband's arms one evening, in a hayloft, while he played with her hair, Anya gazed at the myriad stars above them. It was a clear night, and breath-taking in its beauty.

"Happy?" Kreon asked, nuzzling her neck.

She smiled, "How could I not be? Life feels normal again and so much better."

Returning to Fürth a week later, they began the task of constructing a life together. Kreon acquired a position as a kitchen aide at the local American canteen to support his new bride and the baby on the way. There was a jounce to their step at the thought of becoming parents and over another happy family event: Hannah was getting married to her elder swain.

The nuptials were a low-key affair, as no one felt quite optimistic about the union except the bride. Twenty years Hannah's senior, Tomas Heitch was known to like the bottle. What attraction he held for Hannah, no one could fathom.

"Why is she marrying that old buzzard?" was the question preying on her relatives' minds. Her friends seemed to understand her reason to some degree: Hannah loved mothering people. Who better to "mother" than a weak, old man who needed her?

The wedding day brought dazzling sunshine but a gnawing breeze. Hannah, with ruddy cheeks, wore a demure, tweed suit and carried a sizeable bouquet of flowers from a local field. She, too, was pregnant and had yet to inform her family. The nervous husband and Anya and Kreon were the only ones who knew. At the brief, civil ceremony the sisters gazed at each other and felt pleased with their lives.

Later, at the reception in their grandparents' garden, a thoughtful Hannah took her sister's arm and said, "This day reminds me of when we ate our treasured cookie crumbs. I feel rich again."

"As do I," Anya responded and squeezed her sister's hand.

The day gifted them with a sweet reprieve from life's interminable twists and turns.

As Hannah's wedding reception progressed, Kreon was tapped on the shoulder by Anya's grandfather, while enjoying a beer with guests outside.

"Kreon, come and join me in my study," Johann whispered, his voice sounding grim.

Respectfully excusing himself, Kreon obeyed the summons. Johann was sitting at his desk, his face in a serious frown.

"Sit down," he ordered the young man. An ominous newspaper lay open on the desk and Johann pointed to it.

"You are aware of what is happening in Greece?" he asked Kreon.

"Yes. Some of it, but not all of it. I have been hopeful of hearing from my sister but, thus far, no word. I fear a letter telling me of her situation in Athens may be a long time coming."

Johann nodded at his words.

"It is troubling and frustrating, Johann, and I am not sure what to do," Kreon continued, "I cannot travel there to see her. I have no idea what has happened to her and her family. I do not know where to turn."

Johann intercepted, "Kreon, I am sorry to tell you this, but my colleagues in Nuremberg have informed me that the conflict in Greece, especially in Athens, has turned treacherous and is expected to be on-going," he gazed at Kreon sadly and continued, "The Nazis and British have left, as you know, but Greece is now engaged in a brutal civil war between the Greek Communist party and those wishing to maintain more democratic ideology. And Athens, as you might have heard from your own comrades, is at the center of this maelstrom. The British and the United States are supporting the democratic side while Bulgaria, Yugoslavia and Albania are shoring up the Communist faction of the country. Meanwhile, Stalin and Tito are at each other's throats. We have no idea what will happen. We can only pray your family is and remains safe."

What Johann did not dwell on were the deaths and injuries

Athenians had sustained during the initial conflict, which had occurred in early December of 1944. He did not want to add to Kreon's distress.

"When things calm down, the mail service may improve. I am sure you will hear from your sister, Kreon. You must stay positive." Johann placed an encouraging hand on Kreon's shoulder to bolster his spirit, "Being a U.S. citizen, perhaps the U.S. Army can help you through their mail delivery system."

"I have asked," he told Johann, "And I did give them a brief letter to send to my sister. I will have to be patient for any reply."

"Let us hope that will be soon. I will keep you informed of any news I hear."

"Thank you, Johann. I deeply appreciate the information and your concern. Might I ask to look at your newspaper?"

"Certainly. Read it here at my desk. I will let Anya know what you are doing; but do join us soon for supper."

"I will," Kreon extended his hand, "Thank you again."

Johann shook it and gave him a nod, then closed the door as he left. Kreon read the headline and his heart lurched.

CIVIL WAR RAGES IN GREECE. ATHENS UNDER SIEGE.

CHAPTER FIFTY-SEVEN

For Kreon, the sloth-like days of summer, filled with worry when no letter arrived from Athens, left him with a restless spirit and a nagging sense of doom.

For Rosa and her daughters, summer proved a time of reckoning. She tried hard to ferret out the location of her prodigal husband and settle things once and for all with him. But no one seemed to know where Oswald was. Neither his mother nor his brother, who lived two towns away, were forthcoming with information as to his whereabouts.

After days of sleuthing, Rosa and her daughters were having a chatty lunch at the pub where she worked, when Oswald sauntered in and casually stood before them. They gaped at him as if he were a spectral apparition. Oswald remained firmly planted before them, and Rosa's eventual scowl was soon mirrored by his own. He did not acknowledge Anya nor Hannah, simply treated them as sideshows to the main event.

"Girls, I would like to speak to your mother alone," he stated in a brusque, dismissive tone.

They turned to their mother with a twinge of alarm.

"Go ahead, I will be fine," she reassured them, "Take your plates to the booth in the corner. I doubt your father will ravage me."

Anya and Hannah almost choked at the thought, while their father's frown deepened. Grabbing their food and cutlery, they heeded their mother's directive without another word. Settling into the rear booth, the sisters kept a keen eye on their parents' movements and perked up their ears for voluble signs of trouble.

Their father, meanwhile, seated himself in the chair Anya had vacated.

"So, what brings you here?" Rosa observed him with cool contempt.

"I heard you were looking for me," he replied, matching his nonchalance to hers.

"Yes, I was. We have things to discuss," she told him.

"I want a divorce," Oswald stated it so matter-of-factly that he stunned Rosa into silence. He scrutinized her face, as Rosa's eyes widened in dismay. When she regained her senses, her voice was filled with wrath.

"*You* want a divorce?" she hissed, "Those words rightfully belong to me! How dare you!"

"Quiet down, it's not the way you think. I thought I would spare you the effort of trying to spit those words at me," he said.

"Spare *me*? What kind of noble joke is that?" She nearly spat the words at him as she leaned forward ready to fight. Oswald sighed, predicting her response.

"Rosa, we are both too tired to talk in circles anymore," he said quietly, "Our daughters have no great love for me, and our marriage died with the war. I simply want you to file the papers on your and the girls' behalf and be done with it. That's all." He looked at her with clear eyes and without a desire to clash heads. It was not defeat on his part; it was simple recognition of the truth.

"I will not contest it," he continued, "You can choose whatever reason you want for dissolving our marriage. It might take some time, though. City Hall is a mess right now with the takeover of the American army."

Rosa leaned back in her chair and sized up the man sitting opposite her with clarity and benign disillusionment. He had aged. He looked a bit sorrowful but not regretful of his decision. She felt a pang of guilt, which surprised her.

"Where are you staying?" she asked.

"At my mother's. She is getting old and needs looking after."

Rosa nodded. It was like him to go where he felt needed. She realized that had been the basis of their marriage. Perhaps it was even the basis of his joining the Nazi party.

Had they made him feel wanted and needed? Something she, perhaps, had failed at during their turbulent twenty-year marriage?

"Thank you, Oswald."

"For what?" He was perplexed by this unexpected response.

"For being there when I needed you. For leaving when you knew it was time."

He gave her a sad yet understanding nod, rose from his chair, bowed his head curtly, and walked out of her life.

When Anya and Hannah rejoined her, she explained the situation to them. Anya had conflicted feelings, while Hannah looked morose and shed some tears.

"Does this mean we're no longer a family? That our future children will not have a grandfather?" Hannah asked.

"No! No! I expect he will still be there for you as your father, if you wish it, and will want to see his grandchildren." Rosa avowed, but was not secure in her conviction. "Look, you, Anya and I have always had each other and always will. We are a family and will always be a family. Your father will not be excluded, if he wishes to see you or his grandchildren."

Hannah was appeased by the words, but Anya remained silent. She thought of all she had been through with her father, and she sensed she and her unborn child would have to contend with his probable abandonment. After all, she would be giving birth to a foreigner's child.

CHAPTER FIFTY-EIGHT

The unrelenting stresses of life have a way of damaging the vulnerabilities of the body, and a brief night later Anya woke in excruciating pain.

"Kreon!"

She reached for him as she tried to raise herself up. Roused from his sleep and startled by her cries, he scrambled for a light.

"What's wrong?"

Gazing at her, he felt his heart lurch. Anya was writhing in pain and struggling for breath.

"Ambulance...get," she fell back and screamed.

Pulling the covers from her, Kreon was alarmed to see the sheets spattered with blood. At the sight, he whirled out of their bedroom, down the stairs, and banged on the landlord's door, yelling for help.

"My wife needs an ambulance!"

The dazed landlord and his wife assured him they would call immediately, and Kreon rushed upstairs to remain at Anya's side until it arrived. She was moaning with her eyes screwed shut in agony.

The ambulance arrived within minutes. The medics surveyed her condition and placed her on a stretcher, cautiously maneuvering it down the stairs. Kreon rushed to the hospital with her, holding her hand, praying she would survive. Anya clung to his hand as if it were her only lifeline. Her pain was all-encompassing, and, in her delirium, she thought she would die.

"Don't leave me. Not now. Not ever," he cried as he watched her struggle. Placed on a gurney in the ambulance, looking pale and slight, her body seemed to pool into the sheets. When they arrived at the hospital and Anya was rushed into surgery, Kreon plunged into a private hell.

Please, God. Not again. I cannot live with another death. I cannot live without her.

A torturous time later, as Anya lay sedated in the recovery room, the operating surgeon informed Kreon as kindly as he could, "The baby was lost. It was early on, an ectopic pregnancy. We will explain it to you and your wife when she is feeling better. These things happen. We repaired it in time. Your wife will be fine. We expect she will be able to have other babies."

Kreon nodded, too weary to register the doctor's words. All he wanted was to take Anya home, and hope she would withstand the wound to her spirit as well as her body.

She did. Once physically healed, Anya was determined to become pregnant again and fill the void of the child they had lost. Kreon would not hear of it, too terrified to put her at risk. Anya, however, remained steadfast in her desire to bear a healthy child.

"I want us to be a family," she pleaded. "I want to have a baby and bring new life into our world. I am as sick of death and destruction as you are, Kreon. I want us to build a happy future."

"What if this happens again? What if I lose you? I could not bear it. I will die."

"No! No, you will not! And I will not! The doctor said we could try again. Please, Kreon, I want to hold our child in my arms. Something good must come from all of this. My arms feel so empty."

Her sorrow became so acute, he finally acquiesced to her wishes. Once Anya warmed their bed, he no longer complained about her persistence. By fall, another baby was on the way. And when Christmas came, she and Hannah sat side-by-side, hands stroking their rounded bellies, feeling like winners of a grand lottery.

CHAPTER FIFTY-NINE

In June of 1946, on the second anniversary of D-Day, Eleni Rosa Kalanis, all seven pounds of her, was liberated from her mother's womb. She was named for her paternal and maternal grandmothers, and her first name was shortened to the Germanic "Leni". It took two days for their infant daughter to be born; and, when the delivery was over, Kreon, looking drawn, felt as if he had gone through the pangs of birth himself.

The parents held their breath as the doctor clasped Leni by the ankles and dangled her upside down. Having made her entrance with a blue-tinged face, she was placed in this position, receiving several hearty slaps on her tiny pear-shaped behind, to turn her visage pink. Leni did them one better. Emitting an outraged cry, she turned a fuming red instead. The medical attendants and her parents gave a sigh of relief. A bawling Leni was soon comforted in her mother's arms, while her thankful father smiled with delight. Little did the tyke know he had wished for a blonde-haired, blue-eyed, little angel like her mother. God gave him a dark haired, olive skinned, brown-eyed wonder instead. Startled to see a miniature of his face stare back at him, Kreon fell in love with his Doppelganger. Later, after being bottle-fed, he swore she grinned at him. The nurse tried to explain his little daughter was most likely experiencing gas, but Kreon would have none of it.

Within days, and several visits from family, Anya, and Leni

(wrapped in a soft, white blanket her mother had crocheted for her) were discharged from the hospital. Grateful and over-joyed, her parents brought Leni home to Mathildenstrasse, little knowing that being born in post-war Germany exacted a price.

The child would battle major medical problems three times before she was two. Lack of proper nutrition and a weakened immune system made her susceptible to whooping cough and pneumonia, but it was an allergic reaction to powdered milk that almost killed her in the first weeks of her life.

Anya, like other young women in those post-war days, suffered from the ill effects of malnutrition and emotional trauma. (Also hazardous to the health of the populace was drinking water polluted by the blood of dead men and animals that had seeped into the ground and several waterways in Europe.) The new mother found she was unable to breastfeed her child adequately. A store-bought formula was recommended and bottle-fed to Leni instead.

One night, after the child had been fed with the new formula for the first time, her father heard her whimpering in her make-shift crib, while an exhausted Anya remained sound asleep. Picking Leni up and cradling her, he padded to the kitchen and placed a slice of orange to her lips to suck on, hoping it would soothe her. It did not. In the dim light he noticed Leni's hands and face were swollen, and she was beginning to gasp for air.

Waking Anya, he placed their tiny daughter in her arms and rushed to call for the doctor. Hearing of the child's symptoms, the doctor immediately arranged for an ambulance to transport her to the hospital. This distressed her parents even more. They were frantic to find out where their daughter would be sent. Children of mixed breed marriages allegedly perished after admission to a certain hospital in the city, and they feared Leni might be transported there. Kreon informed the doctor of their dire concern, relating the tragic story of their friends' German-Greek children.

"Both girls were taken to this hospital on separate occasions and neither child came out alive, although neither had suffered from a life-threatening illness," Kreon informed the doctor. When the ambulance arrived, Anya pleaded with the medics to take them to another area hospital instead, one Anya believed safer. In consideration of her acute angst, the doctor had already given them specific instructions and they complied.

Arriving at the emergency room, members of the hospital staff placed Leni on a gurney and swiftly began medical care. It frightened the tot beyond measure and her terrified eyes seemed to scream 'Mama! Mama!' as they wheeled her down the hallway toward a room for critical care. Anya held onto Leni's curled fingers for as long as she could, but then had to let go. Separating her hand from that of her child's was as wrenching as separating her soul from her body.

The emergency medics were quick to bring Leni's severe allergic reaction under control, and it was not long before she was wheeled into another room for rest and observation. The doctor informed her relieved parents that substances in the powder had caused Leni's throat to swell and would have suffocated her before morning. Kreon's wakening to his daughter's soft cries, and his quick-thinking actions, saved her life.

Leni spent several more days in the clinic for treatment. The clinic was run by Catholic nuns. Swishing around in their black and white habits like giant birds of prey, the sight of them frightened the infant. It was only when her parents hovered nearby, and she felt their loving touch, that Leni fell into a secure and quiet sleep.

When the crisis passed, the child was nestled in her mother's arms and returned home with precise instructions and a new formula to ensure the infant's recovery.

In the ensuing months, as Leni toddled around like a bumbling cub, it was apparent she loved visiting her great-grandparents' house. It brimmed with boisterous activity and provided the child with a much-appreciated luxury... a decent chamber pot. The one at home had a cracked edge which grazed her tiny buttocks when she sat on it.

When Rosa noticed Leni's displeasure with using a chamber pot at all, she told Anya, "She is only a babe and will use it when she is good and ready. Do not rush her!"

Defending herself, a distraught Anya explained, "Mama, my fingers hurt so much when I rinse out her dirty diapers in the cold water. I am using up coal to constantly heat the water. She has to be out of diapers as soon as possible."

Rosa looked at Anya's red hands, "You are much too young to suffer from arthritis, but best beware of chilblains. I will find more coal for you, and some cream for your hands. If your hands get worse, please see the doctor."

"Thank you, Mama. I will," she promised, hugging her mother.

Rosa's worried look did not go away.

With the progression of spring and warmer weather, Anya's trouble with her cold hands subsided. After washing diapers and finishing morning chores she often headed with Leni to the Bermann home for an afternoon visit. Johann and Babette doted on being great-grandparents, or "Urgrossvater" and "Urgrossmutter" as they were now called. The house, as usual, brimmed with life as a gaggle of goslings tore around its kitchen or the backyard.

A wellspring of idyllic childhood memories was planted in this environment. Leni especially loved the garden, the chickens, the tree-filled park across the street, and the open fields that led to the nearby villages and the forest. As she grew, it became an endless springboard to adventures with family and friends. She never felt lonely or frightened in these bucolic surroundings nor deprived in any way.

A single treasure she shared while at play with her cousins was a plain, white, wooden box with wheels and a pull-string attached. Depending on the season, they would head to the park across the road and fill it with flowers, pinecones, twigs, leaves, or snow they had collected. Its contents would then be transformed into miniature abodes for the illusory creatures that pranced in their heads – fairies, goblins, and wood sprites.

There were other delights. Each day, the children looked forward to the shepherd as he led his flock of sheep back to his farm in the late afternoon. He would bring the herd to a halt with his wooden staff and allow them to pet the wooly creatures while listening to the lambs' bleats. Whenever the children sounded their own "baaaaahs" in return, the echoing bleats of the sheep triggered unending giggles from their captive audience.

At dusk, the lamplighter would appear with his ladder and light the streetlamps until they radiated a comforting glow against the dark. On summer evenings when Anya and Leni stayed late, they would sit by the open window and wave a cheery hello to him.

When the family members were not "adventuring", the preparation of meals kept the adults busy while the children played around the front stoop until suppertime. Meals were concocted from the rations that were provided. Ofttimes it would include the plump "Knödel" (dumplings) that were molded from finely grated potatoes and served with a bit of "Braten" (browned meat) and sauce. On Sundays, their Urgroßmutter would bake "Kuchli", puffed squares of pastry that were dusted with powdered sugar. She would layer them in her wash basket, one atop the other, and dole them out like the precious delicacies they were.

A greater delight was the occasional tub of ice cream that Kreon acquired from the American canteen and brought to family gatherings. Babette would add a bit of water to thin it, ensuring all could enjoy the treat. She knew when it came to ice cream, everyone was smacking their lips in anticipation.

Unfortunately for Leni, daylight hours in the countryside always flowed into evening and signaled the return to Mathildenstrasse. It was not that this area of their town was particularly ugly; it had survived the war with less damage than most cities in Germany. However, the streets were strewn with piles of rubble here and there, like a mosaic gone amok. It was gloomy, and the air smelled of dust. Leni often begged to stay behind at her great-grandparents. She always squirmed in her mother's arms when it was time to leave.

CHAPTER SIXTY

The sight of the damage around Fürth, the knowledge that 95% of the center of Nuremberg had been destroyed by bombs, the fright of Leni's illnesses, and the chaotic, postwar economy strengthened Kreon's desire to improve or alter their living condition. While he dreamed of opportunities in America, Anya hoped they could thrive in her native country among family. Obtaining a decent job in their area proved difficult, however, although Kreon tried. Work in the canteen offered no future. Everything was still in ruins and progress was not as fast as they hoped. Not just buildings, but democratic laws and edicts and a new government and viable economy had to be resurrected. A modern phoenix had not yet emerged from the ashes, underpinning Kreon's longing to emigrate to the United States.

Reestablishing Anya's citizenship became crucial to this goal. It could only be accomplished by getting her paperwork and birth certificate in order and presented to town headquarters for reinstatement. As head of a family contemplating a move to another country, Kreon was spurred on by visions of a more prosperous and secure life for them. Providing decent food on the table, proper clothes for their backs, and a warm hearth to come home to instead of a drafty garret apartment in a demolished country became his aspiration.

Anya and Kreon also feared for their daughter's safety. Because

Leni was a "Mischling", mixed breed, the child of a double race, the dread of extermination by subversive Nazi sympathizers would not leave them. Leni's ethnicity was apparent. Like her Greek father, her olive skin, dark hair, big brown eyes, and distinct features were not easily hidden.

One night, on a stroll back to town from the Bermann's house, a drunken fellow waved a pistol at them and laughed when he noticed Leni being carried in her father's arms.

"Ach! Ein schwarzes Mischling! Hahaha!"

They escaped injury by remaining calm and treading past him as peaceably as they could while he weaved down the street, brandishing his weapon in the air.

A shot made them jump, as a discharged bullet hit brick.

It was obvious to Anya and Kreon that Nazism did not die the minute the conflict ended. Although war criminals were being brought to justice at the Nuremberg trials, they suspected Nazi doctrines would sprout again like an aggressive weed immune to complete eradication. Leaving for America became a critical issue in the Kalanis household. Kreon was like a tethered horse ready to sprint through the gate, while Anya's spirit preferred to remain in the stable.

As the sluggish bureaucratic machine droned on, several visits to the American Consulate in Munich were required. This resulted in constant delays and roadblocks. A frustrated Kreon made a bold attempt to hitchhike to Prague, Czechoslovakia when he heard the necessary immigration papers could be obtained at a speedier pace there. The trip proved fruitless.

To add to their dilemma, Anya's ability to join Kreon in this exodus was constrained by the U.S. government's implementation of restrictive immigration quotas, and creation of a paper wall of regulations, to control the influx of immigrants. For financial and economic purposes, sponsorship was required beforehand to ensure that incoming refugees would not become a "public charge." In addition, as the head of the household, Kreon needed to be employed for a steady six months before he could bring his family over.

By 1947, the U.S. administration was willing to loan passenger money to American nationals who wished to return to the States (albeit the loan had to be reimbursed later). The Kalanis family tried to leave together, but it was not to be.

Both Anya and Kreon realized a decision and sacrifice would need to be made if they wanted to move forward with their lives.

Months of disappointment later, Kreon sat his wife down and spelled it out plainly, "Anya, I need to go alone if I am to establish residency for us in America. There is no other way."

She listened miserably to his words, "Are you sure? This is so difficult. With you gone and another baby on the way, I don't know if I can bear it."

Embracing her, he assured her, "Yes, you can. We will get through this."

His words were braver than he felt, remembering her miscarriage. At twenty years of age, Anya had already borne so much.

"You are strong and have such a supportive family surrounding you, I know you will be in the best of hands. If I do not seize this opportunity for our future, it may never come again. I have written letters to relatives, and I have the opportunity of obtaining passage to America."

Kreon showed her the letter in his hand.

Anya began to cry. "How many more separations are we to endure? Is this dream of America worth all our anguish?"

"It will be. I promise! I want a better life for you, for Leni, for our future child; one where we can all thrive, not just exist and scratch around to make ends meet. One where we can live in freedom and peace; not worrying about another war breaking out. Circumstances are still so fragile in Europe. Can you understand that?"

Her forlorn eyes answered his, "Yes, I understand. Leaving Germany, leaving memories of the war behind is understandable. But leaving my family, eventually putting an entire ocean between them and us, is not painless. Can you understand that? Meanwhile, being separated from you again, is an Alptraum...a bad dream."

As Kreon labored through the paperwork and began packing for his future trip, a shroud of gloom enveloped their home. Anya's family, too, felt despondent but tried hard not to interfere. This was a decision Kreon and Anya had to make for themselves. Many prayers were lifted toward heaven in the ensuing days.

The appeals were not only for themselves. Kreon craved for word of his sister and her family. As if in answer, a letter miraculously appeared. It was dated three months prior.

CHAPTER SIXTY-ONE

My dearest Kreon,

I have been in receipt of two of your letters recently, and they filled my heart with great joy! Married and with a little daughter...how wonderful for you! God bless you, and may you all be in the best of health! We are surviving here. Alexi sends you greetings, and your little nephew and niece send their uncle a big kiss.

As you know, the situation in Greece is horrendous. We are safe for now and expect to stay that way by staying off the streets as much as possible and keeping our mouths shut and eyes open. How ironic we got rid of the Nazi scourge and another scourge, perpetrated by our own people, appeared. You know where my heart lies in this battle. Hopefully, the civil war will reach an end in the coming year. Stalin, by agreement with the British and the United States, wants the war to end, while Tito wants to battle for the Communists until the last. Four years we have had to endure this travesty in our nation! When will these wars ever end? I pray they do, and we will see each other again.

For now, it is best that you remain in Germany...or will you be heading to America with your family? Please try to get word to me, so I know where you are.

I do have one bit of good news. Who do you think

appeared at our door around Christmas? Your friend, Nico! He is well and as spirited as ever. Unfortunately, his left leg fell victim to German gunfire and had to be amputated. He has since been discharged and has a room at a decent boarding house on the outskirts of Athens. He said to tell you that he still intends to meet up with you someday in America, so you better be there when he arrives! I have no doubt he will make it. You are his family, and he will find his way to you.

Anyway, my dear Kreon, my heart is with you. May God keep you and your family in his care. I have faith someday we will be reunited. We send you and your family our deepest love and wish you good fortune throughout your life. Stay healthy and stay safe. Please write when you can. I miss you dearly.

Your faithful sister,
Vasiliki

Kreon pressed the letter to him, grateful to God for keeping his sister and family from harm and hoping it would always be so. Before his departure, he wrote Vasiliki one final letter to tell her of his plans.

CHAPTER SIXTY-TWO

Kreon departed for America in late April of 1948. Holding Leni between them, Anya tearfully kissed her husband goodbye as he boarded the train for Hamburg, Germany to meet the ship that would carry him across the Atlantic. She and a bevy of relatives waved in silence as the train chugged down the tracks and into the future. Leni, not yet two, just stared and wrinkled her little brow at all the commotion.

The existence of mother and child after Kreon's departure drifted into quietness. Leni ambled about looking for her Papa, but Papa was not there to lift her into the air and catch her anymore, and she wondered where he had gone. Anya did her household chores nary saying a word. The silence was only relieved by the frequent visits to the Bermann home, where the noise of cousins cavorting, and mothers cooking or baking for the hoard, relieved their downheartedness.

When the days passed into weeks and her father did not appear, the local shepherd often found Leni sitting on the stoop by herself instead of joining in the fun. The lamplighter would see her standing motionless at the window, barely acknowledging his presence, while she stared wistfully down the street.

"Would you like me to bake you some Kuchli?" Babette would ask when she saw the child moping about, as the puffed and powdered pastry was Leni's favorite.

But Leni would shake her head with a glum "Nein". The Kuchli were baked anyway. Her great-grandmother knew the aroma would tempt Leni's nose and her small fingers would grab one. Babette smiled when she caught Leni nibbling one as she tottered off. Leni's unhappiness was momentarily forgotten.

Anya, in turn, wrote in her journal to allay hers.

CHAPTER SIXTY-THREE

Mein Lieber Kreon,
Der schöne Tag ist nun vorbei
Ich lege Mich zur Ruh.
Zieh auch Du die Decke über
Und schliess die Augen zu
Schlafe wohl und traum von Mir,
Wach Morgen auf gesund
Bin in Gedanken stets bei Dir
Kuss innig Deinen lieben Mund
Mit Liebe
Deine Braut, Anya

My dear Kreon,
This beautiful day is now over,
as I lay down to rest.
Pull your blanket over as I do
and close your eyes.
Sleep well and dream of me.
Come morning, wake up well.
In my thoughts I am at your side
Kissing your dear mouth
With love
Your bride, Anya

CHAPTER SIXTY-FOUR

One fine morning, an unexpected ray of sunshine illuminated Leni's world at Mathildenstrasse. She discovered a greengrocer had set up shop a short distance from the entrance to their building, and his outdoor stand was filled with colorful fruits and vegetables. Curious about this exotic display, she wandered over from her usual spot on the front stoop and caught sight of something she had heard about from a cousin but never tasted. There, nestled in one of the wooden displays, was a bunch of bright yellow bananas. Oh, how she longed for one!

Roused to action, she clambered up the stairs to their attic apartment, burst through the kitchen door, and asked her Mama if she could have "Geld" (money).

"You want what?"

"Banana!" she bubbled out.

"Well, I guess a banana is something special." She watched eagerly as her mother opened her change purse and handed her a few Pfennigs. "Here, go get your banana. Just bring me back some!"

She beamed at the coins in her hand, then scuttled down the three flights of stairs and scurried over to the greengrocer with joy.

"Banana, bitte." He looked at the few Pfennigs Leni displayed in the palm of her hand and shook his head.

"Nein. Nicht genug!" ("No. Not enough!") Then he turned away to help his other customers.

Chuffed, she clambered back up the stairs and held out her hand toward her Mama, "Mehr, bitte."

Anya hesitated, sighed, and looked at the small palm with the pitiful Pfennigs laying there. Then she looked at Leni's woebegone face.

"Oh, alright. Did he say how much?"

Leni shook her head. Her mother opened her change purse again and handed her a few more of the precious Pfennigs. Emitting a fervent "Danke schöen!" Leni scuttled back down the stairs.

The greengrocer was busy, but she pulled at his apron and stretched out her Pfennig-filled hand to him.

"Banana, bitte."

He looked at her hard-begotten offering and seemed annoyed.

"Nein, nein, Mädel. Es kostet mehr! Du brauchst zehn Pfennig."

Ten Pfennigs? Leni could not count, but her hand was full of several. More! He wanted more?! As he turned back to his other customers, she thought he was the meanest man she had ever met. Leni had a hard choice now: give up or get her banana. She scooted back up the stairs.

Stretching out her hand, she looked up at her Mama with the saucer eyes of a kitten begging for milk.

"What is it?" Anya inquired, "Don't tell me you need more?!"

Leni nodded her head and gazed dolefully at her mother, not saying a word.

"That grocer has some nerve! Is that banana from the King of the Jungle? Made of gold? Must you have it, child?"

Leni shrugged and remained silent.

Anya looked at her daughter's face, "Oh, alright. I guess it's not every day the grocer has bananas."

Her mother took a few more Pfennigs out of her purse.

"But that is the last of it. Understand?"

Leni nodded in obedience and scampered back down the stairs.

With the weight of the coins in her palm a bit heavier, she showed the collection to the greengrocer.

"Ja, ja, Kleine. Das ist gut!"

Leni smiled. He took the ten Pfennigs from her hand and placed her prize in it.

This time, she scooted up the stairs as fast as her wee legs would take her. With boundless anticipation, she handed her banana to her Mama. Anya let Leni help peel it, and they took one slow bite after another. It was very good.

CHAPTER SIXTY-FIVE

As spring gave way to summer, Leni's melancholy over her father's departure turned from hopeful anticipation of his return to restless boredom. When weeks passed by without sight of him, she grew accustomed to his absence and rejoined her cousins at play. Most often the backyard of the Bermann household provided the diversion. Selecting the jewels of the garden, the girls would pluck flowers to have their mothers weave into floral crowns. Once the blossoms were woven together, they would grace the young ladies' heads with an array of color and fragrances.

"How do I look, Mama?" a proud Leni often called out, as she twirled around.

"Like a lovely, little princess!" her mother would profess while watching her daughter do her merry dance.

Joy seemed to be creeping back into the household, especially when Anya shared the news with the adults in her family that she was pregnant again. She decided to keep the news from her relatives and Leni for a while in case the pregnancy did not go well.

Summer had them all dancing after the rains of spring passed. Lush carpets of green graced the land, and the vast meadows, fragrant with sweet hay, offered up a symphony of pastoral music: cows mooing, birds chirping or crows cawing, and chipmunks, squirrels, and deer rustling amongst the trees, bushes, or blades of grass. Horses clopped down the street, bees buzzed, sheep bleated, and geese honked as they chased the children and nipped at their legs. The barefoot renegades ran like dervishes through the fields, trying to avoid bee bites or goose nips, and their merriment could be heard throughout the season.

One warm Sunday, the family ventured to the nearby forest for a placid day of gathering mushrooms, wildflowers, and pieces of wood for their ovens. On the way home, their task, once fulfilled, was rewarded with a stop at a local Bier Garten for refreshments. The heat of the day and their exertion deserved a token reward. Seated on wooden, slatted chairs or on a parent's lap, the children watched their fathers and mothers drink golden beer from the glass steins that were served by a dirndl-attired waitress.

"Could I have a sip, Mama, please?" Leni begged.

"Don't you think you are much too young?" her mother responded with an arched eyebrow.

Leni vigorously shook her head, "Please?"

Anya nodded her approval, then held the glass stein to her daughter's lips.

An eager Leni gulped down a mouthful and nearly choked when it hit her gullet.

"Blechhh! Bitter!" With screwed up nose, and her tongue repelling in and out, a repulsed Leni looked at her mother in bewilderment. Everyone around her chuckled.

"Would you like a lemonade instead, dear?" Anya asked with a feline grin.

"Yes! And with more sugar please!" her daughter insisted.

A lemonade with added sugar sounded so refreshing, and Leni hoped it would get the nasty taste out of her mouth. When it came, it was served as usual, without benefit of ice cubes, and she quenched it down quickly. Ice cubes or ice-cold beer were not part of the offerings at German pubs, as the American soldiers sitting near them had discovered. The Germans considered ice cubes and ice-cold beer or soda an American quirk; something that could hurt their stomach, and they could not fathom this oddity. Moderately cold was the best the barkeep could do. When an American soldier often asked for "Eis" (ice), he discovered, to his surprise, he was served a scoop of ice cream in a dish.

Warm weather highlights also included the appearance of a local puppeteer in Leni's great-grandparents' neighborhood. The maestro would set up a puppet theatre in the field out back to entertain the young ones. They would laugh and scream at the antics of Punch and Judy as each puppet took a swipe at the other with a miniscule baseball bat.

There was also the family pet to be enjoyed. At the Bermann house a white German shepherd named Peter stood sentry. A loving and gentle protector, Leni and her cousins fussed over him as much as he did them. Fighting over who would lead Peter on his afternoon walk was a daily scuffle.

"I'm the oldest and strongest; I should lead him!" declared one lad, barely over five feet tall.

"But it's my turn!" shouted another contender.

The girls were more effective in taking their turn; they cried whale-sized tears.

When summer segued into the colors of fall and then the white of winter, a small wooden box on a pull-string was again filled with twigs and dead leaves, and mounds of snow to be fashioned into homes for the elves and fairies living in the forest and decorated with primitive findings.

Seldom were the children lacking in enchantments. Their imaginations, neither constrained by nor bereft of fertile ground, conjured up the rest. A hot cup of tea, flavored with a tad of sugar and fresh farm milk, became the beverage of choice after their outdoor adventures in chilly weather.

The parents tried valiantly to keep their offspring out of trouble and content. But with children it was always a guessing game as to what they would do or how they felt.

Anya just hoped that Leni would not fall into a depression again over the absence of her father. Kreon, having arrived safely in

America, was settled in a boarding room, and trying valiantly to find suitable work. He had written of his joyful anticipation of another child on the way, but also of his concern for Anya's health and their future. She wrote back that he should not worry; she was beginning to feel the baby stir inside of her.

Busy playing with her cousins, Leni did not take much notice of her mother's sprouting stomach. By late summer, it could not be ignored any longer. She discovered there was no longer room for her to sit on Mama's lap, and the invitations to do so had ended. Quite puzzled by this turn of events, Leni poked at her mother's belly and jumped backward when it moved.

"Baby in there?" she pointed out while staring at Anya's noticeable lump with mounting confusion and apprehension.

"Yes, and you were in there once too," Anya informed her.

"Me? In there?" she asked in dismay, "Did you swallow me?"

Anya pondered how much she should explain to her inquisitive child at this age and thought it best to confer with the women in her tribe first.

As Leni watched her mother's belly grow during the ensuing weeks, Anya often let her feel the movements of the baby inside her. It mesmerized her young daughter, especially when the baby kicked.

"Did you feel that?" her mother asked when a tiny foot seemed to visibly squirm inside her.

Leni tried to stay clear of the kicks, expecting feet to burst through her mother's stomach at any moment.

"How does baby come out?" she inquired.

Anya looked at the women around her for support in explaining things without frightening or confusing her little girl further.

Urgroßmutter sat Leni upon her knee and informed her: "If you put a cube of sugar on the windowsill, the stork will deliver the baby all bundled up and bring it to our window."

Leni, upon hearing this, gaped at her mother and then the windowsill several times. She grew saucer-eyed at the probability of such an event.

Not even three yet, Leni wondered how a baby in her mother's stomach could be taken by a stork and put on a windowsill. Seeing her daughter's bewilderment, Anya sighed. It was time to explain things a little more clearly.

On a crisp November morning, Anya's stomach emerged through the kitchen door looking like an over-stuffed cabbage. She was moaning. Then a puddle of water appeared on the floor beneath her.

"Mama's peeing! *Contraptions* coming!" Leni shouted to the bevy of female relatives sitting at the Bermann's kitchen table. She beamed with pride at making this educated announcement. Then bedlam ensued.

Everyone scurried toward Anya as Tante Bette rushed to Johann's study to call for a taxi. The men, sitting out back to enjoy a beer and the last vestiges of warm weather, barged in as they heard the news and wound up feeling useless as the women clucked about. When the taxi arrived, Rosa and Tante Bette marched out the door with Anya, while the others waved good-bye.

An anxious Leni remained on the front stoop holding tightly to her Tante Gunda's hand. Mama had groaned several times and looked like she was hurting. Leni did not want to think of something hurting Mama.

"Should we wait for the stork now?" she asked, but Tante Gunda did not answer and took her inside. A mystified Leni requested permission to put another sugar cube on the windowsill just in case he arrived.

"The stork has to come here!" she explained.

Instructed to be good while staying behind at her great-grandparents, Tante Gunda kept an amenable Leni occupied by encouraging her to play with her cousins in the backyard.

Later, when Tante Bette returned without her Mama or Oma,

Leni overheard her conversation with the others in the kitchen.

"We made it to the hospital just in time!" Tante Bette recounted loudly, "The baby was almost born in the taxi. The nurses placed Anya on a gurney and, whoops, there he was! He came out wailing like a screech owl!"

Noticing Leni standing by the back door, Tante Bette drew the girl to her side and jubilantly revealed, "Leni, you now have a baby brother! Mama and baby are fine, and your proud Oma stayed with them."

Everyone was excited at the news, but Leni wondered where the stork was. The sugar cubes were still on the windowsill. It was all very confusing.

CHAPTER SIXTY-SIX

Little Demetrios Kalanis was born in early November of 1948. Named for his paternal grandfather, he was called Demetri for short. When Anya brought him home, Leni looked at the small, squiggly thing wrapped in a knitted blanket, then looked up at her mother.

"How do you like your baby brother, Leni?" her Mama asked.

"*That* was in your belly?!" Leni exclaimed. She peered into the makeshift bassinet and declared, "He doesn't look like me."

"No, you look more like Papa and Demetri looks more like me."

"He's going to be pretty."

"Thank you, sweetheart."

"But he's stinky."

"I think he needs a diaper change."

"Did he poop in his pants?"

"I am afraid so."

"Yuk! Look, he's grabbing his feet!" Leni started to giggle, "He's funny!"

"And smelly. I better change him." As she did so, a sudden squirt of water hit the air.

"Mama, he's peeing!"

As her mother tried to reach for a cloth to cover up Demetri's leaky faucet, Leni started laughing and could not stop. Neither could Anya. Demetri was getting them wetter than they wanted to be and now, with a little twist of his body, he was aiming for the wall.

"Mama, watch out! He is too funny! Hahaha!"

Anya finally got the situation under control and managed to clean herself, Leni, and her son up. Swaddling Demetri in his baby blanket, she ordered Leni to sit down, and placed her little brother in her lap.

"Here, hold his head like this, and be careful not to drop him. Babies can squirm out of your lap very easily."

"He's like a monkey, Mama."

"That he is. Our little chunky monkey."

"I like him."

"Do you?"

"Yes. He makes me laugh." Leni smiled up at her mother, as Demetri began chewing on his fingers.

Anya smiled back. She had reached one of her goals. And she was content.

With Demetri's birth behind her, Anya focused on trying to get herself and the children to America as Kreon wished. Her first task was to get the necessary paperwork in order. Her quest soon became a merry-go-round of never-ending possibilities and momentous roadblocks. She felt buried in her "To Do" list. She, Leni, and little Demetri had returned to their lonely apartment on Mathildenstrasse, and the gloominess of winter and Christmas and New Year's without Kreon was settling in. It was her husband's letters that gave Anya the strength to keep going.

Unbeknownst to her, Kreon, struggling with homesickness for his family, had considered giving life in Germany another chance. After reuniting and staying with Greek relatives for a brief period, he had headed to New York City to find gainful employment. His broken English proved a hindrance.

CHAPTER SIXTY-SEVEN

My dearest Anya,

I hope someone will be able to translate my German writing into something you can understand. I am trying to learn more words each day with the German/English lexicon I purchased.

What joyous news to hear of our son's arrival! I wept with delight and thanked God to hear that you and Demetri are fine, and that my little Leni loves her baby brother very much. I can only pray that my parents in heaven know of their grandson's birth. How much it would have meant to them! How much it means to me to be blessed with a daughter and now a son. I cannot wait to hold you and our children in my arms. I miss you so unbearably much.

Things are improving here day by day. After moving from Lowell to New York City, I have taken a job as a dishwasher in a nice restaurant while I seek a machinist position. (Beware...after this I might never want to wash another dish again!) The job does not pay a great deal, but I am saving as much as I can for us. I recently found an inexpensive room to rent in a home in the Bronx, which is a section of New York across the East River. You can find it on the map I sent you. The landlord is a decent man and sends his regards to you.

Last weekend, I took a bus to Lowell, Massachusetts to visit with Aunt Fotini and Uncle Andreas and their family again. They always greet me warmly and my aunt spoils me with the Greek food I love. Their sons and daughters are now grown and treat me like a brother. I look forward to taking you there some day.

I admit leaving Germany has been difficult for me, and I do miss the quaintness and beauty of its villages and countryside. Here in New York, except for Central Park at its heart, one sees mainly concrete, stone, and glass in the streets, along with majestic buildings, traffic noise, and countless people milling about. But there is such a vitality to it! There is no destruction, no deadening of the senses; only a feeling of growth and opportunity wherever one looks. The city promises so much to so many!

I will keep looking for a good manufacturing job. A steady income would be such a blessing to our plans.

Anya, I pray every day that all goes well for us. I know that taking this huge step is not easy for you, nor is it easy for me, because I miss your family too. But here we have a chance to build a better life for our children. We must be brave and forge forward, and forge forward without doubt in our minds.

Greetings to family and friends. Kiss Leni and Demetri for me. I hold you in my arms.

Love, Your Kreon

He continued pounding the pavement for several weeks more, until serendipity finally blessed him.

Dearest Anya!

I recently heard from a colleague that a German-owned company in Astoria, New York was seeking machinists and paid a good wage.

I, of course, immediately put in an application. And yesterday, I was called in for an interview with the manager, who spoke German, and he hired me on! There are many German-American workers in this factory. I know I will feel at home here. Anya, think of it! I have steady employment in my field and an income we can thankfully live on. What a blessing to our plans!

When I pass Immigration's "six-months of employment" requirement, we can be together again! I am so excited for us. I hope you will be too. Please continue with getting the paperwork done. I cannot wait for our reunion. Kiss the children and your entire family for me.

Much love, Your happy Kreon

Anya read his exuberant letter over and over, the paper wilting in her hands. Tears spilled upon it as she thought of what this letter asked for...a commitment, a firm decision to leave, a resolve she was not sure she had.

Her family rejoiced at the news. Anya smiled; but her mother noticed it was only half-hearted.

CHAPTER SIXTY-EIGHT

A letter filled with instructions from Kreon arrived a few weeks later. Anya, having given Demetri his bottle, placed him in the basket that served as his bed. (As with Leni, she was not able to nurse him because her body was still malnourished and could not provide milk. This time, she and the doctor were cautious about what formula to feed the new baby.)

She was dressing a frowning Leni in the itchy, woolen tights that the child hated when the doorbell rang. The unexpected noise startled them both. Trying to pull up the leggings on Leni, it rang again, then a third time, before a loud pounding ensued.

"I am coming!" shouted Anya, frustrated by the interruption.

"Papa!" Leni yelled, fleeing toward the door, as Anya rushed ahead of her and flung it open. The postman stood there with his face flushed from carrying a huge package up three flights of stairs. Anya thanked him profusely for his efforts and gave him a few, spare coins from her purse.

The size of the package left both mother and child stunned as it sat on the hallway floor.

"Oh my. We will bring it to your great-grandparents' home to be opened there, as your father instructed in his recent letter. I will get Onkel Werner and his son to help us carry it."

"What's in it, Mama?" Leni inquired as she ran her minute hand over the sizeable carton.

"We'll have to wait and see, dear."

"Must we wait long?"

When Onkel Werner arrived with his son, Heinz, Leni scurried behind them as they grabbed opposite ends of the heavy twine that secured the package. Her mother, meanwhile, wrapped Demetri in his blanket and cradled him in her arms as they walked down the stairs. In the streets, it was a matter of gingerly navigating the piles of rubble, large and small, and the dismal remnants of the buildings damaged during the war. Leni knew that many people and buildings had been crushed in the war. Her Papa had not come home yet. She tugged at her mother's coat sleeve and asked, "Has Papa been crushed in America?"

"Goodness, child, where did you ever get such an idea? Come! Hurry! We have to catch up with Onkel Werner and Heinz."

When they did, Leni watched as her mother and Onkel Werner whispered to each other, then turned their eyes on her. Their meaningful looks were disquieting.

Fear struck minutes later when her uncle and cousin tumbled over a pile of bricks and her mother gasped in alarm. The package! Leni was now certain bits and pieces of her Papa were in it. They looked so serious as they righted the package, she could think of no other reason for their anxious looks.

Finally arriving at the Bermann household with no other mishaps, they found it filled with family happy to see them arrive. Urgroßvater quickly came to their aid and placed the huge carton on top of the kitchen table, while everyone stared in awe at its size. Leni, growing ever more fretful over its contents, begged them to "please open it!".

As her great-grandfather undid the cord with care, he folded it and put it in a kitchen drawer for later use. Layers and layers of white tissue paper came next. Leni grabbed it all and bunched it into her arms.

"Papa?" she asked with nervous anticipation as she gazed into the box.

A lovely, new dress, dark blue with white polka dots, for her mother was pulled from it to the delighted dismay of the onlookers. Leni yelped with relief realizing her Papa was not broken after all. The giant box was filled with presents from America.

"Mama, you will look so beautiful in that dress," Leni proclaimed, and everyone agreed with her astute fashion sense.

The myriad gifts, as Johann unearthed them from Kreon's package, were greeted with astonishment and placed into grateful hands: tins of cocoa and candy, boxes of tea, soap that smelled of flowers, nylons like the Army wives wore, a warm coat for Anya, a snowsuit for Leni for the cold winter ahead, and a stuffed teddy bear and clothes for Demetri (who slept through all the excitement). Kreon had thought of everyone and everything. There were packets of coffee for the brood and pipe tobacco for Johann (both sewn into the lining of Anya's coat to be secreted through Customs). Leni examined the lining of her snowsuit, but it contained no marvels.

Her Urgroßvater pulled one last gift from the carton. It was wrapped in white tissue paper and had a small card attached to it. Holding the parcel toward Leni, her mother read the message:

"Für meine kleine Tochter." (*"For my little daughter.'*)

Staring up at Johann, Leni gazed at the wrapped gift with amazement.

"For me? Open, bitte!" she implored.

Looming over her with his mane of white hair and handle-bar mustache, Johann placed it in her hands with exaggerated ceremony. An impatient Leni grabbed it from his hands and removed the wrapping with the eagerness of the three-and-a-half-year-old child she was. All eyes were focused on her father's gift.

Inside was a coloring book. It was not just any coloring book. It was bigger than any coloring book anyone had ever seen, and it came with a big yellow and green box. With trembling hands, Leni recognized what the box contained. The Army soldier had called them *Kray-oh-lahs*. He had brought some to a neighbor's child, a friend of hers. It had been a box of ten; but this box was much larger.

There was a number on it. It was not to be believed. Her mother told her it was a box of forty-eight crayons!

"Mama, that's all the colors of the world!" Leni cried out, to the amusement of everyone around her, "America must be rich! Is Papa working for the King?"

She turned to her mother with joy. "Mama, look at all the pages in my book!"

"Which one would you like to color first?" Anya asked, as she smiled at her exuberant daughter.

"All! All!" Leni shouted, gazing at the fascinating pictures.

Turning page after page, she and her Mama chose the one with which to begin. Leni's eager cousins helped her choose the colors. By evening she completed two pictures but had eaten little of her supper. And she barely noticed as her relatives ambled over to view her finished artwork.

"My, my," Tante Hannah tittered, "look at the pretty princess in pink, green, blue, and yellow! But tell me, who's that ugly person over there?" She pointed to a witch colored in black, brown, and purple slashes.

"That's Mrs. Hitler," Leni answered, quite full of her new-found talent.

Everyone roared and her head shot up as she wondered what was so funny. To her, grownups seemed strange at times. She shrugged and turned to the next page.

Before long, aunts, uncles, and cousins started to yawn and exit out the door. Only her Mama, Oma and great-grandparents remained in the kitchen, ready for a relaxing cup of tea. Leni, still immersed in her gift book, began coloring a new picture. Noting this, her Urgroßvater approached her.

"Leni, don't you think it's time to put that away?" Johann suggested.

"Away?" she asked, without looking up, orange crayon in hand.

To her dismay, her Urgroßvater withdrew her coloring book from under her busy hands and assembled the crayons back in their box.

"Yes, away," he answered. "We'll put them in a safe place in the cupboard, and you can color a picture every Sunday."

"One picture every Sunday..." she repeated dazedly, "*One picture every Sunday?!*" She could not believe such unexpected cruelty! Her great-grandfather was a stern man, but she never thought like this! And her mother, who was watching, was allowing him to do it!

Begging them to let her take the coloring book home, her heartfelt pleas were met with firm resistance. There would be no argument.

"ONE PICTURE EVERY SUNDAY?!" She stamped her foot in protest for several more days and sprouted a pout so dour it threatened to make a cabbage of her face.

As the weeks passed, Leni submitted to the routine of the Sunday coloring sessions and peppered the day with limited grumblings, fearing Urgroßvater would take away this rationed privilege if she complained too much. Leni realized that if she respected his bidding, he remained true to his word and allowed her to color one entire picture every Sunday. Once she had eaten her Sunday meal, which she did as fast as her stomach and her mother's protests would allow, and wiped the table clean, he would stride toward the kitchen cupboard and place the coloring book and crayons before her. She, in turn, would give him a curt nod, much like a Queen dismissing her courtier.

Her young mind continued spinning around Sunday. Monday was the worst day. On that day, Anya would assign Leni chores to make the day go faster. There were featherbeds to fluff, soot to wipe off the windowsills, and the stairwell banister to be mopped and polished. The passing of each day brought more chores but increased excitement as Sunday with her coloring book approached.

One weekday morning she and her mother were surprised to find the rooftops laden with snow. Harried pigeons were plucking around in it, trying to find feed, as Anya watched the cooing birds from the garret window.

"Will Papa return in time for Christmas?" Leni piped up, her voice a hoarse whisper. She was shivering on the cot in the corner of their miniscule kitchen, despite being wrapped in a thick blanket. Her mother regarded her with concern as she listened to the coughs and sniffles Leni was emitting as she lay there. The child seemed to always be catching cold.

"Too easily," Leni heard her mother tell Oma when her grandmother came to visit. "She needs decent food and proper medicine. What am I going to do? I hope Demetri does not get sick too. I wish Kreon were here."

"Stay strong," Oma advised, patting Anya's hand. "You were strong during the war. You can be strong now."

By Wednesday, Leni was developing a fever. By Friday, her chest ached each time she breathed. It hurt even more when she coughed, and she felt terribly tired. The doctor was called for, examined her, and somberly stated it was pneumonia. He left medicine for Anya to give to Leni every few hours and instructed her to bring her to the hospital if she had serious trouble breathing.

When Anya administered the medicine, Leni could barely lift her head from the pillow.

"Mama, coloring book?" she whispered.

"Shush, don't worry. It will be waiting for you," a consoling Anya told her as she placed a cool cloth on Leni's hot forehead and covered her up. "Urgroßvater told me you will be allowed to color in two pictures next week."

"Can't he bring it to me?" her eyes begged.

"You must get better first. Now try to sleep." She waited for her daughter's eyes to close. When Leni's coughing fit abated and she slept fitfully, Anya sat back in her chair, rested her head in her hands, and sobbed.

Thoughts of her coloring book drifted in and out of Leni's fevered haze, as she moaned in her sleep. Through the doctor's frightening visits, through the burning fever and the nightly awakenings, through the terrible ache that had spread to her back, the bright splashes of the coloring book beckoned.

As Christmas neared, Leni showed glimmers of improvement, and everyone praised God. To cheer her and spur her on, Anya placed a miniature plastic doll in Leni's hand on whose tiny chest she had carved two little XX's.

"See, your dolly is sick too. She needs taking care of. Think you can do that?"

Leni nodded, as she lay back against the pillow and held the doll to her. In taking care of her little charge, Leni's own sickness soon eased.

By Christmas Eve, she was well enough to be bundled up by her mother, carried to a neighbor's car by Onkel Werner, and taken to her great-grandparents' house to join in the family celebration. She held her dolly close as she was placed on the parlor sofa to view the family Christmas tree. It was not an abundant tree, perhaps only three feet tall, and situated on a corner table. Decorated with a few colorful ornaments, it was alight with small burning candles. Leni thought it beautiful, and, with her family surrounding her, watched in wonderment as it flickered and glowed in the room. Alas, the dripping candles were soon extinguished to prevent a fire. The merriment of the holiday, however, continued with the munching of food and the sharing of gifts her father had sent.

Later in the evening, still nestled on the couch in the sitting room, Leni listened as her family sang Christmas carols. In addition to "Stille Nacht" ("Silent Night"), her cousins sang a hearty rendition of "Kling Glockschen, Kling-a-ling-a-ling". Her favorite carol, though, was "Leise Rieselt der Schnee" (Quietly Falls the Snow). In her childlike imagination the lilting melody and its images brought all the loveliness of the season to life for her:

"*Leise rieselt der Schnee; Stil und starr ruht der See; Weihnachtlich glänzet der Wald; Freue Dich, Christkind kommt bald!*"

The song spoke of softly falling snow, a silent and tranquil lake, Christmas glistening upon the woods, and a call to rejoice because the Christ Child was coming soon!

Propped against an immense feather pillow, Leni spent the rest of Christmas Eve finishing one of the pictures she had missed, thoughtfully inviting her cousins to help choose the colors.

Completing it, she gazed toward her mother, "Can we send it to Papa?"

Anya smiled and nodded her approval.

When bedtime came, Leni refused to remove the warm robe her father had sent. Instead, she kept it wrapped around herself as she lay in the spare bedroom with her mother that night, while Demetri slept in his basket nearby. There was no need to return to Mathildenstrasse since Christmas was being celebrated with relatives the next two days. Clutching her dolly and an envelope addressed to "Papa", she fell asleep. There was little rustling in her chest, and all was at peace.

Falling into a deep slumber, she dreamed her father was with her that night. Relating the dream to her mother in the morning, Leni confessed she wished the dream had come true, and he were standing there with them when she awakened.

"I don't want you, me, and Demetri to be lonely anymore...can't Papa come home?"

Anya stroked her daughter's head in sympathy but could not give Leni the answer she craved.

CHAPTER SIXTY-NINE

Between Christmas of 1950 and the spring of 1951, the uncolored pages in Leni's coloring book were dwindling. She was determined to finish every one of her "masterpieces" so she could present the entire book to her Papa when she saw him again. Assured by her mother that he was working hard in America and saving money to return soon, Leni tried to increase her output.

"Urgroßvater, can I finish the rest please?" she asked with as forlorn a face as she could muster to win his sympathy.

"Nein, Leni, there are still several Sundays left for you to stay busy."

She glowered at his lack of approval and could not understand why Urgroßvater was being so unfair!

By early spring, with her spirits seriously flagging, Leni was surprised to be gifted with a pet of her own. It was a shiny, black bunny kept in an enclosure in her great-grandparent's backyard. A red ribbon and tiny gold bell adorned its neck. The petite rabbit became her treasure, and she named him "Hansi". Visiting his cage daily, Leni often let him play in her lap or hop around as she sat in the garden enjoying his antics.

When Easter Sunday came and the family sat down for their holiday supper, Leni rushed her meal, asked to be excused, and spurted outdoors to play with her pet. To her puzzlement, Hansi's cage was empty, and he could not be found. Frantic, she ran back to the house and notified everybody that "Hansi is missing!"

Taking Leni's trembling hand, Urgroßmutter sat her down gently and explained that Hansi was now safe in her tummy. Horrified, Leni howled like a banshee, and everyone came running.

"I wanted to see my bunny, not have him for Easter supper!" she wailed.

It took the good part of an hour to unruffle her ruffled psyche.

Having witnessed Urgroßmutter chop the head off a chicken with one fierce whack, then chase it around the yard with her hatchet swinging in her arthritic hand as the bird ran headless away from her, Leni questioned why a chicken could not have been chosen again.

"Why my bunny?" she whimpered.

"Leni, it was the only meat we had left to put in the stew. I am so sorry. We did not know how to tell you, and I know this was not the best way," Anya informed her little girl while rubbing her sorrowful head. Leni had not noticed the chickens were gone too. Sniffling away her sorrow, it struck her for the first time that they might be poor if they had to eat her pet.

The thought of poverty continued gnawing on Leni's mind when her mother took her for a bath in the communal washhouse out back the next day. Her great-grandparents' neighbors did their laundry there or used the claw-footed tub for their own baths. It was a small brick building with a chronically wet cement floor and a lock on the door. That day Mama bathed her but did not have a dry change of underwear to cover her with. Leni had to walk back to the house with her naked bottom scarcely hidden beneath the cotton play dress she wore. Even at her young age, her delicate nature was mindful of appropriate attire. Mortified, Leni hoped no one noticed her lack of panties, and prayed that God would dry the ones her mother held before anyone noticed and pointed a finger or laughed.

CHAPTER SEVENTY

Summer went all too fast, and winter too slow. On a soggy April morning, while an impatient Anya was trying to dress her squirming daughter, the doorbell rang.

"Achh! Must someone always come at the wrong time! Sit down and let me get these boots on you."

"Maybe there's a package from Papa!"

Anya sighed, dropped the boots, and walked toward the door.

Kreon had written often, sometimes with pictures of himself in America. The photos always delighted the family. Several letters also bore money, allowing Anya to buy more food or order more coal. And then there were the welcome packages containing clothing and surprises for all.

But there had been no post from him in well over two weeks, and it worried her. Maybe there would be a letter or special delivery today.

She unlocked the door and opened it, expecting the postman. But it was not the postman. It was Kreon at the door! Anya nearly fainted.

Standing tall in a smart blue coat with a white scarf around his neck, he looked handsomer and healthier than she remembered him to be. Gawking at her husband, she remained immobile, not trusting her eyes.

"Well, is no one going to greet me hello?" Kreon spread out his arms, grinning broadly.

Anya emitted a shriek and sprang into them.

Leni, still in a daze, watched and waited. Standing as still as a totem pole, she feared if she made any noise or movement, she might awaken, and her Papa would disappear. When he picked her up and hugged her tight, Leni scanned his face in disbelief.

Papa is truly here!

Leni clung to him until he begged for air. Both parents laughed as she threw up her arms and surrendered her grip. Anya took Kreon's arm and they sat on the couch in the kitchen; he with Leni on his knee.

"Will you stay, Papa?" she pleaded; but her question was lost in her parents' chatter. Her mother had so many questions!

As soon as they recovered from the surprise reunion, all three departed for the Bermann home to celebrate Kreon's homecoming with family.

When Babette and Johann opened the door to the unexpected guests on their stoop, a huge burst of cheer greeted Kreon as he stepped into the arms of his German relatives. The usual gang was there, and he was as delighted to see them as they were to see him.

Once the greetings abated, Kreon strode through the room to finally meet his son.

Little Demetri Kalanis had been sound asleep in his great-grandmother's lap, but as his father's footsteps approached, his eyelids fluttered open, and he yawned.

Kreon bent over to lift the baby into his arms. He marveled at the boy he had always dreamed of. The child that would carry his father's name forward. Strong emotions welled within him. Anya stood next to her husband, holding his arm, knowing he was trying not to break down and cry in front of all these people. But neither one could help the tears from brimming.

The baby looked like Anya, fair in coloring with delicate features, but Demetri's dark eyes were those of his father and grandfather. They looked up at Kreon, questioning him, contemplating whether to gurgle or cry at this big creature enfolding him in his arms. Demetri chose instead to yawn again and make his father laugh. His son seemed rather unimpressed by all the attention and fuss.

Later, when the littlest Kalanis deigned to wake up fully and acknowledge his audience, Demetri, less than a year old, squirmed mightily in his beaming father's arms and let it be known that he needed a diaper change.

The tow-headed tot resided at his great-grandparents house daily, so Babette and Rosa could help take care of him. (It alleviated the necessity of Anya having to cart Demetri, Leni, his stroller, and a cluster of sundry items up and down staircases and back and forth to the apartment in Fürth. Each day, when their visit was over, Anya and Leni were able to return to Mathildenstrasse unencumbered, and ready to head for bed.)

Once cleaned up and refreshed, Demetri, too young to comprehend who this stranger was who was grabbing at him, clamped himself to his grandmother's bosom while his eyes assessed this unfamiliar person. Coaxing him away from his grandmother and into Kreon's arms did not work. Demetri had no intention of venturing forth from his place of safety.

Kreon studied his son and was pleased that he looked like Anya. He quietly sat down and watched Demetri, while Demetri watched him in return. At most, a peaceful detente had been reached.

Noting the gap between her father and brother, a purposeful Leni positioned herself upon her father's knee. In an impressive timbre, she bid Urgroßvater bring her coloring book and crayons to the table (although she was fully aware it was only Wednesday and not Sunday).

Beseeching her father with "Papa look!" she lay her finished pictures before him. Viewing her handiwork with care, Kreon found himself blinking and wiping his eyes. The devotion she had put into this project was obvious. Leni, beaming with pride, assumed her father was wiping his eyes so he could see the pages better.

"Looks like this coloring book kept you quite busy. I am proud of you," he remarked.

Smiling at his words, she took her box of forty-eight "Kray-oh-lahs" and held it toward him.

"Papa, you pick the colors. We can finish the pictures that are left," she announced with a wicked gleam in her eye and a voice buttered in smugness.

Urgroßvater had no choice in the matter now. Her father was home, and she decided to tell him how mean great-grandfather had been in allowing her to color only one picture every Sunday!

Informing Kreon of this grievance, she was shocked when, instead of being angry, he turned to Urgroßvater, and they winked at each other! Stricken, Leni jumped off his lap.

Why did Papa wink? How could he do that!?

Instead of outsmarting Urgroßvater, she had been outsmarted!

Scowling, Leni recalled her mother had winked every so often too when the coloring book was placed before her.

Scrutinizing her father, she concluded she would never understand grown-ups and certainly did not appreciate his reaction. Clever as she was, she had not yet learned the secret language of "The Wink", and it goaded her.

Indignant and injured, she confronted her Judas:

"Papa, why were you and Urgroßvater winking at each other? He was so mean to me! I had to wait and wait and wait to color just one picture each Sunday! It wasn't fair!" she exclaimed, pouting and fuming. She was turning into a dust devil, Kreon noted.

"Was he really so mean to you, Leni? Come sit back on my lap." He picked her up, despite her protests. "Now listen...time moves very slowly, does it not, when someone you love is away? And the days without people you love can make you terribly sad, right?"

Leni pondered this and granted him a reluctant bob of her head.

"But..." Kreon continued, "if you have something to look

forward to that makes time go faster, it helps, does it not?"

Leni thought about the lonely days missing her father, about the sick days, and the sad days, and how the Sundays and her coloring book were always there to look forward to.

"You see," her father explained, "if you had finished all the pages of the coloring book at once, there would have been nothing to look forward to as the long days and weeks passed while I was away," he studied her face, "Do you understand?"

Leni did not answer. After a few moments of thought, with brows puckered in contemplation, she slid off her father's lap and ambled toward her great-grandfather. After scrutinizing his face with the intensity of a criminal judge, she hiked herself up onto his lap and gave him a hug.

CHAPTER SEVENTY-ONE

That evening, Leni was informed her Papa was visiting only a short while. He was on an "Urlaub" (vacation) from his job as a machinist in America and would need to return there in two short weeks.

Leni did not know what a machinist was but thought it a grand job as her father wore a fine new suit and new shoes. He also brought new articles of clothing for them in his trunk, which was delivered the next day. Her favorite gift was a yellow bikini which she planned to wear all summer in the heat.

With a steady job awaiting his return, Kreon wanted his wife and children to join him in America as soon as possible. But there was still much to be done and sheaves of forms to fill out.

With both parents focused on obtaining the elusive visas, it often led to Leni being put in the care of a relative, a neighbor, or a friend, usually on the spur of the moment. While Demetri remained blissfully nestled in the Bermann home, nursing his bottle, and napping the hours away, Leni had begged to stay in the apartment in Fürth close to her father.

It was during one particularly hectic day, with Kreon having to travel to the consulate in Munich at the last moment and Anya needing to present important papers at the city hall in Fürth, that Leni got lost in the shuffle. Knowing her restless daughter would be a distraction while she answered questions and filled out voluminous forms, a harried Anya was desperate to find someone to watch Leni while she was gone. Her appointment, at 1:00 at Fürth's city hall, left no time to run to her grandparents' house. As chance would have it, Frau Keller, in the building next door, was exiting when Anya darted toward her with Leni in tow.

"Oh, Frau Keller, I am so glad to catch you! Could you possibly watch Leni for me this afternoon? I need to rush to the Rathaus to meet with the magistrate's assistant, and it would be difficult to have her there while we process all the forms."

Mrs. Keller looked at the desperate mother and the restless child.

"Well, I am running errands myself, but Rolf is home from school and can watch her for you. Rolf!" she shouted up to her son, who stood at the second story window watching them, "Komm runter sofort!" She repeated, "Come down here immediately!" when he made no motion to move.

When Rolf, the Keller's sixteen-year-old son, ambled down the front stairs, Anya was a bit hesitant. The boy seemed pleasant enough whenever she saw him, but today he appeared a bit sullen and not too enthused by his mother's command.

"Don't worry, Anya. He's good with children; always taking care of his young cousins." She turned to her son, "Rolf, please take care of Leni for a short while, until I get back. I, or Frau Kalanis, should return by late afternoon."

"Sure," he responded impassively, and took Leni's hand. He had played ball with her once in the street, and Leni hoped they could play again. It had been fun, until her mother had interrupted and called her home.

Anya was relieved to see that Leni was smiling and was being agreeable with her temporary sitter.

"Thank you, Frau Keller and Rolf. I will be back as soon as I can!"

"No worries!" waved Frau Keller, as both women walked in opposite directions to conduct their errands.

CHAPTER SEVENTY-TWO

In this world, the wall between Heaven and Hell is diaphanous at best. Of course, Leni, at her delicate age, was not aware of that yet. She trusted the hand that was offered and followed its lead.

"Can we go out and play?" she asked.

"Yes, later," he replied, mollifying her as he pulled her along.

One step at a time, they climbed the staircase while she held onto his fingers. Turning the lock, her caretaker led her through the wooden door of the Keller apartment. He sat his charge on the couch and, turning on a light, began playing shadow games on the wall to amuse her. This went on for a while as she giggled at the phantom animals his hands created and listened to his sing-song lyrics.

"Alle meine Entchen schwimmen auf dem See...." ("All my little ducklings swimming on the lake".)

She clapped with joy, as a duck appeared on the wall.

"Are you hungry?" he asked. "There are some wonderful Schokoladen cookies in the kitchen."

That diverted her attention immediately.

"Oh, yes, please!"

"Well, let's go and have some with a glass of milk!" Gratified by her enthusiasm, he walked her into the kitchen. "Here, let's sit you on the table and I'll find the goodies." Lifting her up, he smiled as her eyes brightened with the thought of a chocolate cookie and milk.

When he placed them on the table next to her, it took little time for Leni to gulp down the treats and finish the glass of milk he had poured.

"Well, you certainly enjoyed that!" He grinned and wiped the milk mustache from her lips.

"I did. But my stomach feels funny from eating so much."

"Oh dear, well we'll have to fix that, so we can go play ball outside. Don't want you to be sick."

"No. Mama says it's naughty bubbles floating in my stomach because I eat too fast."

"Well," he tickled her nose, "we'll make those naughty bubbles go away. Lie down on the table and I will rub them away! Then we can play ball!"

Her Mama had sometimes made them go away, but only by giving her water to drink as she sat on her lap.

"The table?" Leni asked.

"It will be alright," he reassured her, "It will help flatten out your tummy and free it of mean bubbles! Then we'll go outside and play."

She did as he asked, and he laid her down gently.

As his hands began to pull her panties past her stomach, her brow furrowed into a question.

"Don't worry, I just want to rub all around your tummy, so it doesn't hurt you anymore."

With delicate precision, only the pretty white socks and Mary Janes Papa had brought her from America remained on her feet. Her shoulders shivered, but her tummy felt better at his warm touch. Soon the hands began to touch her in places she was not used to. Then something down there began to hurt.

The glaring lightbulb hovering overhead suddenly changed his face. A scream rose from Leni's throat, and she shrieked in terror, "Mama! Mama!" as the face above her turned into a monster.

She kicked at him to make him stop.

"Mama! Mama!"

Mama never came. Mama was not there.

She twisted and turned her small body in anguish. He was trying to hurt her down there, but she struggled against it. In the grip of his madness, something rubbed against her small chest as he pinned her down. His wild eyes grew closer.

"Mama! Mama!" she screamed again.

She was suddenly startled into silence. Something white and sticky spurted across her face. Within moments, the beast disappeared and, breathing deeply, was replaced by the boy she knew.

The beast was calm now, he said, "It's okay. I was just trying hard to scare those mean, mean bubbles away."

She stared at him without a blink. The look unnerved him, so much so that he did not hear the front door open as he tried to clean her up. He had not dressed her yet.

"Yoohoo! Rolf, where are you? There was no line at the grocers, so I am home early."

His horrified mother froze at the kitchen door. Her son was in his underwear, soiled rags on the floor, and the unmoving child only half dressed.

She sprang at him in fury, "What have you done?! My God, Rolf, what have you done?!" She pulled him away from the table and the girl.

"I've done nothing," he declared.

"Nothing? Look at her! She's frightened out of her mind and barely moving!"

"What do you care, mother?" He spat the words, leaving her stung.

Frau Keller looked at her son, as if for the first time, "What do I care?"

"Yes!" he shouted, "Yes! What do you care? She is only a Mischling! Nothing more than a mongrel! They are all dogs, the lot of them! And they should be treated like dogs! They will destroy our German race!"

Frau Keller's eyes bore into her son, then she lashed at his face with such ferocity that Rolf flew over a chair and crashed onto the floor. She did not care if he ever got up again.

Inhaling sharply, she took the now shaking girl into her arms and began to dress her with care. The warmth of Mrs. Keller's hands restored some feeling to Leni's arms and legs. When she was dressed properly and her hair combed, Frau Keller led her outside, while Rolf picked up his clothes and slinked to his room.

Outdoors, the sun shone brightly, but Leni did not feel it.

"Would you like to go to the park with me for a while and see the swans until your mother returns?"

She looked up at Frau Keller, whose hand was shaking in hers, and gave a slight nod.

And so, Leni spent a quiet hour on a bench watching swans glide on the pond and flowers sway in the surrounding gardens until her mother came home and they met her on the front stoop. Leni was then returned to a world where nobody knew. The invisible branding of her face had become a secret, even onto herself.

The face of the monster was eradicated... annihilated... ...shunned from the conscious recesses of her mind.

CHAPTER SEVENTY-THREE

Days later, Leni was quietly sitting in the garden at her great-grandparents' home, watching her cousins play, while her mother and grandmother chatted over a cup of tea.

"I am worried about her," Anya confessed as she stared out the window.

"How so?" asked a concerned Rosa.

"She has been so quiet and listless the past few days, and last night she screamed in her sleep."

"Well, children her age do go through moods and are prone to night terrors. I remember you having them."

"Hmmm...I don't know. I think it is more than that. The other day we bumped into Herr Keller and his son, and she nearly ran off on me. When I caught up with her, she was quivering like a frightened puppy. They walked off before we could chat, and the boy had a suitcase with him. I have barely seen Frau Keller and, when I do, she flies off like a wasp is chasing her."

"Didn't you say they took care of Leni the other day?" Oma inquired.

"Yes. But when I ask Leni about it, she refuses to say a word and walks away from me. I have no idea what to do. She is usually so lively. This is certainly not like her."

"I think you need to have a talk with Frau Keller," Rosa stated firmly.

"I guess I do," Anya agreed, although with growing unease as her instincts gnawed at her.

When Kreon arrived that evening, and Leni had been put to bed, Anya mentioned her concerns regarding their daughter. As her worries unfolded, Kreon decided they needed to speak with Frau Keller as soon as possible.

The next morning, after dropping their daughter off with her grandmother, and without heralding their arrival, they appeared at the Keller's door.

Seeing the pair standing there, Frau Keller became agitated as she inquired into the nature of their visit.

"We would like to come in. We need to speak with you," a resolute Kreon informed her.

Frau Keller flicked a furtive glance over her unexpected guests, "Well...yes. Yes, of course."

As they stepped into the foyer, she led them into her sitting room and invited Kreon and Anya to sit on the couch.

"Would you like some refreshment?" she offered as they watched her wring her hands.

"No, that won't be necessary," Anya stated, stopping Frau Keller from disappearing into the kitchen, "Won't you please sit down with us. We have some questions."

"Questions? What kind of questions?" Frau Keller's voice took on a strained tone, as her eyes flicked around the room as if she were searching for an escape, realizing there was none.

"I...I don't know how to say this," Anya paused, "but something seems to be bothering our daughter since you and your son watched over her the other day. Leni has become quiet and evasive, unlike her usual self. And she had a terrible nightmare the other night which left her screaming in her sleep. Did something happen while she was here?"

Frau Keller looked down at her hands and said nothing.

"Frau Keller, we are aware that Leni can be high-spirited and unruly at times, so if you or your son gave her bottom a spanking or hit her, we need to know." Anya placed a settling hand on the woman's arm to calm her obvious nerves. "We just want to find out why our daughter has been so silent, so we can coax her out of this mood."

Frau Keller looked up at both with tears in her eyes and a pained expression on her face.

"What is it, Frau Keller?" Kreon asked, his tone steady but grim.

His intense stare unnerved her, and she burst into tears.

"I'm sorry. I am so sorry!" she exclaimed, shaking her head to and fro while cupping her face in her hands.

"Please tell us," Kreon implored, trying to keep his voice as calm as possible, although inwardly he was beginning to roil. Anya's own anxiety was already getting the better of her.

"I found him...them, in the kitchen. Anya was on the table half-dressed. I do not know what came over my son! I really do not know what possessed him!"

Kreon sprung up like an animal smelling blood. Anya grabbed his arm in alarm, trying to get him to sit down, but he would have none of it. Her own heart was stricken.

"What happened?" he asked in a voice simmering with volcanic ire, "What happened, Frau Keller?! Did he?"

"No! No. He did not hurt her in that way. I checked," she stumbled on the words, "when I dressed her. I noticed nothing...I," her words suddenly dribbled away, and then there was silence. She could not maintain the lie.

"I will kill your son when I see him!" Kreon spat at her, eliciting wails from the woman and tears from his wife.

"I am sorry! I am so sorry!" Frau Keller exclaimed over and over.

Kreon stared at her with unmitigated disgust, "Sorry? Sorry? Your filthy son will be reported to the police."

"No! No! Please do not do that! They will kill my son!

Please...no!" Frau Keller begged.

"Your degenerate son nearly raped my daughter and shocked her into the state she is in. Where is the mercy in that?" Kreon glared at the woman venomously, "and you were going to let him get away with it!"

"No! Please, please listen. My husband has taken our son up north. Rolf will live on his grandfather's farm. His grandfather is a stern and uncompromising man, and a harsh taskmaster. He will straighten the boy out. You will never see my son here again. I promise you!"

Towering over Frau Keller with his fists clenched, Anya felt sick to her stomach at the thought of what Kreon might do. Had Rolf been there, she had no doubt he would have pummeled the boy without restraint. She dropped her face into her hands, wanting the ugly scene and the ugliness of Frau Keller's words to go away. Anya was reaching her limit, and she knew Kreon had reached his.

"Kreon," her pleading eyes begged him, "It is time for us to go. There is nothing further to be said or done here."

Frau Keller said nothing, quivering in her seat, attempting to stay motionless.

Kreon stalked around her, contemplating her words, contemplating his next move. He ripped at the woman with words, especially words against her son.

It was Anya's pacifying voice and touch, that caused his temper to eventually slacken. Seeing his wife's wracked face, Kreon turned from his prey like a panther that had gorged on its kill and no longer found itself hungering for more. Sated, he headed for the door.

Anya rose to follow him. Without acknowledging Frau Keller further, they left her alone with her thoughts and with her conscience.

When they reached home, the turn of the lock was a welcome

sound. The children were under the care of their grandmother, and their apartment was calm and inviting. It was a place where they could shut the world out. Both drifted toward their bedroom. An exhausted Anya lay across the bed, her mind numbed by the revelations of the day, while a subdued Kreon joined her. Neither made a sound as they let the soothing atmosphere brush over them. Anya was drifting off to sleep when she heard the first sob. She rolled over and was startled to see Kreon cry; cry in such a way that his lungs were gasping for air and the pain appeared to be tearing him apart. She had never seen him like this before, and it distressed every fiber of her being.

She rose and placed her arms around him and lay her head on his shoulder.

"Kreon, tell me what you are feeling." She could sense his suffering, which was akin to her own. "Leni will be alright. I feel it in my heart."

"Will she? It is just..." he could not go on.

"Just what, Kreon? Tell me...I am listening. Tell me, please," she stroked his arm. Watching him cry in such a manner cut through her.

"For years I dreamed of having a family; and now I have one. Every day I have tried to protect and take care of you and the children as best I can. Every day I try. But I nearly failed. Our little girl was nearly raped by a lunatic who found our child so worthless that he subjected her to the vileness in him. And I could not protect her! Everywhere I turn, there seems to be a shadow of the war that haunts me, some underlying evil that has not yet been suppressed. I want to get us out of this God-forsaken country as soon as we can. I want us to be whole, not separated all the time. I want us to begin life with a clean slate; not with the shadow of Hitler, the Nazis, the Third Reich, the Holocaust, these demented young men, hanging over us, suffocating every pore of our lives. America, I want us to go to America so we can breathe again."

Anya understood what he was saying and what Kreon was asking of her. But she could not think, could not answer. Instead, she kissed his lips, kissed his face, kissed his forehead, returned to his mouth and tongue, and answered it with hers, until she felt his arms tighten around her, and they sank back on the bed and made love, made love so deep that it erased the pain and the memories and the evil, and brought them to a state of quietude.

CHAPTER SEVENTY-FOUR

Kreon's remaining vacation days, before taking leave of Germany, were filled with private outings with his wife and children. The evening hours were reserved for visits with Anya's family, friends, and long talks into the night.

During their daytime walks, Kreon paid special attention to Leni, taking her on his shoulders and making her laugh as only he could, while Anya peaceably pushed a sleeping Demetri in his stroller. Leni was coming out of her lethargy, chattering more each day, and slowly becoming as delightful as a bluebell sprouting in the garden. It eased her parents' worries.

Time sped, and his visit was soon over. Kreon's ship to America was waiting in Hamburg, one of Germany's port cities.

The morning of his departure, Leni walked with her parents along the Pegnitz River near her great-grandparents' home while Demetri stayed in his grandmother's arms. The boy had grown used to Kreon being around but had not yet had the opportunity to truly bond with his father. Rosa felt this was best for the child, as Demetri would only be baffled and hurt by Kreon's disappearance should he become too attached to his father in such a short stay.

Anya had hoped to take snapshots along the picturesque stream with both children, but Demetri, in full infant mode, refused to be compliant. She planned to send the vacation pictures she had taken to Kreon later. Resigning herself to the fact that her son would not budge, she caught up with her husband and daughter as they trailed along the river's path.

It was a breezy spring day, as they rambled along the banks of the Pegnitz and basked under the brilliant blue sky. Puffs of white clouds were inched along by cool gusts of wind that tousled the hair of mother and child.

"Give me a lovely smile," Anya entreated, as Kreon and Leni posed near the riverbank. Leni, wearing a pretty, floral dress and her Mary Jane shoes from America, did so gladly. Kreon kneeled by her side and placed a protective arm around his little girl as the breeze appeared to give her a chill. With a click of the camera, Anya was pleased to capture her husband and child. Kreon, however, did not smile. He knew it would be the last image of father and daughter together before his long journey. Leni felt his sadness, as well as her own. Glancing across the river toward the stone bridge that led into town, she dreaded the sight. Its path would bring them to the Bahnhof (train station) in the center of Fürth, where they would have to say good-bye.

By late morning, after Anya succeeded in snapping a picture with Demetri and other family and friends, Kreon hugged those staying behind, and headed for the bridge with Anya, Leni, Rosa, Urgroßvater and a handful of aunts and uncles in tow. Various cousins and Demetri remained behind with Urgroßmutter, too wrapped up in their play at their young age to be caught up in their Onkel Kreon's exodus. Anya's father was the only family member who was completely absent. Oswald had seldom been seen since her parents' divorce. Brief and awkward encounters in town served as their only connection.

As Kreon's departure neared, Leni's chin began to quiver. He was at the head of the procession into town, and, by everyone's expression, Leni sensed the heaviness of the occasion despite everyone trying to be cheerful. They were aware Kreon would not return, not for a long while. They would have to travel to America if they wanted to see him again. Anya, noting Leni's sad face, encouraged her to "be brave", but Leni was not sure what being "brave" meant. All she wanted to do was cry.

As they continued traipsing into town, Leni's slight arms were laden with wildflowers to be presented to her father before he boarded the train. Carrying the bouquet with utmost care, she felt her hands and shoulders begin to tremble. She tugged at her mother's arm.

"Mama," she asked plaintively, "Where is Papa going again?"

"We've already told you, dear. He's returning to America."

"But where is that?"

"We showed you where on Papa's map."

"I forgot."

Anya squeezed Leni's hand to calm her, but Anya's voice sounded sorrowful as she did so.

"Far away, Leni. Papa is going far away."

"Why is he leaving, if it makes you cry?"

"Don't ask so many questions, right now. Run ahead to your Papa."

The bustling Bahnhoff was impressive: people scurried every which way, waving, kissing, and crying; locomotives lingered on tracks as great puffs of steam hissed in the air; and conductors announced arrivals and departures in voluble voices. Leni listened as whistles blew and trains chuffed in and out of the cavernous station. Gazing up at her father, and nudged by her mother, she handed him the flowers. Her eyes grew wide and luminous as tears gathered. One would have thought, noticing the tyke, that some cruel person had thrown her favorite teddy-bear onto the tracks, and it could not be retrieved. Her father, watching her with concern, bent down to kiss his daughter's wet cheek.

"Why are you leaving, again, Papa?"

He studied her and placed her small hand in his. "Mama and I already told you," He reminded her kindly.

"I forgot."

Picking her up, Kreon hugged her to him.

"Because I love you and want to make a good life for my little girl, your brother, and your Mama."

Leni was confused. *People leave you when they love you? Didn't he want to be here with us instead?*

"When will you come back, Papa?"

"I will see you soon. Do not worry."

Leni could not recall the rest of the day. It remained a blur. One moment, her Papa was surrounded by everyone hugging and kissing him; the next moment he was gone. As the train pulled away, she waved and waved, until there was no need to wave anymore.

That night, mother and daughter returned to their garret apartment. They both hated returning there. They hated the stillness. It would only be the two of them again at Mathildenstrasse. They hated the loneliness that the absence of a husband and a father brought. They hated feeling vulnerable and scared. As Anya held her child in her arms, Leni caught their image in the small mirror over the kitchen sink.

Anya was crying copious tears as she clung to her child.

The bewildered child patted her mother's cheek.

"Don't cry, Mama. Don't cry."

As the summer faded, Anya enrolled Leni in the local nursery school run by the nuns in a church hall. It offered games and singing.

"It will be fun. Wouldn't you like that?" her mother asked, but Leni was not keen on going and shrugged. Anya cajoled her into it.

At school, the pious nuns, keen on propriety and piety, intimidated Leni. Their black and white regalia was always ready to swoop down on her for the slightest misdeed. To add to her misery, several children taunted her with, "Where is your father, Mischling?

Do you even have one?"

"My father is in America! And I have a coloring book and Kray-oh-lahs from my Papa! And a pretty dress! Do you?" she would shout.

The great plumes would then descend upon her with admonishing squawks, and she would close her eyes and think hard about the coming weekend. Her Papa would be with her then. Well, not really. But she prayed hard to wish him there. He would not make her go to this awful school!

Leni's prayers had results. Anya withdrew her from nursery school within two weeks. Notice of an infestation of head lice among several students, and Leni's daily grousing and pouting, led to Anya's decision.

CHAPTER SEVENTY-FIVE

While Leni played happily at home once again, Anya's pacing around the apartment increased. The addition of her son to the Kalanis family, she discovered, necessitated the submission of extra paperwork to the American Consulate. When matters finally progressed, Anya was requested to come with her children to the American Consulate in Munich for their medical examinations. After an arduous railway journey with her children and Rosa in tow, she was dismayed to be told Demetri had not passed the examination, and his visa was, therefore, deterred. Demetri, felled by the chicken pox weeks earlier, had a residual pock mark still visible on his body. As a result, they were sent back to Fürth minus approval for him to travel to America. The Consulate informed Anya that Demetri was to be "Pocken-frei" (pock-free) before she could reapply for his visa.

Dispirited and cradling Demetri in her arms while Rosa led Leni by the hand, Anya was on the verge of screaming as they lumbered back to the train station for the long trip home. Arriving late that evening, they walked from the Bahnhof to Marienstrasse, not having the energy to venture further. Exhausted, the two women carried the children upstairs, placed Demetri in his basket, changed into nightgowns, and fell across the bed. A drowsy Leni lay between them, glad to be under warm covers.

Sitting in the Bermann kitchen the next afternoon, a frustrated

Anya raised her voice by three octaves, as she relayed the dismal outcome of the previous day.

"One little pock mark and they refuse to let us go! I cannot believe it! Verdammt! I wonder if we will ever get the chance to go to America?"

Rosa and Babette sat there and let her fume. They wanted to comfort her and offer a hug, but she looked so fierce, they feared for themselves.

When her outburst was spent, Anya sank into the nearest chair. Placing her head in her hands, she looked as forlorn as a child who has been told that Saint Nicholas and the Easter Rabbit are just figments of her imagination. An unconcerned Demetri lay curled in the wash-basket beside her, taking a nap, blameless as could be.

Watching him, Anya sighed, "How lucky he is to be of an age where you can be oblivious to all this. I wish I could be that carefree. What is it going to take for us to get to America?" she asked Rosa, hoping her mother would say something to soothe her turmoil.

"You know the answer," Rosa stated, "A sponsor, a steady job, lots of paperwork, a bit of money and medical clearance. You and Kreon have managed the first four; the last one will come too."

"I miss my husband," Anya cried, dejected at the thought of facing more roadblocks, "We have been separated so much."

Rosa patted her distraught daughter's hand.

"I know. Stay strong. You will make it through this. The American Consulate simply does not want to risk letting any disease, especially an infectious one, enter their country."

"I understand, Mama. But it was *one* dried up little pock mark. *One* little pock mark has delayed all our plans!"

Rosa ventured another reassuring pat on Anya's hand, hoping her daughter would calm down. As she did so, both she and Anya became aware of Babette twitching in her chair.

"Why do you want to go to America of all places?" Babette asked, "I saw pictures. There are wild Indians and only huts to live in. What kind of life is that for you?"

Rosa and Anya looked at Babette as if a turnip had grown out of her ear.

"What?" Rosa remarked, taken aback by her mother's assertion, "Where did you get that idea?"

"From a book Kreon showed us," Babette explained, feeling a bit discomfited as they continued staring at her.

"That was a history book!" Rosa chided. "Cowboys, huts and Indians existed over 100 years ago in America. Not now!"

"Well, I thought...." started Babette looking flustered. She had never studied America much. Her homeland and family were all she had time for.

"America is very much like this country," Anya corrected, "Just much, much bigger, with taller buildings and more jobs. Kreon is doing well there."

"I know he is doing well! That is good!" Babette retorted, embarrassed by her lack of knowledge. Observing Anya's sad face, she softened her tone.

"I have an idea, if you want to listen," she said to her tempestuous granddaughter.

Anya and Rosa perked up their ears. If the matriarch of their family had an idea, it must be respected. The three stared at her in anticipation.

"Why not go over to visit America with Leni first, since you both have been cleared for travel. Stay awhile. See if you like it. Leave Demetri here with us. You know we will take good care of him. Then, if all is to your liking, you can return and take him and your belongings with you. He should be well enough to receive his clearance from the American Consulate by the time you return."

Anya and Rosa looked at each other. It was a feasible plan and it made sense. Why not?

"Kreon is working at a steady job," Babette continued, "He is making good money. He could repay any loan needed to make the trip, could he not?"

The three women, with a quizzical Leni in their midst, stared at each other for a few moments without uttering a sound. Then Anya sprang into action and asked her grandmother for pen and paper. She wanted to write to Kreon immediately!

CHAPTER SEVENTY-SIX

By late fall of 1950, Anya's decision to visit America with Leni reached fruition. Kreon sent the required money for tickets, and their ocean voyage was scheduled for the end of December. They would leave from Bremerhaven on a freighter called the *George Washington*. Their fare was reasonable, but the purchase was not as good a decision as Anya thought. Crossing the Atlantic in winter was a challenge she had not completely fathomed: a freighter was lighter than an ocean liner, and the seas were rough in winter. However, the tickets were affordable, so she ploughed ahead.

At their leave-taking shortly after Christmas, Leni never let go of her mother's hand. Anya realized it was the only gesture that made her four-year-old daughter feel safe and secure. She, herself, wished she could hold someone's hand as they embarked on this strange, new adventure. They were going to see America! Kreon would be waiting!

Needing to leave Demetri behind was heartbreaking, but Anya was consoled knowing he would be safely nestled in his grandmother's arms and great-grandmother's ample lap. He also seemed quite nonchalant about their going. With two ladies-in-waiting and a great-grandfather, aunts, uncles, and cousins surrounding him daily, they would be missed like two eggs in a fertile chicken coop. *No great worries about him*, Anya guessed. Yet, this sense of solace did not stop her from crying profusely when she hugged him goodbye.

Holding Demetri, she brushed back his silky hair as he gave her a lop-sided smile. He smelled of baby powder and she could not stop kissing his ruddy little cheeks, as his chubby fingers tried to grab onto her face.

Oh God, what am I doing? How can I leave my baby boy behind?

"Come," Rosa said, taking Demetri from Anya's arms, "You will be back before you know it. Seeing America first is a good decision."

Anya stood up, took a deep breath, and nodded her head.

"This is so hard, Mama."

"I know. Try not to dwell on it. Demetri will be kept busy and well-taken care of."

As Anya wiped at her eyes and gathered her bags, Leni moved toward her brother and gave Demetri a generous peck on the cheek as he squirmed in his grandmother's arms. Leni wondered if her little brother understood what was happening. With so many relatives around him, she doubted he would miss them or even know they were gone. The thought made her sulk. She wanted to be missed by her brother.

"Come, Leni, we are ready to go," her mother told her. Leni held Demetri's hand one more time.

As they bundled up in their coats, Rosa handed her granddaughter a small cardboard suitcase in which was packed a "Sand Kuchen", a delicious pound cake she had baked.

"It is one of your favorites. You can eat it on your trip," Rosa told her.

Leni beamed, "Danke, Oma."

Indeed, it was a favorite treat of Leni's, and she was already savoring it. Her mother smiled, noting that German pastry seemed to comfort the girl through many a trial in her young life. Although the Sand Kuchen came with instructions to enjoy it on the trip over, Leni decided to save it and share it with her Papa in America. After accepting the gift, a profusion of heartfelt, good-bye hugs followed. Leni, melting into the warmth of her grandmother's arms, started to sob. She did not want to let go. Nor did Rosa.

After many reassurances of "We will be back soon!" at the Bahnhof in Fürth, Anya boarded the train with her daughter, and they seated themselves near a window and waved. Handkerchiefs were fluttered in return and kisses blown, as the locomotive pulled out of the station enroute to the port city of Bremerhaven in the north of Germany.

Arriving by nightfall, mother and daughter slept in barrack-like quarters provided for seafaring passengers. In the early morning, the freighter *George Washington*, awaited them.

While people shuffled here and there on both pier and ship, Anya and Leni scurried up the gangplank onto the main deck of the freighter. Leni clasped her mother's hand as if it were a life-raft. It was an unsteady life-raft at best, for Anya's hand was quivering too. The commotion aboard the freighter was overwhelming. Seeing their angst, a ship steward came to their aid. Looking over their ticket information, he led the way, all the while speaking in German to Anya's relief.

Guided down clanging, metal steps and along nondescript corridors, they came to a stop as the steward pointed out and unlocked the door to their modest stateroom. Anya, gazing out of its porthole, was disturbed to discover their quarters were barely above sea level. The steward assured them their room was secure, while a porter knocked on their door delivering their essential suitcases. He informed Anya that her sizeable trunk was stored in the ship's hold for safekeeping.

"Danke for your help," she said, opening her purse with shaky fingers to hand each man a customary tip.

"You are welcome," they each replied in her native tongue, bestowing her with a gracious bow before exiting.

Sensing Anya's nervousness, the steward added, "If you would like, I can return in a short while to guide you back to the deck to see the ship depart, in case you have forgotten the way."

"Thank you, you are very kind, but I think we can manage."

"I will be on deck if you require further assistance, Frau Kalanis. Have a good day." He bowed again, and she smiled in return, feeling a bit reassured. Leni, meanwhile, leaped on the nearest bed, testing its bounce-ability.

After the steward closed the door, and her daughter was reprimanded, Anya rummaged through the suitcases and put away their needed clothes. The room contained a bunk bed, a round table with two chairs, a built-in closet, a chest of drawers, and a miniscule shower/bathroom in which to tidy up.

Listening to the ruckus outside, Leni asked cautiously, "Can we go upstairs and watch the ship sail away? Please, Mama."

"Yes, just let me get this finished. They won't sail until everyone is on board."

"Well, I hope they hurry!"

Apparently, my daughter is feeling more confident too, Anya noted, now that they were settled in.

When they clattered back up the stairs, trying not to lose their way among the hoard of passengers and porters with suitcases trouncing about, they covered their heads with woolen scarves to ward off the winter chill nipping at their ears. The freighter's mooring was unfastened, and the ship began to inch out toward the vast ocean. Watching the woeful faces on the dock, tears streaming down their faces as they waved a last goodbye, Anya's heart winced thinking of the people she had left behind. She would have to leave them behind forever if the decision became a permanent one. *Would the separation be worth the sorrow?* She had no answer to her question.

Anya shortly discovered crossing the Atlantic on a freighter during winter was more of a nightmare than a dream. Within hours she turned a moldy green and upchucked breakfast, lunch, and dinner in the days that followed. This necessitated Leni being watched over by willing passengers and crew members during Anya's days of misery. Leni, fearful of venturing beyond their cabin, often refused to leave her mother's side. She would rather stay with her sick mother than not see her at all; and she did not like being with strangers.

One night the turbulent sea proved just as cataclysmic for Leni. While sleeping in the upper bunk, which she had begged her mother to do instead of sharing the lower one, the ship heaved and hoed with such gusto that Leni was catapulted onto the table and chairs below then hurtled to the floor. Her mother's scream startled her awake, and Leni screeched in return.

"Are you alright? Oh my God! Try to stay still until Mama can check you over."

Anya picked her squealing daughter up gingerly to prevent any further injury and sat her on the lower bed.

Fortunately, having been in a deep sleep with her body totally relaxed, nothing was broken. Minor bruises, however, were expected to appear after her unbridled flight to the floor. Scooping Leni up and calming her sobs, Anya, and the steward who came to their aid after hearing the commotion, assessed the situation. He placed a willing Leni back in the top bunk, but this time with a guardrail in place. Anya, during the interim, ran to the bathroom to do battle with her stomach.

Two afternoons later, with Anya weak and wan, a sympathetic lady from across the hall escorted Leni to the children's shipboard Christmas party. Members of the crew, dressed as Santa and his elves, handed out a toy, baked goodies, and chocolates for each child to relish. Leni was gifted with a stuffed elephant made of red oilcloth. It was quite unique and one of the nicest presents to be had. Beholding her gift with awe, Leni assumed she received the special prize for being airborne in the middle of the night.

Several days afterward, the *George Washington* slipped into New York Harbor in time to celebrate the New Year (1951) in a new land. Leni and a thankful Anya could not contain their excitement as they stood on the ship's deck and watched it glide into New York Harbor. The tall buildings left them breathless. And the sight of the Statue of Liberty, which Kreon had described so eloquently in his letters, filled them with reverence. Anya, looking forward to the steadiness of land under her feet, searched for Kreon's face amid the waiting crowd at the dock. He was there.

When the ship docked, it took a while before they were permitted to disembark; Anya knew it would be worth the wait. As soon as clearance was given, the passengers strode down the gangway and filled the massive Custom House that was bursting with personnel, luggage, carriers, and family waiting to greet them. Anya sighed with relief when she set foot on solid American soil. Within a short time, the new arrivals lined up at the gates, had their paperwork scrutinized, and were thrust into their new world.

Then the blessed moment arrived.

"Papa!" Leni yelled as she spotted her father. Running through the throng, with her mother yelling after her, she soared into his waiting arms. A blissful Anya, weaving her way through, floated into them. Husband and wife, father and daughter were together again. All that was missing was Demetri.

A porter wasted no time in aiding them with their luggage, (informing them that their trunk would be forwarded to their home by the next day) and hailed one of the taxis waiting outside to take them to their destination. Kreon gave the driver the address of the residence where he lived in Queens, a borough across New York City's East River. As they pulled away from the shipyard and into the streets, mother and daughter were astounded by the sights that greeted them along the way.

"Kreon, how many people live in New York City?" Anya asked, aghast at the crowds and towering buildings flanking them on each side as they gazed out the taxi's windows.

"Millions, Anya. What you see are mainly high-rise apartments and office buildings for the well-to-do. As we leave the city, you will see more normal-sized buildings and homes."

Kreon was right. Anya was glad to see patches of grass and a park here and there as the cab driver brought them to the place Kreon rented and called home. The "apartment" was a miniscule, finished basement in a lovely two-story house that featured a narrow garden out back. It contained a double bed, a cot for Leni, a bathroom, small table, and a hotplate and undersized refrigerator for cooking. The owners were Greek.

Anya contemplated her new domain.

"I am to cook on this?" she exclaimed, pointing to the hotplate.

Kreon smiled, "Only to warm up food or your tea. The landlady said you are welcome to use the kitchen upstairs whenever necessary."

"Whenever necessary? What about when she is using it?"

"I guess you will have to work that out with Mrs. Syros. She is easy to get along with, Anya, as is her husband and young boy. I usually ate out or made sandwiches for myself. I did not cook often. Mrs. Syros was kind enough to bring me a plate with extra helpings whenever she cooked a big meal. It would last me for days. I have the feeling she will try to fatten you and Leni up too."

Kreon's smile was infectious, and Anya noticed his face and stomach were fuller since leaving Germany.

"Now come, let's take a walk around the neighborhood and eat dinner in a proper restaurant!"

He pulled both of his girls into his arms and off they trotted.

CHAPTER SEVENTY-SEVEN

Anya adjusted to the constraints of their living quarters, being informed by Kreon that if she conceded to moving permanently to America, finding a larger apartment would be the first order of business.

Their landlord and landlady, Mr. and Mrs. Syros, proved pleasant to be around and were helpful in getting Anya and Leni settled in. The two ladies often found themselves cooking meals together and sharing both kitchen and dining room to feed their families. The only thing Anya could not abide was the putrid smell of octopus being cooked whenever Mrs. Syros decided to prepare one for supper. Anya would then beg Kreon to take them for a hamburger and a long walk to allow their living quarters to be aired out.

Leni too was often invited to come upstairs and play with their son, Georgie. He often strewed his toys around in their sizeable living room or throughout the garden.

At first, Leni enjoyed the visits, amazed by the many toys the boy owned; but after a while she balked at joining him.

"Don't you like playing with Georgie?" Anya asked, seeing her daughter sit listlessly on her cot.

"Not really," Leni replied. "He doesn't share. And he keeps pushing me away when his mama isn't looking." As she spoke the words, her eyes welled up.

Anya sat next to her daughter and put her arms around her, "Tell

Mama what's really bothering you."

"He's not fun like my cousins. I miss everyone at home. And I miss my brother. I miss Demetri!"

At the sound of his name on her tongue, Leni broke into tears.

"Now, now," her mother crooned while hugging her tight, "I miss your little brother and everyone too. Very, very much."

In fact, there had been nights when Anya worried about being so far from her son and cried silently into her pillow while her husband and daughter slept.

"But we came to America to see your Papa and see if we liked it here. Give Papa a chance to show us America while we are visiting. Maybe it is a place we will grow to love. Okay?"

Leni wiped her nose on the back of her hand, while her mother produced a handkerchief to clean it up and dry her tears, "Okay."

"Now," Anya proposed, "should we go for an American ice cream cone?"

During that spring and summer, Anya and Kreon kept Leni active, especially on the weekends. Kreon introduced his family to his friends at his workplace, and they often received invitations to their homes to meet their family. There were also outings into New York City (Rockefeller Center and Central Park being Leni's favorites); ferry rides to Staten Island (where seeing the lights come on at dusk throughout the city was especially enthralling); having fun strolling the boardwalk at Coney Island; and laughing at the animals in the Bronx Zoo. What impressed Anya most were the American supermarkets.

"Good Lord, so much food and so many choices! How do they manage to sell it all? One supermarket could feed half of Germany!" she joked, as her eyes tried to take it all in. Kreon was delighted at her and Leni's amazed response to everything they viewed.

With Kreon's respectable income and progress on his job, the girls were also doing serious shopping and wearing finer clothes. Leni was soon the proud owner of an American cowgirl outfit replete with toy gun and hat. By late spring, she was whipping along the streets on her first tricycle, compliments of her father's generosity. Anya warned her husband not to spoil the child, but Kreon just laughed seeing the joy he brought to his young daughter. Leni, he knew, would remain well-behaved; he and Anya would ensure that. Life was busy and good. All the activity kept homesickness at bay for a while, but as summer neared its end, they could no longer ignore what was piercing their hearts.

Kreon recognized the wistful glances they tried to hide when they received a picture of Demetri in the mail, as he felt their pangs too. He had not seen his son in almost a year. That night, after Leni was put to bed, Kreon sat his wife down.

"I think it is time for you and Leni to return to Germany for now, Anya. I am hoping by next spring we can make a final decision. I am earning good money here. But if you feel you and the children will not be happy in America, we must decide what our next step will be. We cannot go on like this."

Anya sadly agreed.

By late summer of that year, 1951, she and Leni boarded the *S.S. Rotterdam*, a Dutch ocean liner, and set off on their return journey to Fürth. Leni's cardboard suitcase was packed with little gifts for her cousins, mainly packages of gum; and Kreon had tied a giant, swirled lollipop on it for her brother. The lollipop was the size of Demetri's head.

Leaving Kreon again was torturous for all three. As wife and child waved good-bye to him from the ship's railing, he looked so forsaken in the crowd of faces, it made them cry. He mirrored their feelings.

"I am getting weary of always parting," he told Anya the night before her return journey, as he watched their daughter sleep.

"As am I, Kreon, as am I," she confessed, holding him tight.

They returned to their bed one last time.

CHAPTER SEVENTY-EIGHT

Voyaging out to the Atlantic that day, the sheer size of the ship enticed Anya and Leni to explore it. It was majestic and quite regal compared to the freighter that had transported them to America. Kreon was able to procure better accommodations this time. Anya dubbed it "a splendid city on water" with people milling about in nice clothes, stewards in sharp white uniforms, shops and restaurants at its center, and a swimming pool on its upper deck. Their cabin was far more comfortable too. Anya was especially pleased: good weather and the sturdiness of the ship was guaranteed to make their journey smoother this time. As a precautionary measure, she carried motion sickness pills and a few crackers in her purse, but prayed she would have no need of them.

Their days at sea were bestowed with sparkling waters, turquoise blue skies, and the wondrous sight of porpoises flipping through the air. Passengers were also treated to several American movies in the onboard theater. The first starred Jerry Lewis and Dean Martin. Having learned some English, Anya and Leni thought the movie quite funny. But it left Leni wondering if all American men were that silly. Her Papa, she decided, was certainly not.

Arriving back in Fürth less than two weeks later, they were met with an exuberant response to their homecoming. High-spirited hugs and kisses were plentiful. Both mother and daughter squashed Demetri in their arms until his stream of giggles transformed into impatient squirms.

Leni's tricycle arrived with her, and her cousins begged for a ride. Her brother received his own pint-sized tricycle but was not yet ready to pedal it down the street.

"It's fun to be home again, Mama!" Leni professed, glowing with joy over the reunion. Anya smiled but felt encumbered as she surveyed the jubilance around her. Her decision, she realized, would impact so many lives.

A few days after their arrival, the burden on her shoulders growing ever heavier, Anya asked her mother to take a walk with her in the surrounding countryside. Packing sandwiches and a bottle of lemonade for them to share, they ventured out into the woods. The weather, blessedly, was temperate and relaxing.

After a few minutes of strolling in quiet reflection amid the fields and trees, Rosa glanced at her daughter's face. Surprisingly, Anya no longer looked perturbed. The struggle in her daughter's mind seemed to be over.

"You have decided to leave, haven't you?" Rosa asked, saddened by the thought.

"Yes," Anya replied, looking off into the distance as if she could already see her future.

"With a whole heart?" her mother inquired in a forthright manner.

Anya turned toward Rosa and paused, "I think it would be nice if we spread our blanket and sat in the shade of that tree for a while, don't you?" pointing to the edge of the forest.

They did as Anya suggested, and each took a refreshing drink from the bottle they shared between them. Their mouths were dry, and there would be much to discuss.

"Mama," Anya began, "you know more than anyone how it pains me to leave my family; but if I'm to build a life with Kreon and our children, I have to go. I will miss my German life and everyone in it. I will miss the beauty of my homeland. Part of me will be left behind forever when I leave. But I will not miss the bad memories, nor the poverty, nor the sickness that destroyed our country and nearly our sanity all those years. It is time for a fresh start. I wish it could be here. But it cannot. My husband wants us to start a new life in America."

"What about your wants?" Rosa asked.

Anya turned her head away, gazing out over the land, and did not answer.

Rosa drew a deep breath and patted her daughter's hand, as she too gazed across the field.

"I will not lie and say I am happy with your decision, but I will not interfere in the decision you have made. I understand it."

"Thank you, Mama," Anya said with deep emotion.

"You are not my little girl anymore. You belong with your husband. Kreon has sacrificed so much for you, and you must do the same for him and your children. It will take several more years for Germany to rebuild itself. With Kreon settled in a good job, he can finally offer you the stability you crave. You have never known it while you were growing up." Rosa looked at her daughter with pangs of regret.

"Oh Mama, do not say that! You were always there, as was our family. You were my shields, my posts to hold on to when the terrible war and the Nazis swept around us. I could never have survived without you! You taught me how to be strong," Anya emphasized as she gripped her mother's hand. The love in that moment was bittersweet, and they embraced fiercely before letting go.

"I will visit you someday, my darling girl. And no doubt your adventurous cousins might follow your lead. You will not be rid of us that easily!" Rosa proclaimed with a heartrending smile on her face.

"I will expect no less of you or them, Mama. And my arms and door will forever be open."

Soon thereafter, on a sunny and hopeful day, Anya, and Rosa, with Leni and Demetri in tow, trudged again to the American Consulate in Munich. A precocious Leni was aware her mother had made a final decision. She knew they were to live in America forever. Mama had explained it all to her: Papa had a good job, America offered a better life, Mama wanted them to be a family. What Anya had not mentioned to anyone but Rosa, was her desire to get away from the memories of the war. With things still unstable in Europe, thoughts of another government taking over, another political struggle or upheaval shredding her world, troubled Anya often. She wished her family to be safe, thus she started packing.

In April of 1952, Anya with Demetri, age three, and Leni, nearly six, prepared to leave their hometown of Fürth and head north to board the *S.S Italia* for the United States of America. Anya finally had their passports and visas in hand

CHAPTER SEVENTY-NINE

How does one say a final "Good-bye"? It was something Anya had never done before and prayed she would never have to do again. Leaving people and the places she loved, not knowing when or if she would see them again, was heart-stopping. She drew in deep breaths of air, hoping the sadness would not suffocate her. A sharp pain in her heart threatened to tear it asunder.

Many dear people embraced her at the train station, unsure of a future reunion. Because of their age, Urgroßmutter and Urgroßvater were the most disconsolate of all. As the elders hugged the little group of three good-bye, it was a hug for the ages.

When it came time for Rosa and Anya to part, mother and daughter clasped each other with fervent promises of future visits, "if God is willing." Then Rosa pushed Anya and the bewildered children toward their train before an avalanche of emotion engulfed them. They boarded in haste and waved a final farewell from their compartment window.

With an unknown future hovering over them, Anya and her children made their way to the shipyards of northern Germany. That night they slept in the familiar barracks designated for overseas passengers. The children curled in their mother's bed, foregoing their own, and remained silent.

The next morning, after a sparse breakfast (for they had little appetite), the three took a walk along the lengthy dock to view the ship that would carry them to America. Gazing up at the mammoth hulk, mother, and daughter, along with little Demetri, sensed the enormity of what they were doing. As the dark waters surrounding the harbor lapped noisily against the immense ocean liner, it caused mother and daughter to experience panic for the first time, as well as an uncommon vertigo. Seeing Leni weave, Anya grabbed her hand and held her tight. Demetri tugged at his mother's skirt and would not let go. They were departing for good. Surrounded by fellow immigrants, Anya guided her children up the gangplank. Once all passengers and staff were accounted for, the ship was steered out of the harbor toward the open sea. Everything familiar was drifting away from them, and their sadness pierced sharply.

On board, everything was still in chaos. Fellow passengers scurried up and down the decks while suitcases were delivered by porters to cabins all over the ship. People called aloud for help at every corner, either needing directions or searching for misplaced luggage. Demetri stared, befuddled by the massive disorder.

"Where are our big boxes?" he asked in confusion.

Anya explained that their steamer trunks were in the hold, which Leni, the 'seasoned' traveler explained was in the belly of the ship. Demetri wondered where the belly was on such a big boat. Leni did not have time to answer, as the crowd jostled them about. Brother and sister held as firmly as they could to their spot in the main corridor, reluctant to move for fear of being swallowed up by the throng. Their mother's hands clasped theirs, and their hands gripped back.

The dramatic parting of the past few days soon left its mark. Falling into a deep sleep that first night on the ship, Leni drifted into the menacing arms of what would become a recurrent nightmare. She explained her nighttime shrieks to her mother the next day.

Between nervous gulps, she revealed, "I was standing near a giant ocean. The waves were coming closer and closer. Then they grew higher and higher. In the end, they were fearsome and crashed all around me!"

Leni had screamed "Mama! Mama!" at that point and woken up her mother and made her baby brother cry. Anya had calmed them both and cradled each until they fell asleep again. She, herself, was frazzled and fell into bed overcome with exhaustion. Sleep engulfed them all within moments.

At the break of morning, they found the ship clipping across the sea through sparkling and frothy waters. Mama helped dress them in preparation for breakfast in the vast dining room, which left them goggle-eyed. It was luxury beyond what they were accustomed to. Every tabletop was swathed in a white linen tablecloth and adorned with spotless, white china plates and gleaming silverware and a delicate vase of flowers. Leni felt like a princess when they were guided to their seats. Within minutes their plates were laden with eggs, bacon and "cross-ants" as Demetri dubbed them, and jam, and a pile of delectable pancakes, and fruit. The aromas were tantalizing, and they dined on this feast with relish. The children watched their mother sip English tea (instead of coffee, which Anya's stomach disapproved of) from an elegant cup and mimicked her refined movements with their sturdy mugs of hot chocolate.

With bellies filled to bursting, the satisfied diners agreed to take a long stroll around the ship's upper deck. The weather was glorious, and, as the ocean liner maintained a steady course, they basked in the sun and breathed in the briny sea air. It did much for their disposition by freeing their hearts and heads of the tangled cobwebs inside.

In mid-stroll, Leni and Demetri spotted dolphins skimming through the pristine water, then jumping in and out of the frothy waves. They rushed toward the railing to view the incredible antics of these sea mammals, while their Mama pointed and shouted, "Look! They are jumping again!" Leni and Demetri whooped with delight.

Three hours passed before they returned to their cabin to have a brief rest before lunch and then, much later, the evening's dinner. Their stateroom was a decent size and they moved about it freely.

The room had a bunkbed on each side, a table and four chairs in one corner, and a closet and bureau for their clothes. An adequate bathroom adjoined it. There was also a round porthole from which Demetri and Leni could view a smidgeon of ocean and sky if they stood on a chair and stretched their short legs.

From day one, Demetri decided he wanted to sleep in one of the upper bunkbeds, and Leni was not about to dissuade him. She was quite content to snooze in the lower one across from Mama, so as not to repeat the accident she suffered on the *George Washington* freighter. She watched as her mother fastened the guardrail along Demetri's bed before he went to sleep. This time there would be no rude awakenings in the middle of the night. Demetri never tumbled off.

The one thing the children could not get used to on the ocean liner was its interior maze of hallways. They led from one staircase to another to another to another until they did not know where they were nor which way to turn. Leni made sure she and Demetri did not lose sight of their mother, for she was certain the hallways would lead them astray and they would never be found nor heard from again.

To the Captain's credit, and Mother Nature's benevolence, the voyage proceeded without incident and lasted a little more than a week. Meanwhile Demetri and Leni had the opportunity to meet and play with other children on board and settled into the *S.S. Italia*'s daily routine without a fuss. The refreshing sea breezes braced the travelers, and the sun warmed everyone's spirit as they scurried around the ship. The huge vessel, the passengers were informed, was only four years old; and they marveled at its modern features which included a lounge, sundecks, library, shops, a movie theater, a beauty salon, and huge indoor and outdoor swimming pools. It was impressive and beyond Anya's expectations. Kreon, she guessed correctly, had ensured they would be comfortable on the trip over and lack for nothing. Anya surmised he had scrimped and saved as much as he could for their tickets.

"Mama, will we have a swimming pool in America?" Leni asked.

Anya chuckled, "Not right away. Someday maybe. Who knows what America and your father have in store for us!"

The thought of Papa was heartening. Despite all the on-board activity, sharp pangs of homesickness befell them at unexpected times, and they resulted in the onset of sniffles again. Anya tried hard to be discreet about her own tears and, of course, her worries. She made a marked attempt to keep them focused on the prize at the end of their journey: They would see their father again, and she would have her husband back.

CHAPTER EIGHTY

W e're here!"
Such simple words for such a momentous occasion:
May 7, 1952.

An elated Leni uttered them with glee as the *S.S. Italia* glided into New York Harbor. Anya, overcome with emotion, pulled her children close to her. They were situated on a bench with other passengers at the stern of the boat, their legs covered with woolen blankets to ward off the morning chill. Leni could not contain her excitement, while Demetri sat still, a bit overwhelmed by it all.

Realizing they were edging into port and disembarking within the hour, the passengers were brimming with anticipation. Most cheered boundlessly as tugboats directed the ship into the harbor, while others viewed the city before them with flutters of anxiety and disquiet.

The sky and sun, pale in color on this day, cast faint sparkles on the grey water while light sprays of seawater and the teeming smells and noise of the city surrounded them. Within moments the lead tugboats emitted a loud toot, signaling that the *S.S. Italia* had circumvented the lapping swells of the Hudson River and was nearing its destination.

Noting this, Leni grabbed the startled Demetri by the hand and shouted "Komm! Komm!", as they burst from their Mama's embrace and raced toward the front railings. Anya yelled for them to slow down and wait for her, but, in the grips of Leni's exuberance, they did not follow orders. Holding onto her brother with one hand, Leni swept the air with the other.

"Demetri, look! That is the Statue of Liberty we are passing! And over there in the city is the Empire State Building, the tallest building ever!"

She pointed toward the city's skyline, playing the part of the know-it-all elder sister. Demetri's gaze lurched up and a look of both awe and confusion streaked across his face. Leni recognized that look. She and her Mama had it once too. Demetri was wondering what they were doing in this place. He kept staring as if looking for his great-grandparents' house.

As her offspring stood at the railing beguiled by the view in their own separate ways, Anya began photographing them with the camera Kreon had sent her in his Easter package. Noticing her, the children smiled dutifully into the lens, then turned to wave at the people on shore. Demetri copied Leni's movements, although with less enthusiasm.

"Wave harder!" she shouted, "Maybe Papa can see us!"

They were dressed in their best for him. It was important to look their smartest, Mama had counselled, so he would be proud of them when they arrived. Leni was clothed in a blue velvet coat with white fur trim and matching bonnet. Demetri was in a plaid, woolen jacket that had been sent from America, a woolen cap that had a brim, and corduroy pants that were a bit long, but which he could grow into. Mama was clothed in a long, blue coat with a velvet collar. Today it protected her from the blustery currents of the wind, as the sun tried to peek through. Kreon was waiting at the dock. It was three days after his birthday, and he was getting the best present of all. Or so Anya assumed as they prepared to go ashore.

CHAPTER EIGHTY-ONE

A miracle occurred when they stepped onto U.S. soil and rushed into the waiting arms of husband and father, respectively: Mr. and Mrs. Kreon Kalanis, along with their two young children, Leni, and Demetri Kalanis, became a full-fledged family in America. It appeared to be a fairy tale ending.

Despite appearances, Kreon and Anya were wise enough to know that life was not a fairy tale. Life, they had learned, was much like a kaleidoscope. With each twist and turn it rearranges its colors and patterns, and often surprises you. They knew that their future would bring new challenges. Their current elation, however, would not let them dwell on what those challenges might be nor how difficult to overcome.

On the day of their arrival, the first struggle the family faced was ensuring that their names were spelled correctly on their paperwork. They did not want their baptismal names Anglicized, misspelled, shortened, or completely fractured as they shuffled through each checkpoint in the vast Customs Hall. The ship logs were filled out at each ship's point of departure by busy clerks notorious for incorrectly spelling passengers' names as they rushed. Kreon was vigilant in ensuring his family name remained intact. He would not allow his father's name, bestowed upon his son and future progeny, to be mutated into any other form.

In their new world, they chose to remain Kreon, Demetri, Anya, and Eleni Kalanis.

After their papers were examined, and their passports and visas stamped by Customs personnel, Kreon and Anya proceeded to claim the suitcases and steamer trunks that belonged to them. A friend of Kreon's was there to aid in transitioning the family to their temporary home base.

A drowsy Demetri and Leni, overcome by the commotion around them, tried to stay alert in the cab of their Papa's friend, a friend who proved to be a true humanitarian in Anya's mind. Mr. Perras helped pack up their belongings and transport them from the New York pier to the lone room their father temporarily rented in the Bronx. Carrying the suitcases and trunks up three flights of stairs was a Herculean effort on the part of both men. Anya, trailing behind with the children, hoped all Americans would be as generous in spirit as this man was.

Overwhelmed by the day's events and their new surroundings, mother, father, and children soon drifted off into a fitful sleep. Sister and brother slipped into bed with their Mama to cuddle. Their father slept on the small couch opposite the bed with his legs dangling over the edge. Anya chuckled inwardly when she realized Kreon had lost his penchant for sleeping on a floor and had opted for something semi-comfortable. Cramped was the only word for their present quarters. The next morning, they woke up in a semi-conscious state, scarfed down a breakfast of tea, jam and toast, and went off hunting for a permanent residence.

While traversing the Bronx and Queens via subway and bus, Demetri seemed perturbed by the discordant sights and sounds whirling around him.

"Why are there so many buildings and people? Will the cars run us over? Why are they honking so much?"

He did not like the noise and clamor and was stupefied by it. There were sizeable apartments in several tall buildings for the parents to examine, and the height of each building left him dumbstruck. As his father guided them through the maze, using his rudimentary English to help his family navigate it, Demetri could only stare at his surroundings all day and frown.

"Where are the trees and flowers?" he was desperate to know as cars whizzed by from every angle. "Where are the sheep kept? And the cows?"

Everything was built of stone, glass and concrete and it bewildered him.

"There are no sheep and cows," Leni told her inquisitive brother, sounding as if she was an expert on the subject.

The myriad cars that whooshed by them on the streets were predominately yellow and Demetri wondered why. Kreon explained they were taxis, vehicles people with extra money rode in. Someday, he promised, they would ride in one too. Leni assumed they did not have extra money, but wished they had because walking endlessly on concrete pavements hurt her feet.

It was a blessing when, near the end of the day and before Anya's and Demetri's childlike impatience erupted, their parents found an apartment they liked and could agree upon. After signing the lease and paying the contracted amount, the family returned to the rooming house in the Bronx where everyone collapsed in exhaustion. Anya rubbed her aching feet, and the children plopped on the couch, while Kreon poured glasses of Coca-Cola for them in celebration.

Within days, essential furniture was purchased, and the family settled into their new two-bedroom apartment on the top floor of a three-story complex in Queens. The rent was $85 a month, a moderate sum within their means. The children were relegated to the bedroom facing the main avenue, while Kreon and Anya took the bedroom to the rear. It had two windows, a closet, and a fire escape that faced the parking lot and playground out back.

Kreon and Anya soon discovered that the neighborhood they lived in consisted of a smattering of various ethnic groups. Around the corner was a small synagogue, but no Christian church was located nearby.

"Do you think we can find a Lutheran Church in the area?" Anya asked her husband, concerned about enrolling the children in eventual catechism classes and raising them in her faith (as was agreed upon).

"I have heard there's one not too far away," Kreon assured her, "We might have to walk to get to it though, until we purchase a car. I also heard a new church is being built closer to home, so do not worry yourself about this."

Peering out the front window as he spoke, Anya longed for her native countryside. All she saw before her were similar brick buildings separated by wide walkways that sprouted squares of brown grass and metal benches. She was pleased to realize their building was a better situated one. The area at the rear was bordered by residential homes with lovely, little gardens and blooming trees; a lone Eden amidst the asphalt that surrounded the other boulevards. Anya could see the houses from their living room window and dreamed of residing in one someday. Turning wistful, she knew it would be several years before they could make that dream come true. She and Kreon needed to earn and save as much as they could to achieve such a goal.

CHAPTER EIGHTY-TWO

Flushing, New York

May 10, 1952
Liebe Mama,

I hope my letter finds you and the family in the best of health. How is everyone? I miss you all! I so look forward to hearing from you! Please write soon and as often as you can. Kreon and the children miss you a great deal too!

Leni, Demetri, and I arrived safely after a smooth voyage over the Atlantic. We are in good spirits although still very tired and overwhelmed by our new surroundings. There has been much to do in the days since we set foot in America.

Kreon and I managed to find a decent apartment with two bedrooms in a nice neighborhood right away, and our new furniture will be delivered within the week. With the money Kreon saved, we have purchased a simple dining-set; twin beds and a dresser for the children's room; a bed, a dresser and wardrobe for our bedroom; and a couch and armchair for the living room; and, naturally, lamps for each room.

I cannot thank you enough for packing so many needed items in our trunks! The pots and pans, the utensils, the cups, the towels and washcloths and the blankets and the feather pillows have come in especially handy. Leni and Demetri helped me make beds out of the blankets and pillows as we are "camping" in the rooms until our furnishings arrive. We are presently using the trunks and suitcases as our dining table and chairs. The children consider it great fun and are being very imaginative with the rest! Pudding served in cups, or wearing a pot on their head, seems to be their favorite amusement. Tomorrow I will go shopping with Kreon for other needed items and more groceries. I still cannot believe we are with him again. The company he works for is doing well, and his job is secure and pays a good salary. We are blessed.

I do not allow myself to think too much of my life and family in Fürth, because when I do, a terrible wave of homesickness surges in my heart, and it does not serve me well. I must get on with my life in America and with my little family. We are finally together!

Mama, please stay well and write soon. Send my love to one and all. I am always with you in spirit. And tell Hannah I look forward to hearing about her third baby! Kreon sends good wishes too, and the children big hugs!

Your loving daughter,

Anya

CHAPTER EIGHTY-THREE

Anya stayed as busy as she could to keep her mind from drifting back to Germany. A used sewing machine had been quickly purchased, and her deft skills with thread, fabric, skeins of wool, knitting needles and a crochet hook soon helped her decorate their apartment as warmly as their pocketbook would allow. Curtains, pillows, bedspreads, and doilies were colorful additions to the rooms, thanks to Anya's talents.

As they settled into their new home, they were grateful to be a family again, although life in New York proved a major adjustment for all. Aware their move to America was considered permanent, the finality of it was distressing to Anya. A return trip to Germany would not be financially feasible for many years to come. This new life, Anya, and even Leni and Demetri, began to realize, was *it*. Like young horses led from the barn to the open range for the first time, she and the children were saddled with conflicting thoughts and emotions.

Kreon found their leap astonishing. Anya and the children had moved from bucolic surroundings to an energetic and frazzling city; they had left behind a huge family and become a minimal one; they had relinquished the familiar and stepped wholly out of their comfort zone into the unfamiliar. Giant leaps such as theirs, he knew, usually exacted a price. And the price soon became evident.

Demetri lost weight, Leni began sleepwalking, and Anya had

intense moments of homesickness. There was no telephone in their home yet, nor the ability to pay for trans-Atlantic calls. Letters that often took a week to ten days to reach their destination were their only connection to their family back home.

Kreon, of course, was relieved that they were with him; yet he had to make an adjustment too. Two young children scurrying about him each day was something he was not used to. Rules had to be established in his household, and his demeanor became stern to ensure his son and daughter remain civilized and not the rambunctious, wild cubs they showed signs of becoming.

Once the clamor of resettling had died down, manifestations of the past reared up in disturbing ways. There were nights, much to Anya's bafflement, when Kreon cried out in his sleep calling for his father. She learned to wake him with a comforting voice and calm him with tender assurances that it was only a bad dream.

One such episode woke Leni. While Demetri was sound asleep, Leni was roused by the disturbing noises coming from across the hallway. Her parents' door was closed, but she treaded on pussycat feet toward it, turned the knob and peeked in. She noticed her father was whimpering in his sleep while Mama stroked his head. A soft nightlight illuminated the room.

"Kreon, everything is all right," her mother whispered into his ear, her voice barely audible.

Mesmerized, Leni watched her father open his eyes and raise himself into a sitting position, then rub his face with his hands. His hair appeared wet, and droplets of sweat were beading on his forehead. He seemed dazed and confused.

"I was dreaming...I was dream...oh God, won't these visions ever leave me alone?" Kreon cried, rubbing his eyes with increased fierceness to wipe them away.

"What was it about this time?" Anya asked softly.

Leni heard her father take a deep breath, as she peered through the crack in the door.

"I was dreaming," he paused and looked around as if disoriented,

"I was dreaming that I was in a building…running down its staircase, and the Gestapo was chasing me. I could hear their heavy boots and the sound of snarling dogs. I had to get out of the building, but there were strobes of light crisscrossing the stairwell. I was only safe when I reached a landing and hid myself in the shadow of its farthest corner. As I stood there, trying not to be seen, I realized there were a few seconds when the lights turned off. I tried to time each moment so I could make it to the next landing without being seen. But the men and dogs were coming closer. Then…"

Kreon hesitated, while outside their door their undetected daughter gulped in fright.

"Then what happened?" Anya inquired, continuing to stroke him in comfort.

Leni watched her father swipe his wet hair from his face as he turned toward her mother.

"I wasn't sure I would make it. The dream ended. And I wasn't sure I would make it." Feeling the shiver of his body, Anya put her arms around him.

"You did make it, Kreon. You made it! And now you are safe. You are here with your family, and you are here in America. There is no one chasing you. There is no need to run anymore."

They remained quiet for a while. When Kreon lay down again, Anya pressed her body against him. He was suffering a keening of the heart, and she held him close.

"You are safe," she repeated, "We are both safe with our children."

"Mama?" Leni uttered at the door, startling her parents.

Anya looked up to see their daughter framed in the doorway. Trying to remain calm, she requested as kindly, but firmly, as she could, "Leni…please go back to bed. Papa just had a bad dream. Go on…go back to your room. Papa and I are going back to sleep. Everything is fine."

Leni did not want to return to her room; she wanted to cuddle in bed with them and make Papa feel better. But, wisely, she did as she was told. Padding back to her room, she tried not to wake Demetri, but he stirred and sat up, sniffling in the dark.

"Where were you?" he cried.

"Pssst, better whisper," she instructed, as he sniffled again. "Are you crying?"

"Ja."

"Why?"

"I woke up and you were gone!"

"I went to the bathroom." She did not want to explain her visit to their parents' bedroom door.

"I thought you had gone away and left me alone again."

"Again? Oh." It dawned on her why he was upset. She sat on the edge of his bed, "But I always come back, don't I? I would never leave you for always. I'm your sister. And I'll always be your sister."

"Promise?"

"Yes. If you promise to always be my brother."

She could hear the smile in his voice.

"I promise," he said.

"Pinkie-swear?"

They locked pinkies for a moment, and Demetri was calmed.

"Now go to sleep before we get in trouble," Leni whispered, drawing Demetri's blanket up to his chin and wishing him "good night". He turned to his side and closed his eyes.

As she crawled under her own blanket, Leni hoped everything would be all right.

"Please, God, make Papa and Demetri feel better. Make them feel safe again."

Drifting off to sleep, one word stuck with her that night: she wondered what the Gestapo was. Instinctively she knew it was something terrible, and she should not ask her father about it if it gave him bad dreams.

CHAPTER EIGHTY-FOUR

While their father readied himself for work the next morning, Demetri and Leni sat down for breakfast with their mother. Anya gazed at her sleepy-eyed youngsters with concern.

"Papa sure snores like a lion," Demetri pointed out, "Roarrr! Roarrr!"

"You never heard a lion snore!" Leni roared back, annoyed with his assessment of the situation. She had not slept well.

"Those weren't snores," Leni informed him. Anya gave her daughter a warning glance not to say anything more. Facing her son's inquisition, Anya simply informed Demetri that their father had been dreaming about the war.

"It is to be expected," Anya explained, "The war was a great sadness for him and others, but you must not be frightened by his nighttime sounds. He is just having a bad dream."

"Was it a *really* bad dream, Mama?" Demetri asked.

"Yes. Like the bad dreams you and your sister sometimes have," she told him, "Now go give your father a hug before he leaves for work."

Kreon was surprised by the sudden onslaught of small arms embracing his leg and waist as he stepped into the kitchen.

"What is this?! A plea for me to bring home ice cream?"

His face was beaming as they followed him to the door and kissed him good-bye. Anya was pleased at the way they waved him off.

"I think it would be nice if we explored our neighborhood today; perhaps stop at the park. Would you like to do that?" she asked her brood of two.

"Yes, I guess that would be nice," Leni replied, although with not much enthusiasm.

"I would!" piped up Demetri, "I don't want to stay here." He jumped from his seat and ran off to get ready.

"Mama, do you ever dream?" Leni wondered, as she drifted into a solemn mood.

"All people dream," Anya replied, hesitant about saying more.

"Do they have good dreams or bad dreams?" Leni continued.

"People usually have a little of both, your Mama included," Anya answered truthfully.

This made Leni feel better. At least she understood that dreaming was normal and not just something she and Papa did. This emboldened her to admit to her mother that her dreams were just as scary as her father's.

"Mama, I still dream that I'm standing by the ocean and the waves are coming closer and closer and getting bigger and bigger and I'm afraid they will drown me. What do you dream about, Mama?"

Troubled by her daughter's confession, Anya took Leni's hand with concern and began, "We all sometimes have upsetting dreams. I dream...." but a whirling dervish in the form of Demetri stopped her from finishing.

"I dream about flying and there are birds all over the sky following me!" Demetri blurted as he charged into the room with arms spread and flapping about.

Cross at the interruption, Leni gave him a withering look. Anya simply raised an eyebrow at him, and turned back to Leni's query, "I dream that the people we love and left behind in Germany come to visit, and I am so happy to see them. But then I wake up and they are gone."

"Does it make you sad?" Leni asked, aware her Mama was not

smiling.

"Of course! I miss them very much. Don't you?" she asked.

"Yes, I do too," Leni admitted with a sizeable lump in her throat.

"Me too," professed Demetri with drooped wings and downcast eyes.

Breakfast did not appeal to them that morning.

Days followed where Demetri and Leni appeared physically more fragile. Neither of the children complained of any ailment, but the sight of their thinning bodies became a great worry for their parents. Demetri was losing the most weight between the two, which Anya attributed to unspoken homesickness. More than three years of Demetri's childhood had been spent at his great-grandparents home surrounded by cousins his age, farm animals, and rural scenery. In Germany, he saw his mother and sister during the day, and then they would disappear, and now they were always there. He had experienced limited contact with his father, and now Papa was always there, too. He did not mind their presence, but the move to America and subsequent adjustment for him was monumental. Leni, on the other hand, had interacted more substantially with her parents and been exposed to America before their recent journey. She was a smart young girl of almost six and had an inkling of what to expect and how to wend her way through it. Demetri did not.

The readjustment plagued both children to different degrees, and their immune systems were weakened by the stress. Damp spring weather brought on colds and scratchy throats. Having little money for doctors, mustard plasters on their congested chests and wet rags around their ankles to bring down any fever were the go-to remedies. As a preventive measure against anemia, for they looked wan, their parents began feeding their patients a daily dose of cod liver oil to pump them up. Thick and slimy, the liquid concoction tasted like rancid fish as it slid down their gagging throats. The putrid 'medicine' was followed by a swift gulp of orange juice to kill the repulsive aftertaste. Leni and Demetri made sure to pinch their nostrils tightly together, as their parents aimed a sizeable teaspoon into their mouth each day. It was the only way they could swallow it without gagging.

The cod liver oil 'somewhat' contributed toward the embellishment of their bodies, but it was the local bakeries that deserved most of the credit. Anya, beyond her own flair for baking, bought whatever special delicacies they could afford from these shops (the preference being strawberry shortcake, black & white cookies, rum cake, or custard-filled Napoleons). The children were slowly plumped out by developing a sugar habit.

Having conquered the battle with the spring colds, another critical problem arose for Kreon and Anya: Leni's nocturnal journeys. It began with Leni sleepwalking into her parents' bedroom at inopportune times or gliding into the living room at night to stare at the birthday doll her grandmother had sent. But when Leni, in her dreamlike state, began to unlock the door to their apartment and head up the stairs leading to the building's rooftop, her parents became alarmed. Much like Johanna Spyri's famous book *Heidi*, about a young girl taken away from her grandfather and the beautiful Alps and brought to the big city of Frankfurt against her will, her perplexed parents wondered if Leni was longing for the mountains of her German homeland. Both the fictional Heidi and their very real daughter, Leni, wandered toward rooftops searching perhaps for the very same thing. However, this habit was not acceptable.

Kreon tried to solve the dodgy problem by installing a chain-lock high up on their apartment door. Leni solved that problem by pulling a chair up to reach it.

"Kreon, what are we going to do?" a distraught Anya wailed when they caught their child in the hallway again, "What is making our daughter do this? We cannot stay up all night, every night!"

"We will have to," a grave Kreon, appraising the situation, informed her, "Perhaps we could take turns watching her through the night. Or perhaps installing a bell on the door might work."

"I can watch her at night. I want you to go to work and stay alert when using those factory machines! I do *not* want you exhausting yourself. I can rest during the day."

"Well, let her sleep in our bed just for tonight. Tomorrow I will install a bell, and we will see if that helps. This disorder cannot last forever. I am sure she will calm down, and it will subside. Wait and see. I know this change is difficult for the three of you. It was the same way for me when I first came here. I do not recall sleep-walking...but then no one was around to tell me otherwise."

Anya rewarded him with a look of disdain instead of the grin he anticipated.

Leni never made it to the rooftop. The bell worked. Adapting to her new surroundings each day, she grew more tranquil. And the nighttime wanderings soon ebbed then ceased. Kreon concluded his daughter's eventual need for a good night's sleep, undisturbed by the startling tinkling of a bell, overrode her need for a midnight stroll.

CHAPTER EIGHTY-FIVE

Leni's sixth birthday, and her first in America, fell in early June. Unburdened by colds and nocturnal strolls, she was eager for the day to arrive. In celebration, her mother escorted her and Demetri to the local playground for moments of merriment until their father returned from work. The playground boasted a mushroom-shaped, metallic fount that cascaded water over the children standing around it. She and Demetri ran under the sprays in their shorts, laughing like raucous hyenas while getting drenched. Anya provided towels, and a basket of sandwiches, apples, and soda, to enhance their afternoon fun.

That evening when their father returned home, he placed six red roses (Leni's favorite) and a Donald Duck comic book into his daughter's hands. She looked at the precious roses with astonishment and thought them and the American comic book the most wondrous of gifts. A birthday cake topped with plump strawberries, whipped cream, and six glowing candles also awaited her. Its sweet, spongy, goodness graced her lips and fingers (and Demetri's) as much as it filled her stomach.

After shutting her eyes and making a secret wish, ("Please let us see our family again"), and gobbling up her slice with great relish, Leni parked herself on her father's lap. Taking the comic book in hand, she began her own personal and creative recitation of the story, as reading was not yet one of her acquired skills. In her imaginative rendition, Donald Duck went to Deutschland and fought in the war with his bow and arrow and came back to America with a bunch of Indian feathers as a prize. It was a big hit with her family. And, thus, their first spring together heralded what they hoped would be a happy summer.

CHAPTER EIGHTY-SIX

When summer swaggered in, wrapped in hot, lazy, uncomfortable days, it brought a pinch to Leni's teeth. The developing toothache was one of several she had suffered as a child back home in Fürth. Back then, Anya had taken her to a local dental clinic for an examination. She was surprised to be sent home with instructions to give Leni half an aspirin and do nothing until her baby teeth fell out. As for Leni, she hoped they would never have to return. At the center of the reception area was a three-tiered table displaying a host of dental pliers as well as the teeth they had pulled.

By summer in America, Leni's permanent teeth were becoming a serious problem. Her jaw was too small to contain them properly, and they emerged in an irregular pattern. Some teeth grew in on top of each other, some grew in sideways, and her top two front teeth presented themselves with black gashes right across their center. She looked as if she were wearing braces. Her jaw was also slightly misaligned, which resulted in a lisp that would take eventual speech therapy to correct. It made Leni self-conscious; the pictures they sent home to relatives showed her with a pursed mouth or half-hearted smile.

With her tooth throbbing, and feeling miserable, it was clear to Anya and Kreon that Leni needed to see a dentist right away. Her parents had heard of a Dr. Cohen residing in the building around the corner. He operated a dental office out of his apartment and was known to charge reasonable prices and have evening hours. Kreon paid the office a quick visit and, in his limited English, requested that Leni be seen for treatment as soon as a slot was available. There was an opening at 7:00 p.m. that evening.

Arriving at the scheduled time, holding her father's hand, Leni's stomach churned. The dentist led them through a canvas curtain that served as a door to his work area. Seeing the huge dental chair and the instruments that surrounded it, Leni's pupils dilated to the size of dinner plates. Dr. Cohen pointed to the chair and instructed her to sit, while Kreon was requested to remain in the waiting area. As her father let go of her hand, Leni felt squeamish and wanted to run. The dentist, sensing her fright, nudged her toward the throne of red vinyl with its chrome trim. The intimidating chair and the ominous instruments dangling around it, were guaranteed to make any child feel like they were on a slippery slope to hell. Leni was no exception.

Placing a sizeable paper bib around her, Dr. Cohen poked around her gums and teeth with what Leni assumed was a crochet hook. With a burning cigarette dangling from his mouth and his sour breath nearing her face, Leni, fearing the ashes would land on her tongue or fall in her lap, pushed him away. Dr. Cohen would have none of it and came in for the kill. In a commanding voice, he instructed her to open her mouth wide...as wide as she could...and approached her with pliers. Realizing the offending tooth was going to be pulled right out of her head, she braced herself for the invasion. When he yanked it, Leni was neither good nor brave, instead she emitted an earsplitting scream as blood dribbled from her mouth. When the pliers came at her again, she screamed a second time, spurting red specks at him. Angered, Dr. Cohen pulled her from the chair and slapped her across her cheek.

"Shut up! People will hear you!"

Her father certainly did. Kreon came flying into the makeshift room, scooped Leni up and yelled words at Dr. Cohen that were not translatable to decent English.

"Take her out of here before she scares my customers away!" Cohen ordered between clenched teeth.

An enraged Kreon spit a volume of unpoetic words at the dentist, while Leni cried on her father's shoulder. Rushing to carry Leni away, droplets of blood appeared on Kreon's shirt, while Leni's once spotless, white blouse was trickled with red.

When they arrived home, her distraught parents tried to calm Leni and examine her mouth. Leni continued to cry, squirm, and bleed. Her mother grabbed cotton swabs from the bathroom and a washcloth to stem the flow. As she did so, a shocked Anya informed Kreon that the tooth had been pulled, but so had a piece of the gum surrounding it.

With an ice cube wrapped in a washcloth, Anya made a valorous attempt to staunch the bleeding and numb the pain without getting bitten for her efforts. Leni remained whimpering and gulping back tears, while Kreon seethed. With an anguished look, Anya asked him, "Why did he have to treat her this way?"

Before her husband could answer, Demetri came to see what the commotion was about and stood there in panic.

"Will I have to go to the dentist too?" he asked, terrified at the prospect.

"No! Never this one. Never!" his adamant father assured him.

When the bleeding stopped, Anya guided her daughter to the bathroom and had her rinse her mouth out with warm salt water. It stung, and Leni cried some more.

Brushing the damp hair away from Leni's face, Anya embraced her child until the tears subsided.

Exhausted from the ordeal, Leni was put to bed early with her mother's gentle instruction to "go to sleep." Cradled in Anya's arms, she did so, while Kreon put Demetri to bed with repeated assurances that he would not have to go to "*that* dentist".

Joining her husband in the living room later, Anya curled up next to him on the couch, and Kreon was dismayed to see her cry.

"What's wrong? I promise I will never take her to see that man again. I could beat him for treating her that way!" he proclaimed.

Anya sighed, "It's not just the way she was treated. I fear the question might be *why* was she treated that way? I'm sure that other children have screamed in that dentist's chair and not been slapped."

Kreon observed her with growing concern, "What are you saying?"

"I am wondering if it is because my children and I are German. Dr. Cohen is Jewish, and we are the only Germans that I know of in the immediate area. What if he hates Germans and took it out on Leni? He sees us around. He must know who we are."

Kreon sat back shocked at her words. It took a moment for him to say anything in reply.

"You are speaking of racism in reverse, Anya...of some sort of anger over, and retribution for, the Holocaust? Do you really think that?"

She stared directly into his eyes, "Yes, Kreon, I do. Being German, I live every day in the shadow of what Hitler and the Nazis did. We Germans will always live in that shadow. It will always be a poisonous part of my heritage."

"Anya..." He tried to interrupt, but she would not allow it.

"Kreon, let me speak my thoughts, right or wrong. You work with Germans all day in the factory. I must go out and watch people stare at me when I try to speak English in a store and my accent is obvious. It is not always a kind eye that greets me."

"What about our neighbor, Mrs. Weinberg? She has taken you under her care and been immensely kind to us. The neighbors have not given us any trouble, have they?"

Anya had to admit they had not been unkind; they had just been curious or indifferent toward her.

"I think," Kreon continued, "that this repulsive clash with Dr. Cohen has upset us greatly, and we must be careful not to overthink it or overreact. Perhaps he had a terrible day. To call him a bigot might cause great trouble. We can only hope something like this does not happen again."

He tried to put her at ease by putting an arm around her and pulling her close.

"We will see," she remarked with little confidence in her voice, "we will see."

"I must admit, our daughter did scream loud enough for his customers in the building to hear. Perhaps atonement for his bad behavior will come when they cancel their appointments!" He produced a slight smile as she punched him on the arm.

Leni, lying in her bed across from her dozing brother, tried to go to sleep, but her gum was still a dull ache, and her mind was restless. Later that night, when Anya crept into the room to check on the children, she was dismayed to find Leni still awake.

Seating herself on the edge of her daughter's bed, she placed Leni's hand in her own.

"Are you in pain, sweetheart?"

Leni shook her head, "It's hurts only a little. The ice pack helped. I just can't sleep."

"What is keeping you up then, child?"

"That dentist scared me," Leni paused, "His eyes looked so frightening."

"Do not worry about that horrible man. You will never have to see him again. Papa and I are terribly sorry we did not take you to the clinic. However, they only had an opening on Friday. With your tooth aching so much, we did not think it wise to wait until then."

"It's okay, Mama. I know we have to save money."

"Oh Leni," a sob caught in Anya's throat, "I promise we will take you to a better dentist to get your teeth fixed. Papa wants me to try to get you into the clinic tomorrow to make sure you do not get an infection in that wound. The money is not important. You are!"

Anya kissed the forehead of the little girl who was growing up way too fast, just as she had done. It grieved her.

"Now go to sleep. You need to rest."

"Will you stay with me, Mama?"

"Yes. I will stay with you for a little while," Anya said. "Sleep well. Mama is here."

As Leni grew drowsy and drifted into sleep, a disturbing shadow of strange eyes crept into her restive mind, and there it slumbered.

CHAPTER EIGHTY-SEVEN

Leni's gum, and the gap from her missing tooth, healed before long. Her parents were happy to hear her babbling away again, although her brother capped his ears. By late summer, she had absorbed enough English to enter first grade at the local public school. Their neighbor, Mrs. Weinberg, and her two children, Daniel, and Leah, helped with their lessons. Anya still stumbled with her pronunciation skills and her English was rudimentary, while Kreon got by with his fractured English. His co-workers spoke German most often and that proved a hindrance to furthering his fluency.

On the first day of school, Anya accompanied a nervous Leni and escorted her to the assigned classroom. Anya let go of her little girl's hand with reluctance, knowing what a momentous step it was for her child. She had watched her daughter dress excitedly in the new outfit she was wearing: a white blouse with Peter Pan collar and short, puffed sleeves; a red plaid skirt; white tights; and her newly shined, Mary Jane shoes. She had plaited Leni's hair into careful braids with a small, red clip at each end. With her new knapsack on her back, filled with a blank notebook and sharpened pencils, Leni was quite the picture of an eager student. Anya, full of hope and pride, watched her daughter take a seat amid the other arrivals. She gave Leni a smile and a kiss on the forehead and wished her well before she left the room.

Leni did not see her mother wave goodbye; she was too busy

gazing at the blackboard with anticipation.

Within minutes, a fresh bunch of adolescents scampered through the door (mothers in tow), and, with a mixture of excitement, indifference, or downright fright seated themselves.

With her students finally settled in, the teacher, Miss Kent, introduced herself and asked each student to stand when their name was called. One by one, they were introduced to their classmates on an easy first-name basis. Most were greeted with hoots and hollers by their friends.

When Leni's turn came, Miss Kent mentioned her name was "Eleni, but she likes to be called Leni. Leni has come all the way from Germany to live in America with us." There were no hoots or hollers, just silence as the children stared at her with intense curiosity. Leni's cheeks burned, and she bowed her head feeling discomfited by the marked attention. With that awkward initiation, her education in America began.

Returning home in the afternoon, her mother greeted her with a welcoming hug and maternal curiosity, "How did your day go, Liebchen?"

Leni sat down on the couch next to Anya and mentioned the lessons of the day and showed off her notebook filled with a few letters of the alphabet. She made her first day of school sound as exciting as she could and said nothing of her uncomfortable morning.

In the ensuing weeks Leni discovered grade school was not a stroll through a country garden; there were briar patches along the way.

Feeling timid, she became so reluctant to raise her hand in class that, one day, when nature called, she waited too long to assert her need. Wetting her pants right there in her seat in front of the class, she cried from shame and did not know what to do.

The teacher, alerted to the mishap by snickers in the room, called for an assistant to take over, and steered a sniffling Leni to the nearest ladies' room. There, within minutes, Miss Kent washed the necessities in the sink and Leni's underwear was restored to her...quite damp, but wearable. With kindness and caring, the teacher, familiar with unruly bladders, instructed Leni to not be afraid to raise her hand when she needed to go to the bathroom. It was okay, Miss Kent maintained; she would always be glad to take her to the bathroom.

Upon returning to the classroom, to Leni's further embarrassment, the assistant sat her on the window ledge where the heat vents could dry her damp underwear. While Miss Kent resumed the lesson. Leni faced the entire class from that perch and wanted to die. Her underpants dried, but the indignity of sitting in such notable view left her face wet with tears the heat vents could not dry.

That evening, relating her tale of woe, Leni begged not to have to return to school.

"It was awful! I would rather stay home. I won't have to raise my hand and let everyone know I have to go to the bathroom!" she pleaded, "I am so much happier being home!"

She felt betrayed when her parents chose to have her return to the scene of her humiliation the next morning. It was good for her character, they said, although she did not know what that meant. She unwillingly did as she was told and kept her head low when she entered the classroom and saw nosy eyes peeking at her. Luckily, within days, her discomfort was put to rest; two other water-logged children replaced her on the window perch. Thereafter, all three made sure to raise their hand.

CHAPTER EIGHTY-EIGHT

When finished with her schoolwork, Leni taught her mother and brother the American words she picked up each day; otherwise, they spoke German at home. Her father had trouble conquering the English language, but it was more than just working with Germans all day long. He was fluent in Greek and German and had a gift for foreign dialects, but English, his true native tongue, was difficult for him to master for some inexplicable reason. He grasped most of what was spoken in English; but he was not as articulate in the language as he wanted to be. Leni, his frustrated tutor, could not figure out why. She, her mother, and Demetri were surpassing him in this language skill.

Confounded by his slow progress, Leni confronted him point-blank, "Papa, why aren't you learning more English?"

Kreon looked with frustration at his daughter, "I am trying!"

"No, you are not!" she retorted in a huff, "You speak English like a little boy."

That night when he repeated Leni's words to Anya, an epiphany hit him.

"Do you think that my trauma as a young boy has kept me from developing my English?"

Anya put her magazine down and contemplated his question.

"You mean that you might be psychologically trapped when it comes to learning English? Hmmm, it is a strange possibility...or a good excuse. I have been informed that I sound like a little girl. But, unlike you, I plan to learn more and learn it correctly!" She stuck out her tongue at him like a two-year-old and made him laugh.

"It is what it is, Kreon. We will absorb it at our own speed, as will Demetri. Our daughter is just a wizard at it; bless the child."

Leni was picking up English with amazing speed, as well as the ability to read it. This skill helped her parents deal better with mundane matters such as grocery shopping.

"No, Mama, the oranges are fifty cents a pound, not for each."

Acting as their intermediary, Leni ofttimes felt like the parent instead of the child. It was disconcerting, and when she mentioned it to her teacher in a student-teacher meeting, she learned it was something many immigrant children faced when they were the first to conquer the English language.

The Kalanis home eventually sounded like a mini-United Nations: German, Greek, and English flew around until their conversations were a jumble of each, and Leni thought it a miracle that they even understood each other.

Through summer and fall, teaching English daily to her mother and Demetri remained Leni's foremost responsibility. Although her mother would always retain a charming accent and manage (again with charm) to screw up words, like pronouncing cake "cockie", Anya got the gist of it and Demetri did too.

With the leaves of autumn came a big surprise; one which aided them further in their quest to master English.

A truck and two sturdy men delivered an unanticipated package one Saturday afternoon. With sweat beading on their brows, the deliverymen lumbered up three flights of stairs and managed not to damage or drop it. Kreon was quick to answer the door when they rang, and quicker to direct them toward the living room. Anya and the children looked askance at the intrusion.

The bulk the couriers set down along the center of the wall across from the couch was swathed in heavy padding. Anya, Demetri, and Leni had no idea what to make of it. It was not until the deliverymen proceeded to uncover it, that a roar of recognition and delight reached the rafters. It was a television! The TV was housed in a polished wood cabinet and featured a built-in record player and radio on one side. Kreon watched their eyes light up like pirates unearthing a treasure chest.

"Kreon, why didn't you tell me?" a stunned Anya asked.

"Because you would fret about the money, and I wanted to surprise you. I have been saving for it for the past few months and bought it on sale with the help of friends."

"Oh my!" Leni exclaimed, barely able to breathe. Demetri, in his enthusiasm, spread his sticky fingers on the screen and tried to hug it. Kreon scooped Demetri up before he could use the screen for a canvas.

"Papa...a real television," Leni said in disbelief. Then she began to cry.

"Oh no," Kreon said, placing Demetri in Anya's arms, and bending to place an arm around his little girl, "What's wrong?"

"It's so beautiful," Leni cried, "I can't believe it." Dropping her head on her father's shoulder, she sobbed and laughed at the same time.

Watching Anya tear up too, Kreon simply stated, "It is ours. It is real."

Leni hugged him tighter, "Thank you, Papa. Thank you," she whispered.

Demetri simply yelled, "Yay!"

The television not only entertained them but made Leni's linguistic duties easier: A TV puppet named "Rootie Kazootie", as well as "Kukla, Fran and Ollie" became her teaching assistants. Her mother then progressed to advanced words by watching "Queen for a Day" and "I Married Joan". Demetri chose to learn to speak like a true Native American by watching "The Lone Ranger".

"My name is Kee-mo-sabbee!" he declared, after picking a feather from his bed pillow to stick in his hair.

Monday nights became special for Leni. After Demetri fell asleep, she was permitted to sneak out of their shared bedroom to watch the screwball antics of "I Love Lucy" with her parents. Afterward "Victory at Sea" was televised, but she would be sent back to bed then. The show focused on newsreels of World War II, and Kreon and Anya preferred not to expose her to such graphic accounts. With a TV now in their home, the children were intent on absorbing their present culture, but their parents made sure to keep one of their feet planted in their past. German traditions were maintained wherever they could be.

In addition to the television set, their apartment burst with music from the phonograph player and their growing collection of LPs and 45s. The radio was often played too. Kreon adored music in the house and would often encourage them to "Put on a record!" Soon Greek, German, American music, or whatever suited their mood on any given day, burst forth. As sounds of mandolins, accordions or American guitars filled their home, and artists of international renown sang their songs, Leni developed a love of dancing and bopped, shimmied, or polkaed through the living room to each exhilarating beat. Picking up the lyrics of numerous songs from all genres and dancing to them became her exuberant pastime. The old and new music of Germany, though, was the family's favorite. It transported them back home for a while.

As English grew to be their primary language, the children acquired a love of American movies. Leni was enthralled with anything Walt Disney, while Demetri doted on Hopalong Cassidy. She and her mother had seen "Snow White" in Germany in a makeshift, post-war theater that consisted primarily of a large room, a few chairs for adults, and a carpeted floor for the children. In America, the first film she viewed at the local movie theater was the animated "Cinderella". For 70 cents she viewed the main movie, a featurette, a cartoon, and was able to watch the entire movie over again without paying extra.

Being exposed to such a colorful fairy tale had its downside. The next morning, Leni sat on a stepstool by the kitchen window gazing woefully at the dismal and rainy day. She longed for a fairy godmother to appear and whisk her to a beautiful palace far away.

Begging her mother to go see the movie again, she was met with a firm "Nein. It costs money, and we watched it twice yesterday." And that was that. Leni fled to her room with a dismal heart. She wished they were rich. In her childlike state of mind, she had not yet realized they already were. The family coffers were meager, but their life together was not.

An unexpected treasure came in the form of their caring neighbor, Milly Weinberg. She had taken them under her expansive wing and clucked over them to make sure they acclimated to their surroundings and continued blooming. Their maternal watchdog often reminded them of Molly Goldberg, the wonderful character they watched on "The Goldbergs", who was the iconic mother-hen stuffed with wisdom and all good things.

Mrs. Weinberg undertook educating Anya about the New England area and its history to pique Anya's curiosity and get her mind focused on the here and now. One day, while seated in the Kalanis home, she decided to quiz Anya on her new-found knowledge:

"In what New England state did the American Revolution begin?" Mrs. Weinberg asked.

"Massa-two-schitz," Mama replied, while Leni bit her tongue.

"Yes," Milly nodded diplomatically, "Massa-choo-sitz," hoping Anya would hear the difference in pronunciation.

Anya proved grittier throughout their resettlement in America than even she, herself, imagined. Kreon expected no less, having been at her side during the war. By the fall, she had, with unwavering diligence, found a few local house cleaning positions for $1.00 an hour. She did not find the work hard nor demeaning. The ladies who employed her were grateful to have help with their ever-growing brood and household and treated her with respect. Scrimping and saving, she aided Kreon in making life as comfortable as they could for their own family. They still dealt with homesickness for Germany at times, even Kreon, but they ploughed on. However, one October day their homesickness and Germany could no longer be held at bay.

Kreon came home from work around 4:00 p.m., while Leni was busy dusting the furniture (her assigned household chore after school). He stopped as usual to retrieve the day's mail from the row of built-in mailboxes situated on the ground floor of their apartment building. He was pleased to find a letter from Rosa in it, knowing Anya and the children would be delighted.

Demetri, occupied at the Weinberg's home playing with David, was staying there for supper.

Leni, finished with dusting, prepared to do her homework when her Papa came in. He was smiling and waved a blue "Air Mail" envelope in front of her.

"A letter from Oma," he announced jovially. Wasting no time, he sat down in his favorite chair, opened the envelope with relish and read its contents. Leni waited with anticipation for the latest news. Instead, she became anxious when his face fell, and he said not a word.

"What's wrong?" she wanted to know.

Kreon gazed at her, appearing stricken.

"Papa, tell me what's wrong!" she pleaded.

"There's been a death," he stated in disbelief, almost whispering the words.

"Who, Papa? Tell me!"

More information was not forthcoming. Kreon simply folded the letter and put it in his pocket as he rose from his seat. His face had gone pale, and he was shocked.

"I'll explain everything later," he muttered in a daze, then looked at her dumbly.

Leni became flustered at the morose sight of him.

"It will be time for your mother to come home from work soon.

Do not say anything about the letter until I have the chance to speak with her alone, okay?"

Leni nodded numbly, perplexed by his request. They began to set the dinner table together in silence. It was only a short while later that Anya rang the doorbell. As usual, she was all smiles when they opened it and greeted her. After engaging in mundane chatter for a few minutes, Kreon mentioned a letter had arrived from Rosa. Overjoyed at first, Anya grew alarmed when Leni looked dismal and her somber husband took her by the arm into their bedroom, sat her on the edge of the bed and closed the door.

Leni waited in the living room, then heard her mother's cries. After a while, her father stepped out and told her to come in. Anya lay on the bed sobbing. He nudged Leni toward her, and she climbed up and curled herself into her mother's outstretched arms.

"Tante Hannah is dead," her mother wailed, holding her tight.

Leni was taken aback, "Oh Mama!"

Both cried, holding tightly onto each other.

Kreon felt acute sadness wash over him.

CHAPTER EIGHTY-NINE

Meine liebe Anya und Kreon,

It is with terrible grief that I write these words to you. Our dear Hannah has died.

She suffered a severe asthma attack while pregnant with her third child. Her doctor had warned her not to get pregnant again as her health was already compromised by her weight gain from bearing two babies and her respiratory problems. But you know how much Hannah loved children and would not heed. The ambulance service that rushed to help her, as she went into distress, was not supplied with an oxygen tank. They told us that post-war equipment for ambulances was still hard to come by. Both Hannah and her unborn child died on the way to the hospital. It has been devastating, and I wish you were here to hold, as I know this news will bring you great pain.

I ask God every day why this happened. Hannah was so young and such a good person! And now her two children are motherless with a lout for a father who abandoned them weeks ago. No one can find him. I am still living with your grandparents, and we have taken in the children and will try to find them a good home. Farmer Thomas and his wife are considering taking them in. For now, there will be room for them in the attic bedroom.

More than this I cannot write. We are inconsolable but will do the best we can. I hold you in my heart. Do not despair. Stay strong for your own children.
   Your mother always,
   Rosa

When the children went to bed that night, Kreon soothed them to sleep then returned to Anya sobbing softly in her pillow. He lay by her side and, as she rested her head on his shoulder, let the anguish flow from her mind.

"I wish I could be with my mother...." she cried, her words scraping across Kreon's heart.

He stroked her head and soothed her to sleep as he did with the children.

The vast distance that separated them from the rest of their family during those terrible days of sorrow could not be bridged. There was no money, not even to borrow, and a sizable bank loan was not in their means.

Anya's grief and homesickness were palpable. They all felt it. She ached to embrace her family and be able to grieve with them, especially her mother. She knew there would be more losses of loved ones to be faced, for her great-grandparents were in their advanced years. But the death of Hannah, her only sister, at such a young age, leaving two motherless children behind and taking the unborn one with her, was a tragedy too unexpected and brutal to fathom.

"I do not understand God anymore, Kreon. I try to find answers, but my search is bottomless and futile."

He, silent in his own grief, took long walks with Anya and the children to heal their spirits. They moved forward one intolerable step at a time. It was all they could do. There were moments of benevolent calm and moments of blistering pain, each subject to the whim of the day. To maintain their sanity, Kreon resumed his work at the factory while Anya returned to her house cleaning jobs. Leni went to school. Demetri played with his friend, David. At home they oscillated between mundane chatter and deep silence. There was no music in the house.

CHAPTER NINETY

Although their parents strove hard to give Demetri and Leni the idyllic childhood they never had, lately the children's days were peppered with outbursts of anger by Kreon and annoyance by Anya. Leni, more than Demetri, seemed to gather the brunt of it. Anger over her aunt's passing had made her sassier at home, and she suffered for her newly acquired skill. Their father's hands did not refrain from giving either child a well-earned spanking, or a tongue lashing like the sting of a whip if they disobeyed. There was also an ever-present broomstick in the closet which served more as a threat than an actual means of punishment. The threat sufficed. Leni and her brother learned their manners. Disrespect toward their elders was not tolerated in the Kalanis household no matter what the excuse.

A new rule was also established: When their father came home from work, after welcoming him, it was necessary that he be allowed to relax and unwind before bombarding him with questions, requests, and tidbits of their day. If they did not comply, they would see the tired, cantankerous side of his nature at the dinner table as opposed to the more personable one. Anya tried to ensure that Kreon remained unruffled, but, in her own irritated state of mind, did not always succeed. Attempting to recover and return to normal after the loss of Hannah was a strain and made them all edgy.

On better days, Anya and Kreon would take the children on

outdoor excursions. On colder evenings, they would play simple board games or hide-n-seek in the apartment with the lights dim. During the latter, Demetri and Leni hid under their beds, in a closet, or in the laundry hamper to foil their parents. One evening, it was their Papa's turn to hide.

"Bet you can't find me!" he challenged, as brother and sister covered their eyes and counted to ten. Kreon decided to hide behind the living room drapes but, to his disappointment, they found him straightaway. His feet were sticking out from under the curtain along with the bulge of his manly torso. The children giggled for the first time in weeks.

At school, or through work and neighbors, mother and daughter began forming tentative friendships to bring them out of sorrow. Demetri, all of three-and-a-half and a moppet of sandy curls and brown eyes, was more like a puppy dog, friendly and happy being greeted or petted by anyone paying him kind attention. He, too, was making a few new friends in the neighborhood.

It was a shock then when Leni came home from school one November afternoon bruised, shook up and crying.

CHAPTER NINETY-ONE

Hey, Nazi pig!" had been flung at Leni by a bevy of schoolboys, along with a volley of ice balls aimed at her body and head.

Kreon and Anya were shaken out of their status quo by seeing their daughter in such a state. After Leni had been cared for, questioned, and put to bed along with her frightened brother, Anya lashed out in fury against the unfairness of it all.

"Tell me, Kreon, tell me why our child is being treated this way? Tell me! What has she done to be attacked like that? Tell me it is *not* because she is German! Calling an innocent child a "Nazi pig" is the worst kind of bigotry!"

Kreon did not respond because he knew it was wiser to remain mute against her rage, and because he could not refute her accusation.

"How can they think all Germans are Nazis? They could have blinded our daughter! Did you see her face?" she cried.

"Anya don't..." Kreon pleaded as he reached out to soothe her.

Her voice quieted but not her mind, "I can't help but think their parents have demonized all Germans because of the horrible things the Nazis did to all those poor people. But it reminds me so painfully of what Hitler did with the Hitler Jugend...indoctrinated them to hate the Jews and become bullies and terrorists. And what now? Are our neighbors going to come full circle and punish *our* children? Children who had nothing to do with the war nor the Holocaust.

When will it end, Kreon? I feel like we will always live in the shadow of a nightmare. We brought our children to America to be *safe*!"

Kreon, pained by her suffering, took her by the hand and seated her next to him attempting to calm her.

"Anya, it is as distressing to me as it is to you to see our daughter treated this way. I will do *everything* I can to stop her getting hurt like that again. But reality is a harsh taskmaster. The horror that these people, or their family members, lived through is so deep and raw a wound in their mind right now, we need to understand the intensity of their heartache and accept it. Perhaps the world will learn from this tragedy; perhaps someday we will all remember it with our intellect and not vengeful emotions. But, right now, we need to explain the situation as best we can to Leni, so she understands why this happened to her. We need to make her understand that it has nothing to do with who she is as a person. You know boys can be brats. They probably heard bits of conversations at home about Nazis and picked up on it. Bullies will say anything and enjoy yelling hateful names at whomever they decide to pick on."

Anya rubbed her forehead and her weariness showed.

"You are just making excuses. I am tired, Kreon. So much has happened. So much is happening. And so much will happen. We cannot seem to escape the war," she uttered in defeat, "Hitler took so much from so many, but not only in lives. My country's culture, its heritage, its pride has been destroyed by this lunatic and his followers," she sighed, despondent at the thought.

"It will change. Maybe not right now, Anya, but someday it will," Kreon replied, firmly determined to help make it so, although he did not know how.

"I suppose there will always be finger-pointing," she acknowledged sadly, "And as long as there is finger-pointing, we will never recognize the frailty in each other. Neither side did anything to prevent the Holocaust, did they, Kreon? Neither the German population nor the six million victims suffered from *apathy*. I think, with rifles and retribution aimed at our head, we were all paralyzed by fear. Armed men can turn people into lambs or lemmings. It is recognition and acceptance of that fact, and of our mutual fear, that will lead to understanding and acceptance between German and Jew, don't you think?" she asked trying to make coherent sense of her thoughts and emotions.

"It is perhaps a truth we should consider," Kreon replied, not wanting to stop the flow of words he knew she needed to express. She had bottled up so much for too long.

"Kreon, your father was destroyed by the Nazis. Why did you marry me, a German?"

"Because I loved you. Still love you. And, because I love you, I will never point a finger."

The next morning, a composed Anya helped dress Leni, taking care not to touch the bruises on her daughter's body, although the child winced once or twice. Anya shuddered at the ones on Leni's head and face while brushing her hair. Taking a few hours off from work, Kreon accompanied his wife and daughter to the school principal's office. Mrs. Weinberg accompanied them to ensure proper communication took place, and to keep Demetri in check.

The principal's secretary, seeing Leni's face and downcast eyes, and sensing the parents' mood, decided to whisk them right in. Mrs. Weinberg explained what arose the day before, and the principal took immediate and grim action. He already had an inkling of who the culprits were. Like most swaggering bullies, the four boys had bragged to their classmates about their recent picadillo, and word had reached the uppermost office. It was not long before they landed in that very office and were stripped of their impudence.

When the principal asked Leni, "Were these the boys that harmed you?" she gave a brief and shy nod of her head while holding on to her father's hand. The boys, seeing the damage they had done, were entreated to apologize to her in a sincere "or else" manner and were threatened with immediate expulsion from school if they ever did anything like it again. When they heard the principal call each of their parents and explain what had happened and their part in it, they squirmed and twitched, for they knew their backsides would soon be as red as any bruise they had inflicted.

Before they left, Leni's parents were instructed to have the child checked by the school nurse. If any notable injury was found, they were encouraged to see a doctor or go to the hospital immediately.

"Will the nurse poke me, Mama?" asked Leni with some trepidation. "I don't want to be poked at. It might hurt."

The efficient but kindly nurse made the exam as painless as possible, but Leni winced every so often as the tenderest spots were touched.

"There are no broken bones, just a lot of bruising. I would recommend ice packs and some aspirin if she is in too much discomfort. I would also suggest you keep her home for a few days until the discoloration on her face fades a touch and the pain diminishes. I am sure her teacher will be glad to send along the daily lesson plans so Leni can keep up with her class while she is healing."

Relieved that there was no sign of serious, physical injury, Anya, Kreon, and Mrs. Weinberg thanked the nurse for her time and care.

"Here, I have some eye drops for Anya," the nurse extended the small bottle to Anya. "You can put them in up to four times a day to help soothe her eyes. And make sure to take her to a doctor if she feels further pain in her face after this week. However, I think she will be fine," she assured them, patting Leni on the back as the family and Mrs. Weinberg departed.

Leni was secretly thrilled at being able to stay home and spend time with her mother. She wished she could always stay home. She did not even mind the achiness of her tender wounds because she could read in peace. And when her lesson plans were done and she finished a nap, she could sit up with Mama and Demetri to watch an afternoon show on their TV.

Returning to her classroom a week later, Leni feared being attacked again. But the boys had been dealt with at the hands of their parents in a memorable way and would not be assaulting anyone again in the foreseeable future. Knowing her ability to wreak havoc on their lives, the chastised ruffians kept their distance from Leni. As she sat at her desk, some classmates eyed her with suspicion, some with compassion, and some with a frown. She withstood it all because her father had instructed her to "Keep your head high!"

At home, it was a painstaking effort on her parents' part to explain why the boys had been so cruel. They told her about the war as best they could without traumatizing her further; but the incident at school had made Leni hyper-conscious of being *different*. German-born, the offspring of a Lutheran mother and Greek Orthodox father, wearing a gold cross instead of a Star of David, she could not escape her heritage. In class, there was discrimination. She remained the last to be picked for project teams headed by her classmates. This led to a sense of exclusion and embarrassment as she waited for her name to be called, only to hear it at the very end. Meanwhile, learning to read and books became her best friends. She thirsted for an escape from rejection and loneliness, and, after the ice ball incident, thirsted for knowledge.

In bits and drabs, Leni learned of the Nazis, the Holocaust, and of Adolf Hitler. She had already learned first-hand about the brutality and irony of prejudice.

"I don't like what I have been taught, Mama," she stated plainly one day to the dismay of her parents.

CHAPTER NINETY-TWO

When December appeared, the excitement of the holiday season proved a godsend in the Kalanis household. Grey clouds unveiled their silver lining. Leni appeared to be healing from the effects of the ice-ball incident when she came home chirping,

"Whistle while you work; Hitler is a jerk.
Mussolini pulled his peenie; Now it doesn't work!"

With Christmas fast approaching, Kreon put aside money for a good-sized tree, some ornaments, and decent gifts for the children: a stuffed doll for Leni to sleep with and a metal bus for Demetri's plastic soldiers to ride in. Anya's earnings from her house-cleaning jobs were going to supply a veritable feast on Christmas day with a giant baked ham at its center.

Kreon's Christmas bonus was saved for the best gift of all ...the purchase of a decent used car by spring. He had learned to drive with the aid of a co-worker and proudly acquired his New York driver's license.

"We will be traveling next year!" he promised his brood.

Aware their father could not drive a car across the ocean, they inquired, "Where to?"

"We will go on a vacation to Lowell, Massachusetts to visit our Greek relatives. You will have fun with your other cousins!" he proclaimed.

"We have other cousins?" a gleeful Leni asked, while Demetri looked confused.

"Yes! Several. And aunts and uncles! They are all nice people and fun to be with," an enthused Kreon assured them.

As they listened to their father's stories about their family in Massachusetts, the thought of Lowell excited them as much as Christmas did.

"I can't wait!" Demetri proclaimed, while Leni beamed behind him.

The first week of December brought snow, to the children's delight, and a package arrived from their Oma in Germany. Neither parent nor child had the patience to wait until Christmas Eve to open it. Placing it on their small dining table, Anya swiftly handed Kreon scissors to cut away the cord and brown paper wrapped around the parcel. Inside were a multitude of goodies: German Kaffee (coffee) for the grown-ups; two tins of chocolate-covered Nuremberger Lebkuchen (German gingerbread cookies); a package of Gummi-Bears for each child; a log of Marzipan that Demetri especially favored; and a "Poesie" album, bound in red leather, containing bits of children's poetry and festive stickers embossed in glitter for Leni. There was also an Advent calendar for each of Rosa's grandchildren to place above their bed. It consisted of a festive scene with 24 paper doors to open each day of the month. Each door contained a seasonal picture, and the final one, opened December 24, showcased the Nativity. German magazines were also enclosed for Kreon and Anya's reading pleasure, as well as some beautiful (and intact) glass-blown ornaments.

"Wow, so many wonderful things!" the children squealed while helping their mother place Oma's gifts under the tree and the ornaments on it. There was also a letter from Oma to be read.

While their parents settled on the couch and Anya unfolded its crisp pages, the children curled at their feet in anticipation of news from home, each praying it was good news. Anya first skimmed the letter on her own, before reading it openly to the children. She did not want to upset them with any bad news, as Rosa was always forthright about what was unfolding at home.

CHAPTER NINETY-THREE

December 2, 1952
Meine Lieblings,

I pray my letter finds you in good health and happy. It has been such a difficult time for all of us this past year, and things are progressing as best they can. Except for an occasional sniffle here and there, as it is colder than usual this winter, we are all doing fine.

Hannah's two, Reser and Hildegard, are adjusting to living with me at their great-grandparents' house. (The attic room is working out well.) They, naturally, are depressed, confused, and missing their mother, but I keep them as busy as I can to keep them from being overwhelmed by sorrow. They are in the company of their cousins often, and seldom ask for their father. (He has not shown his face since Hannah died! May Fate give him what he deserves!)

The news of your new life in America certainly does not sound easy nor free of problems, but I pray it improves with each passing day. How are you managing?

How are my darling grandchildren? I miss you all so dearly.

I will write more when Christmas is over. It has been feverish here with all the children focused on holiday projects, and Oma Babette baking day in and day out. (She never stops!) I am still employed at the factory, as you know, and trying to help each evening with dinner and so forth.

Meanwhile, conditions in Fürth, as well as the whole of Germany, seem to be progressing as best they can. The rebuilding of our nation's towns and cities is providing work for the unemployed, so one can see an improvement in our economy, but not as quickly as we would like. How is Kreon doing at his job?

Let me know if you enjoyed your package. I mailed it in early November so it should arrive for the Christmas season. I wish I could send more. Your own package arrived yesterday, but we will not open it until Christmas Eve. Reser helped me carry it from the post office because it was too big for me to carry alone. The children cannot wait to see what is in it. I look forward to handing out the coats and toys you mentioned. It does not matter if they are secondhand. They will not care, as they have so little now, and it will make them so happy. Vielen, vielen Dank, Lieblings!

The family and I wish you a blessed Christmas. We are always with you in spirit. Write soon and send a picture or two!

Much love and warm hugs,
Oma Rosa

Their grandmother's generous package inspired Leni and Demetri to purchase gifts for their parents too. Each day, the children clamored to do extra chores for extra money beyond their weekly allowance of a quarter each. Once they felt they had enough pennies saved and Christmas was drawing closer, Mrs. Weinberg took them to the local dime store to purchase their surprise packages. A bag of walnuts was chosen for their father, and a housekeeping magazine for their mother.

The celebration of Advent was also on the agenda each Sunday evening prior to Christmas. A green wreath adorned by four red candles was placed on a large white doily in the center of their TV cabinet and surrounded with other greenery. One candle was lit the first Sunday, then two the second, and so forth, until all four blazed and guided the way for the Christ Child's appearance on Christmas Eve. Christmas music was played on their phonograph and tea and cake and freshly baked cookies were served.

The preparation for that day, the streets and stores festooned with lights and festive window displays added to the pulsating joy of the season. Despite the challenges they had to overcome the past few months, no one in the Kalanis home was immune to it.

As it turned out, it was a quiet Christmas. The unseasonably warm weather, then the cold, then the warmer temps appearing again, had given everyone the sniffles. Nothing acute, just a collection of mild headaches, runny noses, and several "achoos" here and there. It was with a subdued heart and a grateful manner with which they opened their gifts that Christmas Eve and greeted Christmas Day.

CHAPTER NINETY-FOUR

January of 1953 appeared with little snow and days of blandness, much to the disappointment of the children. But one day their father came home from work bounding with good news.

"Anya, I have met this very nice gentleman at the bus stop, and he is German and has a wife and two young daughters, and they live not far from us...only two streets away....and he wants us to come visit and meet his family!"

"What? Go to the home of perfect strangers?" Anya asked, a bit alarmed.

"Not strangers. They are from Frankfurt, to be exact. German immigrants like us!" he responded with joy.

Anya could not help but smile at Kreon's exuberance, and the wide-eyed interest of her children.

"Well, then I suppose we must go!" she exclaimed.

Kreon kissed her, and the children clapped their hands with glee.

When Sunday approached, they bundled up, and with a tin of freshly baked cookies in Anya's hand, knocked on the door of Peter and Frieda Brandt and their two children Greta and Ursula. It was friendship at first sight.

The Kalanises and Brandts soon blended into an extended family.

Greta and Ursula, just a few years older than Leni and Demetri, took each child under their wing. "Tante Frieda" and Anya would grocery shop together to save money (e.g., splitting the cost of a pound of butter, with each taking two sticks from the package of four and divvying up whatever other sundries they could manage.) "Onkel Peter" guided them on outings to area parks or into the city via buses and subways to broaden their world. And kaffee-klatches at each other's homes became habitual.

When Mr. Brandt bought his first vehicle, the radius of their sojourns expanded. All eight adults and children often scrunched into his car to ride out to Long Island or to parks such as Bear Mountain in upstate New York.

"Look at the views!" the children would exclaim to the delight of their parents, who were just as enthralled when standing on a platform overlooking a mountain range, or atop a building granting them sweeping views of New York City.

During these many excursions, the adults seldom spoke about the war; they were all too busy acclimating themselves to their new country. Despite their youngsters becoming increasingly Americanized, both sets of parents made sure German was often heard at home, and German traditions continued to be maintained.

One tradition the Brandts, who were Catholic, shared with the Kalanises was their celebration of St. Nicholas Day in early December. The evening began with the four children hiding themselves wherever they could when they heard St. Nicholas' booming knock on the door (Mr. Brandt in disguise). Fearful they might have been "bad" during the year and earn a switch of his stick instead of a plate full of goodies, Demetri and Leni hid under their beds. Leni realized she was growing when St. Nicholas called out one evening, "Where is Leni?"

Greta laughingly answered, "She's stuck under her bed. She got caught on the wooden slat."

Leni's posterior was expanding, to her annoyance, but so was her world.

CHAPTER NINETY-FIVE

Come! Time to get going! Into the auto, everyone!"

Those words from their father's lips thrilled Leni and Demetri because it signaled an adventure ahead. With driver's license and savings in hand by March of 1953, Kreon was ready to purchase a used Dodge sedan. It was white and aqua in color, and the family was beset with joy when he brought it home

Demetri could not wait to get behind the wheel.

"Look, Papa, I'm driving!" he announced, trying to rotate the locked steering wheel by straining his short, stubby forearms.

"Yes, but your legs and feet need to grow more first, little man!" Kreon fired back as he scooped up his son and placed him in his proper seat.

To make their Mama happy and help alleviate her homesickness, Kreon decided that twice each month they would head over the Queensboro Bridge to East 86th Street and visit the Germanic Yorktown section of New York City. Anya, Leni, and Demetri scrambled into the car as soon as Saturday arrived. Between gawking out the window and annoying each other enroute, the siblings entertained themselves by trying to keep count of the yellow taxicabs whizzing by. This Saturday, Leni counted as many as two hundred cabs, which left her, and her brother flabbergasted. Papa had informed them that mostly rich people rode in taxis.

Where were all these rich people going? the children mused.

Parking as close to their destination as NYC parking signs allowed, Kreon and Anya led them on a spree through the German shops in the area. There was Karl Ehmer's delicatessen for savory Knackwurst, Leberkase, and Tee Wurst, as well as German butter and dark bread. The bakery and tea rooms, "Kleine Konditerei" and "Café Geiger", offered scrumptious pastries including their favorite German Krapfen (donuts) and Bienen Stich (Bee Sting Cake) filled with rich custard and crusted with honeyed almond slivers on top.

There was also a German restaurant and a German movie theater, but their favorite was the bookstore. Here they could purchase magazines like "Stern" and the eventual "Bunte" and pour through the pictures and articles of their homeland like sailors coming home from a long trip at sea. Leni began teaching herself to read and write basic German through these periodicals, much to the astonishment of her parents. They thought it was an incredible achievement, but Leni never saw it that way because it all came so naturally to her.

On 86th Street they found the best of their current world and that of their past. Their Papa's driving ability and his new car enriched their life when they hit the open road. The car was revered as a miracle.

When they returned home, they made dinner out of the delicatessen food, ate German pastries for dessert, played a new German record on the phonograph, and pored over the pictures and articles in the periodicals they purchased.

"Saturdays in Yorktown are a feast for my soul," Anya whispered to Kreon as she planted a kiss on his cheek. He was only too happy to oblige.

CHAPTER NINETY-SIX

That spring, their new mode of travel enabled Kreon and Anya to plan their first family vacation. It was to Lowell, Massachusetts to meet Kreon's Greek relatives. The Stanos family now encompassed Papa's aunt, Fotini, her husband, Andreas, as well as their four sons and daughter. Most of the siblings were married and had children of their own. Demetri and Leni were looking forward to meeting and playing with their Greek cousins and being part of their father's family.

On the day they were to leave, misfortune intervened in an unexpected way: their Mama woke up blind in one eye and with blurred vision in the other.

They were stricken. Kreon most of all, seeing Anya so vulnerable frightened. Demetri and Leni approached their mother's bed and began to weep. Anya's arms enfolded them, and she drew them into bed beside her.

"Stay here with your mother," their father hastily instructed, "I am going to get Mrs. Weinberg and see if she can help."

Kreon returned with Milly, who phoned and arranged to have Anya placed in the immediate care of a Park Avenue specialist. The specialist, she informed them, was her cousin and a well-known ophthalmologist. Before Kreon and the children could even grasp the startling turn of events, they found themselves visiting Anya at the prestigious Mt. Sinai Hospital on Fifth Avenue in New York City.

Visiting her in the hospital during those challenging days, Kreon looked forlorn and was silent when he and the children returned home. Noticing his troubled demeanor, neither Demetri nor Leni felt like chatting either. It frightened them to have their mother hospitalized and unwell, and they clung to their father's side. Yet their Mama always smiled when they went to see her. She gave them the feeling that everything would be alright; that this was just a brief misstep in their family's journey.

Through the weeks of her hospitalization, Anya's disease had not been given a name. A possible diagnosis, Kreon was informed in Greek by a hospital interpreter, was Multiple Sclerosis, a frightening and chronic neuro-degenerative disease; but there were no tests that could prove it conclusively. An alternate prognosis the medical staff considered was a brief nervous disorder stemming from the stress Anya had experienced in recent years. Time would determine which it was.

Returning to his wife's hospital room after hearing this, Kreon's face showed his all.

"I know what they said, Kreon. Like you, I was informed this morning."

She flashed him a warning eye, "We will *not* wallow in self-pity! Remember my grandmother's words, 'Do not make mountains out of mole hills; make mole hills out of mountains!'" He grasped her message and said nothing.

No matter the diagnosis, the primary physician initiated pro-active treatment from day one. With special care and mega-doses of B vitamins, Anya regained sight in both eyes. However, she could only see in color with one eye, and black and white with the other. Everyone was thrilled that she could see at all.

When Anya was well again and released from the hospital, she and Kreon discussed their situation.

"I will be fine, Kreon. I am determined to be fine." There were no doubts clouding her mind. "I am in the best of hands. How fortunate we have been to have Milly as our neighbor. She brought me to the best doctor and the best hospital. What more could we ask? Besides, I absolutely cannot leave you. What would you and the children do without me? You would become a clueless Hausfrau."

He took her hand and smiled, but his heart remained secretly heavy. The weight of guilt was preying upon him.

Have I demanded too much of her? Have I been too selfish in fulfilling my own dream? What of hers?

"You know what?" she continued, bubbling with plans, oblivious to the turmoil he was hiding so well, "I think we should travel to Lowell before school resumes in the fall. We all need a change of scene and something joyful to look forward to. It will give me enough time to recuperate, and the weather will still be warm in late August. What do you say, husband?"

Kreon responded with a squeeze of his hand, "Sounds like a perfect plan, wife."

To keep Anya and the children comfortable through the remainder of the summer, Kreon promptly purchased an air conditioning unit and placed it in the living room window. There they gathered and stretched like lethargic cats as the cool air wafted over them on the broiling hot days. The whirring noise that first irritated their ears soon became a Godsend when the mid-summer temperatures rose to above 90. On weekends, they headed for a beach so the children could learn to swim. Sitting in the sand, they let the breeze off Long Island Sound refresh them. By the latter part of August, they were galvanized, packed, and ready for their vacation in Massachusetts.

CHAPTER NINETY-SEVEN

Time to get up!" their father prompted at 6:00 a.m. on the day of their departure, "We have to shower, dress, eat breakfast and pack up the car by 7:00 this morning if we want to avoid heavy traffic. My aunt and uncle are expecting us late morning. So, be good little soldiers and get moving!"

The children sat up, yawned broadly, and wiped the sleep from their eyes before dropping their feet to the floor. Both wanted to sink back into their comfortable bed and attempted to do so.

"No! No! No!" their mother shouted, clapping her hands to wake them fully,

"Get up! Our vacation begins right now!"

The word "vacation" jumpstarted their brains and the rest of their body responded. Anya watched with amusement as Leni and Demetri sprang out of bed, bumped into each other at the door, and ran for the bathroom.

"I'm going first!" Leni yelled.

"But I have to pee!" Demetri yelled louder. Demetri won.

Duly washed and dressed, they sat down for a bowl of cereal topped by a sliced banana. Orange juice was waiting in their glasses. Cod liver oil had been abandoned.

"Mama, what is Papa looking at?" Leni asked, watching her father buried behind a huge sheaf of paper.

"He is studying a map to see which are the best roads for us to travel on today," Anya informed her.

"How far is Lowell?" Demetri wanted to know.

"Pretty far. You better be good in the car and not annoy Papa, or we'll never get there," his big sister counselled.

"About five or six hours away if we take a break along the route," said their father munching on buttered toast as he scanned the map, "We should be there in time for lunch. Finish eating and help your Mama with the dishes and small packages."

Demetri noticed one bag was filled with fruit and the others with cookies, sandwiches, and juice boxes. He decided he would place the cookie bag closest to his seat in the car.

They were on the road within the hour.

The trip north was a revelation. After driving past smaller urban areas, Kreon chose to take a few back roads, where the land morphed into rural hills, dotted with lovely homes in parklike settings.

"Kreon, why did I think everything would look like New York City? Connecticut is so beautiful!"

"As are parts of Massachusetts and even further north. And the beaches of the Atlantic are never far away. We will have to take more rides through the countryside this fall. The colors will leave you breathless!"

Demetri jumped in his seat and piped up, "Look! Moo cows!"

Everyone's eyes turned to the chocolate-colored bovine grazing in the fields. The sight brought a sense of contentment to the passengers. Their minds travelled back in time...back home to Germany...yet here they were in America.

When the car drew closer to Lowell, Kreon felt a rumble of nerves in his stomach. He was unsure of the reception his wife and children would receive.

Because he had not wanted to upset her, he had never mentioned to Anya that his relatives had hoped when he returned to America someday, he would abide by tradition and wed a girl from their Greek community. They had even bothered to select a few candidates for him. Taken aback when Kreon wed Anya before they could protest, he prayed they would respect and fall in love with his chosen wife. The hour of reckoning was less than an hour away.

Upon arrival, they were greeted cordially, amid enticing aromas from his aunt's kitchen. A sizeable leg of lamb with orzo noodles was roasting in the oven and freshly baked koulourakia were cooling on a shelf. Demetri's and Leni's eyes became fixated on the Greek cookies, as they piled into the humble home.

Kreon's aunt and uncle, now in their eighties, both lean of body with slight curves to their spine, fussed as they shuffled around the visitors. They shook hands with Anya, hugged the children, and kissed Kreon on each cheek. When introductions were made, his maternal aunt and uncle insisted on being called "Thea" and "Theo" (aunt and uncle) by Anya, and "Yia-Yia" (grandmother) and "Papou" (grandfather) by the children. Leni and Demetri picked the terms up without a problem as "YAH-YAH" and "PAH-POO" made them giggle and were easy to pronounce.

By evening, after finishing a substantial supper, Leni and Demetri found themselves surrounded by surrogate aunts, uncles, and a multitude of cousins. Life felt normal for the first time since they left their mother country. It was like being home again in their great-grandmother's kitchen.

Alone in their guest bedroom that night, Kreon confessed his earlier plight to his wife.

"Why did you not tell me they were trying to hitch you to a Greek bride? I would have understood and given you up," she piously told him. He did not see the mischievous smirk on her face.

"I was afraid you would send me away, and my life would have been wretched. Two hot-tempered Greeks in the same household are one too many for me!" he cried.

"That would never have happened. I intended to win the prize!" she laughed, and fell on top of him in the bed, setting the springs to creaking.

"Oh dear, what will they think!" Anya whispered.

"That I am exceedingly happy with my wife," he said, and kissed her soundly on her grinning lips.

Amid their daily outings to inspect Lowell and visit with relatives and friends, Yia-Yia began to teach Anya to cook savory Greek dishes in her spare time: Greek lemon chicken (drenched with oregano and lemon juice in melted butter), Dolmathes (grapevine leaves stuffed with meat and rice), as well as Greek meatballs, Spanakopita (spinach pie), and Avgolemono (lemon) soup were amid the proffered meals. While conjuring up this cuisine, the ladies bonded.

The dishes would be alternated with German sauerbraten, potato dumplings, sausages, and sauerkraut when they returned home...and the eventual American hamburgers and hot dogs. Anya was becoming a formidable international cook, Kreon surmised!

While Yia-Yia and their mother prepared supper, Demetri and Leni often headed to the corner bodega to purchase their favorite comic books ("Lulu" and "Archie" for her; super-heroes for him) and a fruity popsicle. Returning to the comfortable chairs on the enclosed porch, they would slurp their ice pops and enjoy their comics until it was time for supper.

At the table, they often found their father chatting in Greek with Papou, while their mother and Yia-Yia served the meal. Throughout the two weeks of their visit, mealtime, and playtime with other members of the family, made for many happy hours.

"I like playing with my cousins, Papa," Leni divulged.

"Me too!" Demetri seconded.

One special morning, Kreon and Anya decided to take Yia-Yia and Papou along on a visit to a lakeside amusement park situated just over the Massachusetts border in New Hampshire. While Papou rested on a bench with Kreon, Anya and the children beckoned their

Greek grandmother to view herself in the long, funhouse mirrors bordering the park's walkway.

"Come, Yia-Yia!" they implored.

With some trepidation, Yia-Yia, walked over and viewed her image from head to foot. Dressed in staid shoes, beige stockings, and wearing a sedate, navy dress that bordered her ankles, the usually reticent and dignified matriarch of the Stanos family broke into unhinged laughter. Her distorted reflection in each mirror had transformed her body into a humorous freak of nature, and she had never seen such optical illusions of herself before. Their peals of laughter were incessant and contagious, and Kreon and Papou soon joined in. Listening to the mirth, Kreon could not help but think that laughter was the international language of angels.

Approaching their last weekend, a visit to a Greek festival in a sprawling park near Lowell was mandated by the entire Stanos brood. Among the pines and nettles, an enthralled Leni found herself eating Greek food, learning a Greek dance, and even learning to sing a Greek song. Her nature easily adapted to the exuberant Mediterranean spirit. Her mother's and brother's nature did so in a more subdued way. As four-year-old Demetri sat in Anya's lap, they found enjoyment through quiet observation of the cultural festivities, while Leni and Kreon plunged whole-heartedly into it.

"Come, Leni, join the circle of dancers!" Kreon insisted.

Leni did so without qualms, as her father grabbed her hand and her other was caught up by a cousin to her right. First moving in a serpentine chain to the sound of Bouzouki music, then forming a giant circle, the participants weaved and skipped to the intricate sounds of the Syrtaki, a Greek folk dance. A gleeful Leni burst into chuckles as she tried to keep up with the steps. Her father and his cousins grinned at her enthusiastic attempt to master the dance. Yia-Yia and Papou, sitting on the sidelines with Anya and Demetri, applauded Leni's effort.

Anya smiled watching the activities, remembering how her children had been crammed into a room or petite garden with their cousins in Germany. In America, the houses and rooms of Kreon's Greek cousins were enormous, with porches and patios spilling onto vast lawns. The impressive homeowners in his family consisted of a doctor, a lawyer, and two government officials. Together, however, they were simply a normal family enjoying each other's company. No airs were permitted. Their easy inclusion of her family warmed Anya's heart toward them.

When time came for the picnic lunch, everyone sauntered over to the stands that offered an abundance of delicious Greek dishes. One booth served the Dolmathes Leni had developed a taste for, another beef and vegetables on skewers with a helping of rice, another Pasticio (squares of Greek lasagna), and last came mouth-watering desserts. Baklava, dripping in nuts and honey amid layers of thin pastry, appeared to be the favorite.

Demetri's teeth sank into the sweet pastry with relish, gobs of it sticking to his lips, teeth, and fingers which his tongue tried to lick away. Anya had to get a cup of water and use her handkerchief to make him look presentable again. Leni demurred to using a fork like her mother and the other grown-ups did, although fingers would have been more fun.

The entire day provided riveting involvement in Greek culture for the fledgling members of Yia-Yia's and Papou's family in Lowell.

With the day over and settled in bed that night, Kreon turned to Anya tired but happy, "I hope you enjoyed your first visit to Lowell."

"I did. It filled a certain void within me, and I am sure it did for the children too."

She kissed him good-night and turned out the light. He turned over and was soon asleep. Anya stayed awake, listening to him breathe, as she stared into the void that lay before them.

The morning of their return to the city, Anya took the children to the corner bodega to select comic books and snacks for the trip. Kreon and his aunt, meanwhile, were enroute to the cemetery to pay his last respects to his mother. Papou chose to remain home and wait in his garden for everyone's return.

Arriving at the cemetery, Kreon gathered a bouquet of red and white carnations from the backseat and brought them to the gravesite. His aunt said a little prayer in Greek, and they crossed themselves as she finished. Stepping forward and trying to maintain his composure, he placed the flowers on his mother's grave.

"It is odd that both my wife and my mother love carnations instead of roses."

His aunt gave him a penetrating look, "It is an enchanting coincidence between the two women you love the most, Kreon. It is not an omen of impending doom."

She took his hand and entwined her fingers with his.

"How is Anya doing? She looks very well."

"She is in the best of hands, Thea."

"Your parents would be proud of you. You chose well and very wisely."

She squeezed Kreon's hand as a shadow passed over his face and his voice grew hoarse, "Thank you, Thea."

"Anya will be fine. She is a strong woman, despite looking like a delicate flower. It is her husband I worry the most about. He blubbers at the oddest times."

He smiled at those words, as did she.

"I will be fine too. I just want Anya to feel safe and content in America. She is trying so hard to adjust, and I feel guilty taking her from her family. Everything has been so difficult for her."

"Give her time and be patient."

"I am trying, Thea. But I hate to see her unhappy in any way."

"She has you and the children as her rock, and we are here too. You are not without family to help."

Kreon gazed at the grave with the Kalanis name on it.

"I wish father could have been laid to rest here too."

"As do I, Kreon, as do I."

They remained standing there, holding hands, silent in their individual thoughts, letting the warm remnants of summer console them.

Meeting up later that morning, Kreon and his brood packed up the car to begin their journey home. Hugs and sincere invitations to come visit again were offered multiple times. Special invitations to spend the Greek Easter in Lowell next spring were extended by all. Reciprocal invitations to visit them in New Yok City were also extended, as the younger members of Kreon's family had never been to Manhattan and longed to see it.

Packed in the car, amid a last outpouring of hugs and kisses, their journey down the byways of Massachusetts and Connecticut toward home was underway.

Contemplative after their departure, it was not long before a curious Leni broke the silence.

"Papa, what is the Greek Easter like? Is it different from ours?"

Kreon, delighted that she showed an interest, was quick to reply, "Yes, in some ways. The Greek Easter is still about the Crucifixion and Resurrection of Jesus Christ, like Mama taught you. The traditions and practices are different though."

"How?" she wanted to know.

"Well," Kreon began, "first, the Easter eggs displayed in baskets and bowls around the house are all dyed a deep red, unlike the bright colors you and Demetri are used to. The red eggs are called "kokkina avga".

"What?" a confused Demetri asked.

"KO-KEEN-AH-AFF-GAH!" Leni yelled into his ear, hoping it would sink into her brother's head.

"That is correct, although you need not shout it," Kreon chided her. "The red color symbolizes the Blood of Christ, and the hard shells represent the Tomb of Christ. When the eggs are cracked open, it symbolizes Christ's Resurrection from the Dead."

"That's really interesting, Papa!" a fascinated Leni professed. This, of course, spurred her father to enlighten the children even further. With amusement, Anya watched her husband transform into a professor.

"Yes, it is interesting. The cracking of the egg is achieved by playing Tsougrisma," Kreon explained.

"Two-grease-mess" Demetri repeated, while Leni gave him a hopeless look and Anya chuckled.

"Tsou-gris-ma," his father clarified, "is a serious egg-tapping game. Everyone chooses their red, hard-boiled egg carefully and then takes turns hitting each other's egg point to point. If your egg breaks, you are out. If you are the last one without a cracked egg, you will be blessed and have luck for the rest of the year."

"Can we crack open a chocolate Easter egg too?" Demetri asked, innocent in his perception of Easter rituals. Leni shook her head, and Anya covered her mouth to not laugh out loud at the seriousness of his question. Kreon, grinning ear to ear, affirmed, "Very good question, but no."

Demetri frowned, "Well, it would taste better than a red egg."

"Oh, but Yia-Yia would bake a special bread for you that smells like Heaven called 'Tsoureki'. It is in the shape of a large braid with a red egg in the middle. And then there are her delicious butter cookies, 'Koulourakia', and a roasted lamb will be in the oven for Easter dinner."

"Why do they have to give everything such funny names?" Demetri wanted to know.

"They are *Greek* names, not funny names," Leni informed him, but that was not enough to squelch her brother.

"I like *German* Lebkuchen better," he rebutted, this time giving *her* the evil eye.

Anya murmured to Kreon, "I hope next spring they will refrain from cracking their heads together."

Kreon laughed out loud and kept on driving.

Describing the Greek Easter to the children had churned up memories of his last boyhood Easter in Lowell. His blessed mother had prepared an out-and-out feast for their dinner, having saved what she could from the weekly grocery money. That evening they dressed up for the Holy Saturday midnight service and congregated with the rest of their kin at the Greek Orthodox Church they frequented in Lowell. The basilica was massive and ornate inside. As the solemn ritual progressed, he had been, as always, fascinated by the magnificence of the priests' attire, and listened closely to the ritual passages they intoned. At the end of the prolonged ceremony, accompanied by cough-inducing clouds of incense, the priests lined up near the altar holding gold-framed portraits of the Virgin Mary and the Christ. Droves of worshippers rose from their seats, ushered their children forward, and headed toward the altar. One after another they bent in humble supplication to kiss the priests' rings, kiss each of the displayed pictures, then cross themselves before departing through the immense carved and gilded doors. Everyone held lighted candles as they exited. The candles remained cautiously held while glowing all the way home. Kreon had tried hard not to drop his, nor extinguish it, for fear of God striking him dead. It was crucial to bring the lighted candle home intact so God would smile favorably upon you.

Outside the church after Holy Saturday, they reunited with the rest of their kin. Then, when Sunday morning came, they went through another Orthodox ceremony to celebrate the resurrection of Christ. Easter dinner at his aunt and uncle's house and the cracking of the eggs followed.

The scenes of that last Easter rose in his mind like wisps of sea smoke on a misty day. Anya's hand on his arm startled him back to reality.

"Are you alright?" The children had been squabbling in the backseat without the usual reprimand from Kreon.

"Yes, I am fine. I have just been thinking," he told her.

"About what?" She looked at him with concern, "You seemed so far off and sad."

"I was remembering my last Greek Easter with my mother, when we were still whole as a family. It was wonderful this week to be reunited with Yia-Yia and Papou, as well as with the cousins. The only Greek relatives we have yet to be reunited with are my sister,

Vasiliki, and her family. I miss her. I cannot believe she has two children, too, that I have never met."

Anya placed her hand over his on the steering wheel.

"Someday our wallet will be fat enough to bridge the Atlantic and the Mediterranean," she reassured him, "Meanwhile, be glad she writes letters and sends pictures, as do we."

CHAPTER NINETY-EIGHT

In New York, during his first visit, Kreon had found and been reunited with his younger sister, Sonia, after learning of her whereabouts from Yia-Yia. He had also met with his brother, Apostolones, who had been renamed "Tomas" by his adoptive parents. The meetings had not gone well. With Tomas, who was known to be a playboy and gambler, no deep bond existed between them, and they did not see each other again. With Sonia, their conversation boiled into bitter rancor over his father's death and her abandonment of their family.

"I needed the money for my fare to America!" she argued.

"You left your family behind to starve!" he shouted at her.

Anya, aware of Kreon's disappointment with Tomas, and his continued resentment toward and dislike of Sonia, did not press the issue. She only wished their wounds would heal.

CHAPTER NINETY-NINE

By Christmas of that year, through Mrs. Weinberg, and her neighborhood chum, Jerusha, Leni received a peek into Jewish culture and the significance of the Jewish holidays like Hannukah and Passover. Anya had read her passages from the New Testament of the Holy Bible, while Jerusha opened Leni's eyes to stories in the Old Testament. And then there was her father, who grew up Greek Orthodox, and she did not know what part of the Bible he followed, if any at all. It was both puzzling and fascinating to her.

When Jewish holidays rolled around, non-Jewish children were expected to attend their classes, but Leni saw no point in going. Only a mere trickle of students showed up, and the lessons covered shallow ground at best. In some classes she was left to doodle in her notebook.

Pleading her case like a lawyer, she presented her case to her parents, "Please can I stay home too? It's so boring at school with so little to do!"

Her parents relented. They preferred she fill her time in a productive manner, which Leni did by bringing home an awe-inspiring stack of library books. Sleuthing with Nancy Drew or reading tales about faraway lands was an education, they rationalized.

On occasion Leni would be invited to participate in a holiday celebration at Jerusha's house, which helped Leni bond with her neighbors. She was made aware of the purpose of the Menorah and

Driedl during Hanukkah, and the symbolism of matzo bread during Passover.

In return, several neighbors were invited to savor a German Christmas by making a pilgrimage to view the Kalanis' holiday tree. The ceiling-high fir was decorated with ornaments and tinsel with Anya's skillful hand (and her children's interference).

"Stop scrunching up the tinsel and throwing it at the tree! You are making a mess of it!" she would yell. Their father was recruited to drape the holiday lights around its rim. The final task was performed by Demetri and Leni. Placing dabs of white cotton here and there on the branches, they attempted to create a snowfall effect on the tree.

"Demetri, Mama said to make the cotton look like snowflakes, not snowballs," his father cautioned.

The final touch was left to Kreon, He had the honor of placing a crepe angel, dressed in white and gold, at the pinnacle of the tree. Unfortunately, as their father climbed on top of their freshly waxed desk to reach the peak branch, he slipped and crashed onto the tree. The 8-ft. tall fir, lights, and ornaments wound up in a heap on the living room floor, topped by their father.

"Kreon!" A horrified Anya was heard screaming two doors down, as she rushed to help him up, praying he was in one piece.

What would I do if he were seriously hurt? blazed through her mind at that moment.

A petrified Demetri and Leni were of little help. Being kids, nearing ages five and eight, it was not easy to discern whether they were more concerned about their father or about the condition of their holiday tree, as they stood there motionless. All were relieved when a stupefied Kreon stood up, was able to move all moveable body parts, and bore only a few scratches.

After cleaning himself up, Anya applied bandages to his cuts, and they proceeded to resurrect the battered mess to its former glory. Kreon braved the height again but, this time, using a sturdy chair with proper non-slip cushioning.

What would we do without Papa? popped into the siblings'

heads afterward. It was not a sentimental question. It was a frightful consideration in their now conscious minds.

As the season progressed, their homesickness sprouted yet again with the arrival of holiday cards, letters, and packages from Germany. Their friends, the Brandts, were spending the holidays back in the "old country" this year, which made their loneliness more poignant, as they wished they could be there too.

On Christmas Eve, as Kreon observed the increasing nostalgia drift over their faces, the snow flurries outside the window inspired a spur-of-the-moment idea.

"Get dressed in warm clothes. We are heading into the city!" he ordered,

"The city...while it is snowing?" Anya remarked, flabbergasted by his suggestion. Leni and Demetri, having no such qualms, percolated with excitement.

"Yes!" A resolute Kreon shouted and shooed them off the couch to get ready.

Amid a flurry of sweaters, coats, boots and mittens, Kreon drove the short distance to the nearest subway station, parked the car in a nearby lot, and led them aboard the train for Manhattan. Only a few passengers were seated in the subway car with them, as the train sped through the underground caverns with clattering speed.

Switching trains at mid-point, they finally emerged on 59th street near the Plaza Hotel. To their delight, a winter wonderland greeted them. Snowflakes were drifting to the ground in a tantalizing ballet. The fountain in front of the Plaza Hotel was emblazoned with white lights and covered with crystalline snow. The lighted windows of the surrounding skyscrapers were scattered like diamonds against the night sky. It was miraculous. The city had been transformed into their own Christmas snow globe.

There was little wind as the flakes fell and landed softly. The streets were silent and empty except for a few rare souls and a lone policeman walking his beat along the avenue. No sign of danger appeared to lurk in the city. And sight of all sights, a skier was headed down snow-covered Fifth Avenue! With ski mask, skies, and ski-boots on, the intrepid soul was gaily maneuvering himself along the avenue with his ski poles. When the policeman, Kreon, Anya, and their offspring waved to him and yelled, "Merry Christmas!", he raised his pole and merrily reciprocated in kind.

Continuing their trek along Fifth Avenue toward Rockefeller Center, only minutes passed before the powdery snowflakes became more profuse. Sticking close to store fronts to keep from being blanketed in white, they were mesmerized by the window displays filled with mannequins in rich winter garb; enchanted forests with trains, elves, or mechanical deer moving about; holiday trees glistening with dazzling lights and ornaments; or magnificent jewels in mirrored enclosures twinkling under radiant spotlights.

"Mama, Papa...Look! Look! Look!" was all the children could utter.

They were breathless and filled with awe when they reached Rockefeller Center with its wide promenade displaying lighted angels and its glassine, sunken skating rink. At the center of it all was the golden statue of Prometheus, the Greek God of Fire, stretched lengthwise under the massive Rockefeller Center Christmas tree. Transfixed, Leni and Demetri sprinted toward it, dazzled by its colossal size and the immense, colorful ball-shaped ornaments dangling from its wide-sweeping branches.

"Everything is so big in America!" Demetri exclaimed.

Oohing and ahhing as they examined the giant evergreen from all angles, Kreon attempted to take pictures before they turned back to the rink. There they watched a handful of skaters do their last glides and twirls before seeking shelter in warmer quarters, and letting a Zamboni clear the drifting snow.

"Papa, can I get a ride on that truck?" Demetri asked, enthralled by its unusual wheels.

"Not today, son, but maybe someday," Kreon told him.

Demetri's eyes lit up at the thought. Little did he know what was waiting for him under the Christmas tree (in miniature, of course).

Leni gazed dreamily at the skating rink.

"I wish I could twirl like they do and wear a pretty costume and white skates."

"I am sure some day you will twirl like a princess on ice," Kreon stated with a promise in his voice.

Leni's eyes lit up at the thought.

Her mother smiled, "And I wish I could sit some place warm and get something to eat."

"That wish I can fulfill right now!" Kreon declared jovially.

"I'm hungry!" both children piped up, while their parents took their hands and led them back to Fifth Avenue.

Just two blocks away, they found a family-style restaurant festooned in rustic, holiday décor. When Kreon opened the door, Anya was happy to see a warm and welcoming dining room filled with country and not modern décor. The children made a swift beeline for a table near the window. When the waitress brought the menus, the happily ensconced family was more than ready to order their Christmas dinner.

The homey bistro, filled with a scant number of patrons, smelled of sumptuous home-cooking and oven-baked goods. Aromatic spices wafted through the air. White candles, encircled in holiday greenery, flickered on each table. They had never eaten Christmas dinner as a family in a restaurant before (although once they did have lunch at an Automat where everyone put nickels in to get their food out of the glass display cases). Anya noted the menu offered a grand array of dishes to choose from. *What to choose?* She decided Kreon should make the selection for them and once ordered, instruct the children to wait patiently for the feast to arrive. However, once served, they dug into their meal like excavators at King Tuts' Tomb uncovering layers and layers of unknown treasure.

Stuffed with succulent pot roast, mashed potatoes, gravy, buttered rolls, and peas, Leni and Demetri looked up after finishing their meal, each with a twinge in their sweet tooth.

"May we have dessert, Papa?" Leni asked shyly, knowing it would add to the bill. Her nostrils, and her brother's, inhaled deeply when they caught a whiff of cinnamon and vanilla from the dessert cart nearby. It was laden with elegant pastries of the most delicate kind, amid generous portions of cake and pie.

"Yes, you may," he said. Beckoning to their waitress, Kreon ordered hot chocolate for Leni and Demetri, coffee for himself and Anya, and generous portions of hot apple pie with whipped cream for all.

The pie was delicious, but not as good as Oma's apple strudel, Leni decided; yet the warm spices and thick juice from the apples were still heaven to her taste. She voiced no complaints. Demetri, however, was more vocal.

"This pie tastes almost as good as Mama's Spritz cookies!" he declared, while everyone chuckled.

After waiting for Demetri to slurp up the last bit of his pie and hot chocolate, Kreon contentedly paid the sizable bill. Their dinner had been worth it.

Putting on their coats, mittens, scarves and hats, the family left the coziness of the restaurant with some reluctance. A swoosh of nippy air greeted them as they headed out the door and continued their journey through the drifting snow.   Walking across Fifth Avenue, they entered St. Patrick's Cathedral through its massive doors. Kreon watched as his wife and children were left breathless by the church's interior. They paused for a moment in stunned silence. Every alcove and vestibule were adorned with red and white poinsettias; and countless rows of burning candles in glass holders were glowing throughout.

"Would you each like to light one?" Kreon asked.

"Oh yes," they whispered in unison, as he placed money in the offering box and instructed each of them to select a candle.

Using the long, thin, reeds of wood that were provided, they lighted their candles, while their mother recited a prayer blessing all the people they loved, as well as the birth of the Baby Jesus. Kreon could tell their thoughts were with Oma and their great-grandparents, so far away, and of Hannah and her unborn child.

"Please take care of them," Anya prayed as the candles flickered. Taking in their warmth and glow, she felt a strange sense of peace in placing their spirits in the hand of the Lord. She smiled at Kreon and gathered her children close.

Wending their way through the aisles of the cathedral, they stopped to view the stained-glass windows, the Stations of the Cross, and the magnificent display of the Christ Child laying in the manger. Throughout their tranquil stroll, treading with care so as not to disturb the devout visitors praying in the pews, the majesty of their surroundings humbled them.

They departed St. Patrick's Cathedral in quietly and began their journey home. Wandering back to the subway station, Anya watched as the persistent snowfall bejeweled Fifth Avenue and the pathways leading into Central Park. The Park glistened with glowing lanterns reflected on the snow-covered lawns and walkways. Looking back at the soaring skyscrapers flanking the avenue before they trotted down to the subway station, Anya realized how much they were beacons of promise and opportunity.

What she appreciated most of all on their mystical tour was the pristine beauty and stillness of New York City on a snowy night. It was a rare event and not an easy one to replicate. Miracles seldom are.

Returning home, they rid themselves of their wet clothes and put on their flannel nightwear and robes to warm themselves. After Anya set up things in the kitchen, Leni and Demetri were offered a tiny dribble of "Glühwein", a hot punch native to their homeland (concocted of port wine, citrus fruit, and cloves), and laughingly pretended to be woozy. Substantial mugs of hot chocolate followed, accompanied by the Nuernberger Lebkuchen (gingerbread cookies) Oma had sent in her Christmas package. A plate of their mother's homemade German butter cookies also appeared. Demetri and Leni wasted no time in scarfing the treats down with immense gusto.

After stacking up Perry Como, Tennessee Ernie Ford, and

German Christmas LPs to play on their phonograph throughout the evening, the family made themselves comfortable on the living room couch. Leni, scanning the wrapped treasures under the tree, was eager to dole them out. She had saved her allowance and again done extra chores to buy her parents and brother some proper gifts this year. For her Mama, she bought a small bottle of "Evening in Paris" perfume from McCrory's Five & Dime; for her Papa, a linen handkerchief with a "K" embroidered on it; and for Demetri, a special, oversized edition of a Superman comic book. She could barely wait to surprise them!

When time came to open the festive packages, her parents made a big to-do over Leni's gifts, which made her blush with joy. Demetri let out a singular (and loud) "Whoopee!" and was soon entrenched in his comic book.

Upon receiving her own treasures, Leni was astonished to be gifted with the doll crib she had coveted in McCrory's window. Her parents had hidden it in their bedroom closet and decorated it with a big, red bow.

"Oh Danke schöen, Mama and Papa! Now I have a proper place for my doll from Oma to sleep!" she exclaimed. Demetri, who had received a set of plastic cowboys with miniature horses, and a model Zamboni that ran on batteries, was busy playing with them on the carpet.

When all wound down, it was well past their bedtime. Yet there was one last ritual to perform: the lighting of all four candles on the Advent wreath. The candles were to light the way for the Christ Child to be born on Christmas Day. This task Leni did with great solemnity as "Silent Night" by the Vienna Boys Choir was played.

It was a perfect Christmas.

The children, sleepy and sighing, were soon curled up on each side of Kreon and nestled in his arms.

Anya stared at the comforting scene. Her children were sleeping peacefully, and she prayed it would always be so. She stared at her husband in admiration.

On this day, he had created magic. It had opened her eyes.

Life would not always be this idyllic for them, she knew. Like any family, they would face peaks and valleys in the years ahead. But on this day, they had a decent roof over their heads, food in the house, a TV, a car, a phone, warm clothes, German and American friends, a Greek family that embraced them, a German family that loved and missed them, and, most valuable of all, each other.

There was also the hope of Anya landing a position as a ticketing clerk in a major department store in the area. It was only a bus ride away and offered a good wage and decent discount on any merchandise she wished to purchase there. An interview had been set up for the first week of the New Year.

She was a wreck about it, often exclaiming to Kreon and Mrs. Weinberg, "I am not prepared to do this yet!"

But they assured her that she could easily learn the job, since she was nimble with her fingers and her English was much improved.

She decided she would be brave and go for that interview. With more money coming in, more could be saved. Perhaps they could visit Germany, or even Greece. And her mother could visit in time. Maybe they could even save for a house in Connecticut where, Kreon mentioned, there were manufacturing companies offering jobs in his field. Life was full of possibilities.

She studied her husband. He looked so content with the children asleep in his arms.

"Kreon, why did you take us to New York City in the snow?" she wondered out loud, as it had been such an impulsive move.

Turning to her, he answered with complete sincerity, as he reflected on the day, "One Christmas Eve, when I was apart from you and all alone, I went into the city during a snowfall to walk the streets in silence. I walked for hours trying to get over the sadness and loneliness of not having you and the children with me. And..." He stopped and grew quiet.

If only you knew how many tears I shed that day, Anya.

"And what?" she asked gently.

He gave her a smile, "...and, today, we are a family."

Indeed, they were, she concurred. And that, for Kreon, seemed enough.

She studied him again. *No, there is one more thing I need to do.*

"Kreon...." she whispered so as not to wake their dozing children.

"Yes?" he replied, drowsy from the evening's celebration.

She caressed his arm with warm affection, and he regarded her cheerful face with an inquisitive look.

Gazing directly into his eyes, she said, "I think it is time I studied for my American citizenship, don't you?"

Her grin widened as she watched Kreon's face light up as magnificently as any Christmas tree.

He said not a word but held her hand and embraced their children tighter. She noticed his eyes were shining.

Watching her husband fill with joy, Anya was reminded of another place and time.

She remembered when she, Leni, and Demetri were aboard the ship that brought them to America.

They had begged to stay up and watch a sunset on deck with the other passengers that evening. It was past their bedtime, but, seeing their pleading faces, she had relented. After cocooning them in their winter coats and a warm blanket, and sitting them in a deck chair, she stood at the railing looking out to sea. The white caps and pounding waves as the ship cut through the waters was exhilarating, and the sunset was more spectacular in color than she expected. Multiple shades of orange, yellow, pink, and lavender blazed before them. When the sun took its evening dip into the sea, the crowd dispersed, and Anya smiled at her sleeping urchins. She made no motion to disturb them. Instead, she watched the sky turn to indigo and listened to the rhythmic waves slap against the ship in the dark.

Leni had stirred at that moment and roused her brother too.

"Mama, I'm cold," she mumbled.

Wrapping their blankets securely around them, Anya took each child under a wing, and guided them to the railing.

"I want you to look up," she instructed.

"Why?" both children asked in unison.

"Just look," Anya replied, "and make a wish."

Above them millions of stars had appeared, dotting the infinite sky with their brilliance.

"Make a wish on a star."

She had done so with Kreon one night.

And on this Christmas Eve in America, she realized they had fulfilled each other's longing.

She had gifted Kreon with a family.

And he had gifted her with a future.

EPILOGUE

Kreon and Anya Kalanis lived a worthy life. They were married for almost 60 years and returned to Germany and Greece often to be reunited with family and friends. Many German relatives settled in America following their example.

Both were well into their eighties when they took their final journey. Each was honored in a separate memorial service with many attending. Although they died eight years apart, their ashes were interred together in May 2012 near their home in Connecticut. It was a glorious day on what would have been their wedding anniversary. They were buried in sunlight, surrounded by their children, their grandchildren, and their great-grandchildren.

It was a peaceful and private affair. In honor of her father's last request, Leni placed a red rose and a white rose on their grave. She would do so each year on their special day.

God bless.

ACKNOWLEDGEMENTS

This book, because of its personal nature, took me a long time to write and, in the writing of it, I owe many thanks to many people. Foremost, my gratitude to Manchester Community College for starting the journey, and to Smith College for a brilliant education and for setting the course.

My deepest gratitude goes to Joan Shapiro for including me in her incredible writing group and introducing me to my creative soul-sisters: Barbara Bergren, Elaine McMahon, Charlotte Pyle, Jennifer Pacquin, Laura Perry-phillipe, Erin Doolittle, Sarah Karstedt, Donna Smith, and Terri Klein. I could not have written this book without you. Your insight, your input, and your guidance kept me motivated and sane throughout the writing, editing, and publication of this novel.

Immeasurable thanks to my original editor, Dawn Metcalf, who, when I thought I was done with my tome, handed me 21 pages of editorial comments showing me that I could go deeper. Many thanks, also, to Liz Delton for the design of a wonderful book cover, doing a final edit, and for formatting the beast! And Melanie Cherniak for her publishing knowledge and guidance.

My heartfelt gratitude also to Renate Lemieux, Marianne Kreuzer, and family members for sharing their invaluable war-time experiences with me.

And a big thank you to my nephews: Brian Karadimas, who gave me the kick I needed whenever my stamina flagged and helped come up with the book's title; and Jason Karadimas, who in facetiously writing my epitaph "Here lies my aunt, she's dead and old; She wrote the books that never sold" spurred me on to prove him wrong. Thank you also to my German Greek American family who waited so patiently.

Last, but not least, a special bow to my personal cheerleader, my beloved and belated "Aunt Mitzi" Natsios. And also to my former English teacher and friend, Marie Gram, who said, "Do it for me, Ellen."

I did.

ABOUT THE AUTHOR

Ellen Karadimas is a former Ada Comstock Scholar at Smith College, Northampton, MA, with a B.A. in Theatre. A first prize recipient of the Denis Johnston Playwriting Award, and several scholastic and journalistic accolades, her career has encompassed the communications and event coordination fields. Born in Fürth, Germany, raised in New York City, she now resides in Connecticut.

REFERENCES

The following reference materials were integral to the details surrounding this book. However, I relied heavily on interviews with family and friends to tell a more personal story.

Christopher Ailsby, *The Third Reich Day by Day* (Chartwell Books, Inc., 2010 and Brown Bear Books Ltd., 2001)

Terry Chairman, *The German Homefront 1939-45* (Philosophical Library, 1989)

Jackson J. Spielvogel, *Hitler & Nazi Germany – A History* (Prentice Hall 1992)

Matthew Hughes & Chris Mann, *Inside Hitler's Germany – Life Under the Third Reich* (Chartwell Books, Inc. / MJF Books, 2000)

Made in United States
North Haven, CT
16 June 2022

20239314R00257